**THE RICH AND THE POOR,
THE CIVILIZED AND THE SAVAGE,
THE LOFTY AND THE DAMNED**

RENNO—Born among white men, raised among Seneca—and destined to be a great chief of two worlds.

DEBORAH—Admired by the ladies and desired by the men of her colony—and taken by force from her people to be a slave to Seneca squaws. Only she could be Renno's woman.

JEFFREY WILSON—Aristocratic and rebellious, he would gladly do worse than a savage—for the pleasure of bedding Deborah.

ALAIN DE GRAMONT—Like Renno, born white, yet a man who incited Indians to spread death among the colonists while serving the French through his treachery.

**SEIZING THE REINS OF DESTINY
AT THE DAWN OF A NEW NATION!**

The White Indian Series
Ask your bookseller for the books you have missed.

The White Indian Series
Book I

WHITE INDIAN

DONALD CLAYTON PORTER

BANTAM BOOKS
NEW YORK · TORONTO · LONDON · SYDNEY · AUCKLAND

WHITE INDIAN

*A Bantam Book / published by arrangement with
Book Creations, Inc.*

Bantam edition / November 1979

*Produced by Book Creations, Inc.
Lyle Kenyon Engel, Founder*

ISBN 0-553-24650-X

Published simultaneously in the United States and Canada

*Bantam Books are published by Bantam Books, a division of Bantam
Doubleday Dell Publishing Group, Inc. Its trademark, consisting of the
words "Bantam Books" and the portrayal of a rooster, is Registered in U.S.
Patent and Trademark Office and in other countries. Marca Registrada.
Bantam Books, 666 Fifth Avenue, New York, New York 10103.*

PRINTED IN THE UNITED STATES OF AMERICA

RAD   20   19   18   17

Introduction

No period in American history is more dramatic and colorful, and few eras were more significant than the century and a half between the establishment of the Jamestown Colony in Virginia early in the seventeenth century and the conclusion of the last of the so-called French and Indian Wars in 1763.

The Colonization of America Series, of which *White Indian* is the first volume, will deal with this exciting time.

Great Britian and France were both expanding their empires, and each was trying to establish domination of North America, sending colonists as well as troops and ships to this New World that Captain John Smith described as a vast land in which the "ocean of trees" was limitless. Spain, her own empire already shrinking, made a determined effort to remain in the competition, and a number of smaller powers, the Netherlands and Sweden among them, also took part in the struggle.

The victims of this incursion were the native

Indians, a noble people who watched in resentful bewilderment as a tidal wave of white settlers swept over their homes and hunting grounds. Some elected to fight all newcomers. Other Indian nations, reading the handwriting on the forest wall, chose to ally themselves with the Europeans, principally the English or the French. The tribes of the northeast, ranging from the nations of the Iroquois League—the Seneca, Mohawk, Oneida, Onondaga, Cayuga, and later, the Tuscarora—to the more powerful independents—the Algonquian, Huron, Ottawa, and Delaware—played prominent roles in the never-ending conflict. In the process, they made important contributions to the development of American culture.

The struggle was complicated by many factors. The 1685 revocation by King Louis XIV of the Edict of Nantes, which had guaranteed freedom of religion to Protestants in France, sent thousands of French Huguenot refugees streaming into the English colonies. The English colonies themselves regarded each other as rivals, and only their mutual suffering ultimately forced them to band together.

The heritage of what has become America was created by the tugs-of-war that took place on the Atlantic seaboard, chiefly within a strip of land that extended inland no more than 250 miles. Here, from Quebec to the Carolinas to the Floridas, were forged the principles and customs that Americans and Canadians today hold dear.

White Indian and the books to follow in the Colonization of America Series salute these gallant people, red and white alike, and acknowledge our debt to them.

Chapter I

As every settler in the Connecticut Valley well knew, even in times of peace, there was no real peace. Indian nations fought each other, then banded together to attack and harass the towns and villages established along the Connecticut River by the English, French Huguenots, Dutch refugees from New York, and a few Scandinavians. From time to time columns of French troops and irregulars, often accompanied by their own Indian allies, marched south, raiding the settlements to keep the people of Massachusetts Bay off-balance and to prevent reprisals in kind. Every frontier dweller carried his flintlock into the fields by day and kept it beside him at night.

Older settlers recalled that almost four decades earlier there had been a period of genuine peace after the Pequot War of 1637, when the most populous Indian nation in the region had been virtually decimated and the colonists had moved into their territory. Lesser tribes, among them the Agawam and Chicopee, had been subdued, too, and Fort Springfield had become

1

the largest and most active trading post in the western part of the Massachusetts Bay Colony.

When at least one hundred members of the militia were at their posts, the log fort on the east bank of the Connecticut River was believed to be impregnable. Thick logs of oak, maple, and elm provided the defenders with ample protection from the arrows and spears of their foes, and Fort Springfield also boasted four cannon. The largest of them, a demiculverin that fired iron balls half the size of a man's head, was notoriously inaccurate, but its roar was so loud that savages who heard the sound hastily left the vicinity.

The problem, as Fort Springfield's officers well knew, was that a full complement was maintained only during bona fide publicized emergencies. The militia consisted of volunteers who were kept busy on their own farms, and most of the time no more than fifteen or twenty gunners and infantrymen were on duty.

The Mohawk, allies of the mighty Seneca nation in the powerful Iroquois League, became embroiled in a dispute with the Ottawa, their neighbors to the north. Not wanting to face the Mohawk alone, the Ottawa called their friends the Algonquian, who ruled a land that extended from the Maine District of Massachusetts Bay to the shadows of the Citadel in Quebec.

Rather than ask for aid from all four of their sister nations of the Iroquois League, the Mohawk showed their contempt for their foes by appealing only to the Seneca, whose very name struck terror in the hearts of tribes from Hudson's Bay to the Spanish Floridas.

To the consternation of his enemies, Ghonka, the Great Sachem of the Seneca nation, responded to the challenge in person. He seldom went to war, customarily going into the field only at the head of the combined columns of the Iroquois, but personal circumstances caused him to seek the diversion that this particular campaign offered.

For ten years Ghonka had wanted a son who would someday join him at the Council of the Strong, but for ten years his dearest wish had been frustrated. His first squaw had given birth to a daughter, but both mother and child died in the epidemic of heat sickness that swept across the land.

Then, two years in the past, Ghonka had taken a new squaw, Ena, many years his junior; because he loved her, he was sure the god of fertility would shower him with blessings, and at the start of the harvest season, when all the signs and portents were favorable, Ena gave birth to a son.

Before the Seneca could rejoice, however, the infant died, and Ena almost lost her life, too.

On that very day, Ghonka received word from the Mohawk of their dispute with the Ottawa, and he left at dawn the next morning, placing himself at the head of a band of warriors three hundred strong, marching alone, a bearlike man with a thick chest and broad shoulders, the five feathers of his high rank protruding from his scalp lock.

The Ottawa paid a terrible price for the Great Sachem's grief, for Ghonka attacked their main town, taking the defenders by surprise, and burned it to the ground, killing more than 150 braves while his own forces suffered only a few casualties. Then he razed two smaller Ottawa villages as his foes fled before him, and drums spread the word through the vast forests of the wilderness that Ghonka was on the warpath.

3

He turned eastward and marched his men for forty-eight hours without pausing to rest. The warriors, accustomed to harsh discipline, did not complain. On the contrary, they enjoyed themselves thoroughly.

They maintained their usual silence as they made their way through the forest of pine and cedar, spruce and hickory, but occasionally they exchanged broad grins. They were the most feared and respected warriors in all the land, and they liked nothing better than showing off their prowess.

Only Ghonka remained gloomy. He set a blistering pace, sometimes taking a few mouthfuls of the parched corn and smoked venison he carried in his pouch, pausing only briefly at rivers and brooks for a swallow of water. Ottawa scalps decorated the loincloths of his warriors, but Ghonka carried none. He needed none to demonstrate his stature.

The drums carried the news of impending doom into the territory of the Algonquian, whose chiefs and senior warriors convened in haste if not in dignity. It was true they had given their pledge to help the Ottawa in their war against the Mohawk, but the Ottawa had suffered ignominious defeat, and now the Algonquian stood alone. Had they faced the Mohawk, they might have been inclined to honor their obligation to the Ottawa, but as one of the oldest braves, a wizened man of eighty summers, pointed out to the members of the council, the Algonquian had no quarrel with the Seneca. And no sensible nation went to war when Ghonka himself led his warriors.

The Algonquian heeded the elder's advice and promptly sent a delegation to meet the Seneca. The braves unstrung their bows and removed their war paint to prove their peaceful intentions.

4

The two parties met beside the shores of Lake Winnipesaukee in the land that the men with pale skins were calling New Hampshire, and there they treated with each other.

The Algonquian offered five hundred strips of wampum, each heavy with the shells of clams and oysters, in return for peace.

The Seneca, being an inland nation, placed great value on this special wampum, but Ghonka exacted a higher price. Even his own senior warriors were surprised when he demanded seven hundred strips of wampum and one hundred necklaces of scallop shells, but the Algonquian sought peace so desperately that they agreed, and that night the two parties smoked the pipe of peace and feasted together.

Ghonka remained apart, still brooding as he stared into the fire.

When the feast ended, the Algonquian departed, and the Seneca made camp for the night. Ghonka continued to sit before the fire, his body motionless, his arms folded across his chest. The fire died down, and his closest subordinates, who had the privilege of sleeping nearest him, were awakened by the sound of his voice.

The Great Sachem was intoning something, his cadence rhythmic but his words unintelligible.

The senior warriors closed their ears, for only Ghonka and the chief medicine man had the right to speak directly to the Great Spirit, the god who was the father of all manitous, and it would have been unseemly to eavesdrop. Besides, the warriors had no desire to invoke the wrath of either the Great Spirit or Ghonka. None were sure which was the more ferocious.

His prayers ended, Ghonka slept for a time. But he awakened when the first light appeared in the sky, and soon the Seneca began the long journey home.

They marched due west from Lake Winnipesaukee until they came to the Connecticut River, and because it was easier to walk along the bank than to thread a path through the forest, Ghonka indulged his braves by allowing them to follow the river as it flowed southward. They had performed well and they deserved the reward.

Thus it was that the Seneca came upon the tiny town and fort called Fort Springfield.

One of the scouts in the advance party doubled back to tell the Great Sachem that a town of the pale skins lay ahead, guarded by a large fort made of logs, its walls so high that it was not possible to determine how many men might be defending the town.

Ghonka had no quarrel with the pale skins, who had not dared to establish homesteads and build villages in the land of the Seneca. Lesser tribes had suffered, but his territory had not been violated. It so happened, however, that he knew the worth of their belongings because both English and French traders had come to him with gifts in recent years.

The hatchets of the pale skins were made of a hard metal that could be honed to a fine edge, and the knives of these intruders from the far side of the great sea were superior. They also had firesticks that could kill or maim from great distances, although Ghonka wanted nothing to do with these weapons. The arrows and spears of his ancestors had made the Seneca preeminent in war, and he had no desire to experiment with new weapons.

Nevertheless, he coveted the other belongings of the pale skins. Perhaps, if he acquired these riches, the emptiness inside him caused by the death of his infant son would begin to dissipate. Ghonka's victory over the Ottawa had whetted his appetite for further triumphs, and the craven submission of the Algonquian had denied him the opportunity to win more glory.

He halted his warriors, and they took up hidden positions in the forest while they awaited the coming of night.

For two long weeks, Jed Harper had been too busy to celebrate the birth of his first child, a son. He had brought his wife, Minnie, to Springfield so the fort's doctor could attend her, and since the child's birth she had remained in the doctor's care because of complications that had set in.

Jed had been forced to return to his farm five miles away. The harvest couldn't wait, so he had labored from sunrise to sunset, bringing in the melons and pumpkins, corn and onions and peas that would provide his little family with staple foods during the long winter ahead.

His work done, he had come to Springfield to bring his wife and baby home, but the doctor insisted that Minnie stay in her room at the fort for another day or two, so Jed decided to remain in town.

It was his bad luck to draw militia duty at the fort, although he really couldn't complain. There had been no Indian raids on the fort for more than two years, and he had only to stand at his post in the watchtower, now and then looking out through a knothole to see if there was any activity in the woods beyond the town. The night was dark, with banks of heavy clouds obscuring the moon and stars, so he couldn't see much of anything even when he tried.

This was a perfect time to celebrate, and Jed had

7

brought a jug of rum to the watchtower with him. Rum was a sure cure for the dreary boredom of sentry duty, and Jed and his friends were delighted to pass the time toasting the arrival of his baby son.

The militiamen scarcely knew what hit them.

Jed sensed something moving behind him and turned in time to see a husky Indian warrior, naked to the waist. Then a stone hammer descended, crushing Jed's skull, and he knew no more.

The efficient Seneca went about their task silently. One group neutralized the fort while another moved from house to house. Ghonka had ordered that no prisoners be taken and no survivors left, and his men obeyed him to the letter.

They were directed to take only cooking utensils and blankets, hatchets and knives. This was the purpose of the raid, and the braves were permitted to snatch only the personal trinkets they saw in passing. No time was to be wasted gathering frivolous items.

In all, 189 men, women, and children died in the slaughter, which would be recorded as the worst raid in Springfield's forty-year history. For years thereafter, no settler, militia officer, or official of Massachusetts Bay knew the identity of the raiders, and no one suspected the Seneca because their homeland was so far away— near Lake Ontario in the western portion of the unsettled area claimed by New York Colony.

Ghonka seemed to be everywhere. He sped up and down the town's three streets making certain that his instructions were followed and that no man took more than he could carry comfortably on the long march home.

Hurrying on to the fort, Ghonka was gratified to note that there was no sign of resistance. His braves were moving from chamber to chamber, silently dispatching the pale skins.

Ghonka came to a small chamber where a young woman had just died in her bed, her blood staining the sheets. The young warrior who had killed her raised his stone hammer to destroy the infant who lay beside her.

Minnie Harper had been changing her son's diaper when the attack had come, so the baby was naked. Ghonka saw that the child was a sturdy, well-formed boy, and on sudden impulse he ordered, "Stay your hand!"

The young warrior lowered his hammer.

Ghonka approached the bed and looked down at the infant.

The baby returned his gaze, and the Great Sachem was astonished to note that there was no hint of fear in the infant's eyes.

Ghonka could not help laughing aloud.

The baby smiled and gurgled at him in return.

That settled the matter. Ghonka picked up the infant and clumsily wrapped him in a blanket. The son he had so desperately craved. Now Ena would have a child to hold in her arms and the future of his dynasty would be assured.

He would call his son Renno, after the god of fertility, whom he would honor for the rest of his days.

Less than a half hour after the raiders struck, they departed as silently as they had come, and the only survivor was the infant who would be known as Renno.

Chapter II

Most of the Seneca lived in longhouses made of clay-chinked logs covered with thick elm bark. Clan members or relatives lived in clusters of such communal dwellings. But the Great Sachem, Ghonka, although a member of the Bear Clan, lived separately with his family, as befitted his rank.

His house, a miniature version of a longhouse, was twenty-five feet long, nineteen feet wide, and had a hide of elk skin covering the entrance, beside which the emblem of the Bear Clan was carved and painted red.

In the stone-lined pit in the center of the dwelling burned a fire that was never extinguished, night or day, no matter the season. The smoke escaped through a hole cut directly over the fire in the center of the roof, and above the hole stood a platform, supported on four legs, that kept out rain or the heavy snow that had been falling regularly in recent weeks. The wind was mild, so the smoke escaped freely and the interior was clear.

A double row of bunks lined one wall, each made of a slab of wood; those on the bottom were covered with skins and furs and used as beds, and those above were used as storage space for clothing, weapons, tools, and other private belongings that were not suspended from the pegs on the other walls.

Renno's bed was only half the size of those used by his father and mother because he would remain under their roof only until his seventh summer, when he would be moved to the longhouse of the boys. Even now he enjoyed no special privileges, just as Ghonka and his wife, Ena, had few prerogatives of rank. A black metal cooking pot hanging from a wall peg, which Ghonka had brought with him from the town of the pale skins two years earlier, was the only visible luxury.

Ena saw to it that Renno slept beneath a soft blanket made of the marvelously warm cloth taken from the pale skins' town. But there were disadvantages to the use of the blanket, too, the worst being the cold shock he felt when he was removed from his bed.

Ena placed Renno in the backsack used for the exclusive purpose of carrying him out of doors, and he relaxed again. The outer portion of the container was tough bearskin, itself warm enough for older people, but the inner layer was composed of the deliciously warm fur of the silver timber wolf, which lay next to Renno's skin.

As his mother moved out into the open, Renno snuggled into the fur, trying to bury his face in it. The air was so cold that his cheeks burned and his nostrils stung, but the discomfort soon eased and he was enveloped by the warm cloud.

He was incapable of remaining quiet for very long, and his normal and powerful two-year-old curiosity had him wriggling in his wrappings until he could peer out and watch the scenery.

His mother's beaded leggings flapped as she walked with purposeful strides, plowing through the deep snow. Soon they were joined by another woman, similarly laden, the mother of his friend Anowara, who was slightly younger and smaller.

The two women exchanged greetings, then walked out past the stockade that surrounded the Seneca town, and after a while they caught a glimpse of their destination.

Renno saw it, too, and promptly ducked back into the warm fur. He hated this place, and he braced himself for the ordeal.

His mother began to sing. In a low melodic chant she called on the spirits of the wilderness, the manitous, to give her child strength and courage. Renno's skin prickled. Ena was a medicine woman renowned for her ability to communicate with the spirits, and Renno felt their presence in the towering trees, and he could imagine them listening to her, then whispering to each other in the wind. Perhaps they were even whispering to him.

"Be strong," they told him. *"Be brave."*

The women, both singing, walked slowly onto the frozen surface of a small lake, and Renno and Anowara were placed carefully on the ice, still wrapped in their furs.

The boy watched as his mother hacked at the ice with a small stone hatchet she took from her belt. A hole had been broken in the ice earlier in the day, but the cold was so intense that a new skin of ice had already thickened. Ena cleared it away, then plucked the child from his cocoon and held him high over her head.

12

The air numbed Renno as it struck his naked body, but he did not struggle, and his face remained impassive.

"Manitous, make Renno strong!" Ena cried. "Sky-woman, see your child and make him hardy!"

Renno folded his little arms across his chest, as he had been taught, then sucked in his breath.

Holding him tightly and maintaining her firm grip, his mother plunged him into the icy water and held him there.

Renno bit back the cry that came to his lips. Silently he endured the heart-stopping shock of the freezing water, the almost warm feeling of the air as his mother removed him from the lake, then the renewed sting as he was plunged below the surface a second time.

Anowara, younger and less sturdy than Renno, began to weep as her mother performed the same ritual. The woman clamped a hand over the child's mouth to stifle her sobs, then continued to hold her hand there until it seemed that the baby would choke. The hand moved briefly to allow the little girl to gulp in a short breath, and the process was repeated until Anowara gained control of herself.

Her mother spoke gently. "Do not cry, little turtle. A Seneca never cries. You will be a strong woman, a brave woman. You will not be one who cries!

"Look at Renno," Anowara's mother continued. "He knows the wisdom of silence. One day he will be a great warrior."

Ena smiled.

Even though she made no comment, Renno knew she was pleased with him as she dried him and wrapped him in his furs. Curling up in this warm place, he willed himself to stop shivering.

His mother looked at him with approval. That was his reward, and he wanted nothing more.

The special scents of autumn filled the forest, where the leaves of oak and maple and elm were turning red and gold, and any Seneca worthy of the name could have followed the tracks of small animals preparing their winter lairs. The last wild raspberries of the season were clinging to their stems, and soon the older girls would begin to gather the sassafras plants.

No one supervised the band of boys trooping through the forest. This was a free day, when they were allowed to find their own amusement and were subjected to no instruction. The older men were in council, and the active warriors were either off hunting or engaged in raids against the Ottawa. Those unfortunate enough to have stayed at home had been rounded up by the women to help clear some new fields that would serve the needs of the growing town. A flock of geese flew overhead, too high for the arrows of the hunters to reach them, as they headed southward from the land of the Ottawa and Huron.

Renno, now seven summers old and included in the company of boys only a few moons earlier, lagged behind. He was young to be a member of this group. Most of the other boys were at least nine, but Ghonka and Ena, knowing Renno was older than his years, had entered him into the company. El-i-chi, their younger son, still only five summers old, was much too young to join the group.

Renno knew that the others expected him to bring up the rear, but he didn't mind because he had plans of his own. He was carrying a small knife, a quiver full of hunting arrows, and a bow, and he was filled with a spirit of independence.

14

He intended to sneak off at an opportune moment and go hunting on his own. If they learned of his plans, the other boys would want to come with him, but they would spoil his fun. With no adult on hand, they would be so unruly that any wild game would scatter. Besides, group hunting offered no challenge.

Ever since spring, Renno had been bringing down squirrels and birds as well as an occasional weasel or raccoon, and on one special day a red fox. When he hunted alone, it was so much easier to remember what he had been taught. He had learned to judge from the depth and imprint of a bear's tracks how recently the beast had made them. Scratch marks on tree trunks told him when raccoons were in the vicinity, and the patterns of disturbed leaves revealed the presence of birds' nests, just as bent blades of grass told him how recently deer had been in the area and in what direction they had been headed. Of course he had never shot any big game. On the infrequent occasions when he had come across bear or elk tracks, he had reported immediately to a warrior, as he had been instructed.

Today the sky was bright, lighting the forest in places where the leaves were already falling. The air was crisp, and Renno was in high spirits as he succeeded in slipping away from the other boys, making his way silently through the forest. He walked rapidly through the trackless woods, taking special note of trees and boulders so he could find his way back without difficulty.

After a time he came to the bank of a small stream, and when he dropped to one knee to scoop up a few handfuls of water, he saw fresh tracks in the mud. Obviously they had been made by a very large bear that had paused to drink at this same spot.

Soon the bears would go into hibernation for the

winter, so this was the season when they ate all the nuts and berries they could find prior to their long sleep. The warriors had said that bears were more dangerous in the autumn than at any other time of year.

As he moved away from the stream Renno heard a rustling noise in the bushes behind him, and he turned just in time to see an enormous brown bear, its fur matted, glaring at him with malevolent eyes.

The boy knew there was no way he could reach his companions in safety. The bear could overtake him. Remembering a man in the town who had lost an eye in a fight with a bear, Renno believed his only hope lay in climbing a tree, so he waded across the stream and headed for the nearest tall oak, but he was too late. The bear's roar made the leaves tremble, and the huge animal charged across the stream, its jaws open, its powerful front paws clawing the air.

Renno felt numb. Resigned to a fight for his life, he began to think that it could not be accidental that the elder son of the head of the Bear Clan should be challenged to a duel by a mammoth bear. The manitous were testing his manhood, and if he failed, if he faltered for a single moment, he deserved to die.

Reacting instinctively, the boy had no time to ponder. Drawing his bow, he discharged arrow after arrow at his enemy, so many that he could not even count them in this time of crisis.

The arrows found their target, but the bear continued to advance, roaring in pain and anger.

The boy gripped his small flint knife by the hilt, the thought of retreat no longer in his mind. The manitous would desert him forever unless he proved his manhood: he had to kill or be killed.

The bear towered over him, and Renno struck at the furry throat with all of his strength. He dodged the huge paw, its long claws raking the air, and still reacting without conscious thought, he sidestepped just as the animal staggered and collapsed at his feet, the knife embedded in its throat.

Looking down at the bloody carcass, Renno gasped for breath. His rib cage ached, his throat felt raw, and he wanted to retch, but he had enough presence of mind to shout the Seneca war cry at the top of his voice, although this last effort exhausted him.

He had no idea how long he stood there before he realized that he was acquiring an audience. Some of the boys were staring at him in openmouthed wonder while others were still arriving at the scene. Even Skahnon-dih, the oldest of the boys and the band's unofficial leader, was deeply impressed.

"It will be hard for us to take this great creature back to the town by ourselves," he said, his tone respectful. "We lack the proper knives. Do you wish us to bring help?"

Unable to speak, Renno could only nod.

His companions ran off as fast as they could.

Alone again, the dazed boy walked slowly around the bear, admiring it and marveling at his accomplishment. The manitous had taken note of his courage and had intervened in the battle on his side, and he offered them a silent prayer of thanks.

Then he heard another rustling in the brush on the far side of the stream, and for a moment he thought the nightmare would be repeated. Surely the manitous would not test him again now that he was unarmed!

A bear cub about two feet tall emerged from the brush, waddled to the stream bank, and sat down, calling plaintively for its mother.

Renno waded across the stream cautiously, but the bear displayed no fear, no animosity, and it made no attempt to run away. No wonder the large bear had been so aggressive! She was defending her cub.

The seven-year-old boy picked up the cub, which immediately snuggled into his arms.

"Poor creature," said Renno. "You have lost your mother. I had no choice but to kill her in war, and now you are my captive. But do not be afraid! I will do you no harm! I will adopt you, and like El-i-chi, you will become my brother!"

That night at the house of Renno's family, a ceremonial meal was laid out in honor of Renno and the bear spirit. Renno sat cross-legged in front of the flames in the place that was usually reserved for the host. The entire meal was special, and Ena saw to it that many of her elder son's favorite dishes were served. After the feast, Renno was expected to make a speech —his first—and he rose to the occasion sufficiently to thank his parents and the manitous, after which he presented the bearskin to his father's sister, Sah-nee-wa, who was the clan mother of the dominant Bear Clan.

At last it was Ghonka's turn to speak. The Great Sachem rose, casting aside his robe of buffalo hide and folding his arms. For the first time he nodded gravely at Renno, using the greeting that warriors reserved for each other, then he stared into the flames of the cooking fire. "The son of Ghonka and Ena," he said, "has done what few warriors have ever done. For the rest of his days he will wear a necklace made of the bear's claws, and they will protect him from harm. Ghonka and Ena are blessed, the Bear Clan is blessed, the entire Seneca nation is blessed because we have Renno as our son. Runners will be sent to all of the towns and villages of our nation to tell them of his deeds. Stand, Renno!"

The boy approached his father and stood before him. The Great Sachem placed his hand on the boy's head. "You have passed the first test of manhood. Other tests will follow in the years ahead. May you meet them as well."

Renno made no reply, aware that he was permitted to speak only when granted the right.

"What will you name the cub?" Ghonka asked.

"Ja-gonh," the boy replied without hesitation.

The entire group laughed.

Ghonka was amused. "He-who-has-a-joyful-heart? Why that name?"

Renno grinned at little five-year-old El-i-chi, who was holding the bear cub on his lap. The younger boy held a gourd filled with cherries soaked in maple syrup, and he was sharing it with the animal. "My own heart is filled with joy," Renno said, "because now I have two brothers. Together we will perform great deeds for the Seneca. Together we will make the people of the Seneca proud of us. Together we will conquer our nation's enemies!"

The adults couldn't help laughing as Renno went out the door carrying Ja-gonh in one arm and leading El-i-chi by the hand. Silent and proud, Ghonka felt more certain than ever that the many gods, including the Great Manitou himself, were watching over the Seneca.

Renno and Ja-gonh were inseparable. The bear slept on the floor of the longhouse in which the boys-in-training lived, eating increasingly larger portions of corn and vegetables and honey and fully sharing Renno's life. When the boy fished or hunted, the bear went with him and was instructed in the countless secrets of the forests and fields. Ja-gonh soon towered above the tallest adult warriors, but he was gentle and he molested no one. Members of the tribe took care never to tease him, never to anger him, and only Renno and El-i-chi were on familiar terms with him.

At the end of two years, Ja-gonh began to display signs of restlessness, sometimes vanishing for several days at a time. Renno went to his father for advice.

"Ja-gonh is grown now and must live his own life," Ghonka said. "Set him free, and he will return whenever you wish to see him or he wishes to see you."

"So be it, my father," Renno said.

That same evening, at dusk, the boy of nine summers and the bear of two went together into the deep forest. It was late when Renno returned, his back straight, his eyes staring straight ahead, and no one dared ask him what he and Ja-gonh had said to each other.

Thereafter, there were times when Renno hunted or fished and his peers heard him emit a call unlike any sound they had ever heard. On these occasions Ja-gonh soon appeared, and the pair sometimes were joined by El-i-chi, who had just been admitted to the band of boys. Even the oldest and most forward members of the group knew better than to intrude on what all of them recognized as a family gathering. They would watch from a distance as Renno spoke earnestly and at length to the bear, with little El-i-chi adding comments from time to time.

No one dared follow when the trio vanished into the forest, for it would have been discourteous to spy on them, and no sensible boy wanted to incur Renno's displeasure. At nine, he was tall, husky, and incredibly agile, so strong and cunning that he won free-for-all contests with boys four years his senior. He had become so adept with hunting arrows that one of the warriors had made him a set of heavier, deadlier war arrows, and no member of the band of boys was his equal in such arts as throwing a tomahawk or aiming a spear.

Ja-gonh, still devoted to him, was gradually achieving his full size and weight and was already a hulking brown giant, as quick as he was powerful. No boy, or combination of boys, could possibly cope with such a team.

As for El-i-chi, his situation was different. A child of seven summers, he was still small for his age and relatively frail and had been sent from his home prematurely. Ghonka and Ena had discussed whether the boy could hold his own among the older children, and Ghonka, sure that Renno would protect and instruct his brother, at last prevailed.

Ena bowed to his wisdom, even though her heart was heavy. But, like Ghonka, she placed her faith in Renno, and he did not disappoint his parents. From the moment El-i-chi became a member of the boys' band, Renno became his little brother's supporter, adviser, and protector, shielding and teaching him, helping him in the arduous process of becoming a true Seneca warrior.

Other members of the band initially regarded El-i-chi with contempt, although they took great care not to mistreat him or tease him in Renno's presence.

El-i-chi struggled to overcome his handicaps. He had trouble keeping up with the others when they ran, swam, or engaged in trials of endurance, and he was so much weaker than his peers that the instructors refused to permit him to engage in free-for-all fights or other competitive games.

Gradually, over a period of three moons, El-i-chi grew tougher and stronger, his muscles becoming wiry, his endurance increasing. He was so imbued with the incomparable Seneca spirit that he never complained to his brother about the secret teasing and vindictive nastiness of the other boys, even though he knew Renno would put matters to rights instantly. A Seneca never whined, no matter what his fate.

The season was far advanced when the band of boys went out into the forest for a full seven days of exercises, a frequent occurrence that was part of their training. Each exercise was more difficult and complex than the one before.

Making their camp in a hollow beside the swiftly flowing waters of a brook, the boys cleared the brush in the immediate area, so they couldn't be surprised by enemies, and gathered wood for the fire that would be made later. Then the warrior in charge of training assembled them.

"Each of you will go out alone," he said. "You will bring back game or fowl or fish for your evening meal; you will take no roots and pick no berries. He who brings back a plump duck or a weasel will feast. He who brings back no meat will fast. None will be allowed to share his food; so those who are lazy or clumsy will go hungry tonight. Go. And return by the time the father-sun departs from the sky for his own night of rest."

The boys scattered, and El-i-chi was relieved to be spending a few hours by himself, for some of the older boys had taunted him unmercifully on the long march from the Seneca town.

Determined to succeed in his day's efforts, El-i-chi headed into the forest, his destination a deep pool fed by a pretty little waterfall that Renno had shown him on a previous expedition. Fish were plentiful there, Renno had said, and the younger boy hoped to bring back a whole string of fish. It didn't matter that he would be able to eat only a few of them, for the warrior in charge of training and his assistant would be happy to cook the leftovers for their own supper.

Far more clever than most people realized, El-i-chi had developed his own method of catching fish, a variation of a technique long used by adults. He searched for a long, straight stick, about as thick as the length of his thumbnail, and after stripping it of smaller branches and leaves, he stretched out on his stomach at the side of the pool, making no move and no sound as he waited.

His patience was rewarded when he saw a spotted fish, about six boy-sized fingers in length, swimming lazily near the surface. Easing his stick into the water, he gently tickled the fish's back with the blunt end, slowly coaxing it nearer the surface as he pulled up the stick. When the fish came close enough, the boy shot his hand into the water, snatched it with a firm hand, and threw it up onto the bank. During the afternoon, he managed to catch five fish, all large enough to be eaten and much more than he himself could consume. He had reason to be pleased with himself.

As he began to search for a length of vine to use for stringing his catch, El-i-chi realized that someone was watching him. Freezing for an instant, he turned slowly and saw Skah-non-dih standing in the shadows of a large maple. The older boy, in his final year of training before taking the tests that would admit him to full membership in the brotherhood of warriors, was by far the biggest member of the band. He was also a bully, although he was always cautious when Renno was in the vicinity.

Smiling broadly, Skah-non-dih leaned against the tree. "A bountiful catch, mighty fisherman," he said.

El-i-chi felt a wave of uneasiness.

The older boy sauntered forward, ostensibly to look closely at the fish. Then, before El-i-chi could even blink, Skah-non-dih threw the fish into the water.

El-i-chi cried out in anger and alarm and took a step forward to restrain his torturer.

The grinning Skah-non-dih picked him up, heaved him into the pool, and shouted, "Now you can catch even more fish!" as the younger boy rose to the surface and began to swim toward shore. "You can take them from their longhouses under the water. Dive for them, mighty fisherman!" he taunted, picking up a handful of stones and throwing them one by one at the child.

El-i-chi was forced to swim in the opposite direction to avoid the barrage as the stones began to splash around him, but one rock caught him on the cheek, drawing blood, and another grazed his shaven head near his scalp lock.

A whimper of pain rose to his throat, and the little boy could not smother it. He submerged, swimming below the surface, but eventually he had to come up for air.

The instant he reappeared, Skah-non-dih began throwing rocks at him again.

"Stop!" El-i-chi cried, breathing hard. "I—I can't stay in the water much longer—or I'll drown!"

Skah-non-dih's taunting laugh echoed across the pool, then it broke off abruptly.

The child shook the water out of his eyes.

Renno and Ja-gonh stood only a short distance away, and El-i-chi, uncertain whether to be relieved or alarmed, saw that his older brother had drawn a flint knife from his loincloth. The bear was standing on his hind legs, towering above the humans, and a menacing growl rose from within him and made the leaves tremble.

Renno's calm was monumental, although the child could see he was poised for combat. All the same, he spoke in a quiet, seemingly unflustered voice. "Anyone who attacks my brother will die."

Skah-non-dih's eyes dilated. "I—I meant no harm," he said. "It was only sport. You know we treat all new members of the band roughly to harden them." He began to back away.

But Ja-gonh lumbered after him, reaching out a paw, his wickedly curved claws extended.

Skah-non-dih tried in vain to smother a gasp of terror.

Renno said something to Ja-gonh in an undertone, and the bear sat down, a puzzled expression in his eyes, and began to scratch himself. He seemed relaxed but still watchful.

"Ja-gonh, my brother, will help me if I need him, but in dealing with you I need no help," Renno said.

Shivering, El-i-chi climbed out of the water and tried to speak.

Renno silenced him with a wave. "I am in charge now," he said as he turned back to Skah-non-dih. "The brothers of my family believe in a fair fight. El-i-chi is only half your size and age. You could break him in two with your hands, just as Ja-gonh could tear you apart with his paws. But the bear is too big and strong for you. I am not as tall as you, and you are heavier, but I am more than a fair match for you. Agreed?"

"Agreed," Skah-non-dih replied hastily. "But I have no wish to do battle with the elder son of Ghon-ka. I offer you the pipe of peace."

Renno ignored the proposal. "You know that I will beat you in any manner of fighting. We will use knives if you wish. We will use spears if you prefer.

Or we will fight in a free-for-all. It doesn't matter. Whatever you choose, I swear to you—in the names of the manitous who guard the spirits of those Seneca who fight with valor and die in battle—that I will kill you." He sounded much like Ghonka when the Great Sachem went into a cold rage. His voice barely rose above a whisper and sounded almost tranquil.

Skah-non-dih sucked in his breath. "May the manitous of the forest be my witnesses," he said, "I swear I will do no harm to El-i-chi."

"If he is harmed, I will hold you responsible." Renno was unyielding.

"I seek only friendship with all in the Bear Clan."

"That remains to be proved." Renno placed an arm around his little brother's narrow shoulders.

Ja-gonh rose to his feet and moved to the other side of El-i-chi, and the trio went off into the forest without a backward glance. Renno's honor had been satisfied now, and he was prepared to let the matter drop. He would explain the situation to the adult instructor without naming his little brother's torturer, and he felt certain El-i-chi would be allowed to share the wild turkey he had snared and slaughtered. He paused occasionally to pick handfuls of berries for Ja-gonh, as a reward for his unfailing loyalty.

Skah-non-dih stayed beside the pool, taking care not to let his feelings show. He had lost face, and his shame so overwhelmed him that he swore vengeance against the sons of Ghonka. He might have to wait a long time, but one day he would repay them for the disgrace they had forced him to suffer.

Chapter III

Mildred Wilson sat, miserable as well as cold, huddling near the fire that was blazing in the oversized hearth in the great hall of her husband's mansion in Cornwall. She and Andrew were devoted to each other, and that was saying a great deal, but other than their three-year-old son, Jeffrey, their lives were bleak, their future nonexistent. They had been naïve to entertain such high hopes when they had been married less than four years earlier.

Smoothing the skirt of her watered-silk gown, Mildred made a conscientious effort to look at the positive side of life. She herself was a handsome young woman, brown-haired and slender, who had brought a substantial dowry to a union in which her funds were not needed. The dashing Andrew, the youngest son of a prominent nobleman whose properties had been returned to him when King Charles II had been restored to the throne a few years earlier, had ample funds in his own right.

They had this rambling house in Cornwall, as well

as the smaller place in London, and a dozen servants on their staff. They could afford all the new clothes their place in society demanded, and they could give dinner parties of which no one need be ashamed. Only recently they had entertained Charles, "the Merry Monarch," and the latest in what appeared to be an endless succession of his mistresses.

But the dissolute Whitehall court of the King was distasteful to Mildred, and life was dreary in Cornwall, where she and Andrew were regarded as somewhat beyond the pale of the upper crust because he had no title of his own.

What bothered her most—because it ate so deeply into the energetic, ambitious Andrew—was that he had nothing of significance to occupy his time. He had thought of initiating a political career and running for a seat in the House of Commons, but the docile Parliament had no real voice in the affairs of Great Britain and approved of everything the King and his ministers wanted.

He held a commission as a captain in the Royal Army, of course, and he was in awe of Prince Rupert, the commander in chief of the army and navy, but Andrew's older brother was also a professional soldier, and he took precedence: Andrew would end his career as a lieutenant colonel who would never gain command of his own regiment, and his brother would go on to become a general.

The sound of hoofbeats on the hard-packed snow interrupted Mildred's ruminations; that would be Andrew returning from his mysterious four-day trip to London. He had been secretive about his reason for going off to the city, saying that he would tell her more in due course, but at this moment she no longer cared, for she had missed him even more than she thought possible.

A few moments later Captain Andrew Wilson came into the great hall, flinging back his silk-lined cape and unbuckling his sword with the jeweled hilt. The snow was still wet on his high boots and silver spurs. He grinned at his wife, embracing her tenderly, and Mildred clung to him for a long time, reveling in his masculinity.

At last he released her. "All is well?" he said.

"I've had no problems," she said, "except that I missed you. But I didn't expect you until later this evening, so I have no refreshment ready for you."

"That's soon remedied. Will you join me?"

Andrew sank into a chair near the fire, draping his leg over one carved-oak arm. "In spite of a dull dinner at my father's and making the customary obeisances to His Dissolute Majesty, I had a splendid time."

"I'm delighted," she murmured, sipping her wine.

"You've never met Johnny Bledsoe—Lord Bledsoe now, since the death of his father. Johnny had rooms across the hall from mine at Oxford."

She waited for him to go on.

"A year ago, King Charles appointed him Minister of Colonies, and even my father—who despises officialdom—is forced to admit that Johnny is doing marvelously well."

Mildred encouraged him with a nod.

"I spent most of my time in London with Johnny," Andrew said, staring into the fire. "And I've learned about some opportunities for investment."

Mildred was surprised because Andrew had never shown any leaning toward the financial.

"Johnny showed me some fascinating statistics. One of the most prosperous and rapidly growing of our North American colonies is Virginia. I'm not particularly interested in it because the principal occupation there is the raising of crops, mostly tobacco, and I can't see myself as a planter." He paused. "The other colony that's doing well is Massachusetts Bay."

Mildred was scarcely familiar with the name of the place.

"Boston, the principal town, is still rather drab, but at its present rate of growth it is certain to become a major seaport and trade center within a few years. My father recently invested in a shipyard there—which is good reason not to do the same."

She couldn't help smiling at his fierce sense of independence.

"I became excited," Andrew said, "by the potential of the far side of the colony, on the west, at the edge of the wilderness. There's a tiny fort there called Springfield. It was totally destroyed in a savage Indian raid a few years ago, but people are starting to trickle back into the area. There are furs that bring a high price on the London market, the opportunities for farming are great, and no one knows what minerals might be found under the ground."

"You've decided to make an investment there?"

"Well," Andrew said, "land can be bought for a mere shilling an acre, about one-twentieth of what land costs in Cornwall. By the time Johnny Bledsoe finished showing me various documents, I was so convinced of the future of western Massachusetts Bay that I paid the Crown at once for a tract of twenty thousand acres, a portion of it facing what's called the Connecticut River."

He had paid an absurdly low price for the property

and had little to lose. Even more important, it was good to hear him expressing enthusiasm about something. "What will you do with twenty thousand acres, Andrew? That's an enormous estate."

"It is large, but by New World standards it isn't enormous. And in answer to your question, darling Mildred, I intend to develop it."

She couldn't help frowning. "It may not be a simple matter to find the right overseer to look out for your interests."

Andrew paused, displaying a trace of nervousness.

"I'm proposing that we go to Massachusetts Bay ourselves, live there, and develop the property," he said.

Mildred could only stare at him in astonishment.

"I'll grant you it won't be easy," Andrew said, "but the taming of the wilderness offers a tremendous challenge. . . ."

She was still so stunned she didn't know what to reply.

"Springfield is growing again, and the fort there will soon be rebuilt. What's more, a man with my military background is rather desperately needed. Johnny Bledsoe assures me that the governor of Massachusetts Bay will offer me the command of the western militia —a part-time citizens' army of volunteers that most residents join."

"I see."

"I'm not asking you to cut down trees or spend your life cooking over a primitive stove. We'll obtain the services of indentured servants, and we'll hire as many others as we need. Why, every gold sovereign I own will be worth several times as much in Massachusetts Bay. We'll be one of the wealthiest families in the entire colony."

Mildred raised a hand. "I'm not necessarily disagreeing with you, my dear, and I do appreciate your enthusiasm. But there are other factors to be considered. Our children will grow up to become illiterate savages."

"Hardly." Andrew had thought of every angle. "When they're small they'll have you to teach them, and when they grow a bit older I have every intention of sending Jeffrey—and any others we may have—back here to England to school. I assure you I shall not shirk my obligations as a father." His voice softened. "And never will I fail to discharge my duties as the husband of the loveliest lady it has ever been my privilege to know."

Her thoughts were still whirling. There were so many aspects to be weighed. "You say this place was burned to the ground by savages only a few years ago? Won't living there be dangerous?"

Andrew nodded, his eyes bright. "Very dangerous. It will become my responsibility, if all goes as I hope, to make the area safe for future English colonists. That's just one of the challenges awaiting us."

If he was unafraid, she reflected, she would be obliged to conquer her own fears, and then she began to spark to the idea. "I think," she said at last, "I might enjoy the experience."

"We have a clear choice," Andrew declared. "We can either stay here and stultify in a decaying society, or we can help create a future on a continent that's largely unexplored."

She stood and placed her hands on his shoulders. "Darling Andrew," she said, "when you put the choice in those terms, you very well know there's no real alternative."

* * *

The Reverend Obadiah Jenkins was one of the youngest men to have been granted a degree in theology at Cambridge University in more than a century. His recently acquired certification as clergyman made it difficult to interfere in the problems of others, but at this moment his conscience demanded that he right an obvious injustice. Still, he tried to concentrate on the roast mutton he was eating at the small country inn near Bradford, in Yorkshire, where he had stopped for a noon dinner on his ride south.

The couple at the next table seemed oblivious to the proximity of a stranger. The girl, who was quite pretty, said angrily, "I'm not refusing to marry Jonathan. I may, or I may not, depending on the way I feel a year from now. I'm simply insisting on my right to do as I see fit."

"You'll marry him, Elizabeth," the burly young man said grimly. "You know very well we're reduced to two small parcels of property—"

"That's all that's left of the estate papa left us because you gambled away the rest at cards!"

"Whatever the reason, and I readily admit my fondness for the gaming table, Sir Jonathan is still our best and only salvation. He may not be young, Elizabeth, but he's madly in love with you. And he's the wealthiest man in the county. You'll ride with me to his manor house the moment we finish this impossible meal in this stinking place, and you will accept his proposal!"

"I refuse!" the girl cried.

Obadiah Jenkins struggled to shut out the sound of their voices and tried to concentrate on his own situation. As it happened, his problem had been absurdly simple. He had been offered two parishes. One, in Sussex, was small, but its members were influential, and if he could expand the parish his future would be assured.

The other offer had been too ridiculous to even consider. His tutor at Cambridge, knowing his resources were severely limited, had shown him a letter from an official in the distant colony of Massachusetts Bay. The residents of a frontier village called Fort Springfield required the services of a Congregationalist clergyman. They promised anyone who volunteered for the post that they would build him a church and clear land for a property he could farm in order to grow his own vegetables and poultry. They also swore they would provide him with meat for his table—in lieu of pay—until such time as they could recompense him in cash.

Some might regard the offer as romantic, but Obadiah Jenkins, although still in his teens, was neither a child nor a lunatic, and he had decided to establish his ministry in safe, comfortable Sussex rather than in some barbaric New World outpost.

"Harry, you're hurting me!" the girl cried.

Obadiah Jenkins twisted around in his seat and saw that the man had caught hold of the girl's arm and was wrenching it behind her back.

"You'll damned well do as I tell you!" the man shouted.

"Please—stop!"

The man wrenched harder and with his free hand slapped the girl across the face.

Obadiah could tolerate no more, and he jumped up from the table. "Be good enough to release the lady!" he said.

"Mind your own business. She happens to be my

sister," said the man as he tried to drag the girl from the table.

"I asked you to release her. Now I demand it." Obadiah continued to speak with quiet authority.

The sobbing girl barely glanced at Obadiah as her brother dropped her arm, turned to confront this person who was daring to intervene, and saw someone so slender and youthful that he looked like a mere boy. "I won't warn you again," he said. "Go away."

"I'll depart gladly if you'll stop bullying this poor girl," said Obadiah.

The brother lost what little was left of his patience. His face, reddened by the ale he had been drinking, became even more florid, and he decided to rid himself of this nuisance before concluding the mission on which his future livelihood depended.

"We'll *discuss* this outside," he said, waving toward the door. He turned to the girl. "I will meet you at Sir Jonathan's house, Elizabeth."

Feeling regretful that he hadn't quite finished his meal, Obadiah left enough money to pay for it, and uncertain of what lay ahead, he accompanied the man to a field behind the stable at the rear of the little inn.

"I'm Harry Allen," the brother said brusquely. He appeared to be in his mid-twenties. "Who are you?"

"Obadiah Jenkins." Obadiah was relieved that he was not wearing his clerical attire.

"Well, Jenkins," Allen said, "I'm obliged to teach you not to stick your nose into matters that don't concern you." He drew his sword and laughed unpleasantly.

Obadiah was forced to draw his own blade, but he felt no fear. Throughout his stay at Cambridge he had obtained his exercise by fencing for one or two hours

35

each day, and he was as proficient in the art of swords-manship as he was in handling firearms.

Holding the blade he had inherited from his father, Obadiah calmly took measure of his opponent. It might be enough to wound him slightly, just to give the man's sister an opportunity to take herself elsewhere instead of committing herself to an unwanted marriage.

Harry Allen didn't bother with the niceties of a formal duel. Instead of saluting his foe and politely crossing swords, he lunged without warning, aiming the point of his blade at the younger man's throat.

Obadiah leaped to one side with barely enough time to raise his own sword and deflect the other's blow. He was enraged by the unorthodox maneuver, and he retreated, parrying a series of wild blows until his mind cleared and he gained some measure of self-control. *Anger,* his fencing instructor had told him repeatedly, *is a duelist's worst enemy: a calm, incisive mind is a sharper weapon than any sword.*

That advice saved Obadiah's life. He beat aside his opponent's reckless thrusts until he gradually came to realize that Allen was no match for him. The man was a rough country squire who relied on sheer force rather than finesse, and it became apparent that he knew little about the fine points of dueling.

Holding his sword high and remaining vigilant, Obadiah kept retreating, parrying, barely touching the other man's blade, and frequently maneuvering so it slid harmlessly along the length of his own.

Allen's inability to draw blood frustrated him, and his face grew redder as he exerted himself. It was impossible for him to admit that this boy could be a master swordsman and he himself only a crude amateur, and he began to use his heavy sword as a cudgel or whip, lashing back and forth with it.

Obadiah's calm gave way to alarm, and he began to fear that his own blade might snap when warding off a blow. Self-preservation demanded that the duel be rapidly terminated, and Obadiah decided it was best to inflict an injury to his foe's shoulder, pinking him just enough to incapacitate him while doing him no serious harm. Switching to the offensive, Obadiah feinted twice and then thrust his blade home.

Allen, not realizing that the momentum had changed, chose that precise moment to lunge again, viciously and abruptly. The sudden movement caused him to shift position slightly, raising his body and moving to one side.

Too late, the horrified Obadiah saw that his own thrust was aimed straight for his foe's heart. He was unable to halt or deflect his drive, and his sword penetrated deep into the man's body. Harry Allen died on the spot, the color draining from his ruddy face as he collapsed.

Too stunned to move, Obadiah finally had the presence of mind to withdraw his blade and wipe it clean on his opponent's clothes. Appalled by the idea that he had killed a fellow human being, he quickly realized that he had placed himself in an untenable position.

This had not been an ordinary duel. There was no referee, no physician, and no seconds to act as witnesses. He had no proof that he had been forced into the fight by a man who had not given him an opportunity to reject the challenge. In the eyes of the world, he could be accused of cold-blooded murder.

Only the man's sister had seen him leave the

inn, and surely she was not committed to testifying against her own brother in favor of a stranger who had gallantly but unwisely tried to prevent her from being abused.

At worst, Obadiah could be hanged; if a court showed him mercy, he might be sentenced to imprisonment for the rest of his life; and even if he were exonerated, no parish in England would accept the services of a clergyman who had killed a man in a duel.

Suddenly the secure position in Sussex evaporated and the life he had envisioned came to an end before it had started. His one hope now was that he could take advantage of his other opportunity and escape to America, beyond the reach of the Crown bailiffs.

Fighting panic and forcing himself to think, he made certain he had left none of his personal property on the field. Relieved that he had paid for his meal, he sprinted to the stable, noting that no one else had appeared in the field. As nearly as he could tell, there had been no witnesses to the duel and its grisly ending.

Obadiah's horse was still saddled, so he started off at once toward the port town of Hull, a little more than fifty miles away. Hull was the principal Midlands port of trade with the New World, and he hoped the twenty sovereigns in his pouch, all he had in the world, would be sufficient to buy him immediate passage to Massachusetts Bay.

When the inn was far behind and he was certain that no one was on the dirt road behind him, he spurred his horse to a gallop, but after racing for a short distance, he saw a lone rider ahead of him and prudently slowed to a walk.

As he approached, he saw that it was a woman riding sidesaddle, and he recognized the girl called

Elizabeth who had been the inadvertent cause of the tragic incident.

He drew up beside her, and she smiled at him timidly.

"Thank you for trying to help me," she said, "but I've decided that my brother is right. I'm going now to Sir Jonathan's house to tell him I've agreed to marry him."

Obadiah tipped his hat to the girl, smiled as best he could, and spurred forward again, but he rode no faster than a slow canter until he lost sight of her behind him. The irony of the situation was not lost on him. Harry Allen had died in vain, and he himself was a murderer in the eyes of the world because a foolish young woman had been unable to make up her mind.

Obadiah couldn't even contemplate the existence he would be compelled to lead in a raw community on the edge of the New World wilderness. Nor could he dwell on what might have been. He had to reach the safety of a ship that would sail before the Crown authorities found him.

Even an abiding faith in the Almighty was scarcely enough to sustain Obadiah Jenkins in this hour of his most severe trial. Nevertheless, he offered a silent prayer that he would not be overtaken and captured.

Andrew Wilson was sorry he had come to Newgate Prison in search of an indentured servant. Conditions here were intolerable. The vast majority of prisoners lived in the open during the warm weather, and then, when the cold forced them into it, they crowded into the ramshackle structures, where they had no choice but to sleep on the floors and to endure the stench of unwashed bodies and the lack of proper sanitary facilities. The slops they were fed once a day did little more than barely keep most of them from starving.

The worst misery of their daily existence was the realization that it was almost impossible to win release. Records were slipshod, the courts were indifferent, and only those who had funds were ever recommended for discharge. Debtors were the most pitiful. They would not be released until they paid their creditors, and while in prison they had no way of obtaining the money to do so.

Having been informed by Lord Bledsoe that it would be a long and difficult task to obtain the service of someone after reaching the New World, Captain Wilson steeled himself and decided to see the matter through. He walked with his hand on the hilt of his sword, ready to withdraw the blade if any of the gangs of ruffians roaming the grounds came near him and his escorts, for the two surly guards armed with short swords looked incompetent, and he felt only contempt for the assistant warden in charge of the party.

Andrew had rejected three candidates without bothering to speak to them. They were brutes, creatures who looked capable of murdering him and Mildred in their beds, and he had no intention of taking such people with him to the wilderness of North America.

"Ah, there's a likely candidate, Your Worship," the assistant warden declared.

Andrew saw a young man in his early twenties sitting on a low stone fence, his once-respectable clothing frayed and torn. Following the direction of the young prisoner's gaze, Andrew saw that he was watching a young woman, a girl even younger than himself, as she drew a bucket of water from a well and drank from the dipper. She was wearing a dark gown that had seen better days, and from a distance she seemed attractive, although painfully thin. There were few overweight inmates at Newgate.

"Stand up, you!" the assistant warden demanded, prodding the young man with a short whip.

The nudge was an unnecessary insult, and the young man flushed as he stood up.

"Tell His Worship your name and the reason you're under sentence here."

"Thomas Hibbard," the prisoner said. "God help me, I'm a debtor. My father died a week after I was married, and I inherited his debts of eighty sovereigns, which I couldn't pay. So here I am and here I'll stay until I rot." Hibbard met the visitor's eyes with a steady gaze. He had somehow managed to stay healthy in this ghastly place, and his speech indicated that he had enjoyed some rudiments of an education.

Andrew liked the looks of the young man, and after weighing the matter for a moment he decided to take the plunge.

Introducing himself, he said, "If you're interested, I'll pay off your debts and take you to the New World with me. You'll be bonded to me for two seven-year periods, and you'll work with me to develop a property I've recently bought on the wilderness frontier. Will you go?"

For an instant hope flared in Tom Hibbard's eyes, then faded again. "I'd give my soul to do it, sir, but I can't." He gestured toward the young woman, who was approaching with a worried expression on her face. "My wife is a debtor, too, seeing as how the law court took away the few sovereigns she brought into our marriage and made her a criminal with me. I wouldn't leave her alone in this godforsaken jungle for all the freedom on earth."

"What's amiss, Tom?" said Agnes Hibbard as she came up to them.

Her husband explained the situation to her, and she nodded, fighting back tears.

"How much are your debts, Mistress Hibbard?" Andrew asked.

"Four sovereigns, but they might as well be four thousand." Like her husband, she spoke with calm civility, and her eyes did not waver.

Andrew didn't hesitate. "Will you come with your husband and join Mistress Wilson and me in our adventure?"

Agnes Hibbard studied this benefactor who was offering a release from the living hell of Newgate. He was obviously an aristocrat, and his character appeared to be reflected in his direct gaze and firm smiling mouth. What was more, she detected a warmth and sympathy in him that she and Tom had found in no one during the year and a half they had spent in this horrid place.

More articulate by far than her husband, she spoke for both of them. "Tom and I accept your kindness, Captain Wilson, and we thank you with all our hearts. You won't regret this, sir, and neither will your lady. It doesn't matter what kind of life lies ahead for us in America. Anything is better than this, and I promise we'll serve you well."

They went to collect their meager belongings while Andrew went to the office of the assistant warden. There he paid the two debts and signed the necessary papers, and he was ready to depart by the time the Hibbards joined him.

They walked beside him to the front gate, clutching their precious release documents, still dazed by their good fortune.

"I'll buy you some new clothes and a decent meal," Andrew said, "and tell you what little I know about the life that lies ahead for us." He stopped short when he realized that they weren't listening to a word he said.

Tears glistened in Agnes Hibbard's eyes, and she gestured beyond the grim walls of Newgate Prison.

"We're free, Tom," she murmured. "Free!"

America was far from what the Reverend Obadiah Jenkins had expected. He hadn't cared much for Boston, any more than he liked cities in England, but this remote countryside in western Massachusetts Bay was different.

The waters of the Connecticut River were so clear he could see the salmon and shad gliding deep below the surface. The forest that stretched toward the horizon to the west seemed to comprise an ocean of trees as vast as the Atlantic. There was game enough for all in that forest, just as the fertile ground would produce corn and wheat, flax and barley and vegetables in quantities liberal enough to support a large population.

Obadiah inhaled deeply as he paused in his task of nailing a roof to the frame of his new log house.

Dangers lurked in the forest, of course, from animals and from Indians. The principal danger, he had learned, lay to the north, where the French, who had established colonies in Canada, had ambitions that caused them to covet the English settlements.

He felt almost no guilt over the tragic incident that forced him to flee to North America. Apparently it was right that he had come here, and strangely, he felt at home. Like his new neighbors, Captain and Mistress

Wilson, who were also building a house, he found the wilderness a challenge.

Had he gone to that parish in Sussex he would have lived a peaceful, uneventful life, but here, he reflected, every day posed new adventures. What he enjoyed most was the knowledge of how badly he was needed.

Glancing at the sun to determine the approximate time, he went into his cabin. He washed in the water he had drawn from the river, changed from work clothes into his clerical garb, and taking his sword and a pistol, he went to saddle his new horse.

As he rode along the bank of the river, Obadiah caught a glimpse of the ruins of Fort Springfield. The Indians who had destroyed the bastion had been thorough, burning it to the ground. He agreed unreservedly with Captain Wilson that it must be rebuilt, and as soon as his own house was finished he would join the volunteers who were already hard at work laying foundations for a new fort that neither the French army nor any Indian force, no matter what their size, would dare attack.

After riding for about a quarter of an hour, Obadiah arrived at a small log house in a clearing, and he concentrated on the task ahead of him. Only a few hundred settlers were scattered throughout the region, and all of them were worried about the Widow Alwin.

They had ample cause for concern. Two of the earliest settlers on the frontier, Ida Alwin and her husband had avoided the massacre at Fort Springfield because of a lucky accident. They had gone off to Boston to meet Ida's brother, as well as his wife and their infant daughter, who were arriving by ship from England. The Alwins' absence from the town had saved their lives, but their troubles had been endless. Learning that her brother and sister-in-law had died on board ship, Ida and her husband had adopted their niece, Deborah. Then their own child had been born. Poor little Walter, still a baby, was discovered to be deaf and mute.

Most recently, Ida's husband had passed away, and the woman lived alone with the two youngsters and tried to do a man's work to keep up her farm. The burden was too great for her, and friends had tried to persuade her to move to Boston where she could earn a comfortable living as a seamstress.

Only recently, Captain and Mildred Wilson had spoken to her about it. The Wilsons' wealth and vast holdings gave them a position of responsibility and respect in the community, but the outspoken Mistress Alwin had told them, none too politely, to mind their own business. Now it was the new clergyman's turn to try to help her, and he didn't relish the task.

She came to the door at once in response to his polite tap. "What a nice surprise, Reverend Jenkins," she said.

"I just happened to be in the neighborhood and thought I'd drop in," said Obadiah. His excuse was lame, but it would be years before he would be able to develop the knack of inventing better reasons for calls like this. "Hello, Deborah."

The blue-eyed child—she was only five or six—had hair the color of ripened wheat. She looked like a toy doll as she curtsied. "Good day, Reverend Jenkins."

Obadiah went to the crib and greeted the baby with a smile and a gentle caress. In spite of his handicap, there was a lively intelligence in Walter's eyes, reflected the minister.

Ida Alwin busied herself pouring tea.

"I'm interrupting you," Obadiah said, "and I wish you wouldn't make a fuss on my account."

"Rubbish," she replied. "It's no bother, and even if it was, we did without a man of the cloth here for so long that I'd gladly bake a cake for you to take home with you!"

He laughed, then turned as the little girl, who had been sitting and reading a book, jumped to the floor. "May I go out and roll my hoop, Aunt Ida?"

"Very well, but stay in sight of the window so I can keep watch on you."

Deborah skipped out, carefully closing the door behind her.

"There ain't too many Indians hereabouts these days," the woman said. "Leastwise nobody has reported any Naturals in the neighborhood. But it don't pay to get careless."

Obadiah Jenkins took a deep breath. "Indeed," he said. "But living here is so hazardous that it imposes a terrible burden on you, Mistress Alwin."

"I don't suffer more than anybody else," she replied in a quiet, firm voice. "Oh, I've had my share of tragedy, but I'm grateful that the Lord gave me a strong back and a willingness to abide misfortune."

His discretion was greater than his valor when facing this formidable woman, and he beat a hasty retreat. "How does it happen that Deborah can read?"

"It didn't just happen, Reverend Jenkins," she snapped, then calmed herself by sipping her hot tea. "I've been teaching her ever since she was a tiny tot, not much older than Walter is right now."

"If you'll forgive the observation, I'm surprised that you have the ability to read."

"I taught myself when I was young," Ida said. "I

46

have a fair hand for writing, too. I talk careless-like sometimes, but now that Debbie is growing older I'm taking more care with my grammar." A wistful expression came into her eyes. "It's my greatest regret that Walter will never be able to read."

"Not at Fort Springfield, I'm afraid." He saw an opening and made up his mind to exploit it. "It might be that there are people in a city who could help him."

"We don't live in a city," she said flatly. "We live here."

"Mistress Alwin," he said, "I came here this afternoon with the intention of trying to persuade you to move to Boston where you could earn far more with your needlework than the bare living you make here. Now that I know you can read and write, I'd like to point out that even better doors would be open to you. During my short stay in Boston I was told by any number of people that they have a great need for teachers there. I myself had more offers than I could count."

"But you refused them and came to Fort Springfield, sir," she said promptly. "Will you allow me to be rude and ask your reasons for turning down those offers?"

She was clever to place him on the defensive. "I am an ordained minister," he said, "not a schoolteacher, and I have God's work to do."

"That's fine, Reverend. You have God's work to do, and I have mine, and I must do it myself, in my own way! Last week it was old John Bailey, and the week before it was the Cruickshanks. Two days ago Captain Wilson and his pretty wife just happened to be passing by, and they started in on me. They all mean well, but most people don't seem to know they're being rude when they stop minding their own affairs and start offering advice to those who don't want it and don't need it."

"Someday, in five or ten years, there will be enough people in Fort Springfield for you to work exclusively as a seamstress, Mistress Alwin," said Obadiah. "Until then, you'll have to work your farm."

"I know farming."

"To be sure, but the work is very hard. And you have two small children who depend on you, one of them suffering from physical problems."

"I don't neglect Walter or Deborah, and I never will!"

"But your life would be so much more comfortable—"

"I don't seek comfort." Ida Alwin stood and faced the young clergyman, her eyes shining. "Hear me out, Reverend Jenkins. My husband, bless him, and I cleared this land with our own hands, felling trees, uprooting stumps, digging out boulders. This land is *mine!* My son and my niece will own it after me, and it will go to their descendants after them. No catastrophe or calamity will ever drive me away from Fort Springfield. You're new to America, but when you've lived here for a spell you'll know what I mean. This land is a part of me now, and I'll live here and die here. This is my home."

Chapter IV

By the eleventh autumn of Renno's life, he was tall and powerful, so advanced for his age that he sometimes defeated adult warriors in games of strength and skill. Ghonka had taken personal charge of his education, and one day each week, when the Great Sachem's busy schedule permitted, he went off into the forest to give private instruction to his son. It was assumed that Ghonka revealed to the boy the secrets of making war and keeping peace, as well as teaching him the tricks of combat that had made the Great Sachem the most honored and feared Iroquois leader in the memory of the oldest inhabitants of the League.

El-i-chi was showing substantial progress, too. Stronger and much sturdier, although still slight for his nine years, he had earned the respect of his peers for his exceptional intelligence and unflinching endurance. He had learned to handle himself in free-for-all fights with older, heavier boys, and even when seemingly defeated he doggedly continued to do battle. One of his more remarkable talents was his ability to walk all day

49

after eating only a handful of corn, just like an adult warrior.

The brothers were inseparable, conducting most of their exercises together, and they had developed such a sensitive rapport that they seldom needed words, for each seemed to divine the thinking of the other.

They were often joined on their journeys into the forest by Ja-gonh, and the trio sometimes spent several days together, but Renno and El-i-chi made no mention of these visits, and in spite of their curiosity, the other boys asked no questions.

After twice failing the manhood tests, Skah-non-dih managed to pass them on the third try, thus making it unnecessary to expel him from the ranks of the Seneca. He was a full-fledged junior warrior now, seldom seen by the younger boys.

Renno had taken his place as leader of the band of boys, even though some in the company were two or three years older. His skills in hunting, fishing, and tracking; his cunning and valor in war games; and his proficiency in sports and trials of strength had won him the place, and none disputed it. The warriors in charge of the band's instruction were struck by his relative wisdom, his sound judgment, and his refusal to become involved in the petty quarrels that frequently erupted.

The members of the band enjoyed the tenth moon of the year more than any other because they returned home to spend time with their families. The season was autumn, when hunting was at its best after the animals and birds had feasted all summer on the bounty of the mother-earth, and the boys were expected to help fill the larders with food supplies for the coming winter.

There were few members of the boys' band who enjoyed the season more than Renno and El-i-chi. Ena made new loincloths and robes, leggings and moccasins and shirts for them, and early each morning, after stuffing themselves with boiled corn pudding and maple syrup, cold meat, and bowls of sweet pumpkin soup, they went hunting, rarely returning before dusk. They always took a pot of honey with them for Ja-gonh.

The brothers developed remarkable teamwork. El-i-chi had a sixth sense for finding game, and Renno dispatched it with sure, quick arrows or lances. On one occasion, with the help of Ja-gonh (who aided them in a manner they explained to no one but Ghonka), they killed an elk. The carcass was so large that, while Ja-gonh stood guard, the boys had to summon help from three adult warriors of the Bear Clan, who carved it and brought it home.

One morning, the boys set out soon after breakfast. The air was crisp, the smoke from the wood fires mingled with the delicious cooking odors, and the leaves were turning. The father-sun appeared on the horizon, and both Renno and El-i-chi were at peace with the world. No boys could have asked for a more glorious day for hunting.

They left the palisade, walked across the fields, and plunged into the forest, not aware that they were being followed by a stealthy Skah-non-dih. For two years he had waited to avenge the humiliation he had suffered because of them, and having observed their routines during this moon, he had chosen today to even the score. Perhaps he would kill them, although he might be satisfied to shame them and make them appear ludicrous. He would decide when the opportunity presented itself.

Renno and El-i-chi made no noise when they walked. Their feet seemed to be guided by magic as they avoided dead leaves that would rustle or small branches that would crack beneath their feet. The discipline of their training had already become instinctive, and they were as silent as the lynx, as cunning as the wolf. Their mastery of the wilderness was almost as great as that of grown braves.

They made their way rapidly toward the south, and then Renno halted his brother with a gesture. In a small clearing they saw the tracks of three deer.

El-i-chi studied the largest set of tracks. "There's our buck," he said, speaking in the special low tone the Seneca used when they didn't want their voices to carry through the forest.

Renno dropped to one knee and examined the hoofprints. "No, this deer is a mature doe," he replied, and he refrained from adding that he hoped it was a doe for the simple reason that his mother preferred the more flattering doeskin to the heavier, more durable buckskin.

As El-i-chi well knew, no one could determine from hoofprints whether a deer was a male or a female. He admired his brother above all people except their parents, but just this once he wished he could be right. He would tease his brother for days.

Renno, who knew what he was thinking, laughed silently and playfully tugged at the back of the younger boy's scalp lock. That tug meant that they had made a wager: the loser would be obliged to cut out the brains and liver that would be used in the curing of the skin, a messy task at best.

The tracks were easily read, and it was obvious that the deer was large. The boys moved with even greater caution, two wraiths making their way through the trees.

They had no way of knowing that Skah-non-dih

had gained on them and was creeping along, following them with equally great care.

Renno glanced at his brother.

El-i-chi nodded.

The tracks were leading them to a rock outcropping rich in natural salt where deer frequently congregated to satisfy their craving for salt, and Renno was almost certain that was where the animal had gone.

The tracks were becoming fresher, and both boys knew they would soon find their deer.

Skah-non-dih knew it, too, and he also followed the deer tracks, sure they would lead to the lick. He wondered if it would be enough to frighten the deer away at the last moment, and then vanish himself. No, for then the arrogant brothers wouldn't realize he had been the one responsible, and he wanted them to know that he had avenged himself against them.

Renno caught a glimpse of the deer and immediately halted well back in the trees, downwind from where the animal was feeding.

El-i-chi stopped, too, even before he saw the deer. He peered through the trees, then grimaced. Renno was right again. The animal was a mature doe.

Renno refrained from smiling. He had won the wager, which was satisfaction enough, and there was no need to make El-i-chi unhappy. Now they had to bring down the deer, and he made a brief gesture, meaningless to anyone but his brother.

The boys separated and approached the lick from different angles. The one who first obtained the clearest and most direct sight line would be the one to shoot the deer.

Remaining between the pair, Skah-non-dih moved closer, too, and all at once saw what they did not.

Someone or something moved slightly at the top of the rock outcropping, then vanished from sight. The young brave froze, staring hard at the spot, and finally made out a tiny patch of copper-colored skin. A human being was lurking at the top of the rocks, and the mere idea that he was taking care not to reveal himself, not putting an arrow into the deer, indicated that he had to be an enemy of the Seneca.

Skah-non-dih was torn. He had been yearning for revenge against Renno and his brother, but he was still a Seneca, loyal to his nation, and if he could kill or capture an enemy brave he would win great glory which might well result in his advancement from the ranks of the junior warriors, who were required to perform most of the difficult and unpleasant tasks on the trail.

Common sense won the battle, and with great reluctance Skah-non-dih decided that revenge would have to wait. He could always find an opportunity to harass the brothers, but the chance to kill or capture a foe of his people and prove himself worthy of promotion was too great to be missed.

He slipped around to one side of the little glade and silently crept up the slope that led to the summit of the rock outcropping.

Eventually, Skah-non-dih caught sight of the man. He was an adult of at least five and twenty summers, a brave who wore the full vermilion and white war paint of the Erie. Truly an enemy.

The Erie, concentrating his attention on El-i-chi, reached for an arrow and fitted it into his bow.

Skah-non-dih wondered how, without being seen, he could cover the fifty feet that separated him from the Erie. He decided that the capture of the enemy seemed too difficult to accomplish; he would get rid of the man with an arrow of his own.

At that moment, Renno, whose senses were always attuned to nuances, looked up and saw Skah-non-dih on top of the rock pile. Not seeing the Erie, he jumped to the conclusion that the older boy intended to shoot him or his brother.

"No, no!" he shouted, the sound of his voice sending the doe into headlong flight, and leaping to one side, he raced toward El-i-chi to throw him to the ground and cover his brother's body with his own.

The Erie, who had just begun to draw his bow, turned for an instant and caught sight of Skah-non-dih standing at the far end of the little rock pile. Realizing that he himself had almost been trapped, he shifted his aim, his bow twanged, and the arrow sang through the air.

Skah-non-dih had no chance. He crumpled to the ground, the Erie's arrow embedded in his throat, and died without making a sound.

Too late, Renno became aware of the real danger. In his scramble to avoid Skah-non-dih, he had foolishly dropped his own bow, and now he saw that El-i-chi, who had managed to race back to the shelter of the trees, also had left his bow behind. Both brothers were helpless, and Renno stood in the open, completely exposed to enemy fire.

The Erie grinned at him as he fitted another arrow into his bow and took aim.

Renno made up his mind to die bravely. He folded his arms across his chest and waited for the arrow that would end his life.

But the shaft was never fired, for there came a rumbling noise followed by a deep-throated roar, and

Ja-gonh stood fully upright on his hind legs and charged toward the Erie.

The great bear battered the man with his powerful paws, and the terrified Erie screamed. Then Ja-gonh sank his teeth into the brave, shaking the man like a dog worrying a bone, and Renno heard a sickening cracking sound as the Erie's neck broke.

Ja-gonh dropped the body, which rolled off the edge of the outcrop and fell to the spot where the doe had been feeding a few moments earlier. The bear stood there, snarled, then dropped to all fours and silently looked down at Renno.

As unmoving as the beast, the boy returned his gaze. "Thank you, brother," he said. "May your winter sleep be peaceful, and may the manitous guard you from all harm."

Ja-gonh turned and quietly trotted away, vanishing into the forest beyond the rocks.

El-i-chi, recovering from his fright, emerged from the woods and joined his brother. "We will not see Ja-gonh again until the buds appear on the trees and the grass begins to turn green," he said. "How can we repay our debt to him? If he hadn't appeared, the Erie would have killed us both."

"Members of a family," Renno replied, "do not measure their debts to each other. Our father helps us in many ways, but we cannot say what we owe him. I am bigger and stronger than you, so I do many things for you now. But the day may come when I will need you more than you need me."

Together they made a sling of vines so they could carry Skah-non-dih's body back to the Seneca town. Renno stared down at the body of the Erie. He hesitated for an instant, fighting a natural feeling of revulsion, then dropped to one knee and cut away the brave's scalp lock. It was still dripping when he thrust it into the top of his loincloth. "This prize belongs to Ja-gonh, not to me," he said, "but for his sake I will carry it."

For a time they trudged in silence, and the burden they carried was heavy. At last El-i-chi spoke. "Skah-non-dih was a true son of the Seneca," he said. "He had no friendship for you and me, but he gave his life for us, so I honor him."

"It is so," Renno replied, but his tone lacked conviction. He thought it odd that Skah-non-dih had appeared so suddenly, seemingly out of nowhere. Perhaps the young warrior had intended to ambush him and El-i-chi but had been distracted by the unexpected presence of the Erie. A buck might shed its horns and grow a new pair, but its hide remained unchanged. So it was with people. Skah-non-dih had made no secret of his enmity, and there was no reason to think he might have changed his attitude toward the brothers.

"It is true," Renno said, "that the Erie would have killed us had Skah-non-dih not taken into his own body the arrow that was aimed at me. Yet I must admit to you that I am glad we owe nothing to him or to his clan. Ja-gonh, our brother, avenged his death."

El-i-chi was impressed by his brother's wisdom. A remark he had overheard Sah-nee-wa make to their father was true. When Renno reached manhood, there would be no warrior in all of the tribes on the earth who would be his equal.

When Renno reached his fourteenth summer, the women of the Bear Clan held a meeting, and there they listened to the words of Sah-nee-wa and Ena. Both declared flatly that Renno, although a year younger than most of those who took the tests of manhood, was ready to face the trials that would determine whether he would leave the band of boys and be admitted to the ranks of junior warriors. The women, who had been keeping the youth under close observation, agreed without dissent, and the result of their ballot was duly reported to Ghonka.

The Great Sachem summoned his war council, the elders, and the senior warriors to a conclave in the community longhouse, and there he presented the boy's case. "Do not send him to the trials because he is the son of Ghonka," he said. "Send him only if he is worthy of being tested."

A small clay pot, ornamented in the yellow and green Seneca colors, was passed from hand to hand, and each man placed a hand over the open top before giving it to his neighbor. Anyone who opposed the admission of Renno to the tests would drop a raw bean in the pot.

The chief medicine man of the Seneca then announced solemnly that there were no beans in the pot. Renno would join the others to face the manhood tests.

Careful preparations were made. First Renno polished the bear claw necklace Ghonka had given him after he had killed his first bear, placing it on a new plaited ribbon of thongs. Then he carefully shaved his head, except for his scalp lock, with a finely honed stone he had spent days sharpening. Finally, he and two other boys who were members of the Bear Clan were summoned to a meeting of the clan's women.

Their mothers offered songs to the manitous, asking for the protection of their sons. Ena's chant was long and involved, as befitted a medicine woman, and lasted for the better part of a morning. Renno, seated cross-legged on the ground at her feet, his hands folded

58

across his chest and his head bowed, remained motionless the entire time his mother prayed.

That evening Ena left the family hut immediately after the meal had been eaten, and El-i-chi made it his business to wander off inconspicuously so that Renno would be alone with his father.

Ghonka took a long time stuffing shredded and dried tobacco into his pipe, then he meticulously lighted it with a coal from the cooking fire. "My son," he said, "you know the ways of old, the ways practiced by our fathers and mothers since the beginning of time."

"It is so," Renno replied, trying to conceal his anxiety. He had spent his life preparing for the manhood tests, and he knew they would be rigorous beyond belief, straining his skills and strength to their limits. If he failed, how could he face his parents, his little brother, or the members of the Bear Clan?

"You know how to live with the manitous of the forest and make your peace with them."

"It is so, my father." The boy's uneasiness increased.

"You have been taught endurance and courage. Now it will be seen if you falter or flinch."

"It is so, my father." Renno had heard grisly tales of the initiation rites. Some boys, even those who had done well in their years of instruction, had failed in their trials and consequently were compelled to spend another full year with mere children.

"The medicine you wear is strong. It will help you." Ghonka touched the bear claw necklace.

The boy nodded.

The Great Sachem's manner became stern. "It is forbidden for Ja-gonh to help you in your trials. Only you will know whether he comes to you when you are alone in the forest. So you must remember that your honor will not permit you to seek or accept aid from him."

"Yesterday," Renno replied, "I met Ja-gonh in the forest, and I explained to him that I must be alone to solve my problems by myself. He understands, and he will not come to me until I have passed my tests and am permitted to wear the feathers of a warrior."

His father smiled broadly. A lesser youth might be tempted to cheat, but Renno's sense of honor was sacred to him, and his word was sufficient.

"When I return," Renno said, "I will be a man." He desperately hoped he could live up to that pledge.

"I have confidence in you," Ghonka replied.

The boy thought the talk was ended and started to rise.

"Wait, my son."

Renno sat again.

The Great Sachem began to search for words, finding it difficult to express himself. The subject he had in mind was delicate and had to be handled in the right way. "I suppose it is your hope that you will see a vision and that it will tell your future."

"Yes, my father." More than anything in the world Renno hoped he would encounter a vision who would give him a glimpse of his future.

Ghonka hesitated, then took the plunge. "It may be that you will not be granted a vision. I want to spare you disappointment. Sometimes it happens that a man does not meet his first vision until he goes on his first war party."

"So I have been told."

"You have seen fourteen winters, no more, so it may be that your time has not come. Some of our greatest and most powerful war chiefs have met no visions—ever in their lives."

"I know, my father."

"It is true that I myself was granted orenda when I was only your age," Ghonka reminisced.

Orenda was magical power that manifested itself in different ways. It was granted by supernatural spirits to a very few Seneca men and women. Both Ghonka and Ena had acquired these powers in their youth, as had Sah-nee-wa, so it was not unreasonable for Renno to hope that he might be similarly favored.

"However," his father continued, "it is not right to expect powers from the spirits. They make their gifts as they wish, not as we wish."

Renno felt a stab of guilt. He had been assuming that orenda would be given to him, even though deep down he knew this attitude might offend and alienate the spirits.

"I will sing many songs for your safe return," Ghonka said gently as he raised his hand in dismissal and blessing.

Renno bowed his head for a moment, then turned away and went off to join the other members of his group.

The next morning, the group headed out of the town, walking silently in single file through the fields and into the forest. These boys knew each other well, for they had played together since they were small, but now no one joked or played pranks, no one shouted or challenged his friends to a race. By the time the tests ended, those who succeeded would be admitted to the company of men, and never again would they indulge in childish behavior.

Parents and friends watched them depart, quietly applauding their demeanor. Their gravity was a good omen.

For several hours they marched together, making

almost no sound as they slipped through the sea of trees. Then, without anyone giving a signal, they halted simultaneously, raised their right arms in farewell, and went off in separate directions.

Renno trotted along, his gait steady, taking care not to expend too much energy. He moved at an even pace for the rest of the morning, and soon his spirits began to brighten. All his life he had learned to rely only on himself, to be courageous, and to survive without help from anyone. Now he felt a surge of determination. He intended to meet every challenge his trial had to offer.

For three days he would see and speak to no one, fasting to give himself greater inner strength. Then he and the others would meet, each finding his own way to the gathering place where the instructor would compel them to face a series of ordeals. This phase would go on for seven days, and then they would fast again for a final four days. During this last period, if the spirits willed it, some of the more fortunate might see the visions every Seneca longed for.

His only weapon was a small knife; those who sought the favor of the manitous could not appear armed in the presence of the spirits. But he felt no fear. The day was warm, and by the time the sun stood directly overhead the heat had become intense, with insects buzzing in every clearing and open space. But Renno was comfortable, and as he jogged he searched for a suitable place to spend his time of fasting. He paused to drink water from a small stream, which was permitted, and he stretched out on the ground to rest, relaxing completely before he set out again.

The boy trotted for most of the afternoon, and late in the day he found a hillside, lightly covered with brush, and decided it was a good place to halt. A brook ran through a small gully at the base of the hill, the scrub was deep enough to cover him and offer protection, yet no enemy could sneak through it and attack him.

For two nights and two days Renno stayed in the same place, fasting, letting his thoughts wander as he contemplated the legends of the Seneca, and sometimes singing one of the ancient chants the manitous had taught to the nation's ancestors. His initial hunger soon passed, and it proved surprisingly easy to turn his mind away from food. Even the wild raspberries on the slope did not tempt him.

His mind functioned clearly, the images that came to him were sharp and well defined, and he was at peace with himself and the world around him.

By the end of the third day, Renno began to feel strangely light-headed. The yellow flowers dotting the hillside became brighter and seemed to glow, and when the wind sang through the trees below the hillside, he could almost hear voices. The breeze seemed to be on the verge of revealing something to him before it died away, only to start again a short time later. When the cool air caressed his skin he had the sensation that, if he tried hard enough, he could float into the air like a bird. At the end of the third day, he broke his fast by eating a few strips of dried venison and a handful of parched corn, but he had no real interest in the food, which he found tasteless. When night came, he looked up at the stars and the waxing moon and he sang the songs Sah-nee-wa had taught him, asking the manitous to grant him visions if they approved of him. Then, unable to stay awake, he fell into a deep sleep.

That night the dreams came. But they were the dreams of almost-vision rather than of vision itself. Some were ugly and threatening, and others made no sense. In one, he stood at dusk before a longhouse unlike any he had ever seen, its smoke hole elongated by a tube on the roof. Even more peculiar were the side openings, which were covered with an extraordinary substance, solid and hard, that kept out wind and snow and rain but was transparent, admitting light to the dwelling as well as allowing one to see the interior of the place from the outside. Nowhere in the world could there be such a magical substance.

The dream went on. The door opened and a woman emerged who reminded him of his aunt because her hair was gray. A single glance at her face was enough to reveal that she was firm, self-reliant, and that she would tolerate no nonsense. Her face, hands, and forearms—the only portions of her body that he could see outside the dress that covered her from her neck to her feet—were pale, the color of the juice of a milkweed pod. Never had he seen a human being with such a peculiar pale skin, and it made him uneasy.

The dream continued. A younger woman—a girl—appeared in the doorway behind the woman. Her hair, which shone in the sunlight, resembled the tassels of cornstalks, and Renno was so fascinated by its golden hue that it took another moment or two for him to realize that the girl, like the older woman, also had pale skin.

While he gaped, his uneasiness increasing, the girl slowly extended a hand to him and said something in a strange tongue. Virtually all tribes could understand each other, even if they spoke somewhat differently, but the girl addressed him in a language that was incomprehensible.

Renno fled, not because he lacked courage, but because the menace represented by these women was beyond his understanding. Even though he knew he was dreaming, he congratulated himself on his wisdom in escaping.

He slowed his pace in the dream, then walked through the shadow country of sleep until he came to another longhouse. This one looked more familiar, with a proper smoke hole in its roof and no shiny, clear substance in its side openings. Without hesitation, the boy decided to go in and ask for shelter.

He entered, and the longhouse was empty. But a fire was burning in the pit, so he sat down beside it to wait.

After a time, the fire spoke: *"Someone has just come in. I believe it is a young man."*

"Indeed it is," the ceiling replied.

Renno's flesh crawled. He had heard of nonhuman objects speaking to people, but only in stories and legends, not in real life.

"I am here," he said aloud, careful not to mention his name. Evil magic could be done by supernatural forces when they learned one's name. "I have come to ask for shelter until morning. Where is the owner of this longhouse?"

The fire laughed. *"When she comes home you'll be surprised! Won't he, ceiling?"*

The ceiling was not amused. *"Young man, be wise, and leave. The owner of this longhouse approves only of young warriors who have courage. To them she gives power. But she kills cowardly braves."*

Renno was irritated, even though he knew he was dreaming. "I am no coward," he said. "Test me and see for yourselves. I will gladly accept power if it is given to me, but anyone who wants to kill me will be killed first. Who is this person who owns the longhouse?"

"She is not a person," the fire replied, crackling

65

with humor. *"She is half human, but her face is not the face of humans."*

Renno, dreaming furiously, immediately thought of the great false-face masks, the strange and twisted carvings that lined the walls of the community longhouse in the Seneca town. They were terrifying, mysterious beings, but sometimes they granted powers, including the ability to cure sickness and madness, to those who showed them respect. Now that he knew the owner of this longhouse was a face, he would have to proceed with great caution. Certainly she had the power to kill him.

The dream seemed endless.

The ceiling laughed. *"I know what this young one is thinking,"* it said. *"He believes the owner will grant him face power."*

The fire snapped. *"Is he a healer, do you think?"*

The ceiling spoke somberly now. *"Not this one. If he proves he has the courage of a lion, she might take pity on him and make him a warrior."*

The fire burned higher. *"Why would she do that?"*

"Because she is part one thing and part something else. And so is he!"

In spite of the heat thrown by the fire, Renno felt a chill. He was hearing something he had never discussed with anyone, something he had tried to lock out of his mind, something more important than anything in his life.

"He does not yet know what he is," the ceiling said, *"but he is not like the other Seneca. The skin under his loincloth, where the father-sun does not strike it, is as pale as the light of the moon. So is his hair."*

The awful unspoken truth was out in the open at last! Renno was different. His hair was the color of corn tassels, like the hair of the girl in the earlier part of his dream. His skin, too, was as pale beneath his loin-cloth as the skin of the girl and the older woman. He cringed.

No one had ever mentioned these matters to him, yet since earliest childhood he himself had known them, and that knowledge had spurred him to become stronger and more cunning than all the others, had driven him to show greater endurance and display greater courage.

Suddenly he heard a low moaning sound that congealed his blood. Perhaps it was only the wind, but he remembered Sah-nee-wa telling him about the noise a manitou made when it was about to reveal itself.

He was not ready to accept a vision. He was unprepared for any verdict that might be rendered. In fact, no warrior had ever been known to experience a vision until the very end of his two-week trials.

Renno fled from the longhouse, and the dream ended.

Although the night had been cool, he awakened in a lather of perspiration. Dawn was breaking, and he returned slowly to reality. He bathed in the stream, then found a rabbit in the snare he had set the previous night. He made a fire, and while the rabbit was roasting he caught two fish in the stream and gathered handfuls of the wild raspberries. His appetite had returned with a vengeance.

When he finished eating, Renno set out for the rendezvous, and as he trotted through the forest he felt that he had reason to be satisfied with his progress. His dreams were confusing, but he had gleaned that the manitous might extend favors to him, so for the present he was content. He had never wanted to be a healer like his mother, and it was good to know he was not being considered for that vocation.

His one desire was to become a warrior as mighty and renowned as Ghonka.

It did not matter that his hair was as yellow or the skin beneath his loincloth as pale as that of the girl in his dream. He was the son of Ghonka and Ena, and in years to come he would give the whole Seneca nation good cause to sing his praises.

Renno had to travel farther to reach the rendezvous than any of the others, and when he arrived he had no chance to rest. The instructor, a senior warrior named Hawen, ordered the boys to run again and again around the lake on whose bank they were making their camp. Some of the initiates, not yet recovered from their three days of fasting, stumbled and tried to remain on the ground to rest, but Hawen promptly beat them with a birch rod until they got to their feet again, and they ran until their tongues were hanging out and they panted like tired dogs.

Renno was determined not to be beaten, and he continued to run even when he felt certain his legs would give way beneath him.

The boys were allowed to halt long enough to eat some dried fish, venison strips, and parched corn, and then they were forced to run again. The exercise continued all afternoon without respite, and whenever they lagged Hawen taunted them.

Hawen, running with them effortlessly, shouted, "I am an old man ready for the long sleep. But I can do what these strong young braves cannot. You are children who should be returned to the care of your mothers!"

Shortly before nightfall he sent them hunting in pairs, and two of the boys soon brought down a buck that provided them all with ample meat. They were exhausted and ready for sleep as soon as they had eaten, but Hawen forced them to dance around the fire, chanting songs that asked the manitous for courage and strength.

It was the middle of the night before the boys were allowed to stretch out on the ground, and Renno, like all the others, dropped off to sleep instantly.

Before dawn, Hawen awakened his charges by throwing cold water into their faces. There was no sign of light in the sky, the moon had vanished, and the boys ate cold venison in the dark. Then they followed Hawen and began to run again, but this time they went only a short distance, halting when they reached a gorge where a waterfall sent sheets of chilly spray down to rocks below. Renno stared at the white water roaring past him.

"Swim!" Hawen called. "Now!"

No one dared disobey, and the boys plunged into the numbing water. Renno almost lost his balance, regaining it just in time to prevent himself from being swept away by the swift current.

They swam for a time, then were ordered to stand still in a pool at one side of the river where the waters surged around their necks. There they remained for most of the morning, motionless shadows whose arms, legs, and bodies gradually became drained of feeling.

Renno had never known such torment, but his features were set, concealing his pain. The others tried to remain impassive, too, even though some could not prevent their teeth from chattering.

"Swim!" Hawen commanded suddenly.

The boys, glad of the chance to exercise, promptly moved off in all directions.

One of the band, weakened by the hours of standing in the water, swam feebly, and the current began to carry him toward a jagged pile of rocks where the water was churning furiously.

Hawen shouted to the boy and threw a small log in his direction with such force that Renno marveled at the warrior's strength, but the log landed too far downstream from the enfeebled boy, and it drifted and bobbed rapidly as it headed toward the dangerous rocks.

Renno recovered from his near trance. Directly overhead he saw a willow tree, its branches trailing far out into the water, and he knew what had to be done.

Oddly, he felt no fear, and he could hear the words Ghonka had spoken many times: "A true Seneca warrior does what he must for his people and himself."

There was no choice. Renno grasped one of the strongest branches and, holding fast to it, began to walk out into the deeper part of the river where the current was perilous.

Little by little he worked his way toward the struggling swimmer. There wasn't much time. His own exercise had warmed him, but the water was so cold it was making him numb again, and he knew he had to act before he lost what strength he retained.

Suddenly he stepped into a hole and lost his balance. He felt the willow branch jerking out of his grasp, and involuntarily he closed his hand over it again, catching it firmly by its soft, tender end.

Using both hands, he pulled the branch toward him, bending it into a half-moon shape, and when he felt it growing taut he was satisfied.

Then he continued to inch his way toward the center of the churning river.

The boy in the water realized that someone was coming to his assistance and the knowledge gave him somewhat greater strength. Sometimes swimming a few strokes, sometimes staggering forward again on his feet as he gasped for breath, he tried to fight his way toward his rescuer as the current continued to propel him downstream.

Every step Renno took was an agony, almost more than he could bear, but he could not allow himself to think of his torment or the odds against him. It was essential that he save his friend; nothing else mattered.

A rush of current knocked the victim down again and moved him several yards closer to the rocks at the far side of the river.

"Don't try to swim!" Renno called. "The current is too swift! Stay on your feet!" Soon he reached the point where he could not go any farther. The willow branch was fully extended, and the muscles in his arms and hands ached as he clung to his lifeline. If he relinquished his hold, he, too, might be dashed against the rocks, but he refused to dwell on that possibility. He was here because he was about to leave boyhood behind, and a man did whatever was necessary for the Seneca, his friends, and himself.

Sobbing for breath, the victim used the last reserves of his energy to work closer, then closer still, until only a few yards separated the two boys.

The critical moment had come. Little by little, Renno relinquished his grasp on the tree with one hand while gripping the branch all the harder with the other. Then, placing his feet wide apart on the rocky bottom of the swift-moving stream, he braced himself, stretching his free arm at water level as far as he could reach.

"Take hold of me!" he called. "And don't miss!"

The other boy lacked the breath to reply, but he understood what had to be done. He would have only one chance to make physical contact with his rescuer. Within the next few seconds, he would have to take hold of Renno's hand or be lost as the river swept him to his doom.

"Now!" Renno shouted.

The victim lunged.

Their hands met and held, and Renno felt as though his arm would be pulled from its socket.

"Clasp your hands around my middle," he directed. "Quickly! I can't hold on much longer with one hand."

The other boy, exhausted but clearheaded, obeyed instantly, leaving Renno free to grasp the branch with both hands again, and the pain in his shoulder eased a trifle. Now, with his friend clinging to him, he fought his way toward the bank.

Hawen and the others stood on the shore, watching silently. No one interfered, and the warrior had no advice to offer. Renno needed no direction.

At last, as the struggling pair neared the shore, Hawen gave a command.

The boys formed a lifeline extending from the bank of the river into the water, the boy closest to Renno caught hold of him, and the whole group heaved, hauling Renno and his burden closer. One last tug brought both boys onto the mossy riverbank, and as they tumbled to the ground completely out of breath, Renno finally let go of the willow branch.

Under Hawen's direction, a fire was built; the half-frozen pair sat in front of it eating venison strips, parched corn, and dried apples; and both boys soon recovered their strength.

The boy Renno had saved tried to thank him, and Renno was embarrassed. "I did only what you would have done for me."

Hawen gathered the band in a circle before the trials were resumed. "Renno behaved like a Seneca warrior," he said, and he could have offered no higher praise.

Then, as though nothing unusual had happened, the tests were resumed, and the boys were required to spend the entire afternoon running up and down high hills, never slackening their pace, never pausing for breath.

The rest of the week passed in a similar fashion. The boys ran incessantly, plunged into cold water, and tested their endurance to the utmost. They ate sparingly, were allowed only a few hours of sleep each night, and were given almost no opportunity to relax.

"In war," Hawen told them, "you will face conditions far worse than you must meet now. He who lags behind or falls by the side of the trail harms all his comrades. If you pass these tests, it is only the beginning. For years to come you will continue to grow stronger. When you march with the Great Sachem, you will know no rest, day or night, and he who cannot keep up the pace will be a disgrace to himself and the whole nation."

On the seventh day, prior to the resumption of testing, there was a break in the routine.

"Today is the final day of trials before you ask the manitous if they will grant you visions," Hawen said. "Today you will not run, you will not climb, you will not swim. Instead, your blood will run to prove it is Seneca blood, to prove you are worthy of being called men."

He walked to a pile of small rocks, which the boys had been sharpening in their supposed free time. Each member of the band was directed to select two rocks and then form a large loose circle.

Hawen began a chant the youngsters had never heard before, and as they became familiar with the tune and words they joined in. The idea behind the song was simple. The boys asked the manitous for help; they requested courage from the mother-earth; they asked for strength from the powerful Thunder Spirit.

They repeated the lyrics endlessly, and the song began to have a hypnotic effect. The members of the band stared straight ahead, their eyes fixed, their postures slumping, their voices becoming more and more wooden as they chanted.

Renno's mind felt clear, strength seemed to flow through him, and he sang even more loudly. I must be the first, he told himself. I am related to Sah-nee-wa, the head of the Bear Clan, the first of clans. I am a Seneca noble. I must be true to my ancestors, to all who have gone before me.

He knew what had to be done, and he did not hesitate. Suddenly he raised his two sharpened rocks, one in each hand, and slashed at his thighs. Blood ran from the gashes and his legs began to throb, but his expression showed no pain, and he did not pause in his singing.

He bent a second time and, smiling as he sang, inflicted cuts on his calves. The blood ran freely, but he did not flinch and his voice did not falter.

The other boys, who were wounding themselves less severely, forgot themselves and their own pain as they watched him.

The son of Ghonka and Ena, the nephew of Sah-nee-wa, had to display more courage than anyone else. The inheritor of the mantle of the Bear Clan had to prove he deserved his privileged standing. He had to set the example. He was no ordinary boy and would become no ordinary warrior. The whole nation would be watching him, judging him to determine whether he was worthy of his parents.

This time, with slow deliberation, Renno gashed his torso.

It became increasingly difficult for him to sing, but he did not pause even though he grew hoarse and began to gasp. It never occurred to him to stop.

The other boys were watching him in admiration and horror, and Hawen was observing him closely, making no secret of his concern.

Renno became too dizzy to stand, so he sat cross-legged on the ground, and now he gashed the upper parts of his arms. Captives of war who died at the stake surely felt no worse than he, but they sang until they expired, and he would prove he was their equal.

Hawen did not want to break the spell, but he indicated with a gesture that it was time to call a halt.

Renno paid no attention.

Eventually he was forced to pause in his chanting to take a breath, and at that moment he heard a faint sound. He looked up at the sky, and there in the glare of the bright sun he saw a soaring hawk, its wings spread. A hawk! The one certain sign from the manitous that he had passed this grueling test!

All at once he felt at peace with himself and the world. Thanks to the power exercised by the hawk, his pain vanished and his smile became genuine. He dropped the sharpened rocks to the ground, folded his arms, and fell silent.

"You are a man," Hawen told him.

Renno's sense of well-being increased.

"All of you are now men," the warrior continued. "You have proved you are Seneca."

They accepted his judgment in pleased silence.

Hawen instructed them to bathe in the nearby stream, and Renno refused to allow anyone to help him as he immersed himself in the water, staying there until his bleeding stopped.

The band reassembled, and the youths helped each other, applying poultices of moss and healing herbs to their wounds. Those who had suffered the least injury built a fire, then went off to look for wild corn, nuts, and other delicacies. Meanwhile, Hawen went hunting and came back with a doe.

The carcass was butchered and roasted, and at sundown the entire group feasted, the new braves gorging on the last meal they would eat prior to the end of their initiation. Some stuffed themselves, downing one dripping chunk of roasted meat after another.

But Renno, although hungry, ate cautiously, remembering the words of Sah-nee-wa: "He who eats too much," his aunt had told him, "causes his belly to want much more at the next meal." By exercising care now, he would avoid the worst of hunger pangs when he began to fast.

Hawen bade farewell to each of the youths in turn, telling them he would seek and find any who failed to return at the end of the four-day vigil. When Renno's turn came, the warrior hesitated; then he said, "If you wish, you may sleep beside the fire and go off to make your camp in the morning. Your wounds are many."

"I am ready to go now," Renno replied.

"Think well before you decide." The warrior was still very much concerned.

"I am ready," Renno insisted, his voice calm.

"Then go in peace, and may you enjoy a fruitful vision." Hawen raised his arm in farewell.

Renno did not go far because he was still too

weak. He made himself a brush shelter, crude but effective, at the edge of a small clearing in the forest, not far from a little brook, and there he went to sleep.

During the night he awakened, sensing the presence of something or someone. Grasping his knife, he peered through the gloom and made out the bulky shape of a huge brown bear. Ja-gonh had understood he was not to interfere during the trials; nevertheless, he was keeping watch over his wounded brother at a time when it would have been difficult for Renno to protect himself.

Pretending not to see or recognize Ja-gonh, Renno drifted off to sleep again, and when he awakened in the morning the bear was gone.

His body was sore and his head very hot, and he made his way to the brook, where he drank his fill, then bathed his body. After gathering moss, he returned to the shelter and applied poultices, strengthened with medicinal herbs given him by Hawen.

For the next three days he spent most of his time resting, leaving the shelter only to drink and bathe. He knew he was suffering from a fever, but his wounds were healing, and he felt no fear.

Whenever he slept he dreamed, but these mental pictures were jumbled and vague, impossible for him to recall in detail when he woke up. Each time he tried to remember them, they faded rapidly, and he gave up the effort, knowing these were ordinary dreams induced by sickness.

On the last day of Renno's vigil he felt infinitely better. No hungrier than he had been at the beginning, he saw that his wounds were healing rapidly. Even more important, his head was clear, the heat had vanished from his body, and he felt refreshed in body as well as in spirit.

It was no accident that the last night of the vigil was spent under a full moon, when manitous were inclined to be more active than at any other time of the month.

After dark, Renno found himself walking through a forest toward the same longhouse he had visited in his earlier dreams, and he knew he had returned to the land of visions. The longhouse was just as he had remembered it, and when he entered he saw that the fire was burning, but no one was inside.

"The young man has returned," the fire said, *"and now he is truly a man!"*

"Sit down," the ceiling said graciously. *"You are expected, and you won't have to wait long."*

Renno saw his dream image sitting cross-legged beside the fire.

The wind moaned in the distance and the sound of it gradually drew nearer.

Renno wondered if he would be compelled to fight a battle to the death with the manitou-woman who was approaching. On occasion, in order to attain the powers of a warrior, it was necessary for a new brave to engage in such a battle.

"You will have no need to fight me, oh brother of the bear," a voice behind him said. "You cannot kill me, now or ever, and you will become a great warrior with the help of another."

Twisting his head slightly, Renno saw that the manitou stood in the entrance to the longhouse, the full moon directly behind her. He felt a chill when he looked at the place where her face should have been and discovered that he could see nothing because a mist of light enveloped her.

"You have come to seek warrior power," the manitou said.

"It is so," said the youth.

"It will be granted to you, but you must wait a longer time for it. It will be given to you when you go on your first war party. It will be the gift of my son, whom you saw high in the sky."

Renno remembered the hawk he had seen after he had gashed himself with the rocks.

"He is the one," the manitou told him. "But I have come now to make you a gift of a greater power. A healing power."

Even in his dream Renno tried to hide his dismay. Never in his life had he felt the slightest desire to become a healer. If it were the wish of the manitous, of course, he would have no choice, and he would then emulate his mother, but he preferred to become a war chieftain of chieftains, like his illustrious father.

In his dream he was able to detect a note of amusement in the manitou's voice. "You will not heal the wounds of the body or the wounds of the mind, young Seneca. Your task will be even more important than that. You have been selected to heal the wounds of the spirit that separate two great nations: the people of the Iroquois League and the strange people who have come from a far place."

Renno tried to digest what she was telling him, but her words made no sense.

"Your task will not be easy, but you have courage and strength. You have much to learn, but you will acquire wisdom. That is the kernel of my gift."

His confusion became greater.

"Now," she said harshly, "I command you to look at my face!"

Renno had to use all of his willpower, even in the dream, to rise and turn toward the vision. The bright light was fading, and he saw that the manitou's lips were twisted, as were those in the great false-face masks. Her huge eyes resembled those of the masks, too, and were hollow.

But it was her strange hair that fascinated him. It was yellow, hanging far down her back, and it looked exactly like corn silk, exactly like his own hair.

The manitou glided toward him, but then vanished into the air, and his dream faded. He knew no more and slept soundly.

When he awakened, the sun was rising. Renno felt strong, and he was not surprised that his wounds were much improved. Soon they would become mere scars, marks of honor. He drank water at the brook, bathed, and then sang a long song of thanks to the manitou. A rustling sound told him that Ja-gonh had been nearby again, but was finally departing, and Renno thanked him, too.

Then he made his way back to the camp of the new braves. He had experienced a vision, part of which he could not yet understand, but for now it was enough to know that he would be granted warrior power when the time came for him to go into battle. No man could ask for more than that.

His comrades were drifting in one by one, and as each approached Hawen he was questioned sharply: "Have you seen a vision?"

There was no need for the warrior to ask Renno that question. He merely glanced at the youth's eyes and motioned Renno to one side of the fire, where two others who had also enjoyed visions were resting.

After a final feast, the fire was extinguished with water and its remains were scattered, so an enemy would not learn that this was a place used for Seneca initiations.

Renno was elected chief of the band, and he

took his place at the head of the line after Hawen presented him with an owl feather that he was now entitled to wear in his scalp lock. He led the company, and they set off at a trot for home, with the instructor bringing up the rear.

The outer ring of sentries, stationed deep in the forest, passed the word that the new braves were arriving, and everyone in the town gathered in the streets. The drums of the sentries announced that all who had departed for the trials had returned, so no family would have to mourn the loss of a son. None had been forced to smear ashes on his face, either, which meant that the entire band had succeeded in passing the tests.

No one cheered more loudly than El-i-chi when he saw his older brother leading the group, still moving at a brisk trot, wearing the coveted owl feather.

Renno grinned broadly, then waved to his brother before turning into the crowded community longhouse. There he soon spotted his mother and aunt, but he had to pretend not to see them until the welcoming ceremony ended.

Ghonka sat on a platform surrounded by his war chieftains and the senior warriors, all wearing full war paint and headgear, and Hawen stood before them to present the newest male members of the tribe.

"Renno!" he called.

Renno stepped forward, folded his arms across his chest, and bowed to the great men of the nation.

Then he stepped forward again, and his father painted a yellow streak on one of his cheeks, a green streak on the other. Henceforth, he and his comrades would have the right to wear such paint, and they would add to it as they fought in battles and performed other deeds of valor.

When the ceremony came to an end, all the initiates were full-fledged junior warriors. Renno accepted the congratulations of many of the older people, then went off to his parents' house. Henceforth he would come here for visits and occasional meals, but he would live in one of the longhouses reserved for the unmarried braves.

The members of his immediate family awaited him. There were tears in Ena's eyes, but she was not ashamed of them, for a woman was allowed to weep on the saddest or happiest of occasions. Sah-nee-wa's eyes sparkled, and she couldn't resist stroking her nephew's arm in a rare gesture of affection. El-i-chi was so excited he danced up and down, bombarding Renno with questions until a warning glance from his father reduced him to silence.

Ghonka, who was seated at the fire, gestured to a place at his right. It was the first time Renno had ever sat in the place of honor.

"Hawen told me that you had a vision, my son."

"I did, my father." With the whole family listening, Renno told of his experience, leaving out no detail. It was understood that the information was a sacred trust and would not be repeated to anyone, even other relatives. Not until the prophecies foretold in a vision were fulfilled was it appropriate to describe them to anyone other than members of one's immediate family.

When Renno was finished speaking, there was a long silence, broken after a while by Sah-nee-wa, who knew more about manitous and dreams than anyone else. "It is good," said his father's sister, "that you will be granted warrior power by a manitou-hawk. There are no fighting powers greater or more enduring than those of the hawk."

Ghonka confirmed her statement with a nod. His own warrior powers had come to him through a manitou-hawk.

"But there is much in my vision that I don't understand," Renno said.

"No man understands a dream until he lives it," Sah-nee-wa told him. "As time passes, your future will unfold, little by little, until all is clear to you."

"What puzzles me," he persisted, "is that in my first half vision I saw the woman and the girl with pale skin. The girl's yellow hair was just like that of the manitou I saw in my full vision. What do you suppose that means?"

Ena exchanged a glance with her husband, then with her sister-in-law, and she and Sah-nee-wa both rose to their feet.

"Come, El-i-chi," Ena said.

The boy was afraid he was going to miss something interesting and tried to lag behind, but a faint frown on his father's brow sent him into the open on the heels of his mother and aunt.

"What I really want to know, my father," Renno said when he and Ghonka were alone, "is the connection between myself and these persons in my dream."

"I can't interpret your visions, my son. Only the manitous themselves know their meaning." Ghonka was stiff and formal.

Renno had the feeling that his father was concealing something. "I know," he said, "but there is something else that has troubled me for a long time, as far back as I can remember. Why should it be that my skin, beneath my loincloth where the sun rarely strikes it, is pale, when all other Seneca are dark? Why should it be that my hair is yellow when the hair of all other Seneca is black?"

Ghonka had long been anticipating such questions, and he had discussed the problem at length with Ena and Sah-nee-wa, but now that the moment had come, he was tongue-tied. Technically Renno had become a man, but he was still too young and inexperienced to be told the full story of his background.

"You are my son and the son of Ena," Ghonka said. "Even during your initiation trials you became a leader, and we take great pride in you."

"Your pride pleases me, my father." Renno's bewilderment increased, and he felt as he had during his vision.

"All is revealed to him who is patient."

"I will be patient, my father," he said, his Seneca-bred self-discipline coming to his rescue. His father saw fit not to answer several direct questions that would solve a riddle. So be it. Renno had made a promising beginning, and the spirits of the Seneca would guide him in the future, just as they had in the past.

Chapter V

When Aunt Ida Alwin gave people a piece of her mind, they listened carefully, without interrupting her. The sinewy gray-haired woman in the homespun linsey-woolsey dress that fell to her ankles (the woman people sometimes called a shrew behind her back but never to her face) stood in the yard of the little church inside the high palisade that followed the contours of the Connecticut River. She was freely expressing herself to the people around her.

Beyond stood the heights of Fort Springfield, rebuilt and expanded since the disastrous Indian raid some sixteen years earlier. There was nothing that reminded anyone in the growing community—which stretched toward New Town, sometimes called Hartford—that catastrophe had struck in this very spot. A score of shops lined High Street, the town boasted two inns and several taverns, and the farms beyond the palisade were rich with crops of corn and wheat, tobacco, vegetables, and barley. The plump cattle and sheep grazing there added to the pastoral scene.

"You're a disgrace to the Crown and to Massachusetts Bay," Aunt Ida said scathingly. "You may call yourselves men, but you deserve to be scalped by the savages, every last one of you! And you womenfolk know better, too. You should make your men do what's right."

The group that was gathered around her shifted uneasily, although her niece, sixteen-year-old Deborah Alwin, was undisturbed as she stood quietly, allowing the spring breeze to blow through her long golden hair. There was a faint hint of humor in Deborah's eyes, indicating that she knew her aunt better than anyone else and realized that her bark was far worse than her bite.

One other person was tranquil. Aunt Ida's eleven-year-old son, Walter, smiled gently, paying no attention to his mother's tirade as he absently watched a flock of geese heading north. Walter, of course, was different. He was unable to participate in the conversation, and although Aunt Ida and Deborah were marvelously patient with him, teaching him and guiding him, no one else knew how much Walter really understood, how lost he might be in his own inner world.

"You act," Aunt Ida said, "as though the danger is ended. You know there are still Indians all through this area and that the Canadian tribes are urged and paid by the French to make regular raids on the English colonies. But you're as defenseless as the chickens in my yard. At least they have the roosters to protect them."

As she paused for breath, one man found his voice. The Reverend Obadiah Jenkins, now in his late twenties, was no ordinary clergyman, and he was rightly regarded by his parishioners as being something of a diplomat. On weekdays he worked the farm he had cleared in the area between Fort Springfield and New Town, and after sundown he visited the sick and attended to his other pastoral duties.

"You may not know it, Aunt Ida," he said, "but I always keep my rifle hidden under the pulpit. I'm sure the Lord approves."

She was not mollified. "I have no doubt He does," she replied, "but He must be annoyed with others for showing a lack of gumption."

One member of the group was particularly uncomfortable. Abe Thomas, a burly youth in his late teens, was known by everyone in town to be sweet on Deborah Alwin, and it was believed that his reason for taking Walter fishing every week was an attempt to win favor with Deborah and the boy's mother.

Slow of speech and shy, Abe was not in a position to talk back to Aunt Ida. He stared at the ground and shuffled his feet.

Jeffrey Wilson, about the same age, was far less inhibited. As the only son of Andrew Wilson, the area's largest and most prominent landowner, he was afraid of no one. He broke laws that interfered with his pleasures and enjoyed mocking authority. At the moment, even though he knew he was playing a dangerous game, he couldn't resist asking with feigned servility, "Are you a spokeswoman for the Almighty, ma'am?"

Tom and Agnes Hibbard, the indentured servants in the Wilsons' employ, were openly shocked and embarrassed.

"I'm sorry, ma'am," Tom Hibbard interjected hastily, "but Jeff don't mean to be fresh."

Aunt Ida knew better, but her dignity made it impossible for her to lower herself to Jeffrey's level, and she was about to turn away when another couple approached the little group. Colonel Andrew Wilson and his charming wife, Mildred, now as always beside him, had succeeded admirably in the New World. His farm was the largest and most productive in the region, he was annually elected as the head of the local militia, and he represented the district in the Massachusetts Bay Assembly. He was a leader because of the example he set, and the entire community gladly followed him.

Only Jeffrey looked exasperated when he saw his parents, for even he lacked the courage to confront and defy his father. Instead he wandered off, his expression insolent.

"Is something amiss here?" Colonel Wilson asked, his voice cheerful.

"I feel like a hornet trying to get through a glass window," Ida Alwin replied. "I counted seventy-three men sitting in church just now, and not a single one had a musket or rifle stacked in the stand at the door. If there had been an Indian attack while we were sitting there, we would have been massacred!"

To the surprise of the group, the colonel nodded. "You have a legitimate complaint, Ida," he said, "but our situation isn't as desperate as it may seem."

"How so, Andy?"

"The thirty men who attended the early service this morning are now on duty at the fort. The day is clear, and they can see the countryside for miles around. A single blast on the warning horn would have brought all the men at the late service to the fort—which they could reach in almost no time—and there we have weapons aplenty waiting to repel any invaders."

The Hibbards looked relieved, as did Obadiah Jenkins and young Abe Thomas.

Aunt Ida's uneasiness subsided, but she looked

around at the group, her manner still accusing. "Why didn't one of you tell me all this?"

"Because it isn't their place to think in such terms," Colonel Wilson replied. "That's my responsibility."

The knot of people began to disperse.

"One moment," called Andrew Wilson. "I'd like to remind all of you that Mrs. Alwin's concern isn't imaginary. She's alive today only because sixteen years ago she went to Boston to meet a ship that was bringing her family here from Bristol. When the Indians destroyed old Fort Springfield, her absence saved her life, and I, for one, don't blame her for being worried."

Mildred Wilson, who had been quietly conferring with Agnes Hibbard, touched Ida Alwin on the arm. "Come back with us for dinner, you and the children," she said. "Agnes and I have a very large roast of beef cooking on the fire at home right now, and we'd appreciate your company."

It would have been ungracious to refuse, and Aunt Ida, always the lady in spite of her sharpness, recognized the gesture for what it was worth and happily accepted.

"We'd love to have you, too, Reverend Jenkins, if you don't mind such a late invitation," said Mildred. "And you, Abe, provided it doesn't upset any of your family's plans."

A few minutes later, Deborah was holding the reins of their team of horses, and Aunt Ida and Walter were sitting beside her on the board of their unpretentious cart as the little family started down the river road toward the Wilson estate.

The girl, careful to take no part in the discussion outside the church, finally broke her silence. "What prompted you to make all that fuss, Aunt Ida?" she asked. "If I knew that the sentries at the fort would alert the congregation at the first sign of Indians, surely you knew it, too."

The woman's chuckle was dry. "Of course I knew it. But menfolk tend to become complacent, like the way husbands take their wives for granted after a few years. They need regular stirring up to keep them awake. Especially when it comes to Indians!"

"You really don't like any of the tribes, do you, even the friendly Indians who live hereabouts."

"I can't abide 'em," her aunt replied. "They're barbarians, all of them, and I've never yet seen one I'd be willing to trust. Every last one of our friends and relatives was slaughtered in cold blood and scalped when my dear husband and I were in Boston fetching you, child. I'll never forget the horrors we saw when we came back."

"I try to look at it from the Indians' point of view," Deborah said with spirit. "We've taken their land, we deprive them of their hunting and fishing grounds, and we pay them with a few kettles and blankets and mirrors. No wonder they become angry."

"This land," the woman said, a rasp in her voice, "belongs to the Colony of Massachusetts Bay, which means to subjects of the Crown who have chosen to live in the New World. And don't you forget it for a minute!"

Knowing it was impossible to change her aunt's mind in this matter or any other, the girl gave up.

Aunt Ida's thoughts veered in another direction. "I wonder why Mildred Wilson included Abe Thomas in her dinner invitation. I was so surprised."

The girl giggled. "I reckon she saw the way he was mooning at me and took pity on him."

"You could do worse than Abe," Aunt Ida said. "He works hard, he stays sober, and he's reliable."

"He's a decent person, but he's dull."

"A self-respecting woman doesn't look for excitement in a husband!"

"I'm not looking for any husband, not for a long time," Deborah said. "There's no law that forces a girl to marry at sixteen or seventeen—or even eighteen. I intend to wait until I'm old enough to know my own mind, and to recognize the right man when I see him."

"You'll run the risk of becoming an old maid, that's what you'll do, child!"

Deborah's light laugh trailed behind the cart. Her aunt's suggestion was absurd. She herself knew, as did everyone else in the whole Fort Springfield–New Town area, that she was by far the most attractive girl in all of western Massachusetts Bay. And only her common sense prevented her from gaining too high an opinion of herself.

Ultimately, she would marry. She was sure of it. But she couldn't and wouldn't accept Aunt Ida's low opinion of men, and her own romantic idealism was so great that she fully intended to wait until she fell in love. When the man who was right for her appeared, she would recognize him, just as he would know her.

Love, Deborah was convinced, was a necessity in this rough frontier area, where day-to-day life was so difficult, where diversions were few and people had to rely only on themselves. No one was going to rush her into the wrong marriage.

She felt a tingle of excitement as they drove through the opening in the stone fence that marked the boundaries of the Wilson property. Directly ahead stood the whitewashed clapboard house that members of the older generation, who remembered England, swore was as solid and handsome as any squire's home in Kent, Sussex, or Hampshire.

There were differences, of course. There were no lawns here and no flower gardens, for every inch of cleared land was used for growing crops. Squash, pumpkins, green beans, cabbages, and onions were planted close to the house. Pigpens and chicken coops could be seen near the sides of the main building, cows were roaming everywhere, and a calf frolicked only a few feet from the front door. In the New World, even the well-to-do stood on no ceremony.

Mildred Wilson was a generous as well as gracious hostess. The kitchen was, in accordance with the custom here, a separate outbuilding, connected to the main house by a covered passageway. Two stoves were used, one stoked with wood and the other with charcoal, and the meal prepared there was lavish.

The guests began with succulent pink melon, and the vegetables in the beef-based soup were seasoned with Mildred's own herbs. The grilled fish had been caught by the colonel the previous day, the roast of beef was superb, and the cheese had been made by Agnes from a recipe she had brought from Yorkshire.

After spending less than a decade and a half in the New World, the Wilson family grew the better part of its own food, as did most people in the area. The colonists had good cause to boast that everything they ate and drank—including beer and wine—was produced locally, the tea they imported from England being the only exception.

Agnes and Tom Hibbard, who served the meal, sat with the family as a matter of course, as did two young men who were working on the Wilsons' farm until they saved enough money to establish homesteads of their own. There was no master and servant relationship at the table, for, as the colonel sometimes observed, in the New World all men were equal. And Mildred put on no airs because her silk gown was imported from Cathay by way of England, while the other women wore dresses of linen, from local flax, mixed with wool sheared from their own sheep.

The festive atmosphere was marred only briefly at the outset by the failure of Jeffrey Wilson to appear.

"He'll be along soon, I'm sure," his mother remarked privately to Andrew.

The colonel made a wry face. "No doubt he's gallivanting, either getting himself into more trouble or visiting one of the trollops in that new house on High Street."

"Jeffrey is high-spirited, that's all," said Mildred.

Her husband shook his head. "He knows what time we eat dinner on the Sabbath. He'll be given no food here for the rest of the day, no matter when he shows up. An empty stomach may teach him manners, although I doubt it."

For a time, the talk at the table was general, and Deborah sometimes used a private sign language to give Walter some notion of what was being said. Inevitably, the conversation turned to the relations of the English colonies with the French colonies in Canada.

"At the risk of sounding less than charitable," Reverend Jenkins said, "in my opinion, the fault lies with King Louis. He professes to be a devout Christian, but he doesn't behave that way. If the stories I've heard from some of his Huguenot refugees are true, he revoked the Edict of Nantes this very year, and he's persecuting people for no other reason than that they're Protestants. I've met several priests from Quebec, and I know they're as disturbed by Louis's bigotry as we are."

The very mention of Louis XIV, France's grand monarch, cast a pall on the company. One of the hired hands muttered under his breath, unwilling to express his thoughts aloud in the presence of ladies.

"I can see, Reverend Jenkins, that you might think of our dispute with the French in terms of a clash between men of different religions," Colonel Wilson said, "but the French who have been settling in Canada live as we do, under harsh and primitive conditions, and I don't believe they've brought the old religious prejudices with them to this side of the Atlantic."

"Then why do they hate us, Andy?" Aunt Ida demanded. "You know as well as I do that they give arms and whiskey to the Ottawa and Algonquian and Huron—and actually pay them besides to make war against us."

"The problem is complex, I'll grant you," said Andrew Wilson, "but it has simple roots. The French are greedy and want more land, so they're trying to expand in our direction."

"Aren't we greedy, too?" asked Deborah.

Andrew shrugged. "Some of our people are as ambitious as the French," he said. "Men on both sides fail to realize that the better part of the continent is yet to be settled. There's ample room for the English here—and for the French in Canada, all the way to the Pacific Ocean."

"With no one displaced except the Indians," said Deborah.

Her aunt was irritated. "Stop interrupting your elders with that nonsense!"

"Debbie's view happens to be my own," the colonel said. "The French are far more clever than we are in their dealings with the Indians. They welcome tribesmen in their towns and on their farms, and they adopt Indian manners when they go to the Indian villages. We'll need to change our whole approach if we hope to win any of the major Indian nations to our cause—as we must."

"Are you speaking of wooing some of the tribes from the French, Colonel?" asked Obadiah Jenkins.

"To an extent. The Huron and Ottawa are firmly in the French camp. If we tried, we might be able to win the Algonquian from them, but I'm thinking in even larger terms. Our frontier is beginning to move westward from Fort Albany in neighboring New York. In the years ahead, we'll need to win the friendship and cooperation of the entire Iroquois League."

"I've heard they're impossibly wild and bloodthirsty," Aunt Ida said. "How can we even think of making them our allies?"

"We must," Colonel Wilson told her. "The Iroquois include the largest and most powerful Indian nations in all of North America. If the French win them as allies, we'll be pushed out. Everything we've done here, everything we hope to accomplish in the future will be destroyed. King Louis won't be satisfied until all the territory claimed by New England and New York is his. So we must establish firm alliances with the Seneca, the Mohawk, and the other Iroquois nations in the next few years, or every English-speaking man, woman, and child in North America will perish!"

In midafternoon, Deborah returned with Aunt Ida and Walter to their own house, a modest dwelling of clay-chinked logs that overlooked the Connecticut River from the east bluff. Ida had been forced to sell much of the property a couple of years after the death of her husband, keeping only a few acres for the growing of vegetables. She earned the family living by making cloth on her loom and by working as a seamstress, vocations in which Deborah was becoming adept.

The house, aside from the kitchen outbuilding, consisted of a large chamber used for eating and living and working, a small bedroom that Aunt Ida and Deborah shared, and, on the floor above, an attic. A portion of this space was set aside for Walter's bedroom, and the rest was used for storage. The house was small but snug. A huge fireplace provided ample heat, no air came in through the chinks, and in summer the glass windows—a luxury few settlers enjoyed—were removed. When rain fell in the warm season, oiled paper was tacked over the window openings.

During their absence, a neighbor had left a note asking Aunt Ida to call on her to discuss the making of a wedding gown for her daughter. The observation of the Sabbath made it impossible to work on the dress, but nothing prevented a discussion of the subject, so Aunt Ida departed.

Walter went up to the attic to practice his reading. Noting the resolve on his pudgy face, Deborah knew that most of the unkind things said about the boy were untrue. He was neither stupid nor lazy, and in spite of his handicap he was determined to improve himself.

The girl fed the horses and turned them loose in the small pasture, then made the wagon secure in the barn. She pumped water for the horses and chickens and filled another bucket and brought it from the well to the house so it would be available for washing that night. Her mind still dwelling on the dinner conversation, Deborah placed the bucket on the floor near the hearth.

Someone in the room moved up behind her.

Gasping as she turned, Deborah stiffened when she recognized Jeffrey Wilson.

His glazed eyes and the odor on his breath confirmed her guess that he had spent the afternoon drinking rum at one of Fort Springfield's taverns.

"You're surprised to see me," he said with a hoarse chuckle.

"When people make a call," Deborah said primly, "it's customary for them to announce their presence by knocking on the door."

"Oh, I've been waiting here ever since the old witch left and you went out to the pasture."

"I permit no one to refer to my aunt as an old witch, particularly in her own home."

"I could call her worse than that," Jeffrey said, laughing again as he drew nearer.

"What do you want?" Deborah demanded.

"You," he said, and he stretched out his arms to her.

Backing away, she felt a surge of alarm, although her expression indicated no fear. Walter couldn't hear her if she called for help, and in any case there was nothing the boy could do to defend her. The nearest neighbors lived too far away to hear a cry of distress, so she had only herself to rely on.

Jeffrey had never displayed any interest in her, but she recalled now that he had been staring at her after church this morning. Apparently it had dawned on him that she was exceptionally attractive.

"You've come to the wrong person," she said, uncertain how to fend him off.

His smile was superior. "You know who I am," he said. "Any girl in Massachusetts Bay or Connecticut would be lucky to get a Wilson."

"Sorry, but that kind of luck doesn't appeal to me." She picked up a chair and placed it between them.

Jeffrey promptly threw the chair aside and continued to advance.

Not until Deborah stood with her back to a window, the base of her spine pressed against the ledge, did it occur to her that she had allowed herself to be maneuvered into a position from which there was no escape. She should have gone to the door—but it was too late now to think of what might have been.

"I find your presence offensive, sir," she said as he pinned her against the window frame. "I suggest you visit one of the trollops at that new house in town."

"Oh, I went there, but I spent the last of my cash on toddies at the tavern, so they threw me out. Besides, I've been looking forward to a tussle with you for a long time. Why do you always act so superior?"

"I find nothing admirable in you, sir," Deborah replied.

"Then I'll have to teach you that there's more to me than you know." Jeffrey placed his hands on her shoulders.

She pushed them away. "Nothing you could say or do would make you attractive to me. Please leave."

"I'll make it worth your while to be nice to me. Suppose I give you a bolt of the finest silk from the East Indies. You'd like that, wouldn't you?"

"I'd refuse it," she said with her customary frankness, "because I take no gifts from anyone. And because I'd know you stole the silk from your mother."

Her words infuriated him, and grabbing her by the shoulders again, he began to shake her.

Deborah knew it was wrong to anger him, and she was afraid it might be even worse to offer physical resistance, although she wanted to claw his face and kick him. At best, he had always been a bully, creating discomfort for those who were smaller and weaker; at the moment, he was too drunk to behave reasonably. If she fought him he might well rape her, and if she didn't—the result might be the same.

Suddenly Jeffrey took her into his arms and buried his face against her throat.

Squirming in a vain attempt to break his hold, the girl felt something cold touch her hand.

She twisted her head to glance out the window, and to her astonishment she saw Walter, his eyes enormous with anger, extending a bone-handled knife that was used for butchering meat. Somehow the child had become aware of the intruder's presence, and he had come down from the attic, sneaked out of the house, and brought the knife from the kitchen outbuilding.

Thanking her little cousin silently, Deborah took a firm grip on the knife handle; then she pressed the point of the sharp blade against Jeffrey's chest.

The steel broke his skin, and he released her, taking a half step backward. "Where the devil did you get that knife? Give it to me!"

"Try to take it away from me," Deborah said in a low, even voice, "and I'll drive it into you to the hilt. I allow no one to paw me, especially a drunken animal who has never done anything to earn anyone's respect." She gave her words additional meaning by repeatedly stabbing the knife in his direction.

Jeffrey retreated. In spite of his muddled state, he wanted to get beyond the reach of this wild, mad girl.

"Leave this house, and don't ever annoy me again," she said. "For your parents' sake, I won't report this unpleasantness to the constabulary, though I'm much tempted. But if you ever come back, if you ever try to press your attentions on me again, I'll kill you with as little feeling as I'd show a copperhead while shooting off its head with a musket. Be warned, Jeffrey Wilson, and act accordingly!"

The door opened and Walter came into the room with a meat cleaver clutched in his hand. He ran to Deborah.

She embraced him, hugging him hard, then stood with one arm draped around his shoulders as they faced the intruder, their expressions identical.

Drunk as he was, Jeffrey could recognize their loathing for him. Well, maybe he had exceeded the bounds of propriety. In any case, this was not the moment to prolong the incident. He would attend to the bitch some other time. Jeffrey hurled himself out the door and ran up the river road to the place where he had tethered his horse.

Deborah and Walter watched as he spurred his horse and rode toward home at a reckless gallop.

Boston, bustling and raw, was the largest city in England's colonies, which stretched from the deep forests of the Maine District of Massachusetts Bay down the Atlantic seaboard to the palmetto-fringed swamps of South Carolina. Fewer than 150,000 immigrants, most of them British but some of Dutch or Swedish descent, maintained a precarious hold that extended no more than two hundred miles inland from the shores of the vast continent.

Of these inhabitants, approximately ten thousand lived in Boston, the largest seaport and trading center in North America. The Reverend Obadiah Jenkins, who had not visited the city in all the years he had lived and worked on the western frontier, saw the place now through the eyes of a colonist, and he was deeply impressed.

Two of the main roads from the waterfront to Beacon Hill—the center of government and finance—were cobbled now, and it was freely predicted that within a generation all the dirt roads in town would be paved. The clapboard houses were substantial, even in the neighborhood where the poor dock workers lived, and log cabins were rapidly disappearing.

It was true that Boston still maintained a frontier mentality. More than twenty ships, most of them English, some of them Dutch, Spanish, and Danish, rode in the harbor, and their crew members gave the community something of an international flavor. But, much to the disappointment of arrivals from England and Scotland who hoped to settle in Boston rather than move on to the edge of the wilderness, the cosmopolitan atmosphere was only skin-deep.

Every man carried a pistol or sword—or both—at all times for his own protection and that of his family, and disputes were frequently settled with bullets or blades rather than in the law courts on Beacon Hill.

Every householder was his own mason and carpenter, and when a man wanted to build a new kitchen or add a room to his dwelling, the men and boys of his neighborhood pitched in to help. Every woman had her own spinning wheel and used one room in her house for the making of clothes and shoes. There was only one cobbler in town.

Cooking was done either in hearths or on woodburning stoves, and few families could afford more than a small number of kettles, pots, and skillets. Cooking utensils as well as needles, scissors, and knives were imported from England and were exorbitantly expensive, a heavy iron pot large enough to prepare a stew for six persons costing seven pennies on the current market.

Townspeople were unable to grow their own food, but prices were cheap. Farmers brought their produce into town from such outlying villages as Quincy; the catches of the local fishermen were bountiful; and fur traders from the frontier invariably picked up extra cash by bringing venison, elk, and bear meat to the Boston market. In every household, a vegetable cellar contained strings of onions, bundles of carrots, long rows of potatoes, and other root plants. Not even the poorest went hungry in this land of plenty.

Official visitors from London were amused by the spectacle of cattle and sheep grazing in the Common; and the only thing that prevented the animals from entering the grounds of the Governor's House was the picket fence around it. The Governor's House itself, a three-story fifteen-room fieldstone building that the colonists refused to call a palace because they insisted there were none in the New World, was the most handsome and imposing structure in Boston.

The colonists' great pride was the sight of the militia in their blue coats, white breeches, and black boots as they paraded inside the fence and stood sentry duty at the entrance to the building. These volunteer troops lacked the rigid discipline of smart-stepping English regular army regiments, but Massachusetts Bay preferred to provide its own soldiers.

The very presence of the militia was a tribute to the farsighted governor, William Shirley. Appointed by Charles II as the King's viceroy for Massachusetts Bay, Shirley had developed an abiding faith in the future of these people and their colony. Perhaps more than anyone else, he realized that Americans were not mere appendages of the mother country.

He encouraged these independent tendencies by appointing colonials as judges and giving them top posts in his administration. They, in turn, supported him without reservation, and the resulting harmony was at least partly responsible for the emergence of Massachusetts Bay as the most prosperous and advanced of England's New World colonies.

Although the weather was still fairly warm, there was a hint of autumn in the air, and Governor Shirley sat in an armchair beside a small fire in the conference room adjoining his private office. He was meeting with members of his council, the commanders of the colony's three military sectors, and their civilian deputies. Included in the group were Colonel Andrew Wilson and the Reverend Obadiah Jenkins, representing the western frontier district.

Tea laced with light rum was being served, the atmosphere was informal, and with several conversations in progress at the same time, there was an exchange of information on conditions throughout the colony. Obadiah Jenkins, newly elected as Colonel Wilson's deputy, was surprised by the lack of protocol.

Everyone stood when Brigadier General William Pepperrell came into the room, his gold epaulets shining. Like Governor Shirley, he disdained the use of a wig, and he insisted that his subordinates speak with candor at all times. For more than twenty years this farmer from the Maine District had been engaging in seemingly endless war with the French and their Indian allies, and he was the acknowledged expert in every phase of that warfare.

"I assume, Your Excellency," said the general to the governor, "that you haven't explained the purpose of this meeting."

"I've been waiting for you," said Shirley. "You know more about the situation than I do."

"Very well, sir." General Pepperrell turned to the group. "Gentlemen, I regret to inform you that Alain de Gramont has returned to the warpath. One of our spies in Quebec arrived a few days ago with word that Gramont has shed his gold and white uniform, shaved the hair from his head except for his scalp lock, and once again donned the war paint of the Huron."

The commander of the Boston District frowned, the colonel in charge of the Central District sighed, and Colonel Wilson expressed the thoughts of all when he murmured, "That's the worst news we could hear."

Obadiah Jenkins and one of the other deputies, both new to the council, looked blank.

It was Andrew Wilson who offered an explanation. "Alain de Gramont is our nemesis: a strange, secretive man who combines the genius of an Alexander the Great with the cunning of a wilderness lion."

"Many years ago," General Pepperrell added, "when he was a young lieutenant, he took command of the tiny French garrison on Mount Royal, near the spot where the village of Montreal now stands. While he and his men were away on a mission, the fort was attacked, and Gramont's wife and baby daughter were killed. He's never been completely stable since, and he's devoted his life—from that day to this—to avenging their deaths."

"Who killed them, General?" asked Obadiah.

Pepperrell sighed. "No one knows for certain. According to the most popular story, the little settlement was assaulted by the Seneca, ancient enemies of the

Huron tribe and the leading members of the Iroquois League."

"It is also said," Colonel Wilson continued, "that the Seneca were joined by a group of white allies, settlers from either New York or Massachusetts Bay. That has never been verified, and all of us think it unlikely, but it happens to be what Gramont himself believes. And that makes it important." He glanced at Brigadier General Pepperrell.

The general leaned forward in his chair. "It is a confirmed fact," he said, picking up the recital, "that after the death of his wife and child, Gramont's grief was so great that he went off into the wilderness and lived with the Huron. We know nothing about his activities, but at the end of about five years, he returned to Quebec and was promoted to the rank of captain."

"Since then," Colonel Wilson went on, "he has alternated, sometimes leading French troops, sometimes acting as a Huron war chief."

Pepperrell opened his hands. "Today," he declared, "Gramont is a full colonel and commands the infantry of King Louis's army in New France. That is, when it suits him. At other times, he rejoins the Huron, and whenever he does we know there's going to be trouble on our side of the border. The Huron raid towns and attack farms in the English colonies, and they spare us only when they assault the Seneca instead."

Governor Shirley spoke for the first time. "I've sent word to the garrison commander at Fort Albany, so New York can brace itself for trouble."

"Will the Seneca be notified, Your Excellency?" Andrew Wilson asked.

The governor shrugged. "That's up to the New Yorkers. The Seneca are their neighbors, although the colonists and the Indians don't have much contact. Their Great Sachem, Ghonka, who heads the whole Iroquois League—consisting of the Mohawk, Cayuga, Onondaga, Oneida, and Seneca tribes—is a tough old warrior who has consistently refused to have dealings with any white men, and he keeps them out of his territory."

"Naturally," Brigadier Pepperrell said, "the French would like to make an alliance with the Iroquois nations, just as we would, but Quebec's biggest problem is Gramont and his private vendetta. We hold a natural advantage which we'd very much like to exploit; however, Ghonka holds all whites at arm's length. We keep hoping that something will enable us to break through his protective shell, but so far he's spurned all our offers."

"Is it possible," Obadiah Jenkins asked, "that Chief Ghonka might be more willing to make an alliance with us if he suffers a severe attack by Colonel de Gramont and the Huron?"

Pepperrell deferred to Governor Shirley, who had developed a profound knowledge of the Indian nations.

"I regard it as possible, but not probable," replied the King's viceroy for Massachusetts Bay. "Even if the Seneca suffered a major catastrophe, they'd turn to the other four nations of the Iroquois rather than to us. All we can do is to keep chipping away at their defenses and hoping that one of these days they'll be open to friendly relations with us."

"In the meantime," Pepperrell declared, "we've got to look out for our own interests. Our militia in the Maine District has been alerted, and all settlements have been notified. I want similar precautions taken throughout the rest of the colony. Gramont is such a sly devil, there's no way of predicting where he might strike. Colonel Wilson's Western District is the most obvious target because it sits on the edge of the wilderness, but I wouldn't put it past Alain de Gramont to put the torch to Boston itself if he thought he could get away with it. One of the greatest dangers is that he's so completely unpredictable."

"All our people must be informed," William Shirley declared. "I'm afraid that if I issue an official public safety proclamation it will be too upsetting, particularly if the Huron come nowhere near Massachusetts Bay. On the other hand, I want every townsman and farmer notified, and I think the best way to deal with the problem delicately is through the districts."

Andrew Wilson slid his thumbs into his belt. "I'll double the guard at Fort Springfield and the smaller garrisons," he said, "and I'll inform every farmer living in the possible path of the Huron. I'll also send roving patrols to keep watch in the forests. Is there anything else that needs to be done, Will?"

Pepperrell shook his head. "I want all districts to follow your example, Andy. Beyond that, all we can do is pray that Gramont and his Huron will leave us alone this time."

Chapter VI

I n his seventeenth summer, Renno had things other than hunting on his mind. Hiding in the brush near the path to the cornfields, he held a brace of wild turkeys he had shot before daybreak, and so far his plan had worked well. If Anowara happened to be working in the fields today, he would emerge from the brush and present them to her.

Not knowing how girls of his age reacted to surprises, he had no idea what Anowara might say or do, and he felt far more nervous than he ever felt when engaging in his customary activities. He had few peers as a hunter, and when he formed a team with El-i-chi, there were none in the town who could match them. Why, then, he wondered, should he be so apprehensive at the prospect of exchanging words with someone he had known all his life?

Before he could ponder the matter, he was interrupted by the giggle of a little girl.

Even before he turned around, he knew that the newest member of his immediate family had been following him again. Late in the spring, when a remote Seneca village had been attacked and almost wiped out by enemies (presumably Huron from the north), the few survivors had come to the nation's main town. Ba-lin-ta, a chubby little girl of eight summers who belonged to the Bear Clan, had lost both her parents in the attack, and Ghonka and Ena, having always wanted a daughter, adopted her immediately. She was adored by the whole family.

Ghonka and Ena openly spoiled her, as did Sahnee-wa, and El-i-chi played games with her whenever his duties as a junior warrior permitted. But Renno was her favorite, and she tagged after him everywhere, sometimes making a nuisance of herself, although she was such a lovable child that he readily forgave her.

"Ha, Renno!" Ba-lin-ta said. "You didn't even know I was behind you. If I were an enemy, you'd be dead, and I'd have your scalp." She fingered the broad belt that held up her doeskin skirt.

He regarded her with all the severity his seventeen years could command. "It's too early in the day for you to be wandering outside the palisade, Ba-lin-ta," he said. "Our mother will be worried about you."

She dismissed his words with a toss of her braids. "Oh, no. If she misses me, she'll know I'm safe with you."

That was the truth, Renno thought wryly.

"But you didn't even hear me, my brother, and I know why," she said.

The child gave him little peace. Now he made the mistake of challenging her. "Why, small one?"

Ba-lin-ta giggled. "You were thinking about Anowara again, even though she won't look at you."

As Sah-nee-wa had remarked at a family gathering the other evening, little girls seemed to understand more about certain complex matters than junior warriors.

"What makes you believe I was thinking about her?"

"Your eyes became very soft, like the eyes of a doe," said the child. "Anyway, you won't have long to wait. Before I came here I found out that Anowara will be working in the cornfields today." And to Renno's dismay, she sat on the ground and prepared to wait.

"I think this is the day our mother prepares the meal of corn with the syrup of maple for breakfast," he said, actually having no idea what his mother might be serving.

"I already ate a cold potato, so I'm not hungry."

Her quick grin told him she was teasing him now, and he couldn't help laughing.

Ba-lin-ta jumped up and hopped from one foot to the other. "I'll leave before Anowara comes, never fear," she said, speaking rapidly, her tone never changing. "But I don't see why you bother. She isn't very pretty, and I've heard that when she was little she cried all the time. I don't. I never cry. I'm a proper Seneca. Do you want to know something else? Many of the maidens imagine that you look like the manitou of the forest. Do you want to know who said it? Iala said it when I was playing a game in the longhouse of the maidens, and many of them agreed. Maybe you ought to give Iala your turkeys." She paused for breath.

Renno shook his head to clear it. Iala, who was also his own age, was by far the prettiest girl in the longhouse of the maidens, but a number of full warriors were vying for her attention. How could he, only a junior warrior, be of interest to her? Besides, he felt more comfortable with Anowara, although talk with any girl made him uneasy.

110

To stop his little sister's chatter, he glared at her, his expression remarkably like Ghonka's when the Great Sachem rebuked someone. "You hear too much and say too much, Ba-lin-ta. Our mother would be angry if she knew how you gossiped."

Ba-lin-ta accepted the scolding sulkily, staring at the ground and scuffing her bare toes in the dust. "I know what I heard. And I know Iala really likes you. I didn't make it up." Then her manner changed and she brightened. "But you are right, my brother. You are always right, and I'll be more careful."

She raced off toward the town, and Renno watched her go, forgiving her impertinence as he mulled over what she had told him. It was flattering to know that Iala had complimented him. Her father was a powerful medicine man, the head of the society that carved the false faces, so she would be a suitable mate for the elder son of the Great Sachem. But it was absurd to dwell on that possibility when she was sought after by so many full warriors. No, Anowara was a more attainable goal, even though she put on airs in his presence.

All he could do was call himself to Anowara's attention, and if she elected not to notice him, that was her privilege. According to ancient Seneca custom, violated only at the risk of incurring the wrath of the mother-earth herself, it was the woman who chose the man she wanted to sleep with or marry. It was his right to turn away if he didn't want to respond, but it was she who invited his advances, and unless and until she did, he was restrained by thongs more powerful than heavy rawhide.

On half a dozen occasions he had presented gifts of food to Anowara's amused parents, who undoubtedly were aware of his interest in their daughter, and frequently he had placed himself in the girl's path. But she had barely glanced at him.

Perhaps his luck was changing. The women were coming toward the cornfields in single file, and he saw at once that Anowara brought up the rear. That would give her the opportunity to linger for a few moments if she wished.

Concealing the wild turkeys behind his back, he gravely greeted the older matrons at the head of the line, treating them with the respect due their age. He nodded to the younger matrons, then inclined his head slightly as each of the unmarried maidens passed him.

Suddenly he stepped into the path, blocking Anowara's passage.

Rather than squeeze past him, she halted. "I am pleased for you that your hunt was successful, Renno," she said politely.

He had to clear his throat repeatedly before he could reply. "Our longhouse has eaten many turkeys lately," he said. "Too many. Perhaps you know someone who might want these." He thrust the turkeys at her.

Anowara's nod indicated solemn pleasure. "In two nights, when the moon is full, there will be a round dance outside the longhouse of the maidens. Cooked turkey meat will fill empty bellies after much dancing. I will cook the turkeys myself, and you will come and help us eat them."

Renno was elated, but it was not seemly to show one's feelings, so his expression remained unchanged. "It is good to dance when the moon is full," he said. "I will be there."

Anowara took the turkeys and went off to join the other women, and as Renno started off at a trot toward town, his mind so full that he paid no attention to his surroundings, he nearly collided with Iala, who had been following the other women at a distance.

"Do you pursue enemies into the town?" she asked, her tone innocent, a hint of humor in her eyes.

Renno stammered an apology and, saying too much, indicated that he would be joining the full warriors at the moon dance.

"I will go to the moon dance, too," she told him, her lovely face indicating that she was calm but alert.

He nodded politely.

She cocked her head to one side and seemed deep in thought. "Anowara," she said, "is my friend and I like her, but she is still a child. I become angry with her because she doesn't know what she wants." She paused, then added with a slight increase in emphasis, "I know what I want."

Iala was so pretty that Renno enjoyed just looking at her, but he was afraid that she intended to tell him which of the full warriors she preferred. A man did not become involved in the gossip of women, so he withdrew into himself, the change in his manner so delicate that only a fellow Iroquois would be aware of it.

Iala was conscious of the shift. "I also know how to wait," she said, turning away.

The warrior who would win her, he thought, would be a fortunate man. Resuming his run to the town, he wondered how soon he would become eligible to join a war party and prove himself worthy of promotion.

Twice he had asked Ghonka to send him off with a war party, but both times his father had pretended not to hear the request, a sure sign that he wanted his son to drop the subject. It would be wrong for the Great Sachem to show partiality to his son.

Renno debated whether to enlist the aid of his mother and aunt. Both exerted considerable influence with Ghonka, and he knew that both were eager to see him advance, certain that he would behave with valor and distinction. On reflection, he decided that his father would be embarrassed if Ena and Sah-nee-wa intervened on his behalf, and under no circumstances could he cause the Great Sachem to lose face, so he would have to exercise patience, a virtue as great as courage and endurance.

The next two days passed slowly, but the tempo of activity in the town increased on the day of the moon dance. Much to Renno's chagrin, for he wished he had won the honor, one of the full warriors brought down an elk, and the meat was roasted over an open fire. But he had the satisfaction of seeing, from a distance, that Anowara cooked the two turkeys he had given her, just as she had promised.

As he was about to return to his longhouse to dress himself for the dance, he saw Anowara and Iala approaching, both carrying wooden platters that were heaped with corn cakes.

He was not surprised when Anowara walked past him without as much as a nod of recognition.

Iala, however, made a point of halting. "I hope you will come tonight, Renno," she said.

"I will," he replied earnestly.

"Good. I was afraid you might change your mind because not many junior warriors have been invited."

Somewhat to his surprise, he found himself confiding in her. "It is my hope," he said, "that soon I will have the chance to win a promotion."

"I know you will succeed," she said.

He returned to his longhouse, put streaks of green and yellow paint on his cheeks, and then donned a clean loincloth, a shirt and kilt decorated with painted pebbles, and leggings his mother had recently made for him. He grinned as he slipped into a new pair of moccasins that were a trifle tight and would need to stretch as he wore them. They were the handiwork of Ba-lin-ta, her first attempt, and they had required considerable private remedial work, done by Ena, to make them wearable.

The full moon was rising high, turning from pale gold to silver as Renno strolled across the town with the swagger of a full warrior, feeling less confident than he looked. He heard the rhythmic throbbing of three drums growing louder as he approached the field behind the longhouse of the maidens.

A smoking fire, the flames leaping high, illuminated the scene. On the far side, the sachems, medicine men, and senior warriors were sitting with their wives, sipping from gourds filled with crushed sumac berries, honey, and water. Those who were parents of the younger people might stay for a time, but the others would soon retire to their own private dwellings and longhouses for an evening of serious conversation, more easily conducted at a distance from the noise of the drums.

A number of maidens and bachelors and younger married couples were already dancing, the men in one line, the women in another, facing each other. The tempo was stately and their gestures and the movements of their feet were stylized as they paid homage to the manitou of the moon. As the evening progressed, the dancing would become livelier.

It didn't take Renno long to find Anowara. Like the other maidens, she wore a calf-length doeskin skirt decorated with dyed porcupine quills. Her shirt was made of soft doeskin into which a flower pattern had been burned. Her hair hung loose, and she wore a white flower in it.

If she saw Renno, she paid no attention to him and instead chatted and flirted with a burly young full warrior who listened closely to her words and nodded in agreement with whatever she was saying.

A spasm of jealousy shot through Renno. She hadn't spoken to him with that kind of animation since they had played together as children.

Iala was smiling at him, and he returned her greeting with a feeble grin. He guessed she knew what he was feeling and was taking pity on him by trying to reduce his hurt. It was kind of her.

Then he froze as Anowara and the warrior moved out into the open space to join the dancers. In a formal preliminary gesture, the man draped his buffalo skin cape around the girl's shoulders. Renno felt as though someone had kicked him in the stomach. Anowara, by allowing herself to be enfolded in the cape, was signaling to the whole tribe that she was not opposed to the warrior's interest in her.

Obviously Renno's attentions meant nothing to her, and heartsick, he lost his appetite for dancing and feasting. He turned away from the firelight into the welcoming darkness, intending to return to his longhouse, when he was startled by a touch on his arm. It was Iala.

"Renno of the Bear Clan, the son of Ghonka," she said firmly, "behaves like a small boy who has not yet taken his manhood tests."

All he wanted was privacy. "By what right do you speak to me as my mother or my aunt would speak?" he demanded.

Iala did not retreat, and he was unable to read

the expression in her liquid eyes. "Is it the wish of Renno to become a sachem when he grows older?"

All his life he had taken it for granted that he would become a leader of the Seneca, so her question was absurd.

"Of course!"

"I believe you will do it. But you must act like one. It is said that a sachem must have a skin that is seven thumbs thick."

She spoke the truth, and he recognized it. Many times he had heard his father make the same remark.

"A sachem does not show what he feels when the worms eat into his heart," Iala said. "It is not right. You must return to the dance and laugh with your friends. You must dance and eat even though your thoughts are in darkness."

Iala was making him feel ashamed. It was important that others not guess what this girl had somehow divined, or he would be teased unmercifully.

"I will go with you," she said.

He was touched, but he could not accept her sacrifice. "It is not right that you give up your own pleasure for me."

Her faint shrug indicated her indifference to whatever satisfactions she sought for herself, and there was no way that he could refuse the offer without insulting her. Besides, it would be flattering to be seen with the lovely Iala, who was coveted by every unmarried warrior.

"If you wish," she said, becoming shy, "I will dance with you."

"I will always remember your friendship," Renno replied gratefully. "Never will I forget that Iala acted toward me as a sister."

His lack of experience in dealing with girls made it impossible for him to interpret the look she shot at him beneath her dark heavy lashes.

The wind grew stronger, the leaves on the trees began to show their pale undersides, and Renno knew that the storm and the night would arrive together. The deer slung across his shoulders was heavy, although he bore the burden easily as he made his way toward the place where the two brooks drew together to make one river. There El-i-chi would meet him and they would make their camp to celebrate the success of their hunting trip.

It began to rain as he reached the junction of the brooks, so he deposited the deer carcass on the ground. A short distance away, he remembered, was a small clearing where stood the ramshackle remains of a primitive hut, a dwelling that had been occupied for years by a strange old Seneca warrior who had shunned human company. Most members of the tribe avoided the place because the old man had died there, and they were afraid it might be haunted by his spirit. But Renno preferred to be dry for the night, if the place still stood, and he reasoned that as the old warrior had been harmless in life, his spirit—even if it were still in the vicinity—would perform no evil toward the living.

Having made up his mind, Renno picked up his deer again and began to run toward the old ruin. The cabin, still more or less intact, was overgrown with weeds and blueberry bushes, and its roof had fallen in. Renno placed his deer in the crotch of a nearby tree to keep it away from predatory animals, then he stepped into the cabin where he found nothing but a dilapidated sleeping bench and some dry twigs and logs. Glad that he and his brother would be dry and that he would be saved the need to gather wood, he began to scrape the old ashes from the fire pit. El-i-chi would smell the fire and come to join him. All at once he stopped. The ashes at the bottom of the pit were still warm.

The youth's skin crawled. Was it possible that, as some Seneca women had claimed, the old man who had lived here was a sorcerer? He knew of a case—or at least had heard of it—in which a warrior who slept on a dead sorcerer's bunk had been consumed by the man's spirit, and by morning had totally vanished. Certainly it would be better to sleep in the open and endure a few raindrops than to run the risk of a confrontation with an evil spirit.

Emerging from the hut, Renno felt certain he heard footsteps above the sound of the rain. Common sense prompted him to place his ear close to the ground, and he grew thoughtful. There were several pairs of footsteps, and they were human. Evil spirits made no sound.

He withdrew a short distance into the forest, loosening his knife in his belt and taking the precaution of notching an arrow into his bow.

As he watched, three tall warriors entered the clearing from the opposite side, their purple and white war paint identifying them as members of the hated Huron nation.

They were laughing and conversing in normal tones, which told Renno they had no idea he was in the vicinity, and unless they noticed the deer carcass, they wouldn't suspect that anyone was near.

Fresh scalps were dangling from the warriors' belts, and one of the men carried a small bundle of clothing and ornaments. It was apparent that they had just conducted a raid, and it seemed likely that their victims were Seneca.

Remembering the virtue of patience, he waited until the Huron went into the hut and built up the fire. As they warmed themselves around it, he inched toward the open window and cautiously peered inside. The bloody scalps were hanging near the fire to speed their drying, and a captured shirt was spread out nearby, its embroidered pattern telling Renno that it was a shirt of his people. Forcing himself to listen to the talk, he soon realized that these foes had conducted a sneak raid on a small Seneca village to the north.

He was not yet a full warrior, but he knew the manitous had selected him to avenge the honor of his nation. He would not fail them.

Carefully he moved from the window toward the open doorway of the hut, shielding his bow—with an arrow already notched into it—from the rain as best he could.

A flash of lightning made the night as bright as day for an instant, and the Thunder Spirit roared overhead. It was the manitous voicing their confidence in Renno, and his own spirits soared. He knew now that he was sure to succeed.

As the peal of thunder died away, he uttered his challenge, a full-throated war cry, and stepped into the open doorway.

Somewhat blinded by the light of their fire, the startled Huron jerked their heads in his direction, but Renno struck before they could move. His first arrow pierced the eye of a Huron brave, penetrating his brain.

A second arrow lodged in the chest of another of the enemy, and he died, too, struggling feebly as he fell to the ground.

However, in the few seconds that had elapsed,

the third Huron recovered from his surprise. He drew a strange weapon from his belt, a metal object with a long barrel and a curved handle, and pointing it at the young Seneca, he squeezed something on the underside of the weapon.

There was a curious clicking sound.

The Huron muttered an oath, hurled the weapon aside, and drawing his knife, threw himself at his enemy.

Renno was ready, and he thrust the Huron's knife hand away, so the stone blade did no harm. That morning before leaving home Renno had greased his entire body with bear fat to protect himself from the chilly weather, and this gave him an advantage. The Huron was a grown man, huskier and stronger than the junior warrior, and as they fell to the ground, each trying to stab the other, the Huron found his young opponent repeatedly slipping from his grasp.

A stone blade narrowly missed Renno's face.

He knew he would be defeated in a long fight and therefore had to strike swiftly. Feinting at the other's throat, he drove his own blade into the man's stomach, then struck him a second time and a third.

The Huron's strength ebbed.

"Let your spirit take warning in the afterworld," Renno said to him. "All who attack the Seneca must die." And showing no mercy, he drove his knife deep into the enemy's throat.

Feeling no elation, Renno hauled himself to his feet. Before he scalped the Huron, he wanted to examine the unfamiliar weapon.

The instrument was surprisingly heavy, slightly longer than Renno's forearm, and the lengthy portion was about as thick as his thumb. This tube was hollow, but there was no opening at the other end, so it couldn't be a blowgun, a weapon sometimes favored by the Onondaga nation.

As Renno continued to examine the weapon, he felt a savage pain in the back of his left shoulder, and almost at the same instant he was knocked to the ground, with a crushing weight bearing down on him.

Squirming and twisting, he managed to turn around, and he found himself staring up at a Huron giant, his purple and white war paint making his face hideous. Straddling Renno's chest, the Huron's knees pressed the junior warrior's arms against the bare earth.

Renno tried to kick himself free, but he could not raise his knees high enough. His wound was bleeding, and as it throbbed he realized he was helpless.

A knife was poised in the air above his face, and it gleamed in the firelight. Like the other curious weapon, it was made of a hard metal.

"Hear me, Seneca youth, before you join your ancestors in the long sleep," the Huron said. "You have killed three of my braves, so you deserve to die."

The pain in Renno's shoulder was almost unbearable, but his face was empty of expression. He continued to struggle, even though, if it came to it, he was prepared to die with courage and dignity.

Alain de Gramont, known to the Huron as Golden Eagle, stared hard at his victim, then laughed softly but harshly, the knife still poised. "Mark well what I say to you!" he commanded. "You and I are not like other warriors. You came to the Seneca from the outside world, just as I came to the Huron."

The man's eyes were blue rather than brown, Renno noted with a shock of surprise, and the skin beneath his paint had not been exposed to the sun for long periods and was pale, far lighter than the skin of an Indian. In fact, it resembled the color of Renno's own skin beneath his loincloth.

"For more cycles of the moon than I wish to count," Alain de Gramont said, "I have met no Seneca warrior, no Mohawk, or any other Iroquois who is my equal. I am Golden Eagle, the greatest of all warriors. Remember my name, young Seneca."

Renno tried to speak calmly, saying, "I will carry your name into the afterworld with me, Golden Eagle."

"You will not be sent to the afterworld now," Alain de Gramont replied, his blue eyes cold and hard. "I have changed my mind. Because you are young and have not fought in battle, you have not yet gained your full strength and cunning. I will spare you now, and in time to come, as you grow older and know the warpath, perhaps you will become the enemy I seek. Long have I waited for the day when I would fight a warrior as strong and courageous and cunning as myself. I will allow you to live now, young Seneca, so you will become that warrior."

Renno knew he was not experiencing a vision. His pain was real, and so was the ferocious pale-skinned Huron.

"I make you a gift, young Seneca. Keep it, so we may meet more nearly as equals when our paths next cross." He drove his metal knife into the ground a few inches from Renno's head, and it quivered there like the stem of a delicate plant shaking in a breeze. "Who are you?" he demanded. "I want to know the name of him who will become the enemy of Golden Eagle."

"I am called Renno," was the proud reply, even though a creeping sensation of grogginess made it difficult for the young Seneca to speak.

"We will meet again, Renno of the Seneca. I give

you the pledge of Golden Eagle, the great warrior of the Huron."

The weight was lifted from Renno's chest, and he was vaguely aware of the pale Huron disappearing into the night. Then he lost consciousness.

After a period in which time had no meaning, he heard someone calling his name, and later he recalled seeing El-i-chi looming above him. What happened thereafter came back to him only in snatches. He seemed to remember being carried on a litter and hearing the deep voices of warriors, including his father. After swimming in darkness again, he thought he heard the voice of Iala repeating his name, and he became puzzled before the deep night descended again.

When Renno awakened, his head was clear, and he heard the sound of women chanting. He tried to sit up, but a wave of dizziness forced him to drop back onto his pallet. The odors of burning tobacco surrounded him, someone was sprinkling him with herb leaves that felt soft and soothing, and then he recognized the voice of his mother.

The chanting halted abruptly, and Ena raised his head with one hand as she reached out to accept a bowl of steaming herb tea with the other. Renno squinted and saw it was Sah-nee-wa who handed his mother the tea.

Ena held the bowl to his lips, and he drank in small sips at first, then greedily.

His head became even clearer, the pounding sensation behind his eyes halted, and the fuzziness that had hampered his vision was gone. He was lying in the house of his parents. Ba-lin-ta was tending the fire, her small face serious, and Iala was crumbling dried tobacco leaves onto the flames. The presence of Iala with the women of his family surprised him.

124

He reached up with his right hand and felt his left shoulder, which no longer pained him. His muscles were stiff, but he could feel no soreness.

He grinned, and his mother returned his smile, as did his aunt. Iala's face remained grave, but there was something in her eyes that made him giddy.

Ena said something to Ba-lin-ta, who raced out of the hut, and soon the air was filled with the noise of wooden rattles accompanying the chanting of male voices.

Renno knew he was recovering from an illness and that the medicine men of the town were coming to help him.

In a few moments the hut was filled to overflowing with men wearing the grotesque masks of the false faces.

"Ashes," said Iala's father, who in some way unknown to mere humans could transform himself into a medium for the spirits of the forest. "We blow ashes so you will soon become well again."

The air was thick with ashes, the soot raining down on Renno. He felt dizzy and light-headed, his chest contracted and seemed to be squeezing his heart, and then a strange thing happened. The false face worn by Iala's father changed shape and assumed an identity of its own.

There were eyes—blue ones—in the hollow sockets of the mask.

The coarse black-dyed-buffalo hair that covered the head of the mask turned a pale yellow, the color of Renno's own hair, as well as that of the Huron, Golden Eagle, who had become his enemy.

All at once Renno knew that this was the manitou who had come to him at the climax of his manhood trial rites.

"Renno, son of Ghonka," the Great False Face said, not in the voice of Iala's father but as that of a woman, "you have made your new test and you have conquered. Now you are a full warrior."

Gradually the face reverted to its inanimate shape, and the chanting of the medicine men echoed through the hut until Renno's ears ached. His mother, his aunt, and Iala fanned him, dispersing the ashes that continued to fall on him.

Then the medicine men departed, still chanting and shaking their rattles.

"Now you will eat," Ena told him, and ceremonially she handed a wooden bowl to Iala.

The girl knelt beside Renno and began to feed him with a long spoon.

He slept until the next day, when he awoke to find his father sitting beside him, holding a handsome headdress with nine feathers trailing from it.

"This belongs to you, my son," Ghonka said. "These are the feathers of the three Huron you killed in the forest. In a few days, when you are stronger, you will wear them, and in your belt you will carry their scalps when you go to the ceremony where you will become a full warrior."

The Great Sachem reached beneath his buffalo cape and produced the metal knife, which he showed to his son.

Carved on the handle was the symbol of a golden eagle. "Do you also have the hollow tube weapon, my father?" Renno asked.

Ghonka inclined his head. "El-i-chi brought it to me after he found you."

"Never have I seen such a weapon."

"You will learn its meaning at the Council of the Iroquois, which I have called." Ghonka offered no further explanation. "Now you will tell me how it happened that this knife was driven into the ground near your head."

Renno related in full the incident with the pale-skinned Huron who had called himself a great warrior.

His father became thoughtful. "It is true," he said, "that Golden Eagle is a mighty brave. Often have I sought him in battle to test my skill against his, but never have we met. He is the most terrible of all our enemies. But it may be that he is right. Perhaps it is your destiny, rather than mine, to meet him in war. When you do, you must show him no mercy for having spared you. You must kill him."

"I hear, my father, and I will do as you command."

Ghonka handed him the metal knife.

Renno took it and placed it beside his pallet. "When the manitous of war arrange my meeting with Golden Eagle, I will kill him with the knife that bears his symbol."

Obviously pleased, Ghonka stood up and left the hut.

A few moments later Iala entered carrying a nourishing stew of buffalo meat, potatoes, tomatoes, and corn.

As she fed it to him, Renno could no longer contain his curiosity. "How does it happen that it is you—instead of my mother or my aunt, or even my little sister—who helps me to become strong again?"

Iala smiled gently and averted her lovely face. "It is true, as Sah-nee-wa says, that even the most courageous of men have the minds of little children."

"Must a man know the minds of women to become a great warrior?" he demanded, annoyed because she hadn't answered his question.

The girl laughed aloud, then on sudden impulse bent lower and brushed his forehead with her lips.

Renno felt as though his face was on fire. That gesture, at least, was plain enough for him to understand, and it was startling to realize that Iala neither pitied him nor wanted him to become her brother. Indeed, she was offering herself to him as only a woman could offer herself to a man, and his heart pumped wildly.

Quickly recovering her composure, Iala began to feed him again. "You will be very busy," she said. "You will become a full warrior, and then you will attend the Council of the Iroquois your father has summoned. If I know you, Renno, you will want to join the war party that will teach the Huron not to raid our villages. After you return, you and I will speak of matters that concern only us."

A delegation of three senior warriors escorted Renno to the community longhouse, where a bright fire leaped toward the smoke hole in the ceiling. Ghonka was seated cross-legged on the platform, flanked by the sachems of other Seneca towns who were already arriving for the Iroquois Council, and his war chiefs and the senior warriors were gathered behind him.

All of the town's full warriors, along with their newly arrived colleagues from other parts of the Seneca nation, were seated in solid rows opposite the platform. Renno caught a glimpse of his mother and Sahnee-wa in the shadows, and Iala and Ba-lin-ta stood beside them, the little girl so excited that she was hopping from one foot to the other.

Renno, clad only in a loincloth, prostrated himself before his father.

He was ordered to rise, and one of the war chiefs made a long speech in which he described the killing of the three Huron braves. The account was exaggerated and inaccurate, since only Renno knew what had actually taken place, but no one cared. The one undeniable fact was that Renno had indeed slain three of the enemy.

Iala's father came forward and painted the initiate's face and torso with green and yellow paint. This was the first time Renno had ever worn war paint on his body. Then Ghonka placed the headdress on his son's head, and Renno himself removed the metal knife from his belt.

One by one every man present took the metal knife, cut the little finger of his own left hand, and squeezed a few drops of blood into a clay jug. Iala's father added honey, water, and the juice of grapes to the blood, chanting all the while in a low undertone that no one except the other medicine men could understand.

Ghonka was the first to sip from the jug, which was passed around the assemblage, and Renno, the last to drink, drained the contents and threw the jug into the fire. The ceremony was ended, and he joined the ranks of the full warriors.

Ghonka embraced him.

By the time the others had congratulated him, Ena and Sah-nee-wa had gone, taking Iala and a reluctantly departing Ba-lin-ta with them. They had been permitted to watch the ceremony because it was so unusual for one of Renno's age to become a full warrior, but the solemnity of the occasion would have been marred had they remained any longer.

A new dignity was Renno's immediate gain. He moved his belongings that same night to one of the longhouses of the full warriors, and he was struck by the quietness of life there. No one raced up and down the aisles between rows of sleeping platforms as was common in the longhouse of the junior warriors. No one shouted, no practical jokes were played, and under no circumstances did any man challenge another to a wrestling match.

Never again would Renno be required to perform menial chores for his mother, attend to errands for her, or even carry water from the well. Younger by several years than any of his new peers, he was their equal. In fact, few of them could boast three scalps in their belts and the feathers of three slain enemies in their headdresses.

Even El-i-chi was slightly in awe of his brother now and asked him plaintively, "When will we go hunting again?"

Renno grinned. "Very soon. Our father has ordered me to rest and grow stronger before the Council meets, but I'll soon be free to do as I please."

"I wish," El-i-chi said, "that I could sit at the Council meeting."

Renno felt compelled to offer him a full warrior's advice. "Be patient, my brother, and you will grow wise."

El-i-chi couldn't help laughing. "If you had been patient and wise, you wouldn't have attacked three Huron all by yourself!"

Renno had no ready reply.

The pace of life in the main Seneca town soon

quickened. Even though autumn was far advanced, hunting parties scoured the forest for game, and senior warriors participated in the hunt. The junior warriors and older girls were sent fishing, and the younger children gathered edible roots in the woods. Large quantities of food would be needed when the visitors arrived.

Additional longhouses were constructed, and a sea of buffalo-skin tents arose in the cornfields beyond the town's palisade. The Great Sachem was ready to welcome his guests to the conclave.

The first to arrive were the lesser Seneca sachems and war chiefs, surrounded by their senior and full warriors. Those of the highest rank moved into the older, more comfortable longhouses of their respective clans, and the dwellings were soon crowded.

The leaders of the Mohawk, who lived to the east of the Seneca, and the Oneida, their neighbors to the west, were the next to appear. Then came the Cayuga, a people who made up for their sparse population by being more tenacious in battle than any of their brothers, and they were followed by the stolid Onondaga, believed by other Iroquois nations to be lacking in humor.

Renno found it strange to be regarded as something of a celebrity. The Seneca boasted about their junior warrior who had single-handedly killed three Huron, and many of the visitors went out of their way to meet him.

"You will become a warrior as great as your father," an elderly Mohawk sachem told him. "You have found favor with the spirits, and they will keep watch over you and help you."

On the day before the conclave was scheduled to begin, Renno was walking to the meeting site with two Onondaga who were members of the Bear Clan, all three of them having been assigned to the group that would build a platform for the leaders. Suddenly he came face-to-face with Anowara.

Now that he was a hero, her attitude toward him had undergone a miraculous change. She smiled warmly and asked him to remain behind for a moment.

The Onondaga moved on without him.

"I haven't had a chance to tell you how proud of you I am," Anowara said.

Conscious of his new dignity and aware that he wasn't required to reply in words, Renno inclined his head a fraction of an inch.

Anowara placed a hand on his arm, a gesture that meant she would invite his advances. In order to make certain he understood her intention, she allowed her hand to remain for several moments. "I have told all my cousins of the Iroquois nations that you are my oldest and best friend, that we knew each other well even as small babies carried on the backs of our mothers."

"That is true," Renno replied courteously, and he thought it strange that his feelings had changed so radically. Anowara was attractive enough, but her beauty paled next to that of the radiant Iala. Besides, for reasons he couldn't analyze, he no longer cared what Anowara thought of him. Scores of girls were making a fuss over him, and he felt indifferent to their praise. It was enough that a man lived up to the obligations of his duty.

"I've also told my cousins," Anowara added slyly, "that we are still the best of friends."

Renno froze. He had no interest now in becoming involved with her, and worst of all, he was afraid her loose tongue might jeopardize his growing relationship with Iala. In order to make himself emphatically clear, he folded his arms across his chest, nodded, and stalked off after the Onondaga.

He didn't look back, so he didn't see the bitter expression on Anowara's face. It made her feel no better to know that she had only herself to blame for losing the newest Seneca hero.

Early the next morning the men of the Iroquois were summoned to the conclave by five drummers—one representing each of the nations. The senior warriors filed onto the field and sat impassively in long rows, and the younger full warriors moved in behind them. The leading medicine men took places opposite them, followed by the powerful war chiefs, each wearing an elaborate feathered headdress and carrying an impressive number of dried scalps in his belt.

The last to appear were the sachems, dressed in their ceremonial buffalo-skin robes. They mounted the platform together and took their places in order of seniority, with Ghonka, the Great Sachem, seated on the left. At the same instant, in a manner no outsider could fathom, the drums fell silent.

The Indian love of oratory prompted long speeches, and one war chief from each tribe delivered a long harangue on the ties of brotherhood that bound the Iroquois. The principal medicine men followed with similar statements, each stressing that the Five Nations were invincible.

When the weak late-autumn sun was high overhead, the Council adjourned while the men ate a light meal. Then they resumed their places, and at last the conclave got down to the real business at hand.

One of the Seneca war chiefs described Renno's encounter with the Huron, and the embarrassed young warrior found himself in the limelight, with scores of warriors looking at him. The purpose of the declaration was withheld until the end, when the speaker reached beneath his cape and produced the tube of metal that had been pointed at Renno. "One of the Huron," the war chief cried, "carried this short firestick! The others carried long firesticks!"

A senior Seneca warrior produced the other firearms, and all three were passed around.

Renno wondered how he could have been so stupid. He had heard of firesticks—magical weapons that made loud noises, spurted fire, and were deadlier than bows and arrows—but it had not occurred to him that the strange metal instrument the Huron had aimed at him had been a firestick, and only now could he understand his father's deep concern.

The display of the muskets and the pistol created a sensation. War chief after war chief leaped to his feet and demanded that the Iroquois dispatch a mighty force without delay to destroy the Huron and, if necessary, their brothers and close allies, the Ottawa. And if the Algonquian decided to take part in the war, they too would suffer.

Ghonka remained motionless, his face wooden, until every war chief had his turn to speak. Finally the time came for him to give his opinion, and a silence fell on the assemblage as he stood.

"My brothers," he said, "hear the words of one who has led you to many victories over the Huron, the Ottawa, the Erie, and the Algonquian. No warriors have the courage and strength of the Iroquois, but if we go to war against our ancient foes now, we will lose."

His statement was so radical, so unexpected, that the surface calm was destroyed. War chiefs and senior warriors alike were astonished, and an angry, disturbed buzz swept back and forth across the field.

Ghonka raised a hand, and discipline was restored. "The Seneca," he said, "will send our own war party to teach the Huron respect for our people. But we are not ready for a big war. The Huron and Ottawa have formed an alliance with the pale skins who live in the town they call Quebec. It is the pale skins who have given the Huron many firesticks and have taught them how to use these weapons. Our bows and arrows are no match for them."

His words made sense, and the chiefs and senior warriors, although still troubled, nodded to each other in agreement.

"The Iroquois must have firesticks, too, and we must learn how to use them," Ghonka declared.

The assemblage roared their approval.

Again he demanded quiet. "I have called this Council for a purpose I will now reveal to you. The Iroquois will not ask the pale skin friends of the Huron and Ottawa for firesticks, for we can get them from other pale skins who live nearer to us. I ask for your agreement to send messengers to the towns the pale skins call Albany and Springfield and Boston. We will meet with these pale skins, and they will give us firesticks. They will teach us how to use them."

There was another roar of approval.

But the Mohawk sachem was thoughtful. "My brother," he demanded, "what will we give for these firesticks? It is wrong for the Iroquois to involve ourselves in the fights between the pale skins of Boston and Albany on one side and Quebec on the other in exchange for the weapons."

The sachem of the Oneida leaped to his feet. "My brother of the Mohawk speaks the truth," he said. "The pale skins are sly and deceitful. If we are not careful, the Iroquois will be fighting their battles for them against the Huron and Ottawa and Algonquian."

Ghonka concurred heartily. "It is wrong for the sons of the Iroquois to die in the wars of the pale skins. They are greedy men, so we will give them what they prize above all else. The skins of beaver and otter, fox and buffalo."

One by one the sachems of the other nations expressed their agreement. All were willing to allow the Great Sachem to negotiate with the pale skins on their behalf and to obtain firesticks in return for animal pelts.

Ghonka offered his pledge, promising to form no alliance with any pale skins.

The sachems voted unanimously in favor of the arrangement. Now it was the turn of their subordinates to protest if they disagreed, but the war chiefs and principal medicine men offered no objections. A few of the senior warriors indicated that they would have preferred no dealings with any pale skins, but they admitted that the Iroquois had no workable alternative.

The young full warriors were present only as observers, and they had no voice in the proceedings, but as he looked up and down the ranks of those who surrounded him, Renno could tell that his new peers were satisfied. He was equally pleased. Even though he couldn't imagine any weapon being more effective than a bow and arrow, he was excited by the idea of obtaining a firestick and learning how to use it.

The five sachems donned special headgear made of elks' antlers, which they touched ceremonially. This act made the agreement binding on all of the Iroquois nations, and the Council adjourned at sundown in time for a great feast prepared by the women.

At dawn, the visitors began to leave, and by late morning the last of them were gone. The junior warriors and older girls of the Seneca town promptly went to work dismantling the temporary living quarters that had been erected for the Council, and quiet returned to the town.

Renno privately hoped that his father would assign him as one of the messengers who would be sent to request a meeting with the pale skins, and he was disappointed when Ghonka selected three senior warriors for the purpose.

The young full warrior had no chance to brood, however. Soon after he learned the identity of the messengers, he and a number of others were summoned to the community longhouse where Ghonka and a war chief, Sun-ai-yee, waited until thirty men, a few of them senior warriors, had assembled. Three junior warriors, El-i-chi among them, stood at the rear, not daring to become too familiar with their superiors.

"You have been chosen," the Great Sachem declared, "to avenge the honor of the Seneca. Sun-ai-yee has selected you to march with him to a town of the Huron and to destroy it."

Renno was elated. At last he would be an active member of a war party!

When the group disbanded, under orders to leave just before dawn on the following day, Ghonka told his sons to remain for a moment.

"El-i-chi," he said to the younger, "it is the wish of Sun-ai-yee that you will be one of three junior warriors who march with the war party. Do as you're told, stay out of trouble, and bring no disgrace upon our family or clan."

El-i-chi bowed his head, his dark eyes gleaming with pleasure. "I will bring honor to my father and the Bear Clan," he swore.

Ghonka turned to his elder son and clapped him on his recently healed shoulder. "It was my wish that you stay at home until the soreness was gone from your shoulder."

Renno hastily flexed his shoulder muscles. "There is no sore place left in my body, my father."

"That is good," the Great Sachem replied, barely concealing a smile, "because Sun-ai-yee begged for the right to include you among his warriors. He said you had earned the right to go with him, and I could not argue with him any more than I could deny you the right to go."

Renno thanked him, aware that, in spite of his disclaimer, his father could have refused.

"You have proved your valor, so take no needless risks," Ghonka said. "I have many plans for your future that you do not yet know."

"I will take no risks except those that must be taken," Renno replied, "but I give you my pledge I will return with more Huron scalps in my belt."

"I have little doubt of it." Ghonka paused, then sighed. "Now I must face the women of our family and tell them that both our sons will march to the land of the Huron. I would rather lead the party myself than hear what your mother and aunt will say to me."

Renno and El-i-chi bowed as he left the community longhouse; then they embraced each other. Their lifelong dream of going off to war together would be fulfilled, even though El-i-chi and the other junior warriors would take no active part in the attack.

Renno went to the longhouse of the full warriors to prepare for his journey, and dusk was falling by the time he went to his family's hut for a farewell meal. Ena and Sah-nee-wa showed no emotion, although they had taken care to prepare some of the dishes that he and El-i-chi most enjoyed. Ena presented her sons with leather bags of parched corn and dried venison strips to carry with them on the trail.

Ghonka was proud of his sons, but he made no mention of their venture, instead talking briefly about the mission he was sending to the towns of the pale skins. "I am inviting these strangers to visit me here," he said. "You will return from your journey before they arrive, so you will be present to hear the talk when we offer them skins for their firesticks."

"What will you do, my father," Renno asked, "if they wish the Seneca to join in their war against the pale skins of the North?"

"You heard what I told the Council," Ghonka replied. "I will refuse. I don't trust the pale skins, so I cannot accept them as brothers."

Ba-lin-ta, seated at the fire between Renno and El-i-chi, could not contain her excitement. "Renno, will you bring me a doll of the Huron?"

"If I can, I will," he assured her, "but I make no promise." It was difficult for a little girl to understand the purpose of war, he thought.

Ba-lin-ta's enthusiasm was undimmed. "I want a Huron shirt," she said. "And a drum, too."

Ena tried to quiet the child. "You can be sure Renno won't forget you," she said.

"And some toys!"

Ghonka intervened. "Ba-lin-ta, the Huron are very much like the Seneca. According to the old legends, we were one people long ago. Evil manitous entered the hearts of the Huron, so they turned away from us and became our enemies, but their toys and drums and shirts are much like ours."

The little girl subsided at last, not wanting to incur her father's wrath, but she couldn't resist looking in silent appeal at Renno.

He grinned and nodded.

When the meal ended, Ena marked the faces of her sons with ashes, and Sah-nee-wa gave them packets of herbs to protect them from malicious spirits. The herbs served a double purpose and were to be consumed in the event of illness.

Renno and El-i-chi hugged Ba-lin-ta and then returned to their respective longhouses. Their father would see them off in the morning.

It was not easy to fall asleep that night, but Renno knew they would spend many hours on the trail, so he forced himself to relax and at last he dropped off. He was awake again long before the departure hour, and he had ample time to daub himself with green and yellow paint, check his weapons, and move out into the open, where his comrades were gathering.

Someone was standing in the dark shadows at the end of the longhouse, and Renno knew at once that Iala had come to bid him farewell. He went to her, and in silence she handed him a small leather pouch.

He opened it and found a carved wooden figure of a hawk. The gift overwhelmed him. He vaguely recalled having told Iala about the hawk, the son of the spirit who had come to him in a vision, that would give him a warrior's power.

He bowed his head in thanks.

Iala took the tiny wooden figure from him, and for a moment their fingers touched.

Renno's whole hand tingled as the girl replaced the figure in its pouch and attached it to his bear claw necklace.

The gift bound them even more closely, and Renno knew that when he returned he would go straight to Iala.

She knew it, too, and she placed the palm of her hand on his chest for a long moment.

Their eyes met and held; then, as silently as she had appeared, the girl melted into the darkness.

Renno rejoined his comarades, and they went to the community longhouse where the three senior warriors who would participate in the raid awaited them. El-i-chi and the other two juniors were there, conspicuous because they wore no paint on their bodies, but they were soon sent on ahead of the party in order to hunt food for the cooking fires.

Then Sun-ai-yee appeared, accompanied by Ghonka, and the two chiefs conferred privately. The war party leader was heavyset, with a protruding stomach, and the hair of his scalp lock was graying, but he was said to be a man of remarkable endurance. He had held his high rank for many years, and the fact that he enjoyed the full confidence of the Great Sachem gave him additional prestige.

Suddenly Sun-ai-yee turned and gestured, and the members of the party fell into line behind him.

Ghonka raised his hand, palm extended, in a farewell to each of the warriors, and his eyes were bright as he looked at Renno.

Most of the town's residents still slept as the war party went beyond the palisade, crossed the cornfields, and plunged into the forest. They moved at a trot, prepared to maintain the same even pace indefinitely. This was one of the secrets of Seneca success, and every member of the group had been trained for this from early childhood.

Sun-ai-yee had no intention of coddling his sub-ordinates, and although he himself had seen more than forty summers, he kept up a blistering pace.

El-i-chi brought down a buck, and he and the other juniors prepared a cooking fire and were roasting the meat in a small clearing when the party finally halted for a few hours of rest long after sundown. The warriors were in high spirits, relishing their adventure; nevertheless, they observed the normal precautions of the trail, conversing in tones that would not carry and keeping a careful watch.

El-i-chi joined his brother, and they squatted side by side, eating chunks of dripping venison. "Iala came to say good-bye to you this morning," El-i-chi ventured, casting a sidelong glance at his brother, his eyes light-ing briefly on the pouch containing the wooden hawk.

Renno merely nodded.

"She gave you a gift."

"She did." It was not seemly to discuss such matters with a mere youth.

El-i-chi suppressed a laugh. "Our mother and our father's sister approve of her."

This was important, and Renno dropped his air of indifference. "I thought so—but what makes you so certain?"

"I heard them talking to each other, and to our father."

"What did he say?"

El-i-chi shrugged. It was the women of a family who arranged the marriages of young couples, and only when a man had strong, valid grounds for protest did he express an opinion of his own. "Ba-lin-ta," the youn-ger brother declared, "has told Iala many times that she can hardly wait until they are sisters."

142

Renno made a wry face. It was unfortunate that girl-children, unlike boys, were not taught the value of dignified silence.

"I'll like it, too," El-i-chi said. "No girl in the whole Iroquois League is more beautiful than she who will become my sister."

"You chatter as much as Ba-lin-ta," Renno said as he reached for another chunk of meat.

El-i-chi chortled quietly, ignoring the rebuke. He emulated Renno in all things, and in due time he, too, would marry a beautiful girl.

Aware of his brother's admiration, Renno softened. "See to it," he said, "that you speak of these matters to no one outside the family."

"Everyone in town knows what you and Iala think of each other," said El-i-chi.

Renno was flattered by the knowledge that he had made a sufficient mark to have aroused other people's interest in his private business. He was comforted that his family approved, and he hoped Iala's parents felt as his did. For now, however, he had to put Iala out of his mind. A warrior who thought of women when he should be concentrating on his mission was courting trouble.

Most of the party slept beside the fire, and the sentries fanned out into the woods. They were awake long before dawn, and they ate the rest of the roasted meat, drank from a nearby stream, and resumed their run. The day passed quietly, and since they were moving through the territory of the Onondaga, there was no need to conceal their presence.

On the second night, the residents of an Onondaga village brought them a hot meal of buffalo stew, making it unnecessary for them to build a fire. Then they came to the land of the Mohawk and spent the third night sleeping in a lodge of their Iroquois brothers.

On the fourth morning of their journey, the atmosphere changed. They were heading almost due north now, penetrating an area used by the Huron as hunting grounds, and soon they would come to the great stream—called the Saint Lawrence River by the pale skins of Quebec.

Leaving only minimal markings on the trail, they lighted no more fires, abstained from hunting, and ate raw fish caught for them by the juniors, augmenting this slender fare with a little dried venison and an occasional handful of parched corn. Each of the three senior warriors now took command of a column of ten men, and there was no conversation at any time, day or night.

Three men stood sentry duty, alert to every sound while the others slept, and the nightly camp was made only in protected places that were more or less impervious to surprise attack. The men spread out at night, too, and each slept with his bow and arrows close at hand.

A morning arrived when Sun-ai-yee passed the word that they were only a single day's march from their destination.

The inside of Renno's mouth felt dry, and he wondered if he would have another encounter with the pale-skinned Huron who called himself Golden Eagle. Perhaps it was just as well if they did not meet. Renno was confident of his abilities in a fight with ordinary Huron, but he felt that he lacked the experience for a confrontation with Golden Eagle. He would be patient, and that day would come.

Following Sun-ai-yee's example, the members of

the party advanced now with great care, their pace a mere crawl as they moved from tree trunk to tree trunk, always remaining in shadows. Such caution was second nature after years of rigorous training.

Before noon, the group halted when they spotted what looked like a long blue ribbon with a silvery sheen, and they knew they had reached the great river and were only a short distance from the Huron town. They drank from a small stream that fed into the river, ate some dried venison and parched corn, and stretched out to rest in the thick undergrowth. Without being told, the men knew that Sun-ai-yee would wait until night to launch his attack.

Renno was one of the sentries assigned to the sector facing the river. His hand on the hilt of his metal knife, he listened for any alien sound as he stared at the water and the banks on either side, closing his eyes occasionally to reduce the strain.

Someone came up beside him, and Renno knew without turning that El-i-chi had joined him.

The younger brother, equally silent and unmoving, needed no instruction.

Renno thought he saw a speck dancing above the surface of the water, swooping high above the tops of the tallest trees, then dipping low again. He lost sight of it, but it kept returning, and he blinked, thinking it would vanish, but it continued to plague him.

He glanced at his brother, a question in his eyes.

El-i-chi scanned the river and the sky above it, then shrugged. Sometimes when one stared too fixedly for a long time, one saw things that did not exist.

Renno touched his brother's arm and pointed.

El-i-chi squinted and stared but saw nothing. He shook his head.

The sky was too bright, Renno thought, wishing that the father-sun would summon some clouds to soften the glare.

All at once something came into his vision and drifted closer, and he felt a sense of wild elation when he realized he was watching a hawk.

The bird came closer, then closer still, flying directly overhead, moving lower in a lazy circle.

El-i-chi saw the hawk, too, and he was awed.

One small feather fluttered to the ground, almost within Renno's reach, and he took a step forward to pick it up. The hawk rose higher, then crossed the river, headed northward, and soon vanished.

There was no doubt in Renno's mind now that he had acquired warrior power. He embedded the feather in his scalp lock, ready to face whatever the future held in store.

When the others awakened, El-i-chi told them in sign language what had happened. Some were inclined to be skeptical, but the new feather in Renno's scalp lock spoke for itself, and thus the appearance of the hawk was accepted as an omen. At the approach of evening, Sun-ai-yee transferred Renno to the first attack group.

At dusk, the Seneca fanned out through the trees, gliding forward soundlessly, and the senior warrior in charge of the first group halted, then pointed.

Four warriors wearing the purple and white paint of the Huron were fishing in the great river; their boat, a craft covered with silver gray birch bark, was pulled up on the shore beside them.

Sun-ai-yee sent two men to determine whether there were any other Huron in the vicinity, and the pair returned with a negative report, so the order was given to proceed. The members of Renno's group took aim and shot, and all four of the Huron dropped almost at the same instant, arrows protruding from their bodies.

The Seneca raced to the riverbank, and Renno used his metal knife to scalp one of the enemy.

Sun-ai-yee ordered the juniors to carry the boat.

They heard voices directly ahead now, and they halted within sight of the town gates. The sun was setting, and the Huron women were returning from the fields. Most were chatting, but several walked apart, as Renno observed, and looked around repeatedly, stone knives in their hands.

It was plain that the Huron were expecting reprisals.

The Seneca preferred not to attack women, as this was a violation of traditional means of warfare, and they did not want to arouse the ire of powerful spirits who might be protecting the Huron community.

So they waited, watching the gates close behind the women.

Renno and the warrior beside him counted three sentries stationed outside the gates, standing silent and unmoving, waiting for some sign that would herald an attack. Other members of the Seneca group counted three more sentries.

The Huron were outnumbered ten to six, a safe margin for the Seneca provided the attack was launched in silence. If the alarm was given, the outcome could be disastrous.

The senior warrior in charge assigned a specific sentry to each of six men, Renno among them. Then all ten members of the advance party flattened themselves on the ground and slithered through the fields of cornstalks and pumpkins. They inched a thumb length at a time, then lay still again before resuming their advance, and now Renno knew the importance of training. He felt no sense of impatience, and his new warrior power filled him with confidence in himself and his mission.

Not until he was little more than an arm's length from his chosen victim did a wave of fear engulf him, drying his mouth. He conquered the sensation, grasped the knife in his belt, and waited, ready to spring.

A cricket—or a remarkably good imitation of one—chirped three times, and the Seneca leaped to their feet, knives in their hands.

Renno plunged his blade deep into the body of the guard, withdrew the knife, and struck again, then yet again. The man died without a sound, and Renno exercised his right and scalped him, adding another trophy to his collection.

His comrades were equally successful, and all six sentries were killed before any could sound an alarm.

As soon as the waiting Sun-ai-yee was assured that the first part of the attack had been successful, he raced forward with the main body of the war party. Several men carried the captured canoe, and they upended it, wedging the prow between two of the palisade logs, then one by one used the boat as a ladder. The rough birch bark gave their moccasins easy purchase, and as they reached the top they dropped inside the wall of the Huron town.

The junior warriors were the last to enter, and their task was to open the gate so the Seneca raiders could make a dash to safety when their work was done.

The others rejoined their assigned groups, with all three units heading separately in the direction of the longhouses.

The town was built on a familiar pattern, and Renno remembered what his parents had said about the similarity of the Huron to the Seneca.

Cooking fires were still burning in the longhouses,

but the intruders had no intention of entering and being trapped inside by vastly superior numbers. The entire operation was so delicate that exquisite timing was needed. Concealing themselves in the shadows, the three Seneca units advanced at a snail's pace, and Renno saw that his group's goal was the community longhouse. A number of Huron men, including several whose paint identified them as senior warriors, had already finished their evening meal and were sitting outside the stuffy building, smoking pipes and chatting before they retired.

The warrior in charge of Renno's group signaled, and the band immediately let a hail of arrows fly at the Huron men. Secrecy was destroyed now. As soon as a number of the Huron died, their comrades realized that the town was being assaulted and without hesitation they ran toward the attackers.

Renno found himself face-to-face with a powerfully built mature senior warrior. Dropping his glowing pipe to the ground, the Huron pulled his knife from his belt.

The young Seneca lunged at him, but the Huron managed to sidestep, trip him, and send him sprawling.

Before Renno realized what was happening, the Huron landed on top of him, flipped him over, and grasping him by the scalp lock, tried to cut his throat.

Only a violent heaving and wrenching saved Renno, but the respite was temporary. He was no physical match for his foe, and the next slash—or the one that followed it—would end his life.

A cold rage filled Renno and exploded within him. His mind still calm, he thought of the warrior power he had been granted; surely that power had not been given to him in vain.

Still struggling, he felt something hot beneath his

hand, and he realized it was the pipe the Huron had dropped.

As the knife started toward his throat again, Renno picked up the pipe and dashed the burning contents into the Huron's eyes.

The man screamed in pain, loosened his hold, and Renno had just enough time to drive his own knife into his foe's chest. He struck repeatedly until he was certain the Huron was dead, then scalped him and jumped to his feet. The entire encounter had lasted only a few moments, and the other Seneca, having created havoc, were beginning to retreat.

Huron warriors were coming out of the longhouses at the far end of the town, and as soon as they organized a cohesive defense it would be a simple matter for them to overcome the small raiding party. Renno took in the situation at a glance and was horrified. The reaction of the Huron was far more rapid than the Seneca had anticipated, and it was not possible to execute a key portion of Sun-ai-yee's plan, which would have insured the safe withdrawal of the invaders.

There seemed little doubt that the Seneca, who appeared to have suffered no casualties, would be able to leave the town safely, but it was equally certain that the Huron would promptly organize a strong pursuit column. Unless the attackers could gain a head start that would then enable them to rely on their renowned speed and endurance, the Huron would track them, ultimately overtake them, and kill every member of the marauding party.

It was essential to carry out Sun-ai-yee's original plan, and Renno, giving no thought to his own safety, turned back. He could hear El-i-chi and several others calling him from the town gates, but it was necessary that he complete the next phase of the mission.

He dashed into the nearest longhouse, where excited women and small children were milling around in confusion by the light of a cooking fire. Hurdling over a little girl of no more than two or three summers, and taking care not to injure her, he dashed toward the fire.

A Huron woman slashed at him with a knife and missed him by no more than the length of his little finger, and a number of the other women drew knives, forming a solid phalanx with the intent to advance on the intruder.

Renno snatched a pot of stew that was simmering at one side of the fire and hurled the contents in the direction of the women, momentarily scattering them. Then he picked up a brightly burning piece of wood, and racing back toward the entrance, he paused long enough to thrust the lighted end of the brand into the rush matting that covered the ground. The matting caught fire almost immediately, and the flames were spreading rapidly as Renno moved out into the open again.

Still carrying the torch, he sprinted toward the gate where the senior warrior who commanded his unit and two other men were covering his retreat. They sent arrow after arrow into the ranks of the Huron, who were already massing for a counterattack.

At that moment the log walls of the longhouse began to burn, the women and children leaving hastily by way of the window openings, punching through the skins that covered the apertures.

Realizing that the entire town could be consumed by flames unless they moved swiftly, most of the Huron warriors abandoned their pursuit of the invaders.

Renno reached the gates and, with the others still protecting him, managed to set fire to the palisade itself.

Sun-ai-yee and the rest of the party had already gained the sanctuary of the forest and were waiting there for their comrades. Renno was the last to join the group, and Sun-ai-yee cast him a fleeting smile, his reward for a task well done.

Without an instant's delay, the Seneca started off toward the southwest, moving considerably faster than their customary trot. They ran for hours, never pausing, never varying their blistering pace. The senior warrior at the rear of the line halted from time to time and pressed his ear to the ground to determine whether the Huron were following. Then he sprinted forward to rejoin his comrades, who knew that, because he gave them no warning, they still had nothing specific to fear.

Not until dawn did Sun-ai-yee call a brief halt, giving his men just enough time to drink from the cold waters of a rushing stream before the march was resumed at the normal Seneca trot.

Confident that they had gained a lead on possible pursuers, the invaders breathed more easily. If their renowned stamina did not desert them, there were no warriors on earth who could catch them now.

For two more days and nights they jogged ceaselessly, the training they had received since early boyhood enabling them to accomplish a seeming miracle that the men of no other nation could match. Only when Sun-ai-yee gave them the signal did they drink from rivers and brooks, and at no time did any member of the party lag behind. Even El-i-chi and the other two juniors, although still in their mid-teens, managed to maintain the grueling pace, and at last the returning warriors reached the land of the Seneca, where sentries stationed in the outer reaches greeted them and drums passed the word that vengeance had been obtained and that the party had suffered no casualties.

The warriors could have halted, gone hunting, and feasted in celebration of their victory while their brothers who had remained at home took up the burden of protecting the area from Huron reprisals. But the pride of fighting men made it necessary for the returning heroes to permit no slackening of their pace. They continued to trot toward their town, each member of the group reveling in his display of endurance.

Certainly there was little danger now. The autumn season was advanced, and with leaves falling from the trees in ever-increasing numbers, the cover provided by the wilderness soon would be vastly diminished. Furthermore, a new Huron strike would be a signal for the beginning of a full-scale war with the entire Iroquois League, and it was unlikely that the Huron and their allies were ready for such a confrontation.

Raids had been exchanged; the Seneca had inflicted greater damage than they had received. The tribe's honor was preserved, and it was unlikely that any hostilities would disturb the peace of the wilderness before spring.

Renno had been concentrating on his running ever since leaving the town of the Huron, but now, secure within the borders of his own people, he could relax.

He had good reason to be satisfied with his accomplishments, for he had fought with distinction in his first military campaign. No one else in the party had taken more than the two scalps he had added to those already in his belt, and had there been time in the heat of battle, he could have acquired still more.

Sun-ai-yee would be certain to report to the Great Sachem and his fellow war chiefs that Renno's prompt and courageous action in starting the fires at the end of the skirmish had saved the lives of the entire band. Not that the young warrior would be given any special award, but his superiors would know that he had displayed valor in combat and that he had shown foresight. In the future he would be given greater responsibilities. It was not unknown for a man to be made a senior warrior while in his twenties, and that became his goal.

The entire population of the town was gathered for the war party's return, and people poured into the open, leaving a lane through which the returning heroes trotted. Men and women smiled and laughed, and small boys darted in and out of the column.

Renno saw his mother and aunt and grinned broadly at them, although it would not have been seemly for him to wave to them until the entire party greeted the Great Sachem.

Next Renno spotted Ba-lin-ta, who was jumping up and down in excitement. It would be difficult to explain to his little sister that there had been no opportunity for him to bring her a trophy.

There was one face he sought as he scanned the crowd, but he did not see Iala anywhere. There had to be some reasonable explanation for her absence, and he was not overly concerned.

The returning warriors came to a halt before Ghonka, his war chiefs, and the medicine men who were gathered outside the community longhouse. There, in an interminable speech, Sun-ai-yee, who was not even breathing hard, delivered a detailed report, recounting everything of significance that had happened on the journey. Renno saw his father's eyes glow with pleasure when his own exploits were described.

When the welcoming ceremonies came to an end, the returning warriors clasped one another by the forearms, renewing their pledges of brotherhood, and then dispersed.

The tired sons of Ghonka and Ena were treated to a feast, and both ate heartily.

"You are truly my sons," was Ghonka's only comment, but he could have offered no greater compliment.

During a brief lull in the meal, Renno finally asked, "What has happened to Iala? I didn't see her at the community longhouse."

Ena and Sah-nee-wa exchanged swift glances, but neither spoke.

Ghonka cleared his throat. "Her father and mother," he said, "have sent her to visit her cousins of the Oneida. She will stay with them for several moons."

It would have been inappropriate to question him further, but Renno was deeply troubled. The looks his mother and aunt had exchanged, combined with his father's carefully measured words, told him that something untoward was happening. His joy faded, and he felt a hard knot of dread.

Chapter VII

The Reverend Obadiah Jenkins sat on an upended barrel that had been converted to a chair, sipped tea from a chipped earthenware mug, and tried to hide his feeling of uneasiness. He had changed into his black clerical clothes after his day's work in the fields, a thing he didn't ordinarily do, but he never regarded a visit to Ida Alwin's house as an ordinary call on parishioners.

Deborah Alwin was directly responsible for his discomfort. The truth of the matter was, at seventeen, she had become a breathtakingly beautiful girl, a rare flower who, he felt, would be wasting her substance if she spent the rest of her life on the frontier. Her beauty, charm, and sound good sense would be certain to win her a secure place in Boston, or even in far-off London, and only in England would she actually find a husband worthy of her attributes.

The problem was that Obadiah didn't want other men paying court to Deborah. Only recently had it dawned on him that he had fallen in love with her, and he was still going to great pains to conceal his feelings from her and the sharp-eyed Aunt Ida.

An impoverished frontier clergyman whose parishioners paid him in the form of eggs, sacks of potatoes, and smoked hams was in no position to support a wife. Particularly one who deserved far more comfort and luxury than life on the edge of the North American wilderness had to offer.

For the present, Obadiah knew he had no local competition. Young Abe Thomas was sweet on Deborah, as he had been for several years. He was a sturdy yeoman, honest but unimaginative, and it was impossible to imagine Deborah consenting to marry someone as plodding as he.

Jeffrey Wilson was more her sort, provided he mended his ways and settled down, but so far he was taking none of the opportunities offered him as the only son of the most prosperous landowner in the area, and Deborah made it plain by her attitude that she despised him.

She stood over Obadiah now, offering him a plate of oatmeal cookies, the golden halo of her hair framing her face; and his thoughts were not those of a clergyman.

"These are fresh out of the oven," she said. "I baked them when I knew you were calling on us this evening."

He had no particular liking for cookies, but because she had baked them he took one and to his surprise found it delicious.

"Has there been any word on the activities of the French?" said Aunt Ida. "I see where Colonel Wilson is still keeping a double sentry formation at the fort."

"He's only taking precautions," said Obadiah.

157

"We've confirmed that Alain de Gramont definitely went off with the Huron, but—so far, at least—they haven't molested any of our settlements, either here or in the Maine District or in New York. We assume Colonel de Gramont and his savages may be making war against some of their Indian enemies. Several of the Algonquian subtribes who are beginning to be inclined in our favor hold to the same theory, but no one can be certain."

"Just so they leave us in peace, the barbarians can kill each other all they please. That's the way I feel," Aunt Ida said. "And if I'm guilty of not thinking Christian thoughts, it can't be helped. Life here is hard enough without being threatened by savages."

Obadiah knew better than to argue with her.

Her son, Walter, now badly overweight, took a handful of cookies and began to cram them into his mouth. Deborah looked at her cousin in dismay, embarrassed, but she didn't want to create an issue in the presence of the minister. She couldn't help feeling sorry for Walter. The boy was capable of doing farm chores because he could be shown by example, and he performed his duties ably. All the same, he was cut off from other people in everything but the basics of living, and a future as drab as his present existence loomed ahead for him.

The girl's darting glance at her cousin made Obadiah more conscious of Walter's presence, and he took the unnecessary but natural precaution of lowering his voice as he said to Aunt Ida, "I've come here for a specific purpose this evening."

The woman merely inclined her head.

"I wonder if it might be indiscreet to talk about Walter when he's right here in the room with us."

Aunt Ida sighed. "Not at all, just so we don't

look at him much, which would make him know we're discussing him. The poor lad can't hear a blessed word we're saying."

"Colonel Wilson and I had a long talk about him the other day," Obadiah said. "He'll soon be of an age when he might learn a useful trade that would help him in later life, and we wondered if you'd be interested in sending him to Boston, where he could be apprenticed. To a baker, perhaps, or a carpenter or a mason. He seems to have a bright enough mind, and we know of no reason why he couldn't learn some occupation in spite of his handicaps."

Deborah replied before her aunt could speak. "I'm afraid it just wouldn't do," she said. "We know Walter well enough to anticipate many of his needs and to interpret others, but he'd be lost with strangers."

"He couldn't survive." Aunt Ida spoke harshly. "And seeing how long it's taking him to learn to read and write, he'd be convinced Debbie and I were deserting him if we sent him away."

The minister was distresssed, but a sense of obligation forced him to continue. "May I ask what you have in mind for him?"

"I have nothing in mind," Aunt Ida replied flatly. "I pray for a miracle that will give him ears and a voice, but the Almighty hasn't seen fit to listen to me. So Debbie and I must do the best we're able. All I can do is hope that—when I'm no longer here and Debbie goes off on her own after she marries—Walter will be able to keep body and soul together by farming this property. The way I see it, he has no real alternative."

"Well," Obadiah said carefully, "you might keep the thought of an apprenticeship in mind during the next year or two. The boy is still young, so there's no need to make any final decision now."

Aunt Ida nodded in seeming agreement, but Deborah knew that her mind was closed.

The conversation was interrupted by a tap at the door. No one in the room had heard the sounds of an approaching horse or cart, but Deborah felt no trepidation as she went to the door. When she opened it, she had to suppress the scream of pure terror that rose up within her.

Standing there were two tall husky Indian braves dressed only in loincloths, overkilts, and leather shirts. Green and yellow paint was smeared on their faces and could be seen beneath their open shirts. Both carried bows, quivers of arrows, and stone knives, but neither made any threatening gesture.

"They're Huron who have come to kill us!" the girl gasped.

Aunt Ida rose, intending to take her musket from its place over the mantel, and Walter reached for the skillet on a wall peg behind him.

But Obadiah Jenkins noted that the braves were making no hostile move, and he intervened. "Allow me to talk to them and find out what they want," he said. "I don't know their tribe, but their paint tells me they aren't Huron."

"Can you speak with them?" Deborah asked in surprise as she made a continuing effort to control her fear.

"I can try," the clergyman replied. "Colonel Wilson has been teaching me the tongue of the Algonquian, which he tells me is the root language of all tribes within many hundreds of miles of us." Taking the precaution of loosening the pistol he carried in his belt, he motioned the immobile pair into the room.

Folding their arms across their chests, the two warriors stepped in, and because it would have been improper to stare, neither as much as glanced at the belongings of these pale skins.

"What do you do here?" Obadiah asked.

The braves smiled in relief at the sound of words they understood.

"We are the messengers of the Seneca, the mightiest nation of the great Iroquois League," the elder said. "We come in peace."

"Then you are welcomed in peace," Obadiah replied as fast as he could put the sentence together.

Deborah and Aunt Ida knew from his expression that although he was wary, he was less apprehensive.

"We bring a message to the sachem of your people," the brave said.

"I will take you to his house," the clergyman said, then turned to the women to explain.

"Don't go off with them alone," Aunt Ida warned. "They're like to cut your throat when they get you on the dark river road."

"I think not, but I'll have to take that risk," said Obadiah. "This is the first time we've had any contact with the Iroquois, who live close to Fort Albany, and it may be important to our future safety to find out why they've come all this way to see us."

"Well," the woman said, "I'd keep my pistol handy if I was you, and I sure wouldn't turn my back to them."

The younger of the braves took note of Deborah and couldn't resist staring at the lovely girl. In the land of the Seneca, a man was permitted to look openly at a woman he fancied even though it would have been rude for him to address her before she gave him some sign of her willingness to receive his advances.

Deborah saw the expression of candid admiration

161

in the Indian's eyes, and although she liked to think of herself as being reasonably courageous, her insides knotted. This savage was making it plain that he wanted her, and it didn't cross her mind that he had never seen a woman with light hair. And eyes that reminded him of Renno.

Obadiah donned his short pea coat and took his stocking cap from the pocket.

"Be careful," Deborah said.

Her concern touched him. "Never fear. I can take care of myself," he told her gratefully.

Oddly, she wasn't too worried about him. He had the physical strength of a farmer and a mind that was more than a match for the cunning of savages. It occurred to the girl for the first time that she respected Obadiah Jenkins as a person rather than merely as a representative of his profession.

The clergyman bowed to the ladies, patted Walter on the shoulder, and led the Indians out into the yard where his horse was tethered. First making as certain as he could that no other savages were lurking in the vicinity, he mounted his gelding and set off at a fast walk.

The Seneca jogged beside him, keeping up the pace with no apparent effort. Both looked with interest at the fort, which was visible by moonlight in the distance.

But Obadiah had no intention of taking them anywhere near the area's principal defense bastion, and instead he conducted them by way of several detours to the extensive Wilson property.

Tom Hibbard was walking toward the main house when the trio arrived, and taking one startled look at the Indians, he began to lift his rifle to his shoulder.

"They're peaceful, Tom," Obadiah called. "I've brought them to see the colonel."

"Who the devil are they?" Hibbard studied the green and yellow war paint.

"Seneca."

Tom whistled under his breath and for the sake of security joined the group.

The two messengers remained tranquil until they entered the large longhouse of the pale-skinned sachem.

Jeffrey Wilson, coming down the broad, curving staircase, took one look at the Indians and bristled defensively.

There was such malice in his eyes that the warriors reacted in kind, returning the young man's insolent glare. There was no need for words. He had challenged them, and they accepted. Sooner or later they would meet him, separately or together, in combat.

Andrew Wilson received the visitors in his study, and after hearing Obadiah's brief explanation, he gave the pair ample time to become accustomed to their surroundings.

The warriors were astonished to find that so many rooms in this extensive longhouse were unoccupied. The walls of books in the study meant nothing to them, but the polished table that dominated the room was apparently used for the purpose of making marks on what appeared to be birch bark. They were fascinated by the hearth, hoping there would be an opportunity to study the smoke hole used by the pale skins.

"We come in peace," the elder of the senior warriors said, and he handed the colonel a small strip of wampum, to which snail shells had been sewn with rawhide thongs.

Andrew Wilson replied, "I greet you in peace,"

and promptly handed them a hand-tooled leather bookmark in return.

They examined it with pleasure, and then the elder said, "I bring greetings to the sachem of the pale skins from Ghonka, Great Sachem of the Seneca, and from the sachems of all the other nations of the mighty Iroquois League."

Speaking the language of the Algonquian fluently, the colonel said, "My longhouse is your home."

The amenities having been observed, everyone sat down, the warriors declining the use of chairs and lowering themselves into cross-legged positions on the floor.

Andrew Wilson, his hair now prematurely white, took the precaution of lighting one of his pipes, and it was passed from hand to hand.

"The Huron, the enemies of the Seneca," declared the Indian spokesman, "have been given many firesticks by the pale skins who live in the town called Quebec."

Listening carefully, the colonel nodded. This was a confirmation of the ugly rumor that the French in Canada were supplying arms to the tribes who were friendly to them.

"Now," said the senior warrior, "the Seneca have a need for firesticks of their own and wish to be taught how to use them. In return they will give to the pale skins many furs of the beaver, otter, buffalo, fox, and wolf."

The colonel exchanged glances with Obadiah and Tom. The English colonies lagged far behind the French in establishing working relations with the various Indian tribes. Every white man knew that the New Yorkers at Fort Albany had failed miserably in their efforts to become friendly with the nations of the powerful Iroquois League.

Now the Seneca, the key tribe of the Iroquois,

were making the first move. The situation was almost too good to be true.

There were obstacles, to be sure. It was Crown policy, established by no less an authority than the King's cousin, Prince Rupert, who was the commander of the Royal Army and Navy, to allow no firearms to fall into the hands of Indians.

To abide by that ruling now, however, would be forcing the Iroquois nations to deal with the French, at the same time causing the English colonies to be hemmed in on the west and south as well as the north, with their backs to the Atlantic Ocean, their only supply and escape route.

This was a question that could only be settled by Governor Shirley after consultation with Brigadier Pepperrell; and Colonel Wilson made a rapid decision. "I will go with you to the town of our Great Sachem," he said, "and I will ask him to listen with favor to the offer you bring to us."

Over the violent objections of Jeffrey, who succeeded in making something of a spectacle of himself, Mildred Wilson gave the visitors a guest bedchamber. She thought it only natural that they should ignore the feather bed and sleep instead on the floor, wrapped in their buffalo robes.

At dawn, Mildred Wilson served them a hearty breakfast, and soon after, the colonel and Tom Hibbard were on the road with the visitors, heading for Boston. The two colonials rode horses, but the Seneca refused the use of mounts, and without tiring trotted eastward toward the capital of Massachusetts Bay. Rather than subject the Indians to inns and taverns and the possible protests of their proprietors, the colonel and his indentured man slept in the open, and all four prepared their meals on campfires. The Seneca, eating roast beef for the first time, were delighted with its taste. Obviously the Seneca had a great deal to learn from their new neighbors.

After several days, the group arrived in Boston and went straight to the mansion of the royal viceroy. Governor Shirley elected to sit on the floor beneath the portrait of Charles II, and Brigadier Pepperrell followed his example, as did Colonel Wilson.

Long complimentary speeches were exchanged, and then the Seneca made their offer.

In a tone he hoped the Indians would regard as casual, Andrew Wilson said, "They're bringing us the opportunity of a lifetime, our first real chance to counter the influence of the French in the New World."

"Do you suppose they'll agree to make a full-scale military alliance with us?" said Brigadier Pepperrell. Long accustomed to contact with the Algonquian, he had no difficulty in hiding his own pleasure.

"They haven't mentioned any such alliance to me yet, Will," Wilson replied, "and I think it may be premature—if not dangerous—to push too far and too fast."

"We'll move one step at a time," said the governor. As always, William Shirley was decisive. "I'll take full responsibility for changing Crown policy, and I'll send Prince Rupert an immediate and complete explanation. I can't imagine the King or the Privy Council objecting to a deal with the largest and most powerful group of Naturals in all North America."

"The Great Sachem of Massachusetts Bay," Andrew Wilson told the Seneca, "accepts the offer of your Great Sachem. We will bargain with him."

The senior warriors nodded gravely, also concealing their elation.

166

"I won't let any Indians get hold of our new long rifles," Pepperrell said, "but we'll take two hundred of the older muskets from our arsenals, along with lead, bullet molds, and powder, and we can throw in some pistols for good measure. It's going to leave us short-handed for arms until we can order replacements from England, but this will be a shortage in the best of all possible causes."

The governor appointed Colonel Wilson as his representative in the bargaining and told him, "Make sure you take several of your young militiamen—preferably sharpshooters—along with you to act as instructors."

"I will, Your Excellency," said Wilson, "and thanks for your confidence. You know I'll make the best bargain I can manage."

"While opening the door to a full-scale alliance," suggested Pepperrell.

"That, too, if I can," Andrew said. "But from what I know of Indians, I'll try to make it appear that the idea originated with them."

"The fewer spokesmen we have for our side, the more the chances of confusion and error will be reduced," Governor Shirley said crisply. "Travel westward by way of Fort Albany, Andy. I'll give you a letter to the New York authorities urging that you act as their spokesman as well and suggesting as diplomatically as I can that they confine themselves to sending a few instructors with your party."

"While you're about it," Pepperrell added, "don't let the New Yorkers cheat you. Their arms depot is the largest in the colonies, and they can match everything we'll be sending."

"Oh, I'll see to it that I bring all the arms—theirs and ours—with me," the colonel replied. "Indians are literal-minded people, and they'd suspect us of trickery if I promised them a later delivery. They're as anxious for firearms to use against their enemies as we are eager to have their help against the French. I've had several days to think of little else, and I'm optimistic that we can work out a contract to satisfy everybody. Except the French. They've been playing at war with us for more than twenty years, never suffering real retaliation, and now we're going to finish what they've started. This is the first move in a fight that will drive either the French or the English from the continent, and speaking for our side, we don't intend to be budged."

After considering the matter, Andrew Wilson decided to take only a small group with him to the land of the Seneca. Obadiah Jenkins was included as a matter of principle, and two younger men were added: Abe Thomas and Jeffrey Wilson. As well as being dependable, Abe Thomas was an expert marksman with both musket and pistol, and even though he was needed at home to work on his parents' farm, he agreed to remain with the Seneca for several months to instruct the Indians in the use of firearms.

"I'm hoping the exposure to a primitive civilization will open Jeffrey's eyes to the benefits he enjoys here," said Andrew Wilson to his wife. "Maybe it will help him settle down."

Mildred was hesitant. "He keeps thinking of the pleasures he enjoyed while he was at school in England," she replied. "What worries me is that he may get into trouble. He's so impulsive."

"He'll be going as a sergeant in the militia, so he won't be along simply as my son. I'm his commanding officer, and I believe I can control him."

Arrangements were made for a delegation of three New Yorkers to meet the men from Massachusetts Bay. The governor of New York and the New York Assembly were enthusiastic over the opportunity to open the closed door that had made it virtually impossible for them to deal with the Iroquois.

Each group was supplying two hundred muskets as well as a number of small arms and quantities of lead and gunpowder. "The Indians will be even more amenable when they actually see the weapons," Andrew Wilson told the New Yorkers. "We'll have a natural advantage in our dealings with them."

The immediate problem was to determine how the weapons would be transported. The most obvious method, carrying the guns in carts, had to be discarded because there were no roads suitable for vehicles with wheels.

Obadiah Jenkins suggested that packhorses be used, and the two Seneca warriors agreed that it might be possible to lead a string of horses through the wilderness, although they emphasized that in many places it might be necessary to cut down trees, remove dead logs, and clear underbrush to provide an adequate trail.

The mission left Fort Springfield on a cold morning when the sky was leaden and a raw wind blew steadily from the west. The men and the heavily laden horses crossed the Connecticut River by ferry, then began their march, and by afternoon they had left the last road behind them and were headed into the forest.

One of the Seneca acted as guide and vanguard, with Colonel Wilson directly behind him, and the other warrior brought up the rear. It was the duty of Obadiah, Abe, and Jeffrey to keep the six horses in line. The trails were still fairly well marked, and the party, eating

and sleeping in the open, encountered no serious diffi-
culties. The Indians went hunting when the first day's
march was completed and brought down a buck, which
would provide meat for days to come.

The New Yorkers were waiting at a rendezvous
near the headwaters of Hudson's River, and the united
groups resumed the long trek westward. In spite of the
advanced season, which produced piles of dead leaves
as a carpet, the evergreens were still thick, the bushes
were tangled masses, and it was necessary to hack a path
through the wilderness for the horses. Thus, a journey
that could have been accomplished within days on foot
lasted for more than two weeks, and only the warriors
showed no signs of weariness.

"I prefer them as friends and dread to imagine
them as enemies," Andrew Wilson remarked to Obadiah Jenkins one night, "and I'm beginning to believe
we're wrong to call them savages. It's astonishing how
well they've mastered this wilderness."

In the late afternoon of the fifteenth day, the party
reached the main Seneca town. Men and women of
the town filled the open areas between the longhouses to
see the new arrivals, and the silence was almost eerie.
These were the first white visitors they had ever encountered, and the Seneca studied them with intense
curiosity. No one spoke, no one smiled, and even the
children watched quietly.

The men from Massachusetts Bay and New York
tethered their horses and were conducted to a small
longhouse used for guests where they unpacked their
personal belongings and stacked the muskets against
one wall and covered them with canvas. The lead bars
for making ammunition were piled nearby, and the
bags of gunpowder were kept far away from the fire.

The colonial emissaries were conducted to the community longhouse, which was so crowded that they had to thread their way through the throng, taking care not to jostle or otherwise antagonize the natives who continued to gape at them.

For the solemn occasion, the Great Sachem was wearing his feathered headdress and his intricately worked buffalo cape. Behind him on the platform were his medicine men and war chiefs, along with representatives of the other Iroquois nations, but it was obvious that Ghonka was the leader above all others.

The newcomers halted in front of the platform, and Colonel Wilson made a speech. Greeting the Seneca on behalf of his own Great Sachem King Charles II, and the King's viceroys—the governors of Massachusetts Bay and New York—he offered friendship to all the people of the Iroquois. He intended to negotiate with them in amity, promising he would neither cheat nor lie. He had brought with him the firesticks that he hoped to offer in trade.

As a grand gesture, he presented to the Great Sachem a sword with a jeweled hilt and a pistol, its handle inlaid with mother-of-pearl.

Watching from the ranks of the full warriors, Renno instantly recognized the tubular weapon as similar to the one the Huron warrior had used to try to kill him.

The Great Sachem admired the sword, removing it from its sheath and testing its sharp edge. He had no need to examine the pistol, whose use he would soon understand.

His own address was relatively brief. The visitors were guests and consequently would be safe in the land of his people. He would deal with them on behalf of all of the nations of the Iroquois League, and he, too, hoped that a bargain satisfactory to both sides could be struck.

The colonel, listening carefully, heard no mention of friendship, much less the possibility that the Iroquois might be receptive to an alliance.

In spite of their caution, the Seneca were lavish in their hospitality. After the brief ceremonies were concluded, the residents of the town, the other Iroquois, and the colonists adjourned to the open fields beyond the palisades where quarters of buffalo meat and venison were roasting over a fire.

The following morning, the colonists amused the Indians by heating pots of water for bathing. Then everyone, including the women and children of the town, went back to the fields, and the visitors were invited to demonstrate their firesticks. It was obvious that the Seneca wanted amenities to be observed and were in no hurry to conduct negotiations.

As a preliminary, the colonel amused his hosts by sticking three Indian spears into the ground, then lopping off their tops with three strokes of his sword. The Great Sachem repeated the experiment with his own new sword, delighted to find it equally sharp.

Obadiah Jenkins initiated the firearms demonstration. Picking up a dried, stunted ear of corn, he balanced it on a branch that he drove into the ground; then he marched fifty paces, halted, and slowly loaded a pistol. No one in Fort Springfield was a better shot with small arms, and members of the militia were sorry that his profession made it impossible for him to become an active member of their regiment.

Aware that hundreds of Seneca were watching him and that he would look foolish if he missed, he waited until he overcame his nervousness. Then he raised the pistol, took aim, and fired.

The discharge echoed across the fields and seemed to bounce off the trees of the nearby forest.

The warriors were wide-eyed, although their expressions were unchanged. Some of the women clapped their hands to their ears, and several small children disgraced their parents by weeping and had to be removed from the scene.

The dried ear of corn had disintegrated.

Now it was Abe Thomas's turn, and he used one of the muskets being offered in the negotiations rather than the long rifle he preferred. He set up two targets as far from the firing area as he could, then returned to the firing line and promptly destroyed both targets.

To convince his hosts that no magic had been employed, Abe gave the musket to the Indians to examine, and the warriors passed it from hand to hand, each peering at the weapon.

There was a mischievous light in the Great Sachem's eyes as he challenged the colonists to a contest.

Colonel Wilson immediately accepted.

Three ears of shriveled corn were impaled on stakes. Then three Seneca warriors came forward, armed with stone hatchets. At a signal from Ghonka, the warriors threw their hatchets in turn, and each struck his target.

The colonists hoped they could match the feat. Obadiah, Abe Thomas, and one of the New Yorkers tried their luck with pistols and managed to hit two of the three targets. The Seneca were winning, even though no one present doubted the superiority of the white men's weapons.

Six more distant targets were arranged, and the

colonists were invited to shoot first. The colonel selected Abe, another of the New Yorkers, and after a moment's hesitation, his own son.

The New Yorker shot first and broke an ear of corn in half.

Abe was next, and his marksmanship still superb, he sent his ear of corn flying in all directions.

The Seneca, always ready to recognize skill, cheered the young militiaman.

Now it was Jeffrey's turn. Conscious of his audience, he moistened his lips and struck an arrogant pose before he raised his musket. His shot sounded, but the ear of corn still stood.

"You pulled the trigger instead of squeezing it," his father said reprovingly.

Now it was the turn of the Seneca. A senior warrior moved out of the ranks when Ghonka called his name, and taking an arrow from his quiver and fitting it into his bow, the brave let fly. The ear of corn fell apart.

A second senior warrior was summoned and repeated the feat.

Then a younger warrior was called into the open.

"My God!" Colonel Wilson muttered to Obadiah, who stood beside him. "He's one of us! He's white!"

The clergyman stared in disbelief. Although he was smeared with war paint and wore feathers in his scalp lock, the young man who had five scalps dangling from his belt was clearly not of Indian stock. He was heavily tanned, but the hair of his scalp lock was fair, his eyes were blue, and his clean-cut features were those of his English ancestors.

The younger colonists were gaping, too.

"I've heard of frontier children being abducted by

Naturals," Obadiah murmured, "but this is the first proof I've seen."

Renno was unaware of the stir he had created. On countless occasions he had practiced the feat he was about to perform, so he shut the audience out of his mind, concentrated on his target, and again the Seneca won.

Under the rules of Iroquois hospitality, it was wrong to allow guests to disgrace themselves, so Renno turned to Jeffrey Wilson, raised a hand palm outward in personal greeting, and speaking the only language he knew, said, "I invite you to face me in a trial of strength."

A sea of nodding heads indicated that the Seneca heartily approved.

Andrew Wilson translated the challenge, then said to his son, "You'll be wise to accept, so we don't lose face."

Jeffrey, already chagrined and angry because his rifle shot had missed, replied loudly, "I accept!"

The colonel again acted as interpreter.

Renno grinned amiably and, stripping off his shirt and kilt, slipped out of his moccasins. With a great show of ceremony, he handed his metal knife to a fellow warrior to demonstrate that he was unarmed.

Jeffrey removed his own shirt, but he decided that his boots gave him an advantage, so he kept them on.

Ghonka explained the simple rules, and the colonel translated. "The first to pin the other's shoulders to the ground is the winner. No contestant is allowed to gouge out the eyes of his opponent or otherwise disfigure him. And just keep in mind, Jeff, we're trying to win the good will of these people."

Ignoring his father's words, Jeffrey saw this white Indian as a symbol of all that he loathed in America.

The Seneca formed a hollow triangle some twenty-five feet long and twenty feet wide around the contestants.

Ghonka invited the colonists to join him, so their view would be unimpaired. He was proud of Renno, but he would wait until victory was achieved before revealing that the winner was his son.

Renno looked at the Great Sachem, waiting for him to raise his hand in the signal to start the match, but Jeffrey neither knew nor cared about signals. All he knew was that his opponent's attention was diverted, so he jabbed Renno in the face with a fist.

Renno was unfamiliar with fistfighting and he took a step backward.

The colonel realized that his son had committed a foul blow, and Ghonka instantly raised a hand.

But before Renno had a chance to respond, his opponent lashed at him again, landing a hard blow to the stomach that doubled him, then sending a smash to his cheekbone that straightened him again.

Groggy and bewildered by the strange tactics, Renno lost his balance and fell to one knee.

His supporters, annoyed by the young colonist's unfair method of fighting, maintained an icy silence.

"The young fool will spoil everything," Andrew Wilson murmured to Obadiah. Then he raised his voice. "Don't use your fists, Jeff! You're supposed to be wrestling him."

Jeffrey did not deign to listen. Instead, he saw an opportunity to end the combat quickly and aimed a vicious kick at his opponent's head.

Renno caught a glimpse of Jeffrey's heavy boot just in time to duck to one side, knowing that if the blow had landed he could have been severely hurt. Outraged by now, Renno slowly got to his feet and backed 'away to give his head time to clear. Never had he known anyone to cheat in friendly combat.

Another shock awaited him. When his eyes met those of his opponent, he found the young colonist looking at him with sheer hatred.

So be it. This was no longer a friendly trial of strength. Renno's personal pride and that of his nation had been assaulted, and he raised his voice in a full-throated war cry.

Every Seneca present not only understood that cry but approved of it. Even Ghonka smiled grimly, hoping his son would teach this brash stranger a lesson.

Colonel Wilson couldn't help sympathizing with the white Indian even though he feared for his own son. Jeffrey had gone too far, and he would have to pay for his transgression. There was no way to halt the fight.

Renno began to inch forward, keeping out of range of the other's fists and boots.

Jeffrey held his ground, looking for an opening.

Suddenly Renno lunged, crashed into his foe, and hurled him to the ground, landing on top of him.

Again Jeffrey used his fists and feet, but Renno ignored the blows. In deadly earnest now, he straddled his foe, caught hold of his hair, and repeatedly struck his head against the ground. Such actions were questionable in a trial of strength, but this fight had become a great deal more.

Jeffrey's punches became frenzied and gradually lost power as Renno continued to pound his head against the hard earth until he appeared to be on the verge of losing consciousness. Then, his moves deliberate, the young warrior pinned the other's shoulders to the ground.

The Indians roared their approval.

Obadiah and one of the New Yorkers had to help Jeffrey to his feet and lead him away.

Abe Thomas was suffused with shame. Jeff Wilson had stained the honor of the English colonies, and that honor had to be restored. Not pausing to weigh the consequences of what he was doing, Abe shouted, "I challenge the warrior to a fair trial of strength in his own style of fighting!"

With great reluctance, Andrew Wilson offered a translation, aware that matters might be slipping out of control.

Renno folded his arms across his chest and nodded acceptance.

Abe stripped to his breeches, taking care to remove his boots, and he gave Obadiah his pistol and knife. Then he moved into the open area and deliberately extended his hand.

The gesture was new to Renno, but he knew what the other meant, and he caught hold of Abe's forearm. For a moment they grinned at each other, two young men who were both in magnificent physical condition. Renno needed no one to tell him that this opponent did not resemble the other.

They waited for Ghonka's signal, then turned to each other and grappled. Neither they nor the increasingly excited spectators knew who was responsible when they sank to the ground and began to wrestle.

Abe had the greater brute strength, but Renno was more agile; the white Indian had a quicker mind and was more cunning, but Abe was stubborn and incapable of admitting defeat. First one gained the advantage and then the other seized it, but neither could pin the other to the ground.

They were so evenly matched that for long periods they seemed almost still as their bodies strained and their muscles rippled. Anyone unacquainted with the rules would have thought the contest dull, but the Seneca, aware of every nuance, watched in breathless fascination, knowing that no warrior in the nation had ever defeated Renno in a trial of strength. The colonists, who had learned of this type of combat years before from local Indians who had since evacuated the district, were equally awed because Abe had no equals anywhere.

Both combatants were drenched in sweat, but both hung on.

Ghonka and Andrew Wilson glanced at each other, and in that moment each knew the mind of the other. These contests were intended for the purpose of establishing a spirit of rapport that would be conducive to success in the pending negotiations. That goal now had been achieved, and the two men knew that it would be best for all concerned if the combat ended in a draw.

"Stop, Renno!" Ghonka called in a low voice that was nevertheless penetrating. "The trial is ended!"

"That's enough, Abe!" the colonel shouted almost at the same instant.

The wrestlers drew apart and staggered to their feet. They looked at each other, laughed, and impulsively embraced, then stood apart as they slowly regained their breath.

After that, the Seneca put on running, spear throwing, and bird shooting exhibitions for their guests, but Renno and Abe Thomas quietly withdrew, their new friendship kindled by mutual respect. The farmer demonstrated how to make bullets and load a gun, and Renno had the honor to be the first Seneca to fire a musket. Then the white Indian responded by showing his new friend how to use a bow and arrow.

That evening, when another feast was held, the pair sat together, each eager to learn the skills of the other's civilization.

Later, when the visitors retired to the guest lodge, a troubled Obadiah Jenkins drew Colonel Wilson aside. "I'm tormented by a dilemma. That young warrior doesn't even seem to realize he's white."

"All I can tell you is that he's recognized as the Great Sachem's son, so we've got to be careful."

"The Lord only knows how he came to be in this remote land, but he's an Indian in everything but his race. My conscience is urging me to reveal the truth to him."

"Far be it from me to argue with the conscience of a clergyman," Andrew Wilson replied dryly. "I just hope it's flexible enough for you to wait until we've made and sealed an agreement with the Seneca!"

The following morning, while Renno and Abe went off together to practice with their new weapons, the other guests went hunting with a party of their hosts. Jeffrey Wilson remained behind, smarting because his father had reprimanded him and because he had lost face in a fight with a savage.

Meanwhile, the Great Sachem and Colonel Wilson withdrew to Ghonka's hut for serious negotiations, and there they remained for most of the day, fencing until they finally reached an agreement. The terms were simple: the Seneca would be given the weapons and in return would pay the colonists two skins for each musket, one skin for the lead and powder necessary for each weapon, and one skin for each pistol.

Abe Thomas would stay in the Seneca town for the winter to teach the warriors how to use and maintain the firesticks.

Neither side would wage open war on the other for a period of at least twelve moons.

For the present, the Iroquois would enter no military alliance with the English colonists. At the same time, Colonel Wilson was assured that it was inconceivable that the Iroquois would go to war on the side of the French, who were allied with the hated Huron and Ottawa.

That night a third feast was held. Abe, who would be lodged in Renno's longhouse, spoke briefly, making it clear that he would not distribute the muskets and pistols until the warriors became familiar with them.

Colonel Wilson, who was translating, added a few words of his own. "Our weapons are very dangerous, and one who does not understand their use can kill by accident."

The next morning, as the visitors packed their belongings and prepared to depart, Obadiah Jenkins took the colonel aside and told him that his conscience could not be silenced any longer.

"I hope you know what you're doing," Andrew said.

"I try to obey the will of the Lord as best I'm able to interpret it. I think it is right for the young man to know his true heritage, and I'll have no inner peace until I've told him." Taking something from his saddlebag and slipping it into his pocket, Obadiah went in search of Renno.

He found the young warrior in the longhouse of the full warriors, enthusiastically cleaning the musket that would become his when he gained greater skill in its use.

"I want to make words with you," Obadiah said in his basic Algonquian.

181

Renno was surprised, but he showed no curiosity, and they walked together in silence to the forest beyond the cornfields.

Obadiah did not call a halt until they came to a small clearing, where the early winter sun was shining. Praying first for divine help, he asked abruptly, "Who are you?"

"I am Renno, a full warrior of the Seneca and a member of the Bear Clan."

"Who are your family?"

"I am the son of Ghonka, the Great Sachem, and of Ena, the medicine woman."

"I have a gift for you." Obadiah reached into his pocket and drew out a rectangle of highly burnished steel, which the colonists used as mirrors when the more expensive glass mirrors were unavailable. "Look well at your face."

Renno took the object, surprised that he could see his reflection in it even more clearly than in the waters of a still pond on a bright day.

"What do you see?" Obadiah knew he had to proceed slowly.

"A picture of my face." Renno grimaced, then laughed as he studied his reflection.

"Look well at yourself, Renno of the Seneca," the clergyman said. "Your hair is the color of my people's hair. Your eyes are the color of my people's eyes. The sun has made your skin dark, but it is really the color of my people's skin."

Renno knew he was not being visited by a spirit. He was wide awake, talking to this pale skin stranger. He was learning a terrible truth, something he had long known and tried to suppress. To face this moment, he needed to call upon all of his courage, all of his inner strength.

He wanted to shrink from the clergyman's revelation, yet the mystery that had troubled him since early boyhood, the mystery that had compelled him to excel in all things and prove himself a true Seneca, was about to be made clear to him.

He remembered the vision with hair the color of corn silk that had come to him in the past, and he asked Obadiah, "Are you a medicine man?"

"In the eyes of my people I am truly a medicine man." Obadiah spoke gently, compassion in his eyes.

Using great willpower, Renno lowered the hand that held the mirror and looked instead at this stranger. What he saw reassured him. This man was no enemy such as Golden Eagle or the young one who tried to fight him unfairly in their trial of strength. This man had kindness and honor in his eyes, and he was not mocking Renno, who felt strangely stripped of his defenses.

"It may be that you belong to the same clan as a spirit who has come to me in the past," said Renno.

"I believe in only one Great Spirit," Obadiah said. "The heavens and the earth are His. He is all-powerful, all-knowing, and all things are possible to Him."

Renno bowed his head. "I will hear your words," he said, bracing himself, even though he already knew what he would be told.

"You are the son of the Seneca," the Reverend Obadiah Jenkins said. "No man will deny it. But your people are my people, Renno, so you are truly the son of my people."

Chapter VIII

For many days after, Renno continued to follow his normal routines; outwardly his life was unchanged. No other warrior could match his growing proficiency in handling a musket, and Abe Thomas also began to instruct him in the use of a pistol.

Secretly seething within himself, offering prayers to the manitous for guidance, and pondering his strange fate, Renno wondered whether he was expert with these extraordinary weapons because he was actually a pale skin. Unable to sleep, lacking appetite even for such delicacies as the roasted liver of an elk, he knew he had to bring his secret into the open, so he went at last to his parents and, behind the closed flap of their hut, repeated what the medicine man of the pale skins had told him. Then he showed them the oblong of polished metal the man had given him, and holding it up to his face, he pointed to his hair and his blue eyes.

Ghonka sat cross-legged in front of the fire, his arms folded across his chest. He was motionless, and his face looked as though it had been carved out of rock.

Ena was the first to react. "The time has come to speak the truth," she said.

Her husband nodded almost imperceptibly and fixed a steady gaze on his son. "Renno is the son of Ghonka and Ena," he said, "but it was not always so. In the beginning, Renno did not come into the world from the body of Ena. He came from the land of the pale skins." Speaking slowly and distinctly, with great dignity, he revealed the details of the raid in which he had spared the life of the infant who had looked at him without fear; he concluded by saying that the baby had taken into himself, at that very moment, the spirit of the child he and Ena had lost.

With great effort, Renno remained impassive, too. "I am the son of Ghonka, the Great Sachem, and of Ena, the medicine woman," he replied. "The Seneca are my people, and for all of my days I belong to the Clan of the Bear. If I did not know this myself, Jagonh, the bear who is my brother, confirmed it when I was still a boy."

Ena wanted to hug him, but she restrained herself.

"But now," he continued, "my heart is sick within me. My place is not like that of any other Seneca warrior."

"If it is different," Ghonka told him, "it is because the mother-earth and the father-sun have special plans for you."

This revelation was so similar to a feeling Renno had long harbored that he was not surprised. But now he became even more confused. Knowing it would be unseemly to ask too many questions, he waited for his father to continue.

"The ways of our fathers and of their fathers before them are changing," the Great Sachem said, "and in the years that lie ahead there will be many more changes. The pale skins came to our land in ships with wings of white cloth that cause them to fly like birds. They have come in large numbers, so many that there are more of them than the pebbles that fill the shores of the great lake. And still they come, more with each moon."

Renno knew he spoke the truth. The towns of the pale skins were growing rapidly, and their farms were penetrating deeper into the hunting grounds of the tribes that lived to the east of the Iroquois.

"The firesticks of the pale skins are strong weapons," Ghonka went on. "They make it easier to kill animals for food and to kill the enemies who would take the lives of our people. That is why I have made the bargain that gives us many firesticks. Soon the Seneca will no longer make war in the ancient ways of our fathers and their fathers before them. We will fight in the ways of the pale skins."

"All the warriors who practice each day with the firesticks know that the words my father speaks are true," Renno said. "One firestick is more powerful than many bows and arrows. One metal knife is the equal of many stone knives."

"After I have gone to join our ancestors," his father said, "the Iroquois will use the ancient weapons only for sport. By that time they will make war only with the weapons of the strangers who come to make this land their own. If we have these weapons and use them, we will live. If we lack these weapons, we will surely die. The day has not yet come when we greet the pale skins as our friends and brothers, but that day will come."

Renno hadn't thought in such terms, but his father's prediction made good sense.

"Those who will lead our people in the years

ahead," Ghonka went on, "must know and understand these strangers to our world. Who is better able to know them than a son of the Seneca who was born in their midst?"

Renno was startled.

Ena intervened. "It is right for Renno to know other things," she said. "I have had many visions, and the manitous have opened the future to me. They have shown me that my son will become a war chief who leads the warriors of the Seneca and the other Iroquois nations to many victories over our enemies."

Renno's spine tingled and his blood raced faster. Nothing could have gratified him more than to know he would lead the Seneca and their allies in battle.

"The manitous have not told me whether our son also will become a sachem. They have said the time is not yet come for me to look that far into the future." Ena paused, then added slowly, "There is much that our son must accomplish first. Renno, you must swear that what I will tell you now will be held close to your heart and that you will reveal it to no living person, not even to El-i-chi, your brother."

"I swear it, my mother," he said solemnly.

"You have been chosen by the manitous to weave the bonds of friendship with the pale skins. That is why you were sent to us when you were a baby. You alone are both a Seneca and a pale skin. The manitous have guided you all your life to prepare you for this work."

No man could refuse to do the will of the spirits without incurring their wrath, and Renno bowed his head. He was exhilarated, yet at the same time he felt uneasy. An overwhelming task awaited him, he felt himself inadequately prepared to face such a challenge, and he knew he had to rely on the manitous to equip him with greater experience and knowledge. For the present, he must simply submit to the inevitable.

"So be it," he said.

"The warrior who succeeds in battle suffers many wounds," Ghonka said. "He who wins has a skin filled with scars."

Renno was familiar with the old saying, but he wondered why his father was electing to remind him of it now.

"The young—and even the senior warriors who are learning the powers of firesticks—know that in time we must exchange the wampum of friendship with the pale skins," the Great Sachem continued. "But there are some men who are older whose eyesight has been dimmed, who cannot see the future as clearly. They would make war on the pale skins and drive them into the great sea."

"It would be foolish to try," Renno said. "There are too many of them, and they have too many firesticks."

"That is what I told the Council, and most men agreed with me," Ghonka said, "but there are some who hate the pale skins so much that they still think as children. There are some among our people who do not like you, Renno, because you came to the Seneca from the pale skins. These men are stupid because none of our warriors are more Seneca than you. But reasonable words do not change their minds. They wish for a return to the days of our ancestors, to a time that is gone forever."

Ena glanced at her husband.

He nodded, almost imperceptibly.

She drew in her breath sharply, then took the plunge. "No full warrior is younger than you, and you have already put five scalps on your belt. Your father and I are proud of you, and most of our people share that pride. But there are a few who do not like you because your hair and eyes are pale. He who hates you the most is the medicine man who is the father of Iala."

Renno felt as though he had been kicked in the face.

"It is right that you should know this," his mother said.

He fought to regain his equilibrium. "Iala," he said slowly, "was sent to visit her cousins of the Oneida so she would not marry me when I returned from the raid on the town of the Huron."

Ena nodded in sympathy.

"We did not tell you, my son," his father said, "because we did not want you to be hurt. But it is right that you learn the truth now. The manitous test those whom they favor so they will know for certain that these warriors have the strength to lead our people."

Renno swallowed hard. It would be more difficult for him to give up Iala than it had been to face any of the trials he had endured in the past.

"Iala will not become your wife," Ena said. "The mind of her father cannot be changed."

"So you must put her aside," Ghonka declared. "You must prove to the manitous that you are worthy of the trust they intend to place in you."

Renno was shattered, and a heavy pall enveloped him. But he had no choice, and his mouth felt dry as he said, "So be it."

The Citadel, the mightiest fortress in all of North America, stood high on a bluff above the Saint Lawrence River and the town of Quebec. This collection of buildings, some of stone and some of wood, surrounded by a high palisade and protected by watchtowers, included barracks, a parade ground, a palace, office buildings, and the smaller houses of high-ranking military officers and civilian administrators. It was the heart, the brain, and the nerve center of New France.

The core of the complex was found in the person of the Comte de Chambertin, the French royal governor who ruled this raw, vast land in the name of His Christian Majesty, Louis XIV. Short and almost insignificant in appearance, the Comte de Chambertin tried to compensate for his plainness by wearing a magnificent suit of handsomely embroidered cloth of gold. His narrow chest was covered with decorations as well as the sash of his high office, and he wore a huge wig that cascaded down his shoulders.

He sat in a high-backed hand-carved chair that closely resembled the throne of his master at Versailles, and he was surrounded, as always, by his personal entourage: these included his official mistress, who wore a shockingly low-cut gown that was absurdly out of place in this community on the edge of the wilderness; an aide-de-camp who had a predilection for wearing women's clothes in the privacy of his own quarters, where he entertained officers of the garrison with similar tastes; and a young half-breed, a girl of great beauty who sometimes enjoyed the questionable privilege of sharing the royal governor's bed.

Colonel Alain de Gramont had no use for any members of the entourage, and it was difficult to conceal the contempt he felt for Chambertin himself.

Smartly clad in his gold and white infantry officer's uniform, a short wig covering his shaved head and scalp lock, Gramont strode into the inner sanctum of the little palace, saluted, and then stood at attention.

It amused the royal governor to keep Gramont frozen for a few moments before waving him to a chair.

"My astrologer predicted I'd have an unpleasant experience this afternoon," Chambertin said peevishly as he hauled the half-breed girl onto his lap and began to fondle her, "but I didn't dream I'd have the ill luck of having to grant you an audience."

Alain de Gramont made no attempt to hide his impatience. "I need to confer with you alone, *Monseigneur*."

"Those who are closely associated with me are known for their discretion."

The girl responded to the comte's ministrations by snuggling closer to him.

Gramont's manner became icy. "Matters of Crown security may not be discussed with anyone except the governor. A directive to that effect was signed by His Majesty himself."

The royal governor sighed petulantly, pushed the girl to her feet, and waved the members of his entourage out of the room.

"What could be so important that no one else can hear what you have to say?" Chambertin demanded.

"One of my best espionage operatives returned today from a tour of the English colonies below the border—"

"In this ghastly weather?" Chambertin interrupted, pointing toward the partly frosted window and the falling snow driven by a strong wind.

"My agents don't care about weather."

The governor sipped his wine, looking offended.

"*Monseigneur*, we face a serious situation. Several months ago, the English in Massachusetts Bay and New York delivered hundreds of muskets to the Iroquois. As nearly as I can glean, about three hundred of these weapons are being used by the Seneca and another hundred by the Mohawk."

Chambertin whistled softly under his breath, and the hand that held the goblet began to tremble. "But this is outrageous! They copy the pattern you created when you supplied firearms to the Huron and Ottawa!"

"Precisely. And the situation requires firm action!"

"When the weather becomes warmer, I assume."

"Naturally. Only small bands of men who know how to deal with the elements can function in winter."

Chambertin watched the snow swirling beyond the window. "You will attack and capture Boston." He made the statement as though the campaign had already succeeded.

Gramont laughed harshly.

The governor looked at him in surprise and raised an eyebrow.

"You forget, *Monseigneur*, that the population of the English colonies is several times that of our own—we're badly outnumbered."

"Then I shall send an immediate request to Paris for several additional regiments of His Majesty's best troops."

The colonel sighed. "Your letter won't reach Paris until the end of April, at the earliest. It will be studied and debated in the Ministry of War until the end of the summer. Then it will be sent to Versailles where it will be passed slowly through various hands, and it will be the beginning of next winter before it reaches His Majesty. With all due respect to King Louis, his military ventures in Europe are far more important to him than anything that happens here in the New World, and even if he agrees to send us more troops, which I doubt, we'll receive only a fraction of what we'd need to capture Boston and New York Town."

The governor was forced to nod in agreement. "I

suppose we should consider ourselves lucky to have two full regiments of regular troops already stationed here to defend Quebec if the English colonies should launch a full-scale campaign against us."

Gramont shook his head. "That's their great weakness. New York and Massachusetts Bay and Connecticut and Pennsylvania are so jealous of each other that they find it impossible to act in concert. Also, they haven't solidified their relations with the Iroquois, and little trust has developed on either side. These, *Monseigneur,* are the weaknesses we must exploit."

"How?" The governor's head was beginning to ache, and he devoted himself to his wine again.

"The English must be brought to believe that they made a mistake in supplying arms to the Iroquois. The growing friendship must be disrupted before they can conclude an outright alliance. Remember the problem we've had with the Algonquian."

The Comte de Chambertin, who regarded all Indians as crude savages, found it difficult to remember one tribe from another, but he was unwilling to reveal his ignorance to this iron-willed subordinate who actually preferred to spend long periods living among the Indians, so he said nothing.

Gramont, who knew the comte well, curbed his impatience. "The Algonquian are far more timid than the Huron and Ottawa," he explained. "They've hesitated when we've asked them to join us because they're afraid of the Iroquois. So, if the Seneca, Mohawk, and the other Iroquois tribes actually take the side of the English, the Algonquian will throw in their lot with the English, too, and we'll be overwhelmed. We need an incident that will force the English to go to war against the Seneca."

"Very convenient, and a neat solution, I'm sure, but I fail to see how such an incident could be arranged."

A gleam appeared in Alain de Gramont's eyes. "In a few weeks, when the weather becomes warmer, let us suppose that a band of Seneca—a large band —launches a surprise raid on one of the English settlements. Settlers will be killed, houses will be looted and burned to the ground, women and children will be abducted. The English will be furious because they have been betrayed, and they'll send an expedition to teach the Seneca a lesson. The nations of the Iroquois League will stand together, you can be sure, and will go to war against the English. They'll hurt each other badly and save us the trouble of waging war ourselves. What's more, we'll earn a bonus, for once the Iroquois are weakened, it will be easier to persuade the Algonquian to become our allies."

"You paint a delightful portrait, Gramont, but I see a flaw. I can't imagine how we could persuade the Seneca to attack the colonists who have given them firearms!"

The royal governor was so obtuse that Alain de Gramont wanted to throttle him. *"Monseigneur,"* he said, "the raiders will merely appear to be Seneca. They will make certain that the English settlers identify them as Seneca, but they will actually be Huron, and they will not change into their own war paint until they have left the English settlement a long way behind them."

"I see." The Comte de Chambertin nodded, but he was still dubious. "It would be a splendid trick, but if the Huron should make errors and allow themselves to be identified, the English colonists well might band

194

together in a major war with us that we can't afford to fight."

"The Huron will make no mistakes," Gramont said flatly, "because I intend to lead the raiding party myself."

Spring came late that year to the land of the Seneca, but at last the grass turned green, buds appeared on the trees, and game became more abundant. Much to the delight of Renno, who was now eighteen, Abe Thomas postponed his departure from the Seneca town for another month.

Renno and Abe had formed a fast friendship, each learning to communicate a little in the language of the other, and now the white Indian would have the opportunity to perfect his already expert marksmanship.

"The reason you're turning into a crack shot is because you have a natural advantage," Abe said.

Renno grinned at him. "I good because I have pale skin?" He could laugh without bitterness now at his unique state.

Abe laughed, too. "No, much as I'd like to think so. It's your vision that helps make you so accomplished —just as you are with the bow and arrow."

On the final morning of Abe's stay, the warriors he had trained gave a demonstration of their newly acquired talents. Immediately thereafter, Renno and El-i-chi were scheduled to depart with the visitor and guide him back to his own home. Out of gratitude, Renno had insisted that he be given the privilege, and El-i-chi had persuaded Ghonka to let him accompany his brother.

Only the fifty best Seneca shots took part in the demonstration. Conspicuous by their absence were the grizzled war chiefs, who were finding it difficult to master the firearms. The vast majority of the participants were the young full warriors, most of them in their twenties. They had been malleable, quick to learn, and equally quick to appreciate the advantages of the musket over the traditional bow and arrow or spear.

Warrior after warrior hit his target while everyone watched, and Ghonka was pleased when El-i-chi showed his prowess. Then Abe and Renno engaged in a contest, and the English colonist won by a margin so narrow that the bullet holes in their targets had to be carefully measured.

After the ceremony Ghonka presented the visitor with a bow, a quiver of arrows, and a stone tomahawk. In a long, dignified speech the Great Sachem told the firearms instructor that he would always be welcome in the land of the Seneca, where he would have the right to hunt and roam freely as long as he lived.

In his newly acquired Seneca, Abe promised to return.

Then, he and Renno went to the longhouse of the full warriors to collect their gear for the journey. El-i-chi joined them, but they were delayed by the warriors' farewells to Abe as the people of the town returned from the fields.

Renno stood apart, and suddenly his blood turned cold. Walking toward him was Iala, prettier and more desirable than ever. He hadn't known that she was home, and he guessed she had returned the previous night.

He took a single step toward her, uncertain of his reception, and then he restrained himself. It was her right to set the tone of whatever future relationship she might want to have with him.

They were so close she could have reached out and touched him, but she walked past him, not even glancing in his direction. A true daughter of the Seneca, Iala was a product of rigid discipline, and she was obeying her father's commands to the letter. In her eyes, Renno no longer existed, and he felt as he had when he was a baby and his mother had ducked him in the icy waters of the pond.

Ghonka was the last to bid farewell to Abe Thomas, who had taught him to use his gift pistol, even though he was still more comfortable with a bow and arrow. The Great Sachem wished El-i-chi a safe journey, then turned to his elder son.

Renno knew instantly that his father was aware of Iala's snub.

Ghonka gripped his son's shoulder and held his hand there for a moment.

Renno was comforted. A few people might dislike him because he had not been born a Seneca, but he was as much a member of the nation as any man. Only today he had distinguished himself with the firestick he would be carrying with him on the journey. The day might well come when Iala's father relented, and then Renno would be reunited with her. Until then, he would never disgrace himself, the Bear Clan, or the nation.

The three young men started out at the customary Seneca trot, but Abe Thomas, who had been trained in a different way, could not maintain the pace, so Renno and El-i-chi reduced their gait to a walk. That afternoon they fished in a stream, and their ample catch provided them with a filling supper.

They took their time as they traveled eastward through the forest, enjoying the weather, the good hunting, and each other's company. During the past months,

Renno and Abe had developed a camaraderie based on mutual respect. Now they trusted each other, too, and Abe was pleased to learn the Indian method of moving swiftly through the wilderness, leaving a minimum number of tracks.

They took turns hunting, and El-i-chi proudly brought down a young buck that provided the group with game for several days. "You're turning into a good shot," Abe told El-i-chi as Renno translated. "Not as good as your brother, but you're in a class with most of our militiamen right now."

They lingered for half a day for no reason other than their enjoyment of the swimming, and as their journey drew to its inevitable end, they were reluctant to part company.

"Come to Fort Springfield with me," Abe said. "My ma will fix you our kind of a feast."

Renno suddenly felt inexplicably shy, and he shook his head. He was not ready to meet a whole company of pale skins. Even if his mother's visions had been accurate and it was his destiny to play a role in advancing the relationship of the Seneca with the strangers who were his blood ancestors, he was not yet prepared to meet them. When the time was appropriate, the manitous would give him the necessary sign.

They paused when they reached the edge of the forest on the west bank of the Connecticut River, and Abe pointed to the fort on the far side. "There's our town," he said. "Sure you won't change your mind and come with me?"

"Someday I go there," Renno said. "Not right time yet."

He and El-i-chi bade farewell to their friend and slipped back through the trees into the dark forest.

They would take their time going home, Renno decided, wishing that the sight of the huge log fort hadn't disturbed him. He had no idea that this was where Ghonka had found and adopted him before burning the original fort to the ground. What disturbed him was the evidence of the pale skins' might. Surely it was right, as his father believed, that the Iroquois nations and these strangers gradually become more friendly.

Abe Thomas was warmly received by his parents, and as the next day was Sunday he went to church with them. Obadiah Jenkins was so pleased to see him that he discarded the sermon he had intended to preach and, after welcoming Abe home, asked him to come up to the pulpit and tell the congregation of his experiences.

Abe would have preferred facing an enemy in battle, but he did his best. "I spent near a half year with the Seneca," he said, "and I no longer think of them as savages. They're a good people, and I like them. I trust them. I'm proud to say I have some real friends in that tribe. Someday, when we all learn to trust each other more, I reckon we'll make an alliance with them that will last a long time."

Obadiah Jenkins thought his remarks were more effective than any sermon on brotherhood could have been, and after the services ended, many people crowded around Abe to greet him and to chat with him.

"I'm glad you haven't turned into a barbarian yourself, young man," Ida Alwin told him with a sniff. "Deborah will be sorry she missed you, but she stayed home with a headache this morning."

Abe summoned his courage. "Maybe she wouldn't mind too much if I pay a call on her one day during this coming week."

Aunt Ida's smile was the only invitation he needed.

Colonel Wilson drew Abe aside to obtain a brief preliminary report from him, and while Mildred Wilson waited for her husband, Agnes Hibbard came up to her and said, "Tom and me had best get started to home, Mildred, so I can put the Sunday roast on the fire. It's lucky we came in the cart, so dinner won't be delayed."

Agnes's devotion to duty was responsible for a tragedy that might have been averted had she and her husband stayed at the church a short time longer.

As they were driving toward the Wilson estate on a deserted stretch of the road that ran parallel to the Connecticut River, a large band of Indian warriors appeared, seemingly out of nowhere, and surrounded the cart. Two of them halted the mare that was pulling the cart, and one grasped the reins.

Tom Hibbard reached for the rifle that lay beside him on the buckboard, but before he could use it, a husky warrior knocked him unconscious with the flat side of a stone tomahawk.

Agnes tried to pick up the rifle as the other savages reached for her, and she attempted to scream, but her cry was no more than a faint gurgle. A knife slit her throat, and at the same instant a spear penetrated her body.

One of the warriors scalped her; another bent down to scalp Tom.

"Do not touch him, my son," the blue-eyed commander of the Indian party ordered sharply. "He saw that we are wearing the green and yellow paint of the Seneca. Let him live to tell others what he has seen. Come quickly. We have much work to do."

The Huron obeyed instantly and followed Golden Eagle as he raced away from the scene of death.

Alain de Gramont was satisfied with the results of his raid, and the thirty-seven members of his party were careful to follow his instructions to the letter. He had chosen the time of the assault perfectly, electing to attack while the English colonists were attending church services.

So far, two farmers had been killed, both with bows and arrows, for the Huron were under strict orders not to use firearms that might alert the Fort Springfield garrison. At both of the victims' homes, other members of their families, including several older children, had been bound and gagged but not injured and left alive so they could describe the green and yellow war paint of the invaders.

Now Gramont and his men set fire to an empty farmhouse, its inhabitants presumably attending church.

The Frenchman was slightly annoyed. He had wanted to take at least one prisoner, and he felt he should have abducted a child or two when there had been the chance. A perfectionist, he regretted leaving any part of a plan uncompleted. Now, with the farmhouse just about to go up in flames, it was wise to return to the forest and start the long march back to Canada.

He led his men toward the river, intending to cross in the canoes they had left in the underbrush, when he saw a young woman standing in the entrance to a small house.

So terrified was Deborah Alwin that she was unable to move. Then, suddenly, she screamed.

Alain de Gramont barked an order to two of his warriors. "Take the woman as prisoner and bring her with us!" The girl was a pretty blonde, and her disappearance would arouse the ire of the English settlers toward the Seneca that much more. A good day's work had been done, and the seeds of enmity between the English colonists and the most powerful of the Iroquois nations had been well and truly planted. All that remained now was to escape before a direct confrontation exposed the ruse and caused a serious outbreak of hostilities between the French and the English.

The colonel had faith in his Huron subordinates and he did not glance again in the direction of the small house as he led the rest of his men to the waiting canoes.

The two braves ordered to capture the girl ran with the speed of bobcats to the house and burst inside, one of them sweeping Deborah off her feet just as she was reaching for the rifle over the mantel.

She fought her brawny captor as best she could, biting, scratching, and kicking, but when she tried to scream the brave unhesitatingly slapped her hard across the face. She was momentarily stunned, for never had she encountered such brutality, and before she could recover, a gag was stuffed into her mouth and thin strands of rawhide were bound about her ankles and wrists. While his companion set the Alwin house ablaze, the warrior slung Deborah over his shoulder, and—in no way slowed by his burden—ran down to the river and got into a waiting canoe, his comrade protecting him from the rear.

The leader of the party, whom she could not see clearly, rasped an order from another canoe, and both craft shot out into the current, turned upstream, and traveled a considerable distance before heading back to the east bank.

When the canoes were grounded, the warriors smashed them, rendering them unfit for further use. In spite of her terror, Deborah noted that the Indians used small hatchets with metal blades, obviously of European manufacture, but in her muddled state of mind she didn't grasp the significance of what she had seen.

Then one of the men picked her up again, carrying her easily on his back, and the party snaked off through the forest.

The numbed girl began to regret the benign attitude she had maintained for so long. She had been wrong to believe that colonists should find ways to establish amicable relations with the natives of North America. Her face still stung from the hard slap, the strips of rawhide bit cruelly into her ankles and wrists, and Deborah had to concede, too late, that Aunt Ida had been right. The colonists would achieve a truly secure foothold in the New World only when they used the force of arms to drive the Naturals out of an area and claim it exclusively for themselves.

All at once, in the distance, Deborah could hear the Fort Springfield bugles blowing and the snare drums rattling. The alarm was being sounded, but she was afraid it was too late.

Her estimate was right. Colonists still standing on the church lawn were the first to reach the fort, where they were joined by farmers from the outlying region. The first task was that of extinguishing the fires in the burning buildings, none of which could be salvaged. The group assigned to Ida Alwin's property had labored hard in the smoking ruins and discovered that Deborah had vanished. Once it was established that she had not perished in the flames, it could only be assumed that she had been captured by the raiders.

Those who had actually seen the invading warriors were questioned closely, and all of them, from the surviving children of the bereaved families to the grief-stricken Tom Hibbard, told the same story.

The raiders wore green and yellow war paint.

Obadiah Jenkins, who would conduct funeral services for the victims the following day, was the first to voice the ugly thought that had occurred to everyone who had become at all familiar with the Indians. "The attackers," he said to the small group assembled in the colonel's office at the fort, "had to be Seneca."

"I don't believe it," Abe Thomas said flatly.

"Why not?" challenged Andrew Wilson.

"Because the Great Sachem, Ghonka, and all the members of his council showed such friendship to me—and to all of us—while I lived with them. The Great Sachem wants good relations with us, and I don't believe he was planning an attack while he was talking to me."

"You're too naïve for your own good, Abe," Jeffrey Wilson said contemptuously. "I wouldn't trust any Natural."

"Well, I would!" Abe retorted. "The sons of the Great Sachem escorted me back here, and I'm ready to swear on Reverend Jenkins's Bible that they're my real friends."

"What I don't understand is what the Seneca would have to gain by attacking us," the clergyman said. "They'll be sending furs to us from time to time in payment for the firearms we sold them, and eventually they'll want more ammunition and gunpowder from us, and I'm sure they'll want more muskets. I can't imagine why they'd conduct a vicious raid that shows them so little profit." He was heartsick over the disappearance of Deborah, knowing more certainly than ever that he loved her. Still, his mind continued to function clearly. "It's in the best interests of the Seneca and the other Iroquois to stay on good terms with us. They have everything to lose in an attack that causes us minor harm. Not that the loss of any of our lives is minor."

Colonel Wilson cut short the debate. "The minds of Indians seem to work in strange ways," he said, "so we'll have to wait until some future time to fathom why the Seneca have betrayed us. We can build new houses to replace the ones that have been destroyed, but we can't bring our dead back to life. Right now our first order of business is to follow the savages and try to rescue Deborah Alwin. Once she's safe, we'll teach the Seneca a lesson they'll never forget, and only then will I stop to wonder why they attacked us."

Renno and El-i-chi prolonged their holiday. There was no need for them to return home quickly; the Seneca were not at war, and game was so plentiful now that a few hunters could easily supply the people of the town with all the meat they needed. Besides, Sah-nee-wa would put any unoccupied young warrior to work helping to plant corn and other crops.

So the brothers traveled through the forest at a leisurely pace, meandering as they pleased. It was easy to bring down game with their new muskets, and they enjoyed this carefree interlude together. This was the life Renno relished above all others, and he rejoiced in the knowledge that he was a Seneca. He could not deny that his skin was pale, but it was impossible for him to imagine spending all his days in the shadow of the great building that the English settlers called Fort Springfield. A man who could not roam where he pleased, at home with the elements, at ease in the wilderness—hunting and fishing when he acquired an appetite and otherwise just wandering for the pleasure it gave him—was no real man. Renno felt that his spirit would shrivel and die if he had to till the fields and spend the rest of his days living in the vicinity of a protective fort.

One night he and El-i-chi found a perfect place to make their camp. They discovered a hidden hollow, concealed by thick, high brush on all sides, that stood only a short distance from a river, and close to the hollow a waterfall dropped three or four times the height of a tall man.

The scene was pretty, berries were already ripening in a sunny clearing nearby, and El-i-chi brought down another young buck. The brothers decided to explore the area and try their luck at fishing in a deep pool above the waterfall that looked promising.

They took normal precautions, for there was always the possibility of being attacked by stray bands of Algonquian or hunting parties of the small tribes that lived in the vicinity. So they always explored together, making sure to light their cooking fire only at noon, when the glare of the sun made it relatively difficult to see from any distance, and extinguishing the flames as soon as they had prepared enough food to last until the following day.

One morning they found a patch of large raspberries, and after frightening away a flock of birds they ate their fill. They brought handfuls back to the hollow to enjoy later, and after cooking and eating several fish with fine white meat, they devoured the rest of the berries.

The sun made them drowsy and they stretched out to rest, but all at once Renno sensed the approach of an alien presence. Putting his ear to the ground, he could make out, even above the roar of the waterfall, the distinct sound of many footsteps moving up the mossy riverbank below the falls.

El-i-chi listened, too, then nodded his agreement, for silence was imperative.

After a time a large party of warriors came into the clearing below the falls.

They were wearing the green and yellow paint of the Seneca, and El-i-chi was on the verge of jumping to his feet and running to greet his tribal brothers, but Renno, still lying on his stomach and peering down at the group below, raised a warning hand.

El-i-chi was puzzled, but he obeyed without argument and resumed his own watchful pose.

Something was amiss, and for a time Renno couldn't decide what was making him apprehensive. The warriors were tall well-built men with bronze skins, and they looked like Seneca. In no way did they resemble the shorter Algonquian, or the Ottawa, who were several shades darker, like the Erie.

Suddenly Renno realized what was bothering him. These warriors were carrying firesticks, but the weapons were somehow different from those that lay on the ground beside him and El-i-chi. It was difficult for him to describe the difference, even to himself, but it was there.

As he watched, the warriors did something puzzling. In groups of twos and threes they stripped, went into the river, and standing below the waterfall, they used moss to carefully scrub away their war paint. It began to dawn on Renno that these braves had merely been masquerading as Seneca, and a hot anger filled him.

With great care, he loaded his musket, long practice enabling him to perform the task silently.

Again, El-i-chi followed his example.

Some distance down the river, Renno saw a captive who was bound hand and foot; the strangers had taken the precaution of making the prisoner additionally secure with a leash around his middle, the other end of which was tied to a tree.

As the warriors began to eat venison strips and parched corn, they removed a gag from the captive's mouth and placed a quantity of food on the ground where the poor wretch would be obliged to eat it like an animal.

The prisoner turned, and Renno saw that it was a young woman whose hair was the color of corn silk, the precise shade of the hair of the Great False Face who had spoken to him in his visions.

It was as though a bolt from the Lightning Spirit had struck him, and his mind went blank, his body tingling.

His feeling returned when a rush of sympathy for the pale-skinned prisoner swept over him. Her eyes had looked tortured, but in spite of her misery he realized she was beautiful.

Perhaps his destiny had led him to this hiding place in the tangled underbrush. Surely it could be no accident that he and El-i-chi had been drawn to this particular place.

Renno's attention was wrenched away from the girl when a warrior, older than the others, went into the water and began to scrub away his green and yellow paint. Another shock awaited the young warrior, for at second glance he recognized Golden Eagle, the Huron war chief, his great enemy.

Renno's anger was transformed into icy rage. He continued to watch, his eyes glittering, and soon he saw proof of what he had already guessed. Some of the warriors were donning purple and white paint. They were Huron!

Turning to El-i-chi, Renno gestured rapidly in the sign language they had perfected as children. El-i-chi nodded, his expression indicating eager anticipation. Like his brother, he felt no fear, even though they were outnumbered by nearly forty to two.

Keeping his musket nearby, Renno reached for his bow and arrows. This vantage point was perfect for attack as well as for observation, and because the odds were great he preferred to launch his assault in the traditional manner rather than with firesticks.

Two of the enemy who had just emerged from the waterfall had donned their loincloths again and were smearing purple and white paint on their cheeks, foreheads, and torsos, and El-i-chi had no need for further instruction as he fitted an arrow into his bow.

The brothers took precise aim and let fly at the same instant, and the two braves crumpled to the ground and died without a sound. The other Huron were still unaware of what was taking place.

Again Renno and El-i-chi fitted arrows into their bows, and again they shot with great care, this time aiming at two other warriors who were standing relatively close to the base of the steep hill, with their backs to it.

Renno's arrow found its target, but El-i-chi missed, his arrow cutting through the young leaves of a tree and landing only inches from a startled brave.

The need for silence was gone now, and Renno reached for his musket. Squinting, he looked down the barrel and squeezed the trigger gently, as Abe Thomas had taught him. His bullet went into the brain of a purple and white painted warrior, and the man toppled backward onto the ground.

El-i-chi was equally successful with his initial musket shot, and both brothers reloaded swiftly but calmly, enjoying this unusual battle. Round after round poured down from the place of concealment, and the bewildered Huron, still uncertain where their enemies might be lurking, grew panicky.

Golden Eagle had emerged from the water at the first sound of musket fire, but his shouted commands did not deter his subordinates, who fled into the forest. Eight of their comrades were dead, and their corpses were left behind.

Alain de Gramont had no choice but to follow his men, reunite them, and lead them back to Canada. For a fleeting instant he thought of disposing of the English colonial girl, but she had served his purpose and he didn't care what became of her. His mission was a success in spite of this unexpected disaster, and the English colonists and the Seneca would soon be tearing at each other's throats.

Throwing his loincloth around him, the colonel picked up his rifle. Renno had been waiting for this moment, and he leaped to his feet, making certain that his foe could identify him. "Golden Eagle of the Huron," he called in a taunting voice, "Renno of the Seneca challenges you to combat!"

There was no sound except the rush of the waterfall as they stared at each other; then both raised their firearms at the same moment—and both missed.

The thought passed through Renno's mind that the manitous did not want the contest to end yet. There would be another confrontation some other time.

Colonel Alain de Gramont, alias Golden Eagle, vanished like a wraith into the forest.

The victorious brothers waited a long time, listening to the retreating footsteps and making certain the Huron did not return, before they cautiously descended from the heights, and Renno rewarded himself with five scalps. El-i-chi took his first three, and both were satisfied with the result of the encounter. Surely now El-i-chi would win promotion to the ranks of full warrior, even though he was only sixteen summers old, and there was a chance that Renno, with an astonishing ten scalps hanging from his belt, would be considered for elevation, unprecedented for one of his age, to the company of senior warriors.

All at once Renno remembered the yellow-haired girl captive and trotted over to her, the dripping scalps sending rivulets of blood down his leg. El-i-chi stayed close behind him, uncertain of his brother's intentions but content to follow Renno's lead.

The trees had partially blocked Deborah Alwin's view of the heights, and she had been able to see only portions of the encounter. None of what she had actually witnessed made sense to her. Some of her captors seemed to have vanished, but these two who were coming toward her, grisly trophies dangling from their belts, wore the same green and yellow paint that she identified with her abductors.

Struggling to a sitting position as best she could and speaking with the last shreds of her remaining dignity, she said, "Kill me now and have done with it."

Renno bent over her, cut her bonds with his knife, and lifted her to her feet. He was surprised because she seemed almost weightless.

Deborah looked at him, startled when she saw the blond hair of his scalp lock, his pale eyes, and his chiseled English features. He was tanned, to be sure, but this man was no more Indian than the leader of the band that had captured her, although that one had taken care to keep his distance from her on the trail.

It occurred to Renno that the girl had spoken the language Abe Thomas had taught him, so he replied as best he could in the same tongue, "Not kill, not hurt," he said. "Safe now."

His English words, even more unexpected than his color, combined with the realization that her bonds had been severed, were too much for Deborah, and she burst into tears.

Renno and El-i-chi looked at each other in puzzled helplessness. Seneca women seldom cried, and even girl-children of Ba-lin-ta's age wept only on rare occasions. The brothers took it for granted that the pale-skinned woman was ashamed of her weakness, so they both turned away from her, keeping their faces averted until she regained her self-control.

At last Deborah's tears stopped, and she was relieved rather than ashamed. There were occasions when crying could clear one's mind, and she realized now that her situation was improved, at least temporarily.

The scalped bodies of a number of her abductors littered the ground near the riverbank, and some of them were smeared with purple and white paint, which made no sense to her.

Obviously this pair had been responsible for their deaths, and she studied them with surreptitious interest. The white Indian, her senior by no more than a year or two, was a strange contradiction. He was a savage, yes, but he was the most handsome male she had ever seen, and had he been a settler living near Fort Springfield she would have been drawn to him at once.

The younger, who was wiry and not as tall, seemed to have the same regal bearing, the same sense of inner dignity that characterized the elder. Both were confident and self-reliant, and in a strange way the girl was reminded of Colonel Wilson and Reverend Jenkins, who were both equally sure of themselves and contented with the places they held in life.

Neither of these Naturals exuded even a hint of the air of menace that she associated with her abductors, although she had no wish to test them by trying to escape through the forest. She had lost all sense of direction, she had no idea where she was, and knew she was incapable of making her way a long distance alone through hostile country. For better or worse, she had to depend on these two savages.

Renno addressed his brother in the Seneca tongue. Pointing toward their hidden refuge above, he said, "Bring our pouches and as much of the cooked meat as we can handle. The Huron may try to seek vengeance, and we must be long gone lest they return. I will collect the firesticks they left behind."

El-i-chi sprinted up the steep slope, and Renno turned to the girl, who looked even prettier now that pink glowed in her cheeks. "You rest," he told her.

The note of command in his voice was so strong that Deborah sat down on the ground at once and rubbed her chafed wrists and ankles. She felt the white Indian staring at her, and she knew she was beginning to blush.

Renno gathered the Huron firesticks, examining them curiously. They were somewhat longer than those of the English settlers, and the stocks were of a slightly different shape. But they worked on the same principle, and he felt certain that once he made bullets to fit them, his people would be able to use them. He made two bundles of the firesticks, binding each with vines.

El-i-chi returned.

Renno motioned to the girl, indicating that he wanted her to rise, and he smiled to show he meant her

213

no harm. Deborah stood, and before she realized what he was doing, he had picked her up and slung her across the back of his shoulders, in the same manner that her kidnappers had carried her. The indignity infuriated her.

"Put me down this instant! I can walk by myself!"

Renno recognized only one word. "Not walk," he replied firmly. "Woman too slow."

Deborah knew she was being chastised, and she had no valid reply to his argument. So, in spite of her ludicrous position, she subsided.

A problem quickly developed, she noticed, when the younger of the warriors, already carrying his own weapons and quantities of food, could not seem to manage the burden of both bundles of rifles. The elder one solved the problem without hesitation. One bundle was left behind.

They set out at a rapid trot, moving considerably faster than the girl's abductors. The white Indian's stamina and endurance amazed her, and she realized that on her own feet she could have made progress through the forest at only a fraction of his speed. She tried not to be too much of a burden and rarely moved or shifted her weight as he continued hour after hour without slowing his pace. No one at Fort Springfield, including Abe Thomas or the burly blacksmith who had only recently arrived, had such physical strength.

Long after sundown they halted, and the girl drank gratefully from a brook before stretching her cramped arms and legs.

Renno sat cross-legged, with El-i-chi opposite him, and beckoned curtly. "Eat," he said, and he handed the girl a chunk of cold cooked venison which he hacked from the remains of the animal's carcass.

The taste of the meat was strong, and the parched

corn was so dry it tasted like sawdust, but Deborah discovered that it gained a measure of flavor when she followed the example of the two young warriors and chewed it for a long time. Somewhat to her surprise, she ate all the food they gave her.

Renno stared at her gravely, his eyes unblinking, in the soft light of a three-quarter moon that filtered through the trees.

Deborah became uncomfortable under his scrutiny.

"Renno," he said at last, pointing to himself.

"El-i-chi," the younger warrior told her.

She curbed a desire to giggle, afraid she might begin to laugh hysterically. "Deborah," she told them, and she had to repeat the name several times.

"De-bo-rah," Renno said at last, pronouncing her name in the Indian manner as he continued to study her.

The girl wanted to hide her face, but she refrained. So far, neither had threatened her, and although she had no idea where they were taking her, common sense told her not to show that she was afraid of them.

The moonlight turned her hair the same silvery shade Renno had seen on the waters of lakes, and it had the same sheen. Not even Iala's hair changed color at night, and he marveled at the appearance of this soft pale-skinned girl who seemed to grow more beautiful even as he looked at her. Her dress was torn at one shoulder, revealing an extensive patch of unblemished white skin, and he couldn't resist the temptation to reach out and touch it.

In spite of her intentions, Deborah shrank from him, and he withdrew his hand at once.

She saw the hurt in his eyes before his expression

became bland, revealing nothing, and she knew he had meant her no harm. He had merely been curious, and it occurred to her that it was possible, even probable, that he had never seen a woman of his own race.

Deborah didn't know how to apologize without creating an impression she might later regret. His knowledge of English was so limited it was almost impossible for her to communicate with him. She wondered whether she should take his hand and touch his fingertips to her shoulder, but he might think her forward. It was better to do nothing.

Renno folded his arms across his chest and looked into space. He realized he had frightened the pale-skinned woman, and his own clumsiness annoyed him. He should have known better than to act so impulsively—it was only that there was something so appealing about her soft skin—and he gleaned that in her world, as in the land of the Seneca, it was the privilege of the woman to define the relationship she wanted with a man.

Technically, this woman was his rightful captive. He had taken her from the Huron and could do with her as he pleased, but her resemblance to the Great False Face with the corn-silk hair was so startling that he had no wish to disturb the manitous or turn them against him.

He had no idea where the Huron had captured the woman, and nothing in her past was of interest to him. She was here, and it was enough that he had assumed responsibility for her. He was uncertain what to do with her after they returned home, but he would seek the advice of his mother and the sister of his father. Ena and Sah-nee-wa usually knew what to do in matters that concerned their own sex.

Unfortunately, his experience with women was

limited. It was true that, in the months since Iala's father had ordered her to reject him, he had paid a number of visits to the special longhouse, where women captured from other nations were forced to give themselves to the men of the Seneca in return for food and clothing. Some of them were expert in the art of coupling, but the pleasures he obtained from them were fleeting. Sometimes he was reminded of the water that helped him overcome a burning thirst. He drank it greedily, but soon he became thirsty again. So it was with the women in the special longhouse.

But why should he be thinking in such terms now? Renno forced himself to face the truth. He wanted this lovely pale-skinned woman. He didn't forget for a moment that it was his right to take her. But he decided to wait. It was wiser to abstain for the moment than to offend the manitous.

The silence dragged on interminably, and Deborah felt an urge to shatter the quiet. This strange young warrior appeared to have forgotten her very existence, and she was faced with a situation she didn't know how to handle. She would wait, even if it took all night, and he would make the first move.

Ultimately, her patience was rewarded.

"Sleep," Renno said, turning to her for an instant.

The girl stretched out on the ground, and she was so tired that soon she dropped off. Her instinct told her he would not molest her, and she was right.

She felt as though she had been asleep for only a few minutes before she sensed him standing over her, and she awakened with a start. The night was very dark now, the moon having vanished, and she had no idea how long she had slept, but it couldn't have been more than a few hours.

Neither of the young braves showed impatience as

217

she cleaned herself in the waters of the nearby stream, and then the elder handed her another chunk of meat and a handful of parched corn.

"Eat," he told her for the second time, and he hoisted her onto his shoulders, obviously expecting her to manage to eat while he carried her.

Somehow she was able to chew and swallow the food, and she knew better than to ask questions. At the very least, the language barrier would make it impossible for him to answer. Again, he and the younger warrior trotted for hour after hour through the wilderness. On the few occasions when they paused, she watched them press their ears to the ground, then display satisfaction, thus she realized they were not being followed by the survivors of the band that had abducted her.

She had to be grateful for that much, even though she had no idea what might happen to her now.

The militia unit from Fort Springfield made steady but slow progress through the forest, and even the optimists among the men thought it unlikely that they would catch up with the Indians who had conducted the vicious raid on the settlement. Nevertheless, they did not give up, hoping that the trail would lead them to a community of the Naturals where they would find and rescue Deborah Alwin.

Their guide and tracker was Abel Finn, a dour farmer who had spent some years trapping animals in the wilderness before he married and turned to more domestic pursuits. He had found the broken canoes in his first wide sweep of the area. Halts were frequent while he studied the patterns of bent grass and broken twigs, and he managed to keep the column on the path the raiders had taken in their flight from the stricken town.

Abe Thomas, who was helping Finn, remained convinced that his former hosts bore no responsibility for the outrage. "We're heading much farther north than the land of the Seneca. Their country lies due west of us, and it don't make sense for them to be taking Deborah somewhere else."

"We'll find out," was Colonel Wilson's tight-lipped reply.

The quietest member of the militia was Tom Hibbard, whose head was still bandaged, and everyone realized that he intended to avenge the death of his wife. He grieved in dry-eyed withdrawal and made his only comment to Abe one night after the group had halted to make camp. "Not even ten notches on my gun butt will bring Agnes back," he said, "but I aim to get them all the same."

After spending a full week in the forest, the party approached a high waterfall that fed a swift-moving little river at its base, and as they drew nearer, a flock of buzzards rose high, their wings flapping, then circled lazily overhead.

"We've found something," Abe shouted, and the main body hurried to the site of the recent battle.

"Don't touch anything," Colonel Wilson ordered as he and his men stared at the bodies of the eight scalped Huron the buzzards had been feasting on.

A brief examination revealed that some of the warriors had been killed by bullets and others by arrows, and the colonel didn't know what to make of these findings.

It was Jeffrey Wilson, disdainful as always, who made the most important discovery. "On some of these bodies," he said, "there are traces of green and yellow war paint. It looks like they were smearing themselves with purple and white paint when they were interrupted by enemies who weren't wasting any time killing them."

Abel Finn and Abe went off to study the tracks of the warriors who had fled, and then Tom Hibbard saw the severed rawhide thongs that had been used to bind Deborah, although the militiamen could only guess they had been used for that purpose.

Renno and El-i-chi had left no tracks that the English settlers could have identified, so there was no hint of Deborah's fate.

After several hours of intensive searching, Finn and Abe Thomas returned. "Colonel," said Abe, "as near as we can make out, the savages ran away from this place in twos and threes. Their tracks are spread out to hell and back over a wide area."

"All we know for sure," Abel Finn added, "is that all of them were going due north—as fast as they could move."

"Can we follow their trail?" asked the colonel.

"There's no way, sir," Abe replied with a shrug. "We'd need ten or twelve experienced trackers, one to follow each trail, and even if we had the men to do it, they'd need weeks or months to trace each one."

"As near as we can make out," Finn added, "these warriors got panicky, and there's no way to track down twenty-five or thirty men who are running separately. Maybe they all got together again way up to the north of here, but maybe they didn't. And the snow will start falling before we can find out for certain where they came from. Long before then the trail will have disappeared as the grass grows taller."

The colonel went off downstream with his second-in-command to discuss the situation.

Lieutenant Donald Doremus, in civilian life the proprietor of the new, highly successful Fort Springfield Inn, was an alert, hardworking pioneer in his early thirties, the only resident of western Massachusetts Bay other than Andrew Wilson and Obadiah Jenkins who had earned a degree from an English university. "I hate to say this, sir," he said to the colonel, "but it appears as though we've come to a dead end."

"I'm afraid so, Donald." Andrew Wilson's sigh was heavy. "What do you make of the carnage?"

"Obviously the raiders were attacked by another band of Indians, probably a force of greater size."

"I agree so far."

"The real problem is the war paint puzzle," Doremus went on. "As nearly as I can piece it together, our attackers were removing the green and yellow paint of the Seneca and daubing themselves with purple and white—"

"The colors of the Huron."

"Correct, Colonel. They were surprised, a battle took place, and the raiders ran away. Their foes either suffered no casualties, or they took their dead and wounded with them."

"So far so good," Andrew Wilson said. "The evidence would seem to corroborate Abe Thomas's claim that the assault on Fort Springfield was made by a tribe other than the Seneca."

"Yes, sir. The Seneca would have headed due west, toward their own homeland."

They were interrupted by Abe, who was carrying a bundle of muskets bound with vines. "Colonel," he said, "we found these guns in the brush only a few feet from the riverbank."

They cut the vines, and each man examined a weapon.

"These aren't our muskets," said Andrew Wilson.

"Abe, did the Seneca have any firearms other than those we supplied?"

"No, sir, not as of a couple of weeks ago," Abe answered with slow emphasis. "And I'm sure I'd have known it if they'd been making a deal for guns with somebody else."

Donald Doremus continued to examine one of the muskets. "This weapon was manufactured in Prussia, Colonel. It carries an even greater mystery. Obviously these muskets were supplied to Indians—at a guess, the Huron—by white men. But I can't pinpoint their identity.

"The most likely suspects are the French," Doremus went on, "because the Huron have become their allies. But we don't know whether or not King Louis's troops buy their arms from French gunsmiths."

"I intend to find out," said the colonel, "and in the meantime I can't discount the possibility that the Spaniards in the Floridas are responsible for these weapons. I'll put a request through General Pepperrell to Prince Rupert in London, and if he doesn't know he'll conduct an investigation. It may be some months before we learn the answer, but I'm sure we'll find out what we need to know."

"What we don't know and may never know, sir," said the lieutenant, "is whether the French or some other nation had a hand in planning and inspiring the attack on us."

"All too true, I'm afraid. Just because the Huron are French allies, it doesn't necessarily mean that the authorities in Quebec can control them. The savages are capable of acting on their own."

"On the other hand," Donald Doremus said, "it seems to me like a deliberate attempt to convince us that the Seneca were attacking us—"

"I've known they were innocent all along," said Abe, daring to interrupt the officers. "Ghonka is honorable, and so are the men under him."

"I'm willing to exonerate them," said Wilson.

"What do we do now, sir?" asked his second-in-command.

"I'm afraid we must give up the chase and go home. We'll strengthen our alert system to prevent another surprise attack, and we'll wait for further developments. If we can ever prove that the French were responsible for the raid, we'll do everything in our power to persuade the other English colonies to join us in sending a major expedition in a campaign to raze Quebec. But we'd need real proof—either that, or another raid when we can take prisoners and find out more from them."

"Until then, sir," Abe asked, "what do we do about Deborah?"

The colonel's face darkened. "I fail to see what we can do," he said. "If she shows up in Quebec, I daresay we'll be notified in due time. The French, for all their faults, don't make war directly on women. The Huron may have killed her, or the enemies who attacked our raiders may have put her to death. It's also possible that she's become the prisoner of the savages who won the battle here. Only the Lord knows what's become of her, and we lack both the men and the resources to search the whole of North America!"

Chapter IX

The outer sentries passed the news on their drums that Renno and El-i-chi were homeward bound, heavily laden with scalps, and bringing with them a pale-skinned woman who was not tied with the rawhide bonds of a captive of war. The entire Seneca town appeared to enjoy the unprecedented spectacle.

The brothers were grave, their demeanor befitting the mightiest of nations, and between them walked the young woman with pale skin and hair the color of corn silk. Her dress was torn, but she held her head high, and none of the spectators knew what it cost her to conceal the fear threatening to engulf her.

Deborah realized that her escorts had arrived at their destination, and she found herself looking at a sea of expressionless Indian faces. She had no way of knowing that their seeming passivity denoted great curiosity rather than open hostility, and that she was the first white woman they had ever seen.

One person in the crowd was seething. Iala instantly recognized a serious rival for Renno's affections.

Obedient to the will of her father, Iala had taken great care to avoid Renno, but that didn't mean she could accept his interest in someone else.

She pressed through the throng, hoping to hear every word of the brothers' explanation of events to the Great Sachem, and for a moment her eyes met those of the pale-skinned girl.

Never had Deborah encountered such a look of hatred, and the Indian girl's loathing for her struck her with the violence of a physical blow. She wanted to shrink from it, to hide her face, but she managed to look elsewhere, breaking the eye contact, and the moment passed.

The Great Sachem was just finishing a meal in the open, and he rose from his place in front of his hut to greet his sons, each of whom extended an arm, palm upward.

"Bow to Great Sachem," Renno told the English girl in her own tongue.

Deborah felt absurd as she curtsied to the grizzled middle-aged savage who wore an elaborate feathered headdress.

The Seneca had never seen such a gesture, and some of the women and children laughed. Ena had to restrain the impulsive Ba-lin-ta, who would have raced forward and thrown herself at her brothers.

The whole community listened as Renno told in full detail the story of the encounter with the Huron, who had disguised themselves by wearing Seneca war paint. He omitted any mention of Golden Eagle, for the developing feud that seemed to be a part of his destiny was not a matter for public consumption. He would tell his father about the confrontation when they were alone.

El-i-chi stepped forward, slashed the vines that

held the stack of four muskets, and handed one to his father. "This is a gift for the Great Sachem. He may give the others to the warriors he chooses."

Ghonka examined the weapon. "Will this firestick and the others like it kill my enemies?"

"They will," Renno assured him, "as soon as I make metal arrows to fit them."

"Then I accept," the Great Sachem replied, and he could scarcely conceal his pleasure. "Renno, my son, is it true that you have killed five more of the Huron?"

"It is true, Great Sachem."

"El-i-chi, my son, is it true that you killed three of the Huron?"

"It is true, Great Sachem."

Ghonka shifted his attention to the pale-skinned woman.

"De-bo-rah," Renno said, "was the captive of the Huron. We set her free and brought her with us."

Deborah recognized her name, even with its strange pronunciation, and her apprehension increased.

"You will make her your slave?" the Great Sacham asked.

Renno became uncomfortable. He was not willing to make a confession of his sympathy for this girl whose skin was the color of his own, so he hedged. "She speaks the tongue of the English, who sold us our firesticks. We don't want them to become our enemies, so I don't know what is to be done with the woman."

Ghonka had never faced such a problem, and he solved it in the only possible way. "Ena and Sah-nee-wa will decide her fate," he said hastily, and then he made further discussion impossible by summoning the medicine men and warriors to an immediate conclave in the community longhouse.

As the men filed away solemnly, Ba-lin-ta, who

226

interpreted her father's words to mean that the pale-skinned woman would become a member of her immediate family, drew nearer to Deborah and grinned at her.

The child's irrepressible smile was the first friendly gesture Deborah had received since her abduction, and on sudden impulse she dropped to her knees and hugged the little girl.

Ba-lin-ta reached out to see if the yellow hair was real, and assuring herself that it was, she burst into happy laughter.

Glancing obliquely at the scene as he went off with the other men, Renno was relieved. Surely his mother and the sister of his father would find the right place in the town for the new arrival.

The first order of business at the conclave was the promotion of El-i-chi to the rank of full warrior. Like his brother before him, he was receiving his advancement at an early age, but the scalps at his belt proved he had earned the distinction. No man protested, the brief ceremony went off without a hitch, and Renno conveyed his pleasure to El-i-chi in a swift glance.

All the full warriors were dismissed, but Renno was requested to remain, and he stood alone in the midst of his superiors.

Ghonka descended from his platform, followed by his war chiefs and the medicine men. The significance of the gesture was not lost on anyone. All, including the highest, held the basic rank of senior warrior, and at this moment all were equals. Every warrior had the right to speak his mind freely, without fear of reprisals or punishment.

The members of the group seated themselves in a double circle, while Renno, still standing, was banished to a place beyond the outer ring. He had no idea what was happening, and he felt slightly awed, but he assumed his most dignified air.

In accordance with his duty as the commander of Renno's company, Sun-ai-yee spoke first. Rising and advancing to the center of the circle, he spoke briefly, as always coming straight to the point. "Renno," he said, "is a warrior of only eighteen summers. But he carries ten scalps in his belt, more scalps than many men carry in all their lives. If the manitous do not strike him down, may he now become a senior warrior of the Seneca."

Renno's spirits soared. Never had anyone of his years been advanced to such a high rank. A senior warrior held a place of command in battle and enjoyed innumerable privileges in times of peace. The mere prospect made him dizzy.

Several elderly war chiefs, all of them now retired, followed Sun-ai-yee. Elders enjoyed universal respect, and everyone present listened to them carefully as one by one they endorsed Sun-ai-yee's nomination.

Renno wanted to shout for joy, but he continued to stand immobile, arms folded across his chest, as though they were determining someone else's future.

Then Ghonka stood. "My love for my son is great," he said, "so I will cast no vote. I do not want it said that I had a part in making him a senior warrior before his time. All I will say is this: if Renno were not my son, I would be the first to vote for his election."

A score of other warriors followed.

Renno noted that Iala's father remained silent. Surely, if he objected to the advancement to high rank of one who had been born a pale skin, he would speak, but he sat with compressed lips, staring straight ahead.

A handful of others also indicated their disapproval in subtle ways, but none protested openly. Out of the entire group of one hundred, the dissenters could be counted on the fingers of one hand.

A silence fell after the last war chiefs and senior warriors had added their unqualified endorsements to the proposal, and Renno stood there, as unmoving as a full-leafed tree on a day when no wind blew.

Then Ghonka mounted the platform. "Let Renno stand forward."

The young warrior moved to a spot below the platform.

"Is it the wish of Renno to become a senior warrior?" Ghonka asked.

"It is, Great Sachem."

"Do you promise to do always what is required of you and to place the needs of the Seneca above your own?"

"I promise, and may the manitous torment me if I fail to keep my pledge!"

"Let him be put to the test," Ghonka said.

Eight senior warriors gathered around the candidate and walked with him to a clearing deep in the forest. There they prepared a stake, driving it into the ground, and after removing his weapons and stripping him to his loincloth, they bound him to the stake with strips of rawhide.

These warriors would stand guard over him in pairs for the next four days and nights to prevent animals from harming him or enemies from killing him. Otherwise they would not interfere, letting the elements deal with him as they pleased.

Renno knew he was forbidden to speak for four days and nights, and he had heard of senior warriors who had remained awake throughout their ordeal for fear they might talk in their sleep. He would be given nothing to eat or drink and was required to stand erect the entire time. If he sagged against his bonds, became unconscious, or went out of his mind, which sometimes happened to candidates, he would be cut down. Then, no matter what exploits he performed in the future, he would remain a full warrior for the rest of his days and would never again become a candidate for promotion.

Had he known what lay ahead, he would have taken the precaution of eating and then drinking quantities of water in advance. But for this very reason, he suspected, candidates were never warned. A senior warrior had to demonstrate extraordinary courage, endurance, and resilience at all times because he set an example for the entire nation.

In his new rank, if he achieved it, he would be given a hut of his own, even though he would probably live in the small longhouse of the bachelor senior warriors until he married. In his new rank he would be entitled to lead warriors of other Iroquois nations as well as his fellow Seneca in battle. Never again would he be compelled to help the women in the fields. In times of peace he would hunt, fish, and practice his skills. He would lead groups in search of buffalo herds in open country. He would be sent as an emissary to other tribes. He would even be eligible to attend meetings of the Council, if requested by the Great Sachem.

Best of all, he would become Ghonka's brother as well as his son.

A few flies and mosquitoes buzzed around Renno, and several bit him, but he paid no attention to such minor annoyances.

The father-sun was warm, but did not heat his blood, at times going into hiding behind high clouds, much as a senior warrior concealed himself in the forest. The mother-earth beneath the candidate's feet was reassuring. And when night came, the moon appeared, its color reminding him of De-bo-rah.

He wondered how she was faring, feeling confident that Ena and Sah-nee-wa were looking after her. It was strange, he realized, that when he had caught a glimpse of Iala in the crowd today he had felt nothing, not even a small pang of regret at having lost her. He wished Iala well, even though she would never become his wife.

On the second day of his ordeal, rain fell steadily for several hours, and Renno felt refreshed. The water cooled him, but he refrained from licking the drops that dribbled down his face onto his upper lip. He felt no need to cheat; he had no desire to cheat. That night the rain stopped, but the moon remained hidden.

Clouds concealed the father-sun on the third day, but Renno did not care. He began to wonder if he might see a vision before the ordeal ended, and he made an effort to suppress the desire to be visited by the Great False Face with corn-silk hair. It was improper to ask for such visits, and by now he had perfected his self-discipline.

On the fourth day the sun was hot, and the candidate began to know torment. He was not hungry, but his lips were split and parched, his throat so dry it ached. His mind was beginning to wander, although he no longer cared. It was enough that he still stood erect and unmoving, not straining against his rawhide bonds.

That night he saw—or imagined he saw—a hawk soaring overhead in the light of the moon. Regardless of whether this vision was real, it sustained him during the last, most difficult hours of his ordeal. The Great False Face had not revealed herself to him, but she had sent the hawk in her place, and Renno was content.

At dawn the following morning, all eight members of the escort were on hand, and Renno's bonds were cut. Sometimes a candidate collapsed when this happened, but Renno continued to stand as he accepted a gourd of water and sipped it slowly. Then they gave him a kettle of soup that he knew his mother had made for him, and he ate it carefully, chewing the meat and potatoes and beans. He could almost feel the strength flowing back into his body.

"Renno, you are a senior warrior now," the leader of the escort said. Each of the others, in turn, exchanged forearm clasps with him. Then they painted his face, torso, and forehead in green, with only a few thin stripes of yellow between the wider strokes. Everyone would know of his new status at a glance.

One of his new peers handed him a musket taken from the Huron, and Renno knew this was his father's gift to him.

His own bow, arrows, and knife were returned to him, and he was presented with a new tomahawk. As a final gesture, he donned the senior warrior headdress, with feathers extending around the crown as well as down the back. He guessed it was the handiwork of Sah-nee-wa.

The others left him, and he addressed a short prayer to the manitous, asking them to continue to protect and guide him. Then he was free to return to the town, where no fuss would be made over him. In fact, the Seneca would behave as though nothing out of the ordinary had happened, even though everyone knew about his remarkable promotion. It was not considered seemly to offer praise or congratulations to a newly elevated senior warrior, whose rank spoke for itself.

Before emerging from the forest, Renno looked around to make certain no one was lurking nearby.

Then he indulged in a long, luxurious yawn. His body craved sleep, so he would go to his new hut, which stood at the end of the row occupied exclusively by senior warriors. Then, when evening came, he would join his family for a full meal. And he hoped De-bo-rah would be there.

Some of the women were already at work in the fields, and Renno paused to greet his mother. She looked at him and her eyes shone. "I am proud of you, my son."

He bowed his head to her, as he would henceforth to no other woman except Sah-nee-wa.

"You look well after your trial."

He couldn't boast, but his slight shrug indicated his contempt for a mere test of endurance. Ena averted her face so he wouldn't see the smile in her eyes. In spite of his exalted status, he was still very young.

"What has become of De-bo-rah?" he asked, unable to keep silent any longer.

"Sah-nee-wa and I have lodged her in the longhouse of the maidens until your father and I speak with you about her. Is it your wish to marry her or to take her into your new house with you?"

Renno hadn't thought in such terms. A senior warrior was expected to know his own mind in all things, but he suddenly felt very unsure of himself. The thought of coupling with De-bo-rah was tempting, but he had no idea what she herself wanted. "We will talk of these things," he said, turning away quickly.

Ena smiled behind his back and shook her head as she rejoined the women.

Renno walked a short distance, mulling over his mother's words, and then his thoughts were interrupted by the sight of a small figure hurtling toward him.

Ba-lin-ta threw herself at him, hugging him fiercely and studying him. "You look wonderful," she said gravely. Renno thanked her.

"Now you can lead a raid on the Erie and bring me one of their dolls," she said, skipping beside him.

"Perhaps." He was making no promises.

"Oh, a senior warrior can do anything he wants. You can even stop the maidens from tormenting De-bo-rah."

Renno caught hold of the child's arm. "What are you saying?"

Ba-lin-ta was wide-eyed. "They've been teasing her ever since she moved into the longhouse. The last day or two she's been working in the fields with them, but she doesn't know our ways and she's clumsy, so they beat her on the face and head. And when they are alone with her in the longhouse, they really torment her. That's what they're doing right now."

He increased his pace.

The little girl had to run in order to keep up with him. "I like De-bo-rah, even though I can't understand what she says. Will you help her, Renno?"

He made no reply.

Ba-lin-ta saw the expression on his face and fell silent. Their father looked the same way when he became angry.

Renno hadn't expected to exercise the prerogatives of his new rank so soon, but he did not hesitate. Senior warriors were allowed to enter any longhouse at any time, so he hurried to the dwelling of the maidens, his little sister close behind.

The flap was open because the spring day was warm, and Renno stepped across the threshold.

De-bo-rah, clad in an ill-fitting doeskin skirt and shirt, her feet bare and her hair a tangled mess, was being made to crawl on her hands and knees back and forth across the open space around the fire. A half dozen young Seneca women were beating her with sticks, pinching her, and occasionally snatching a brand from the fire and touching it to the soles of her feet. They shrieked with laughter whenever she screamed in pain.

Renno was shocked to discover that the principal tormentors were Iala and Anowara, who were treating the pale-skinned girl as they would a Huron captive, and a surge of anger rose within him.

His roar made everyone freeze. Even Ba-lin-ta was frightened.

"What are you doing to the woman I brought to the land of the Seneca?" he demanded in a voice that penetrated every corner of the longhouse.

Some of the young women shrank from him, afraid he would strike them with the flat of his tomahawk. Deborah, who had been praying that her torturers would be called to the fields, looked with gratitude at her deliverer, and it took a moment or two before she recognized him.

Only Iala had the courage to speak. "We meant no harm, Renno," she said defiantly.

"You have done her harm." The sight of the wretched victim filled him with a pity that fueled his cold anger. "Bring her the grease of a cooked goose and apply it to her feet," he commanded.

Iala thought of refusing, but it was a serious matter for anyone to reject a direct order given by a senior warrior, so she gave in and, still managing a swagger, went across the longhouse to fetch a clay jar of grease.

"You will help," Renno told Anowara.

Deborah felt immediate relief when the two girls smeared a thick layer of grease on the soles of her feet,

235

and she fought the tears that welled up in her eyes, for she had learned that the very sight of tears incited these she-devils to greater cruelty.

Several of the young women tried to slip out of the hut, but Renno blocked their path. "Wait!" he roared.

They backed away from him.

"Anyone who touches the woman with pale skin or harms her in any way will be responsible to me."

If he called them before the Council of Women for judgment, they would be in real trouble, not only because he was a senior warrior, but because he was the son of Ena and the nephew of Sah-nee-wa, and both would be inclined to pass judgment in his favor.

"De-bo-rah will not work in the fields today," said Renno. "She will stay here and rest, so her wounds will heal. And remember, I allow no one to molest her."

He watched as Ba-lin-ta helped the limping girl to her bunk, then he turned and left the longhouse and made his way to his new hut, which had been built for him by other senior warriors during his trial. His desire for sleep was overwhelming. He had found no permanent solution to the problem of what to do with De-bo-rah, but at least he had stopped the young women from torturing her. After he slept he would discuss the matter with his parents.

It was quiet in the longhouse of the maidens after Renno walked away. Ba-lin-ta lingered protectively near the pale-skinned woman, and although the child had no right to be there, no one had the courage to order her to leave.

The young women were late for their day in the fields, so they left the longhouse together, none of them looking at their victim.

Iala caught up to Anowara. "I always knew Renno would want a woman with pale skin more than he ever wanted you or me," she said.

Anowara was flighty and fickle, but she had never been mean. "Well," she said, "I can see that a man would think she's very pretty. And you must admit her skin and hair are unusual. So are her eyes."

"They're the same shade as Renno's eyes." Iala was spiteful. "That's why he likes her. He ought to go off with her to the land of the pale skins where he belongs. And I hope he stays there with her!"

Anowara was startled. "But he's a Seneca. A senior warrior. It's a great honor, and he won it fairly."

"It's just as my father says," Iala replied. "When his loyalty is tested, he'll take the side of the pale skins against us. You'll see, someday, that I'm right."

Anowara didn't know what to reply, so she remained quiet, and they walked together in silence.

Suddenly Iala laughed under her breath. "This afternoon," she said, "I'll leave the fields early. Come with me for some real sport."

Anowara looked at her but made no comment.

"I intend to teach Renno a lesson. He thinks he's so important now that he's a senior warrior, but he'll soon learn he's no better than anyone else. By the time I'm done, he'll want nothing more to do with that blue-eyed woman. Oh, I can hardly wait to see his face!"

The conflicts of Europe boiled furiously in the kettle of international politics, with religious as well as national hatreds and rivalries stoking the flames. Soon the conflagration would spread to the New World in ways that no settler could foresee.

King Charles II had died in 1685, and even as

the people of Great Britain mourned the passing of the Merry Monarch, they dreaded the accession to the throne of his brother, James II. James had openly accepted the Roman Catholic faith, and everyone in England, Scotland, and Wales feared that Britain's return to the Church would mean that the monasteries, convents, and other properties expropriated by Henry VIII a century and a half earlier would be returned to Rome.

France, under Louis XIV, continued to pose as the champion of Rome, with the Sun King calling himself a Christian Majesty. Behind the façade of religious differences that went back to the Reformation, every statesman and diplomat in Europe knew that the French and British were engaged in a deadly struggle for world power, which was spurred by the gradual decline of Spain.

The crisis was sparked in 1688, when King James's second wife gave birth to a son, raising the threat of a new line of Catholic monarchs in England. James was deposed, and he fled to France. The throne was given to Mary, his daughter by his first wife, and to his son-in-law, Prince William, Stadholder of Holland, the so-called Protestant champion of Europe. Mounting the throne in London as William III, the new ruler prepared for an intensified struggle with the French.

The first man with whom the square-jawed King William conferred after arriving at Whitehall Palace was Prince Rupert, his wife's cousin, who still retained his posts as head of the Royal Navy and Army. The two men were old friends, long comrades-in-arms. Rupert was not impressed by William's new exalted rank, and the King did not regard the silver-haired Rupert as a dashing and romantic hero.

They sat opposite each other in a modestly furnished room in the palace with no need to put on patrician airs. Both men drank their favorite beverage: mugs of plebeian ale.

"My spies tell me," said Rupert, "that the very day James was deposed, Louis of France ordered twelve new warships built at the Brest yards."

"I heard it was fourteen," William replied with a faint smile.

Rupert shook his head. "There are facilities at Brest for building only twelve warships at a time."

The new King accepted the rebuke.

"I've already ordered a major increase in our own shipbuilding program," said Rupert, "pending your approval, and I've increased recruiting and training, so we'll have men for our new warships as soon as the craft are afloat."

"Do you suppose Louis will allow us the luxury of that much time before he picks a quarrel with us and declares war?" said William.

The prince shrugged. "One guess is as good as another."

"True, I'm afraid." William tugged at a lock of his curly wig. "He takes advice only from people who agree with him, and like all absolute monarchs he tends to believe he's infallible." He sighed. "It's unfortunate."

"It will be for us if we're not adequately prepared. I'm also placing four new infantry divisions, two cavalry brigades, and three artillery regiments in training. The French armies are well trained, well led, and efficient, so I don't fool myself that we can beat them simply by unfurling the Union Jack and launching a major attack."

"The last I saw of your—our—troops, it seemed

that the colonels and younger generals needed more field experience. They've grown rusty during the recent years of peace."

"I'm sending a number of them to Belgium so they can skirmish against the French." Rupert leaned back in his chair and lit his pipe with a coal he plucked from the hearth with a pair of tongs. "We'll be in good shape to face any threat, William. Provided Louis gives us a year or two."

"We'll also need to strengthen our alliances," the King said.

"That's your problem, not mine." As always, Rupert was disconcertingly blunt.

"Well, I can count on my own Dutch divisions, naturally, and I intend to woo the Austrians. Again, that may take time, so we may be forced to endure Louis's calculated insults for a number of months. It won't be easy."

"We have one great weakness that worries me," Rupert said. "Our North American colonies."

"I know very little about the situation there," the King confessed.

"We have colonies scattered up and down the seaboard, as you know. They have a combined population of about one hundred and fifty thousand, and they're getting more and more immigrants every year. Now they'll also be receiving large numbers of Huguenot refugees from France, thanks to Louis's domestic anti-Protestant campaign. Our French immigrants will have more reason than most to join our militia."

"What's the population of New France?"

"No more than seventy-five thousand, not counting the Indian tribes that have formed firm alliances with Quebec."

"If we outnumber them by two to one," William said, "I don't see any real cause for worry."

"Ah, but there is," the prince declared as he emptied his mug.

He waited until a servant came in, refilled the container, and bowed himself out.

"Our colonies are far from united. Aside from the petty quarrels and jealousies typical of any family, they're spread out over such a great area that real co-operation between them becomes difficult. It would take weeks for infantry or militia from the Carolinas and Virginia to march up to the Maine District of Massachusetts Bay, for example."

William became crisp. "What do you recommend we do? Obviously, we can't permit the French to push us out of the New World. It would mean the end for us as a first-rate power."

"Not only that," Rupert said with a grin, "but I'd love to take over French Canada. I'm founding a new company at Hudson's Bay, north of the French settlements, and the profit potential is enormous."

"You haven't answered me, Rupert." William became a trifle sharp. "How do we go about countering the French?"

"Our navy is still limited, and I won't send warships to Boston, Philadelphia, or New York Town until I'm certain that the French fleet will be represented there. As for land forces, I can't spare even one regiment. All our troops are needed here, so the colonies will be forced to depend on their own militia. There's no choice."

"Are they competent?"

"The general in command in Massachusetts Bay, William Pepperrell, is a brilliant soldier. So are some

241

of his subordinates, including Andrew Wilson, whose brother, Lord Beaufort, is a member of your Privy Council. The troops themselves lack the discipline of the Royal Army, but they fight well, it appears, and they've distinguished themselves in a number of minor engagements."

"Then our situation there isn't hopeless," said the King.

"Oh, far from it. William Shirley, the governor of Massachusetts Bay, is doing his best to form a united front, and I've just written him a letter about the increased French threat, which will spur his efforts. Connecticut and Rhode Island will place their militia under Pepperrell's command, I have no doubt, and so will the new colony of New Hampshire, which is rather sparsely populated. New York will at first insist on maintaining the separate identity of its militia, but I believe the New Yorkers will cooperate when they realize how badly they're threatened."

"Then we do have a nucleus over there."

"A solid nucleus, but we need something more," said Rupert. "The French have been more successful than we in wooing the natives and enlisting them as allies. Only recently have we inaugurated the policy of selling firearms to the major Indian tribes. Now I plan to suggest—delicately—that our colonies establish firmer friendships with the savages."

"Why be delicate about it? I'll send a directive instructing the royal governors to establish alliances with the Indians at once!"

"Please don't," Rupert said. "I'm afraid you don't understand the New World mentality, William. Even the governors we send to America are infected by it after they've spent a few years there. Our colonials must be led, never driven, or they dig in their heels and resist."

"Surely they have the sense to see it is in their best interests to obtain the assistance of strong Indian tribes!"

"You simplify because you don't understand their problems." Only one of Rupert's stature could have spoken so boldly to the new monarch. "The frontier settlements in virtually every colony have suffered repeated Indian attacks. Men have been killed, women have been taken into slavery, children have been abducted, and whole towns have been looted and burned to the ground. It's difficult to persuade a man whose father was scalped and whose son has been tortured that he must form an alliance with the very savages who committed these outrages."

"I see . . ." William's annoyance gave way to a mounting confusion.

"Even now," said Rupert, "the colonies are making a great concession by selling firearms to the Iroquois League, the most powerful of all the Indian groups. And the savages are still suspicious of the colonials. Mutual trust can't be created overnight when they've been fighting each other for the past sixty years and more."

"You're probably wise to suggest a closer relationship without pushing too hard," William conceded, "but if a real alliance takes years to develop, our colonies could be destroyed long before then!"

"Once again we come back to Louis of France," Rupert said. "I'm relying on him to solve our dilemma for us."

William knew instantly what Rupert meant, and he laughed aloud. "Quite so. He's arrogant and demanding, and he never thinks of the rights or feelings of others, so his subordinates imitate him."

Rupert nodded.

"The French in Quebec and their Indian allies will go too far, perhaps, and thus they might force our colonies and the major Indian tribes to form an alliance."

"That," said Prince Rupert, "is my precise and devout hope."

Deborah Alwin's blistered feet felt better, and her spirits lifted, but as the end of the day approached, she steeled herself for her next ordeal. Her protector, the young white Indian called Renno, had disappeared, and she was certain her tormentors would take every opportunity to amuse themselves at her expense.

There was no escape, and Deborah knew it. She was tempted to flee into the forest, but she knew better than to imagine that she could find her way safely back to Fort Springfield. The savages would recapture her and would be certain to punish her with even more refined cruelties.

She could tolerate the pain and humiliation if she thought there might be an end to it, but she had seen nothing of Renno since he had intervened on her behalf that morning, and she suspected that even his interest in her was prompted by ulterior motives.

Deborah was prepared to die with dignity. She was determined, no matter what the she-devils did to her, never to weep or scream again, since those reactions seemed to spur them to greater efforts.

Ironically, Deborah, as much as anyone in Massachusetts Bay, had advocated the establishment of friendlier relations with the Naturals. Now she was willing to admit she had been mistaken, that the gulf that separated the settlers from the Indians was too great. These people might have their own standards, but their callousness toward human suffering was so great that she saw no way for those from a more advanced civilization to become truly friendly with them.

The young women began to return from the fields, and Deborah braced herself when she saw her principal torturer, the pretty girl who, for whatever reasons, hated her.

Iala approached her bunk and beckoned. Deborah knew it was useless to ignore the summons, for if she failed to obey she would be dragged from her hard slab and kicked, scratched, and punched. So she stood, waiting for a fresh assault.

Anowara joined Iala, and both girls stood there staring at her and giggling. To Deborah, the sound of that laughter was evil and ominous. Then the Indian girls fell in at either side of her and conducted her into the open.

Deathly afraid, but taking care not to show it, Deborah took heart when neither of the she-devils touched her. They even seemed careful to maintain a slight distance, so perhaps they had listened to the white Indian's warning.

In the gathering twilight, they escorted her through the town. Warriors sitting outside longhouses, women preparing evening meals, and playing children all gazed at the newcomer, but there was no longer a burning intensity to their stares. Perhaps when they took her presence for granted, she might be able to make plans for escape.

Iala and Anowara took the girl to a relatively small longhouse that stood somewhat apart from the other buildings. A middle-aged woman, dressed in a skirt and shirt that were heavily embroidered with

dyed porcupine quills, came to the entrance. The two
Indian girls said something to her, pushed their victim
into the building, and fled.

The woman held a short whip made of several
knotted strands of rawhide, and she conducted the new
arrival to a bunk, pointed to it, and stalked off.

Deborah became aware of sweet-smelling herbs
burning in the fire and noted that partitions separated
the bunks, giving each resident some small measure of
privacy. The women who lived here seemed to bear
scant resemblance to the other residents of the town.
Many had darker skins, most were shorter than the
Seneca, and two were much taller and rawboned, with
very high cheekbones. All were elaborately dressed in
embroidered and beaded costumes.

As they came to her, one by one, to touch her
hair and skin, she noticed that they were wearing
crude cosmetics. Berry juice stained their lips and
cheeks, and smudges of a sooty substance encircled
their eyes.

One of those who came up to her was actually a
man dressed in women's clothing, his movements and
gestures as feminine as those of the others, and not
until much later did she learn that he was a warrior
who had been guilty of cowardice in battle and as a
consequence had been condemned to live as a woman in
this place.

As nearly as Deborah could judge, all the women
seemed to be young, and she was grateful that none
displayed hostility toward her. Two of them came to
her, offering her a gourd of berry juice and a pot of
sooty material. Apparently they meant her no harm,
so she allowed them to amuse themselves by painting
her lips and daubing her eyes.

All at once, the middle-aged woman, who had

been observing the activity from a distance, gave a command in a loud voice and cracked her whip. The residents scurried off to their own bunks and sat on them.

A moment later a burly warrior, his face and body smeared with paint, stalked into the longhouse. He moved slowly up one side of the room, pausing to inspect each of the women in turn, then started down the other side. Deborah noted that the residents returned his gaze calmly, without embarrassment, but she took care to avoid his eyes.

When the warrior completed his tour of the longhouse he returned to a young woman directly opposite Deborah and offered her what appeared to be a leather wristband that had a design of some kind burned into it. The girl looked at it carefully, turning it over in her hand, then said something. A moment later she and the man had stripped off their clothing and, without preamble, were fornicating on the bunk.

Stunned and mortified, Deborah realized that this place was the Indian version of a bordello, similar to the house that had opened only recently in Fort Springfield. Worst of all, she herself was an inmate! No wonder the she-devils had laughed.

If necessary, she was willing to barter her virginity for a safe return to her own world, but she could not tolerate the humiliation of allowing savages to use her body for their pleasure.

The middle-aged woman moved closer, watching her face, the whip in her hand switching back and forth gently. Deborah knew this creature needed no encouragement to beat her into submission. Others were watching the whip apprehensively, and all at once Deborah realized that they, too, were captives who had been forced to become prostitutes.

247

Deborah could see no way out of the maze into which she had been thrust. It was her destiny to become a harlot for savages in a remote Indian town deep in the wilderness.

Renno slept all day, and when he awakened at nightfall he was invigorated and famished as well. Using his burnished steel mirror to assure himself that his war paint was still in place, he donned his new headdress and left his hut. Forcing himself to walk at the stately pace expected of a senior warrior, he went to the home of his parents, and because the evening was pleasant he found the family out of doors as the women prepared the meal over a pit adjacent to the hut.

Ghonka greeted him as an equal, exchanging forearm clasps with him, and both father and son grinned broadly, which they would not have done in public. Renno couldn't remember when he had known greater satisfaction.

He greeted his mother and the sister of his father with the bows that were their due. Then he nodded to El-i-chi, resplendent in the feathers of a full warrior. He would have ignored Ba-lin-ta, according to custom, but she hurled herself at him and insisted on being hugged.

Renno was seated in the place of honor at the left of his father, and he helped himself to food as soon as Ghonka was served. As always, the family ate in silence.

Renno was so ravenous after his fast that he devoured everything in sight, from stew to roasted turkey to grilled venison. He thought he had outgrown his liking for cornmeal and the syrup of maple, but Ba-lin-ta's bowl looked so appetizing that he had a full portion of that, too.

His mother and aunt were pleased by his appetite, and not until the end of the meal, when he wiped his mouth politely with the back of his hand, did they question him about the adventure that had won him his extraordinary promotion. El-i-chi had already told them the story, but they were eager to hear Renno's version, and he related the tale in full, omitting no detail. Then he said to his father, "Tomorrow I will make the metal arrows for your new firestick and mine. Then, if you have time, we will go into the fields for practice." It would have been rude to indicate that the Great Sachem required instruction from his son in anything.

At last the talk veered to De-bo-rah, and Renno became indignant again as he described how he had found her being tormented that morning.

Ena and Sah-nee-wa did not share his concern. "It may be true," his mother said, "that the pale skins do not teach their young to endure pain as we do. But the maidens meant her no harm."

"I'm not so sure of that, my mother," Renno replied. "Iala has a great hatred for me now, although I don't know why, and she has a hatred for the paleskinned woman as well."

Ena merely smiled. Her elder son might be a senior warrior, but he had acquired little understanding of women.

"Is it your wish to marry this woman?" Sah-nee-wa asked her nephew.

Renno grew uncomfortable. "My mother has asked me the same question. I do not know her well enough to make an answer."

The elderly woman looked thoughtful. "It would be good, I think. Then your children would have skins the color of their father and their mother."

"My children will be Seneca!" he replied flatly. "It does not matter whether their mother is white or red."

The family nodded in agreement. The matter required no discussion and was taken for granted.

"What I would like to know," Renno said, "is what should be done with De-bo-rah now. It would be wrong for her to stay in the longhouse of the maidens." He looked first at Ena, then at Sah-nee-wa.

Children were expected to remain quiet while their elders were talking, but Ba-lin-ta was incapable of staying silent. "Oh, it's already settled," she said. "Iala and Anowara took her this very evening to the special longhouse."

Renno was momentarily robbed of his ability to speak coherently.

Ghonka's nod was complacent. "That may be the best for all," he said. "If we return the pale-skinned woman to her own people, they might think us weak. There was much talk of this matter in the council, and all agreed that in the special longhouse she will give joy to many warriors."

"No!" Renno shouted, for the first time in his life disagreeing with his father. It was his right as a senior warrior to express any opinion he wished, but even he failed to understand why the word had exploded from his mouth with such force. Leaping to his feet, he stalked off in the direction of the special longhouse, almost forgetting his dignity. Ena and Sah-nee-wa exchanged smiles.

Ba-lin-ta was frightened, aware that she had spoken out of turn once too often, and El-i-chi glanced nervously at his father. Ghonka frowned, but his wife touched him lightly on the back of his hand.

Suddenly he grinned. "I have a hunger again," he said mildly. "I will eat a bowl of cornmeal with the syrup of maple."

Renno was so disturbed he couldn't think clearly. All he knew was that he continued to sympathize with De-bo-rah. His father was right in asserting that she could not be returned to her own people, but he had no intention of allowing the girl to be kept in the special longhouse. He stepped through the open entrance, and the middle-aged woman called an order, as she always did when a new customer arrived.

Renno looked around the dimly lighted interior and found the girl at once. Deborah sat on her bunk staring down at the rushes on the floor. She raised her head as a warrior loomed in front of her, and she shrank from him, her eyes widening when she recognized Renno.

Renno jabbed a forefinger in her direction. "I brought this woman as my captive to the land of the Seneca!" he said in a loud voice. "Now I claim her as my slave!"

The middle-aged woman knew he was right, and she had no wish to become involved in a dispute with a young senior warrior whose exploits were already inspiring legends. Renno looked at the girl and beckoned, then turned on his heel and stalked out. Deborah followed him, finding it difficult to keep up with his pace but managing to stay behind him. She had no way of knowing that she was observing the appropriate custom when a woman accompanied a senior warrior. All she knew was that she had won a reprieve.

Renno led the way into his new hut, then halted. Now that he had brought the girl here, he was uncertain how to treat her. He covered his confusion by appearing to be confident. He would give her his bunk, at least for the present, and he would use the floor.

"Sleep!" he told her in English, and he pointed to the slab on the opposite wall. Before she could reply, he stretched out on the floor and drew his buffalo robe over him.

Chapter X

Renno took Deborah to the longhouse of the Bear Clan for breakfast, and the girl was surprised by the calm way the Seneca accepted her new status. As far as they were concerned, she was now Renno's woman, and although no one was friendly toward her, she felt no hostility, either.

Then she and her protector returned to the hut. He picked up his bow and a quiver of arrows, said something to her that she couldn't understand, and departed. She presumed he was going hunting, and it was equally obvious that he was leaving her to her own devices. Sitting on the hard earth floor of the primitive little dwelling, she didn't know whether to laugh or weep.

Renno had rescued her from the Seneca bordello before she had been compelled to have sex relations with some brute of a savage, and for that much she was grateful. She was uncertain what he might require from her in return for helping her, but she assumed he would demand that she become his mistress, and she told herself that she would have to accept the inevitable. The very idea caused her to shrink within herself, but she had been on the verge of much worse. Renno was white, even though he was as much an Indian as everyone else in this wilderness community, and she had to admit he was exceptionally good-looking.

Deborah had never allowed herself to think in terms of whether a male appealed to her physically, perhaps because she had never been drawn to anyone in that way. Abe Thomas was a splendid specimen of manhood, but she didn't spark to him. Jeffrey Wilson was repulsive, and she preferred not to think about him at all. Obadiah Jenkins made her feel more alert, more alive, but she had never taken the clergyman's masculinity into consideration.

There was a magnetic quality in Renno that did make her wonder how she might feel if he made love to her. Her first reaction was that she was a brazen hussy who should be ashamed of herself for even thinking about such things, but that was nonsense. She couldn't live with him in the little hut for more than a short time before he would make advances to her, and she would be wise to prepare herself.

Deborah realized that someone was standing in the entrance to the hut, and she looked up from her reverie to see Ba-lin-ta, carrying a bulky bundle in her arms. They grinned at each other, and the child, sure now that she was welcome, needed no additional invitation to enter the dwelling.

Accepting the bundle that the little girl thrust at her, Deborah found several pieces of marvelously soft doeskin, a surprisingly sharp knife, a bone needle, and some small bundles of sinews that, she quickly gathered, were used by the Naturals as thread. "You want me to sew for you?" she asked, indicating a sewing motion in pantomime.

Ba-lin-ta acquired her first English word. "Sew," she said, repeating the motion and pointing to the older girl. It dawned on Deborah that the child had brought her the material so that she could make clothes for herself, and on impulse she hugged Ba-lin-ta, who clung to her happily.

Deborah needed no instruction in the domestic arts, and she set to work making a skirt and shirt. Ba-lin-ta sat cross-legged beside her, watching her, obviously impressed by her skill.

They spent most of the morning together, and as Deborah continued to work, they tried to communicate. After several hours, each was beginning to acquire the rudiments of a vocabulary in the other's tongue. Deborah could only wish she were endowed with the child's facility, for it seemed far easier for Ba-lin-ta to learn English than for her to get the gist of the Seneca language.

The lesson came to a sudden halt when an older woman came into the hut, and Ba-lin-ta promptly skipped away. Deborah had no idea who the woman was, but the kindness in her eyes was reassuring, and when she beckoned, the girl readily left her sewing.

The woman took the newcomer to her own hut for a simple meal of grilled fish and squash, and she was obviously pleased when Deborah practiced the Seneca words she had learned. Ba-lin-ta appeared to share the meal, and Deborah realized that Ena, whose name she had learned, was the child's mother.

After the meal Ena gave Deborah several clay pots, a simple but cleverly contrived device on which meats could be cooked over an open fire, and a few ladles. Together they took these back to Renno's hut, where Ena started a fire in the pit, showed Deborah where firewood was stored, and then conducted her to a series of connecting storage sheds located behind the longhouse of the Bear Clan.

"The food here is for all who belong to our clan," Ena said, accompanying her words with explanatory gestures. "Take what you want; take what you need."

Deborah saw mounds of fresh corn still in the husks and piles of squash and beans and melons, as well as smaller quantities of herbs. It took her a long time before she understood that she was free to use whatever she wanted.

Ena helped her carry the vegetables and herbs back to Renno's hut; then she insisted that Deborah come home with her.

Deborah stopped short when she saw Ghonka—whom she recognized instantly—sitting outside the hut, smoking a pipe. The Great Sachem nodded to her.

The girl couldn't help curtsying to him, and at the same moment she knew that Ena was his wife and Ba-lin-ta his daughter. For whatever the reason, the family of the tribal chief was befriending her.

Paying no further attention to her, Ghonka looked off into space.

Only after Ena had given her a large chunk of fresh venison did it occur to Deborah that Ghonka was actually studying her. It appeared that he didn't want her to know it, so she pretended to be unaware of his quiet scrutiny.

Then El-i-chi came to the hut, greeting Deborah with a smile. He seemed to regard her as a friend, and it began to dawn on her that he was the son of Ghonka and Ena.

Despite his new rank, El-i-chi offered to take water to the house of Renno for his woman.

He beckoned, and Deborah followed him to a stream that ran behind the town; she was still holding the dripping chunk of raw meat. El-i-chi filled two large containers with water and carried them to the new house of Renno. He deposited his burden, reached into a pouch at his waist, and thrust something at the girl, hurrying away shyly before she had a chance to examine it.

It was a small slab of pure salt, obviously taken from a lick and regarded by the Indians as a precious commodity.

Now she had all the ingredients she needed to prepare a meal. Just as life on the frontier had taught her to sew her own clothes, she needed no instruction in the art of cooking. She built up the fire, prepared the vegetables while the flame subsided, and then put the venison on to roast. She had no idea when Renno might return, so she let the cooking of the vegetables wait, although she placed them in clay pots and added herbs to them. She used the salt slab sparingly, crumbling bits from it to be added to the vegetables.

Renno came home carrying a buck across his shoulders, and Deborah detected a quick gleam of surprise and appreciation in his eyes when he saw that she was cooking. He made no comment, however, and went to an open place behind the hut to skin and butcher the carcass. He worked swiftly with a sure hand, then took a large portion of the meat off to the dwelling of Ghonka and Ena.

The meal was ready by the time he returned. Deborah sat opposite him at the fire, discovering that she was hungry after what had been a busy day. She was amused by the domesticity of the scene and giggled aloud when she imagined what Aunt Ida would say if she saw her sitting on the ground cross-legged, dining intimately with a half-naked savage.

Renno looked at her curiously when she laughed, but he made no comment. It was good to know that she was an expert cook, and although he had never tasted squash or beans in the manner she had prepared them, he liked both dishes sufficiently to reach into the clay pots for more.

When he finished his meal, he went back to work on the buckskin. First removing the hair with his knife, he began the process of curing the skin by rubbing it with a mixture of the animal's brains and intestines. Deborah, who was familiar with the process, emerged from the hut and offered him what was left of the slab of salt. He accepted it with a nod of thanks. This pale-skinned girl was less helpless than he had feared. Perhaps the inexplicable impulse that had made him rescue her from the special longhouse hadn't been too bad an error.

Deborah returned to the hut, cleaned the cooking pots, utensils, and gourds, and then went back to the stream to refill the water containers. She brought them back to the dwelling one by one. Renno glanced up from his own labors to observe what she was doing, but he made no effort to help her. She had no way of knowing that a senior warrior would find it beneath him to carry water.

Renno continued to work on the skins long after dark. Deborah finished her chores and retired, feeling some trepidation, but she did not awaken until morning, when she heard Renno going off for a swim. By the time he returned and smeared himself with war paint, a process she watched surreptitiously, she had breakfast prepared. He ate in silence, then returned to work on the skins.

Soon Ba-lin-ta appeared, and Deborah resumed her cutting and sewing of the doeskin garments and began her next lesson with the child in the exchange of English and Seneca words.

Renno entered the hut, hugged the child, and began to build a second bunk. Deborah thought it significant that he was putting another bed in the dwelling. He pretended to be paying no attention to the language lesson, but after he completed his task he listened more and more openly, and finally he dropped all pretense and sat down with the girls. Before long he was joining in the conversation.

His earnestness surprised Deborah, and she realized that he was making a serious attempt to master her language. Surely he knew he was white, she thought, and perhaps that was why he was throwing himself into the effort with such vigor.

Deborah lost all track of time until Ba-lin-ta announced in English, "I hungry."

Stopping everything she was doing, Deborah began to prepare another meal, first going to the storehouses for supplies. The lessons continued while the food was cooking and while they ate. Renno seemed to pick up English words and phrases as easily as Ba-lin-ta, and Deborah envied their facility. She struggled with the guttural Seneca pronunciation and what struck her at first as a jerkiness of speech, but she made better progress than she knew, and soon Ba-lin-ta's pleasure told her that she was starting to make herself understood. Renno remained stone-faced.

Gradually a pattern formed, and when Deborah completed the making of her doeskin skirt and shirt, Renno presented her with the buckskin he had cured, and managed to indicate that she should fashion herself a cape similar to his own, as well as a belt with a pouch and a headband. Ena brought her a small sharp knife and several more bone needles of various sizes.

One day Ena surprised Deborah with a pair of moccasins decorated with dyed porcupine quills. Donning footgear for the first time in days, Deborah couldn't remember when she had appreciated any gift as much. Still, she wondered why the family of the tribe's chief treated her with such kindness.

Eventually Deborah decided that the hut needed a good sweeping, so she made herself a broom with a bundle of stiff straw, a stick, and a length of vine. Ba-lin-ta came in while she was sweeping and raced away again, and a short time later Ena appeared, and then a dozen other women clustered at the door and windows of the hut to watch in obvious approval. Brooms were unknown to them, but by that night every longhouse and private dwelling boasted similar equipment.

The language lessons became an integral part of Deborah's routine. Renno was as faithful in his studies as Ba-lin-ta was in hers, and when he spent a day hunting or fishing, he insisted on a language exchange after he returned at night. However, when a lesson was finished, he had nothing more to say, and Deborah wondered if warriors communicated with women only when dealing in essentials.

She managed to make herself useful, and one day, to Renno's astonishment, she cleaned his Prussian musket for him. "You shoot firestick?" he asked her in English.

She nodded casually, feeling both proud and amused. In her world every woman had to be able to use firearms for her own protection.

He demanded an immediate demonstration.

She pointed to his pistol. "Use small firestick," she said in the Seneca language, preferring the weapon to the more cumbersome musket because the musket's jolt left her shoulder sore.

They went into the fields, and the women at work there forgot their tasks as they watched the white girl shoot at a target, reload, and shoot again. The presence of an audience made her self-conscious, but when she recognized the she-devils who had tormented her, she was determined to make a good showing. In all, she fired six shots, twice hitting her target.

Renno regarded her performance as miraculous, and thereafter he was more at ease in her presence, occasionally struggling to converse about minor matters. She returned the compliment, and their meals were no longer marked by strained silences.

Deborah could not understand Renno's failure to make any physical advances to her. They slept no more than twelve feet apart under the same roof, making it inevitable that they caught glimpses of each other in various states of undress, yet the white Indian never attempted to approach her.

Had it not been for the expression she sometimes saw in his eyes, she would have assumed he was content with their living arrangement. But she was becoming more accustomed to the subtleties of Indian ways, and when Renno's guard was down she knew—beyond any doubt—that he wanted her. Nevertheless, he made no move to take her. She told herself she should be relieved and grateful, but it was unsettling for her to realize that she might be a trifle disappointed.

One day at noon Renno returned unexpectedly early, a buck slung over his shoulders. "Eat at house of Renno's father," he said, and he vanished again.

That evening, Deborah was unprepared when they

walked to the dwelling of Ghonka and Ena, and only then did she realize why the family of the Great Sachem was so kind to her.

El-i-chi was present, as was Sah-nee-wa, to whom everyone—except, at times, Ghonka—deferred. The elderly woman said little, spending most of her time openly studying Deborah, who felt uncomfortable under her unblinking gaze. Something in the old lady's eyes, perhaps the way her mouth was set, reminded the girl of Aunt Ida. They lived in different worlds, but both were formidable, and Deborah was willing to wager that Sah-nee-wa's principles were sacred to her.

Ba-lin-ta amused everyone by her ability to switch from Seneca to English and back to her own tongue, and she did not stop chattering until her mother silenced her.

The meal itself was delicious. Deborah was becoming accustomed to Indian recipes; it no longer bothered her to sit cross-legged on the ground, and she found she was fascinated by these people and their relationships. The settlers at Fort Springfield might regard the Indians as savages, but she was learning otherwise. Their ways were not those of the Old World, but they had their own civilization and obeyed its customs.

Whenever Ghonka spoke, which was infrequently, the whole family stopped eating and listened. His wife and sister were at ease with him; nevertheless, they deferred to him. Renno, whom Ghonka treated as an equal, unfailingly showed him great respect, and both El-i-chi and Ba-lin-ta were in awe of him.

Ba-lin-ta turned to Renno. "Will you give me the antlers of the buck you shot today?" she begged.

Renno shook his head.

"Why not?" Ba-lin-ta asked, pouting.

"I have other uses for them," he said.

"What uses?" the little girl demanded.

Ghonka intervened. "Ba-lin-ta," he said, "it is not right for a Seneca child to question a senior warrior. He may do what he wishes with the animals he kills. It is enough that Renno has promised to make you a pouch. What he does with the antlers is the business only of Renno."

Deborah, who made out the gist of the short speech, saw that Ba-lin-ta had difficulty holding back her tears.

The following morning Sah-nee-wa took Deborah with her to the fields, where the summer crops were ripening. She saw to it that for her own protection the girl remained beside her. Toughened by her own experience on the frontier, Deborah worked hard all day and held her own, thereby winning the respect of the mature women. Only Iala, Anowara, and the others who had tortured her remained aloof, their attitude indicating that, for them, she did not exist.

Before going back to the town, the women went to the little lake to bathe. They undressed without self-consciousness and after a moment's hesitation Deborah followed their example. She had always seen to it that she bathed and swam alone, but a show of English modesty now would be interpreted as discourtesy.

The younger women stared at her openly, and Iala said, "Her skin is the color of the milk plant."

"No," Anowara replied, "it is like a white flower."

"Why do you suppose Renno admires her? How I would love to burn that skin a deep brown color!"

Neither of the girls had any idea that Deborah

could make out much of what they were saying. Now, she thought, concealing a shudder, she understood why they had mistreated her. It was obvious that the girl called Iala had an interest of her own in Renno.

Each day Deborah worked in the fields, and either Sah-nee-wa or Ena stayed near her.

Renno remained at home for a week, and when Deborah returned from the fields she saw him at work with various small instruments on an object she could not identify. He never showed her what he was doing, taking care to conceal the object beneath a small mat, and by now she had learned enough of Indian customs to know it would be rude to question him.

One evening, soon after the last meal of the day, Deborah stood at the entrance to the hut watching the setting sun turn from a glowing gold to a warm orange. She had adjusted well to her new way of life, but she wondered how much longer she would be forced to endure this exile. She was homesick, longing for the sound of Aunt Ida's strident voice and the sight of poor Walter's timid smile.

Renno appeared silently beside her, one hand concealed behind his back. "Renno," he said in the tongue of the Seneca, "gives a gift to De-bo-rah."

The girl took the article he extended to her and saw that the antlers of the buck had been cut into pieces and fashioned into a necklace with a design carved into the polished surface.

She was overwhelmed. Apparently, as Iala had indicated, Renno had been motivated by more than mere pity or compassion when he had twice rescued her.

Her fingers trembling slightly, Deborah put the ornament around her neck and tied it with the thongs attached to the ends. He deserved a reply in his own language. "De-bo-rah," she said in Seneca, "gives thanks to Renno, the senior warrior. She bows before him."

Renno reached for her, his desire at last overcoming his discipline.

His gesture was so abrupt that Deborah reacted instinctively, and she stiffened, at the same moment taking a step backward. If there had been an opportunity to reflect, she might have given in to him. The gift, made with painstaking care, was magnificent by any standard, and a warm glow suffused her. All the same, his move was so sudden that her initial response was automatic, unthinking.

Renno's eyes instantly became opaque, his face drained of expression, and he turned away. Not looking at the girl again, he went to his bunk and stretched out on it with his back to her.

She was regarded by the whole community as his slave, and he could have taken her by force, but his pride wouldn't permit it. She had indicated that she was rejecting him as a man, even though accepting his gift, and that was a woman's right. The Seneca custom had been inviolable for many generations, and apparently this English girl's people observed a similar code.

Very well. He was Renno, the youngest senior warrior ever to wear a feathered headdress, the son of the Great Sachem, the wearer of ten scalps in his belt. He would not allow a mere woman to see that she had caused him pain and humiliation. Soon he slept, or at least pretended to sleep.

The sun dropped behind the sea of trees to the west, and only the banked fire in the hut provided illumination. The horrified Deborah stood motionless, the fingertips of one hand gently touching her lovely new necklace, and in her own misery she was frozen, unable to speak or act.

She knew she had hurt Renno, but she didn't know how to explain that her withdrawal had not been an accurate reflection of her feelings. He had assumed he had the right to make love to her, and after all he had done for her, she could not deny him that right. She sought some way to explain that he had misinterpreted her gesture.

Moistening her dry lips, she said, "Renno."

There was no sound but Renno's deep breathing and the hissing of the coals burning in the fire.

"Renno!" she said more loudly.

He still did not stir.

Deborah was tempted to go to him, but her own strict background prevented her from taking such initiative.

It took Deborah a long time to fall asleep that night. She composed a short speech in English that she hoped would explain her feelings, then she struggled to translate it as best she could into Seneca. Finally she memorized it, repeating the brief statement over and over to herself so the words would come out smoothly. Only then, exhausted by the emotional upheaval, did she drop off to sleep.

When she awoke at dawn, Renno was no longer in his bunk, and he did not appear for his breakfast.

Not until Deborah went off to the fields with Ena did she learn that Renno had gone on a hunting trip with El-i-chi.

"When will he return?"

Ena shrugged. "When the new moon becomes full. It may be sooner, it may be later." Renno's mother guessed they had quarreled, but it was not her place to interfere.

Deborah waited anxiously for more than two weeks, her mind whirling, her feelings alternating between the hope that he would listen to and accept her explanation and the fear that he would want no more to do with her.

As far as she could judge her feelings, she was not actually in love with Renno. In spite of their intimacy, the language barrier that separated them made it impossible for her to know his mind, and his ways were still fundamentally alien to her. All the same, he was the most attractive man she had ever known, he had shown her more kindnesses than she could count, and he and his family were her only hope for the future in this place. Waves of fear washed away her hope, which was reborn and rekindled again until she thought she would go mad.

Seventeen days after he had gone, Deborah heard her first news of him from Ba-lin-ta, who came to the hut early on a rainy autumn morning.

"It's all Iala's fault," the little girl said. "My mother says so." She lowered her voice. "So does my father."

"What is her fault?"

"The problem she has made for Renno."

Deborah's heart sank. Her own pride would suffer a terrible blow if Renno turned back to the nasty Iala.

"Iala is going to marry a senior warrior from a Seneca town to the north. He came here two days ago." Ba-lin-ta grew indignant. "And the very day he came he told everyone who would listen that Renno is a coward!"

Deborah drew in her breath.

"Iala told Mi-kew-il what to say. Just to make

267

trouble. Renno has the courage of the bear. And the lion. And the hawk!" The child's anger was mounting.

"What will happen?" Deborah discovered it was painful to breathe.

"Our father sent a runner to find Renno in the forest. Last night the drums told us they met. Soon Renno will come home."

"Then what will he do?"

Ba-lin-ta looked in wonder at her older friend, who was sweet and charming in so many ways and so ignorant in others. "The pumpkins that still grow in the ground," she said, "will have their vines fed with blood."

Unable to curb her fears, Deborah walked in the rain with the child to visit Ena, who confirmed the story.

"It is the worst of insults," Ena said, "for one Seneca warrior to call another a coward. I know Iala is responsible for this. A long time ago she and Renno almost married." She refrained from mentioning why the romance ended. "Now Iala is jealous of you, De-bo-rah, so she has encouraged the man who will become her husband to tell a great lie. Mi-kew-il is a mighty warrior who carries fifteen scalps in his belt. All the same," she added with a quiet nod, "Renno will win. My visions tell me he will win."

"What will he win?" asked Deborah.

"Renno will prove he is afraid of no man, not even the mighty Mi-kew-il. Tomorrow Renno will come home. Then he and his enemy will fight, and only one will live."

Deborah's flesh crawled at the prospect. Men everywhere were similar, she thought, in spite of differences in civilizations. In the years she had lived at

Fort Springfield, two duels had been fought, one with swords and the other with pistols, resulting in one needless death and a serious injury.

"How can this fight be stopped, Ena?" she asked.

The woman's face became stony. "No one will prevent the fight! I would not allow it. The Great Sachem would not allow it! The honor of Renno, the Bear Clan, and his family must be clean. Tomorrow he will fight Mi-kew-il!"

Deborah was numbed by fear for the rest of the day. Oddly, she had no concern for her own future. Thanks to Renno, her position with his family was secure, and no harm would come to her. But it was Renno's fate that gnawed at her. In spite of his strength, he was young, and not even his courage could compensate for his lack of experience. The little she had heard about his opponent filled her with dread, and that night she found it difficult to sleep.

At dawn the town was awakened by the sound of drums.

Deborah dressed in the new doeskin skirt and shirt she had made, adding a headband and letting her hair fall free. For the first time she wore the necklace of antlers that Renno had given her.

She hurried to the dwelling of Ena and Ghonka, where the family was already eating breakfast, and at their insistence she joined them around the fire, even though she had to force herself to eat a small portion of stew.

Then it was time to leave.

Sah-nee-wa drew Deborah aside and spoke slowly to make certain her words were understood. "Take away the fear from your eyes," she said. "All of the Seneca must not know that the woman of Renno is afraid for him. His enemy must not know it." She paused, then added with emphasis, "Renno must not know it."

She was right, of course, and the girl made an effort to compose herself.

Ghonka donned his feathered headdress and buffalo robe, then looked at each of the women in turn. His dark eyes seemed to burn into Deborah, giving her courage in spite of her fears. Then he turned and left the hut, and he was joined by his war chiefs, who surrounded him as the group started to leave the town.

On this occasion, the medicine men formed a separate unit under the leadership of Iala's grim-faced father. Presumably the principal medicine man sympathized with his future son-in-law, and his subordinates were bound by a strict code to side with him. They went to the opposite side of the field, and there were some—claiming that the medicine men had more influence on the manitous than ordinary people—who believed that Renno had no chance of winning.

But they reckoned without his mother. Ena put a pouch filled with a mixture of dried herbs around her neck before she walked into the open beside Sah-neewa, who carried a gnarled oak walking stick that had been known to cause water to bubble to the surface of dry places in the earth.

Deborah accompanied Ba-lin-ta, and as they followed Renno's mother and aunt, the women and girls of the Seneca came from every direction to fall in behind them. Silent until they moved past the palisade, Deborah asked suddenly, "What is the sign I can give to Renno to show him that I have faith he will win?"

The child considered the question. "Different people give different signs. You are Renno's woman. To show him that your heart joins his heart, you touch the sides of your face with your hands. Like this."

Deborah had no choice. It was not true that she was Renno's woman, even though all of the Seneca, including his family, assumed she had been intimate with him. Now, in order to bolster his belief in himself and to clear up the misunderstanding between them, she had to give him the sign, in public, that would convey to his people that she was truly his woman. Even more important, she would be telling it to him, thereby committing herself to him in the future.

She was uncertain whether she could force herself to make the gesture, but she realized that if it weren't for Renno, she would be a captive of the Huron in Canada, suffering a persecuted existence. Or she would be the victim of Iala and her friends, subjected to incessant torture. Or she would be an inmate of the special longhouse, compelled to give her body to any savage who demanded her as his partner. Her debt to Renno was enormous, and in his hour of need she had to repay it.

The senior warriors, carrying spears, formed two sides of a square on the field, about thirty feet long on each side. Two of their number were about to engage in combat to the death, and it was their duty to prevent anyone from intervening. This was a sad occasion for them, and their somber faces reflected its gravity.

Ghonka and Iala's father took up places on opposite sides of the field, each accompanied by his own entourage. The full warriors occupied one end of the square, and the women and children moved to the last open area. Most of the spectators edged toward Ghonka's side of the field, showing their preference for

Renno, their friend, comrade, and neighbor. His foe was a stranger from another town, so only the friends of Iala and those who feared her father's power with the manitous inched toward the far side.

Deborah caught a glimpse of Iala in a dress embroidered with colored beads and dyed porcupine quills. For an instant their eyes locked. Deborah glared coldly, feeling a twinge of satisfaction when the Indian girl was the first to turn away.

The first of the combatants to appear was Mi-kew-il, escorted by a full warrior of his clan. The challenger was taller than Renno, with a thick torso and powerful arms. Wearing only a loincloth, his body free of paint, he proudly carried a number of scars on his face, upper arms, and chest. He walked with a swagger, sure of his ability to disgrace and defeat a younger, less-experienced man.

Deborah studied him as he saluted Ghonka, and she had to repress a shudder. Mi-kew-il had his counterparts in her own world. She knew from his smoldering eyes and hard face that he was the kind of man who enjoyed performing acts of cruelty.

There was a hush, followed by an almost imperceptible stir as El-i-chi arrived at the scene, coming from the forest. He approached the hollow square formed by the senior warriors, then moved off to join his peers.

Then Renno appeared, lithe and lean, like his foe clad only in a loincloth. Walking quickly into the open space, he, too, saluted Ghonka. Then he turned, deliberately, to search the ranks of the women. Silently, his expression unchanging, he greeted his mother, aunt, and little sister. For an instant his gaze met Deborah's and his eyes became blank.

She could not hesitate, and she raised her hands to

her cheeks, touching them lightly as she returned his gaze.

Renno's manner changed, and he continued to look at her, momentarily oblivious to the crowd. This was the signal he had long awaited, and he squared his shoulders, his eyes devouring her.

Deborah felt a tingling sensation that enveloped her whole being. She was promising to become his woman if he survived, and although Aunt Ida would be shocked and sickened by her abandonment of her lifelong standards, she didn't care. She was pledging herself to repay the greatest debt she had ever owed, and she was doing it of her own volition in the only way she could.

Some of the younger women stirred as Renno and Deborah continued to look at each other.

He was making a promise, too. He fully intended to be the survivor of this combat and to make good his claim on her. He had no idea what had caused this change in her attitude, but now was not the time to speculate on the question.

Tearing his eyes away from Deborah, he looked for the first time at Mi-kew-il, who stood at the opposite side of the hollow square. The man was an ugly brute, almost as strong as Ja-gonh, and Renno knew he would need to use his mind as well as his body to win this fight. His endurance might be as great as his foe's, but few warriors anywhere had a physical prowess that could equal that of Mi-kew-il.

Mi-kew-il repeated his challenge by spitting on the ground, a gesture of supreme contempt. Everything but the combat faded from Renno's consciousness, and he stood alert, motionless, waiting.

Mi-kew-il drew a stone knife, his only weapon, from his loincloth belt. Renno preferred to wait before he used his own metal knife. It was best, he told himself, to judge his foe's style before he committed himself to a course of action.

The older man's face registering his hatred, he began to advance, creeping a few paces, then breaking into a wild dash and lunging at his opponent.

Renno could have sworn he would do this. Warriors other than Seneca could be taken by surprise when a full assault was launched too suddenly, but Renno had been familiar with the tactic ever since he had taken his initial instructions as a boy of seven summers. He continued to stand, still motionless, and not until the man made his final lunge, slashing with the stone knife, did he move. Even then he barely twisted his body out of the path of the onrushing warrior.

Mi-kew-il swept past his foe, his momentum so great that it carried him out of the hollow square. Some of the full warriors laughed at his seeming clumsiness, and no one guffawed louder or more scornfully than El-i-chi. The mockery goaded Mi-kew-il, and his eyes burned as he turned back into the square and made another rush.

Renno knew that Mi-kew-il assumed he would repeat his evasive maneuver, so he altered his response slightly. As Mi-kew-il veered to the right before crashing into him, he ducked instead, then extended his foot a few inches.

Mi-kew-il tripped, crashed to the ground, and sprawled there for a moment. In that instant Renno saw his chance. Whipping his knife from his belt, he leaped, intending to drive it deep into the older warrior's back.

But Mi-kew-il was aware of his own vulnerability at this critical juncture, and he jerked out of the path of the blade, then flipped over and slashed with his own knife.

Still anticipating the quick reversal of fortune, Renno caught hold of the other's wrist.

At the same time, an unyielding hand with a steely grip caught hold of his own wrist. Both men were stretched out on the ground now, each trying to free the hand that held a death weapon.

Renno realized that the other's greater physical strength would prevail, even though he could hold him off for a long time. But he needed to create a diversion. The same notion occurred to Mi-kew-il, who kicked his foe in the groin.

Renno blotted the pain of the blow from his consciousness, willing himself not to feel it. His face was only inches from that of his enemy, so he decided to use that kick to his advantage. He winced, convincing the older man that he was weakened, but even as Mi-kew-il prepared to repeat the kick, Renno smashed his forehead hard against his opponent's nose, splattering blood over both of them.

Mi-kew-il, as befitted a senior warrior of the Seneca, showed no pain, and he wrestled with renewed strength.

They rolled over and over, moving as one from one side of the hollow square to another as each tried to gain an advantage. Their legs thrashing, they were working themselves into a frenzy.

The crowd was breathless, inching forward almost to the line formed by the impassive senior warriors who extended their spears as a barrier to hold back the people.

Deborah was sickened by the brutality; she wanted to bury her face in her hands as she prayed that Renno would overcome and conquer his wily opponent. She was afraid he was no match for the heavier, stronger man, but she kept watching and hoping for a miracle. He had to win.

All at once the two opponents moved apart and, still clutching their knives, scrambled to their feet. They circled each other warily, crouching in order to present smaller targets as they regained their breath.

Renno had amply demonstrated that the charge of cowardice lodged against him was ludicrous, but even if Mi-kew-il withdrew the accusation, it was too late now. Neither of the antagonists could afford to lose face; and honor—even more important to a Seneca than life itself—had to be upheld.

Renno feinted with his knife, and Mi-kew-il leaped backward. Some of the full warriors who were Renno's partisans laughed derisively, and even some senior warriors, supposedly neutral because two of their rank were engaging in the duel, couldn't resist smiling broadly. It was unnecessary to explain the reason for their amusement. Everyone present understood they were accusing the challenger of cowardice.

Mi-kew-il's eyes narrowed, his muscles tensed, and once again he lunged.

This time his drive was not to be denied, and he plunged his knife into Renno's left shoulder.

The shock was numbing, the pain excruciating, but Renno gave no sign that he had been injured. Neither faltering nor pausing to conserve his fast-ebbing strength, he renewed his own assault. Deborah ached for him. Although surprisingly little blood was flowing from his cut, the wound was deep, and she knew he was suffering from a severe handicap.

Renno was more conscious of his disadvantage

than were any of the spectators, much less his foe. A mounting grogginess combined with waves of nausea told him that he would lose consciousness within a short time, and then his opponent would be able to slit his throat, plant a knife in his heart, and proclaim himself the victor. To survive, Renno had to destroy the bigger man instantly.

Mustering his last reserves, Renno threw himself at Mi-kew-il in a cold fury, his left arm dangling help-lessly at his side, his right arm darting and stabbing. His timing and aim had to be perfect.

He ignored the possibility that he would suffer another wound, and feinting again, then yet again, he eluded the other's guard and thrust his blade to the hilt into his foe's body.

Mi-kew-il staggered backward, clutching his mid-riff. Renno saw his chance and struck again, his knife cutting into the older man's heart, and Mi-kew-il was dead even before he crumpled to the ground, blood gushing from his wounds.

Woozy and bleary-eyed, scarcely able to see, Ren-no dropped to one knee and cut off the long plaited rope of hair from his foe's scalp lock. Only now was his honor avenged.

This final symbolic act completed, Renno collapsed.

Deborah leaped forward, pushed aside a senior warrior's spear, and dropped to the ground beside Renno, cradling his head in her lap. His breathing was shallow, and he was very pale beneath his sun-darkened skin.

No one tried to remove the girl from the field, and Ena soon materialized beside her, outwardly calm. "My son lives," she declared.

"He's been badly hurt!" Deborah cried.

"He lives." The statement was flat and unequivocal.

El-i-chi and several other full warriors of the Bear Clan came onto the field and formed an improvised litter by interlocking forearms, each gripping the wrist of another. Renno was lifted onto this human stretcher and carried back to the town at a stately pace.

Deborah and Ena walked directly behind them, and soon they were joined by Sah-nee-wa and a stricken Ba-lin-ta, who was finding it almost impossible to refrain from bursting into tears. Only Ghonka, still surrounded by his war chiefs as he made ready to go back to the town, was seemingly unruffled.

Iala and the members of her family were responsible for disposing of Mi-kew-il's remains. Having lost the fight, he was not entitled to an honorable burial with his weapons, so they would take his spirit and send it to wander for all time through the wilderness, never to rest or know another home.

Renno was taken to the pallet in his own dwelling, and there Ena went to work at once. Opening the pouch she carried around her neck, she crumbled the dried herbs over her son's face and body, all the while chanting an incantation in which she asked the mother-earth and the father-sun to restore his health.

Deborah was impatient with what she regarded as nonsensical mumbo-jumbo. The lack of bleeding worried her, and she thought it essential that hot poultices be applied to Renno's shoulder as quickly as possible.

Before she could intervene or express her thoughts, approaching drums sounded, and soon the small hut was filled with gesticulating medicine men, all wearing carved wood masks with grotesque features. As they chanted, they blew ashes on Renno.

Deborah became infuriated. "Stop it!" she cried, but no one heard her above the uproar.

The medicine men, doing their duty in spite of the sympathies that some of them had shown for Mi-kew-il, finally withdrew. Ghonka came into the hut, joined by Sah-nee-wa, El-i-chi, and Ba-lin-ta. Forming a circle around Renno, they followed Ena's lead and chanted interminably as they prayed to scores of manitous of the earth and the sky, the wilderness and the seasons.

Deborah's alarm increased. Renno's breathing was labored now, his shoulder swelling badly, and touching his forehead, she knew he was suffering from a rising fever. He would die unless he received the right assistance.

"Please," she begged, her desperation making her more fluent than ever in the Seneca tongue, "let me help him in my own way before it is too late."

"No," Ena said. "If it is the wish of the manitous, my son will live."

"Only the manitous can save him," Ghonka added ponderously, then accompanied his wife out of the hut.

They were followed by El-i-chi and Ba-lin-ta, whose sorrow made it plain that they believed Renno would die.

Only Sah-nee-wa remained with Deborah, and she stared hard at the girl. "Is it truly your wish," she demanded, "that Renno awakens from his sleep and becomes strong again?"

"Oh, yes!" Deborah was shocked by the unexpected question.

"I have seen what others have not seen," the old woman said. "De-bo-rah sleeps in this place, but she is not really the woman of Renno. She refused to become his woman, and that is why he went off on his long hunting trip."

It was impossible for the girl to deny the truth of the shrewd observation.

Sah-nee-wa was persistent. "If Renno lives, is it now the wish of De-bo-rah to become his woman?"

Deborah met the searching eyes without flinching, but it required great effort for her to reply. "It is my wish to become his woman."

The old woman continued to study her. "Very well," she said at last, "I will go and tell Ghonka and Ena to permit you to help Renno in your own way."

Deborah took her tattered Fort Springfield dress from a peg and began to tear it into strips. She had recently washed it and had been saving it for her return to civilization, but she needed it now for a more urgent purpose.

Ena came silently into the hut, accompanied by a frightened Ba-lin-ta.

"Help me, please," Deborah said.

Ena seated herself on the ground and folded her arms across her breasts. Evidently she was prepared only to judge, not to assist.

"I will help," Ba-lin-ta said in a small voice.

"Quickly, then, put two pots of water on the fire," Deborah said. "And while the water is boiling, go to the storehouse and bring me a gourd filled with the old juice of the grape."

Ba-lin-ta did as she was directed, filling two clay pots with water and placing them on the fire, to which she added more wood before she sprinted off to the storehouses.

Deborah knew the Indians drank no wine, but they used the fermented grape juice for the preservation of meats and fish for use in winter. She would have preferred the stronger brandywine that physicians at Fort Springfield and elsewhere always poured onto wounds before performing surgery. She had no idea why they did this, but she intended to follow their procedures.

Several hours had passed since the fight. Renno's shoulder was so badly swollen that it was almost twice its normal size, and she could hear a rattle in his raspy breathing.

When Deborah finished tearing the dress into strips, she dipped a strip into one of the pots of water that was now steaming on the fire, and she folded it into a poultice, which she placed on Renno's shoulder.

He was still unconscious, and he made no move.

As the water became hotter, the girl had to use a ladle for her next poultices.

The swelling in the shoulder continued to increase, and there was a dangerous gleam in the eyes of the silent Ena.

It occurred to Deborah that she was taking a great risk. If Renno expired, she would be held responsible, and his family would put her to death, probably with their own hands.

It would be so easy to do nothing now and let him die, but she could not.

Ba-lin-ta returned with the gourd of fermented grape juice.

"More water," Deborah told her, continuing to apply the poultices.

The child followed instructions.

Replacing each burning-hot poultice as soon as it began to cool, Deborah judged that the time had come for the next step, and picking up the gourd of wine, she poured a quantity of it into the open wound.

Then she took the steel knife one of the warriors had replaced in Renno's belt, and plunging it into a pot of boiling water, she held it there until the hilt became almost too hot for her to hold.

Steadying herself for what she knew she had to do, Deborah slowly and deliberately inserted the blade into the wound.

Ba-lin-ta gasped.

Ena's eyes glittered.

Deborah withdrew the blade, and as she did a stream of thick yellow liquid began to pour out. Enormous quantities followed.

The girl cleaned the knife, then placed it with the young warrior's other weapons.

By now the flow of yellow liquid was reduced, and after a time it turned to clean red blood.

She let the blood flow a little longer, then began to place steaming poultices on the wound again.

She had no idea how long she worked, but the swelling slowly shrank until the shoulder looked only slightly larger than normal.

For the first time Renno groaned and stirred.

"Now I will help," Ena said with a faint smile. She rose, plunged a strip of cloth into the boiling water, and calmly removing it with her hand, formed it into a poultice and applied it to her son's shoulder.

A sudden feeling of relief combined with fatigue made Deborah weak.

"Ba-lin-ta," Ena said, "go to our house and bring food for De-bo-rah and me."

Grinning now, the child hurried away.

The tension between the women was gone, and all night they took turns applying hot poultices, halting for only brief periods.

A short time before dawn, Deborah decided the wound had to be drained again, so she used the knife a second time. More yellow liquid appeared, but far less than before.

By daybreak, Renno's breathing and color were normal, and his forehead was cool. His shoulder, although blistered by the poultices that were still being applied, was now its normal size.

"I think," said Deborah, "the time has come to use some of the plants-that-make-good-medicine."

Ena nodded, then went off to her own dwelling for some healing herbs. When she returned, she crumbled them into a powder, and Deborah packed the wound with the substance.

Again Renno groaned, but this time the sound was soft, his suffering minor.

"Now he will sleep the sleep of the strong," Ena said as she stood up.

Deborah rose, too, her joints stiff and her arms and legs aching.

"The woman of Renno is now the daughter of Ghonka and Ena." And Ena embraced her.

Deborah clung to her. These people might be savages according to Aunt Ida's standards, but they were accepting her without qualification now, and she glowed with a deep sense of satisfaction.

Ena departed, sending Ba-lin-ta back with another meal.

Deborah resumed her vigil. She placed a bandage on Renno's shoulder but did not otherwise disturb him.

There was no doubt in her mind that he would recover, and she rejoiced for him. This was not the time to think of the complexities of her own involvement with him.

Renno dreamed incessantly—vague shapes, shadows, and figures appearing before him. Repeatedly they were on the verge of becoming clearer, but the throbbing pain in his shoulder was so intense and so persistent that it was impossible for him to think.

The agony subsided, and he fell into a deep sleep.

As he began to come up again through layers of consciousness, he felt hope that the Great False Face with corn-silk hair would appear before him and reveal his future. Occasionally he thought he caught a fleeting glimpse of the image, but each time it faded and he fell deeper into sleep again.

Then he began to awaken, his mind no longer fuzzy. Now there was only a dull ache in his shoulder, and he felt certain that he caught sight of the Great False Face.

At last the image of his youth had returned to him!

Renno opened his eyes, focusing on the intense blue eyes, waiting for the image to speak. A shock of recognition stung him. The figure bending above him was no image, but a living young woman with pale hair and blue eyes: De-bo-rah!

She returned his gaze steadily, relief and much more in her expression.

Renno tried to understand the look, but he knew too little about females. All he knew was that his destiny lay in De-bo-rah's eyes, and he felt a deep contentment as he dropped off to sleep again.

Whenever he awakened, De-bo-rah was present. Sometimes she gave him water or thin broth. Sometimes she changed the bandage on his shoulder, her touch light and gentle. As he began to regain strength, she fed him his meals, and sometimes he recognized her cooking, sometimes the cooking of his mother.

Ena visited him frequently, confining herself to short stays, and Sah-nee-wa followed her example. El-i-chi and Ba-lin-ta would have lingered for long periods, but Deborah sent them away, and Renno was surprised when they obeyed her without a murmur.

Then, about three days after he regained consciousness, he received a visit from his father.

Ghonka sat cross-legged on the ground beside his son's pallet, silent for a long time.

Deborah hovered in the background.

At last the Great Sachem spoke. "My son fought with the courage of the lion and the bear," he said. "No man has ever fought with greater courage, and no man will call him a coward again."

Renno could have asked for no greater praise.

"The family of Mi-kew-il has burned his weapons and his cape," Ghonka said. "His name will not be spoken again in the songs of the Buffalo Clan. The memory of him has died with him."

Renno nodded gravely. No punishment was more terrible than the erasure of the memory of an individual from the minds of his family and clan.

Deborah could make out Ghonka's words, but his meaning escaped her. No matter, because Renno was quietly pleased.

"The council held a meeting yesterday," the Great Sachem said, "and it was decided that Iala and her family must move to the far town of our people. The medicine men will elect a new leader. By tomorrow the troublemaker and her family will be gone and will never return to this place."

"That is good," Renno said.

Ghonka, becoming increasingly talkative, launched into a detailed account of other decisions made by the council regarding the quantities of meat and grain to be stored for what was expected to be a long and severe winter.

"Do we have enough metal arrows and magic powder for the firesticks to last us for the winter?" said Renno.

"We have enough," Ghonka assured him and went on to tell him about an exceptionally successful hunt that had resulted in the slaughter of forty-three deer and elk. There would be no shortage of meat this winter.

Deborah saw that Renno was tiring, and she intervened quietly but firmly. "The Great Sachem," she said, "will want to pay many visits to his son. But he does not want to stay now because his son must sleep."

Her audacity made Renno fear for her. No one in the land of the Seneca—or anywhere else in the territories of the Iroquois League—ever gave orders to his father.

Ghonka surprised him by chuckling and rising instantly to his feet. "De-bo-rah is right," he said meekly, and he bade his son farewell and departed.

As the astonished Renno grew drowsy, it occurred to him that no one other than his mother had ever handled the Great Sachem with such deftness.

That night Deborah allowed her patient to feed himself, helping him only when she saw that the effort was becoming too great. No matter what time of day or night Renno awakened, she was there, anticipating his needs, helping him.

His convalescence was rapid, and as his shoulder healed, the soreness vanished. But it was still stiff, and Deborah wouldn't yet permit him to exercise it. He found himself obedient to her wishes, even though he couldn't understand why he always did her bidding.

The autumn was advanced when Renno began to take walks, first within the confines of the town and then to the fields and forest. Deborah always accompanied him, and the Seneca came to regard the couple as inseparable.

No one guessed the girl's mounting anxiety. The time was fast approaching when she would be obliged to keep her silent pledge to Renno.

Soon she began to allow him to exercise his stiff shoulder, cautioning him not to push too hard. "You will heal more surely if you mend slowly," she said, and he knew she was right, so he continued to follow her advice.

The day Renno began to shoot arrows with his left hand to make his shoulder more limber Deborah knew his cure was virtually complete. Her apprehension mounted, yet she knew she was required by Seneca custom to make the first move. She had learned that much from her mistakes of the past.

One morning Renno went alone to the fields to practice with his bow and arrow. The day was cold, so Deborah built up the fire. Then she let her hair hang free, and she donned the antler necklace Renno had made for her. Her nervousness so great that she could not sit still, she swept the dwelling, and then she brushed her hair for a long time, removing nonexistent snarls, using a brush made of animal bristles that was given to her by Ghonka and Ena.

Renno returned after several hours and gratefully went straight to the warm fire. "It is the wish of Ghonka and Ena that we come to their house for food this day," he said.

"We will go," Deborah said. "Ena has already told me of her wish."

Now! She could delay no longer!

The girl forced herself to approach him, and she walked over and stood directly in front of him.

He looked at her, a puzzled expression in his eyes. Her silence, coupled with the deliberateness of her movements, was confusing.

She raised her hands slowly to her face, then touched her cheeks lightly.

Renno stared harder at her, comprehension dawning.

The most difficult gesture remained to be performed. Deborah took a deep breath, then removed her skirt and shirt and stood before him in the nude.

For a long moment Renno was as immobile as a carved wooden face mask, gaping at this extraordinary young woman who had saved his life and nursed him back to health. Not only was she beautiful, the living personification of all that was worth remembering in the image that had visited him, but he would be grateful to her as long as he lived for the devotion she had shown him. Now she was giving herself to him freely, and he was overwhelmed. Then his desire for her swept aside all rational thought.

He hurried to the far side of the dwelling and returned with several buffalo robes, which he spread on the ground near the fire. Scarcely able to curb his own feverish haste, he took off his shirt and loincloth.

Deborah was incapable of taking further initiative. The rest was up to him, and he did not disappoint her. Somewhat clumsily, but with surprising tenderness, he pulled her to him.

She responded willingly, even though she was more than a little frightened. Then, as he embraced her, all her fears dissipated and she, too, became immersed in the moment.

They kissed, and then instinct came to their rescue and they became more tender, their lips and tongues exploring gently.

Their bodies pressed together, their desire mounting, and with one accord they sank to the buffalo robes near the burning logs.

Renno knew only that this was far different from his visits to the special longhouse. His relations with the women there had been impersonal, stemming solely from his need to relieve physical urges. Here his emotions were at work, too. He was no longer capable of thinking logically, and as he caressed this lovely girl he felt as though the flames of the nearby fire were consuming him.

By now Deborah had cast aside the inhibitions instilled in her from earliest childhood. If she was a wanton, she no longer cared. All she knew was that she wanted this white Indian as much as he wanted her, and she succumbed to all that was primitive in her own nature.

Just when she thought she could wait no longer, he took her. Their bodies straining, their souls mated, too, and Deborah had no idea that she screamed aloud, any more than Renno knew that his deep moan mingled with the sound of her voice.

In their euphoria, they lingered on the buffalo robes, making love a second time in a leisurely manner, then varying the pace with a third session, swift and violent, that matched yet another surge of passion.

At last the time approached when they were expected at the house of Ghonka and Ena. They used warmed water for bathing, a concession to the world of the pale skins, and at last, fully attired again, they walked sedately across the town. Now it was Deborah's turn to observe the customs of others, so she followed Renno demurely, remaining several paces behind him.

They sat together at the meal, and somehow their shoulders touched frequently, their arms brushed, and without quite realizing what they were doing, they leaned toward each other.

Sah-nee-wa ate calmly, saying nothing, but watching everything, and late in the meal her eyes met those of Deborah.

The eyes of the old woman were eloquent, and Deborah knew now that she had truly become the woman of the white Indian.

Chapter XI

"**K**ing William of England is the natural enemy of France, General!" said Colonel Alain de Gramont, rubbing his hands together as he stood near the blazing hearth in the lounge of the Citadel suite used by senior officers. "His accession to the throne in London guarantees a full war between us. Paris knows it, and we know it. We must be prepared for a struggle that will either win Boston and New York Town for us or will see the Union Jack flying over our heads here. Those are the stakes, General, and nothing less than domination of the continent will be sufficient."

Henri, Duc de Vendôme and bastard cousin of Louis XIV, was an old man with a distinguished military record. His tart tongue had made him so unpopular at the French royal court that he had been given nominal command of the King's forces in the New World. Too old for active service, hating Quebec's cold winters and hot summers, he bore his honorable exile with his customary fortitude. Although he was crippled by various debilitating physical ailments, he still had the analytical mind that had won him a permanent place in the military history of his country. Puffing thoughtfully on his clay pipe, he propped his gout-ridden foot on a stool.

Most of these young glory-seekers were alike, yet the general had to admit that Gramont was different. His hatred for the English and for the Indian nations south of French territories never abated, and he was developing into a first-class strategist. Unfortunately, he was too rough and blunt for service in France, which meant he would spend his entire career in America.

"I have King Louis's personal promise that in the spring we'll be sent two more regiments of infantry and at least one battalion of cavalry," he said. "I think it unlikely that we can squeeze more out of Paris. I quite agree there will be a major war now, but the principal struggle will take place in Europe, not here, and it will be impossible to persuade the high command to weaken the army at home by sending us significant numbers of reinforcements."

Alain de Gramont was contemptuous. "We can't capture Boston with two new regiments of foot soldiers and a few horsemen, sir! You know it as well as I do!"

A faint smile lighted Vendôme's craggy features. "Patience, my dear Colonel," he said. "When a door is closed at one approach to a goal, the wise officer finds and opens another door."

The younger man paused. At least he and his immediate superior shared the same aims, which was more than he could say for the pleasure-seeking Governor Chambertin.

"The English colonies suffer from a similar handicap," the general declared. "London, like Paris, regards Europe as the center of the world. Neither understands that the natural resources and soil of this

continent make North America the land of the future
—and that whoever controls it will achieve true domination. London will give William's new subjects no
more material aid than we can get from Paris. But the
English colonists hold one advantage—their larger
numbers—which we can use to our benefit."

Alain de Gramont was bewildered by the con-
tradictory statement, and he wondered whether some
of the younger officers might have been right when
they whispered that the Duc de Vendôme was becoming senile.

The general promptly demonstrated that he was
very much in his right mind. "We would commit military suicide if we launched a campaign to take Boston
and New York Town. Therefore, we must not go to
the enemy; we must bring the English colonists to us.
Because of their greater numbers, they will be less reluctant to send an expedition into Canada than we
would be to march against them."

"How do we stand to benefit, General?" Gramont
was no longer disdainful.

"They lack our military discipline, and many of
their militia are not accustomed to life in the wilderness, so they will suffer on the march. In these ac-
cursed Canadian winters, they will freeze, and in our
vile summers they will melt."

At last Alain de Gramont began to grasp what his
superior had in mind. He laughed harshly. "And those
who stay healthy will attack the Citadel, an impregnable fortress."

"When they retreat, as retreat they must," Vendôme said, watching the logs blazing in the hearth, "I
feel confident that you and your Indians will know
how to inflict even further casualties on them."

Gramont's eyes gleamed. "My Huron will need

no instructions, and the Ottawa will not be slow to follow their example. We can kill twice as many as will lose their lives assaulting the Citadel!"

"See to it," the general said bluntly, "and all our problems will be solved. The English will become too weak to defend Boston and New York and their smaller towns, and when that happens, even the sleeping leaders of the high command in Paris will awaken to the opportunities that have opened to us here."

"Your plan is brilliant, General. I congratulate you, and I shall lose no time goading the English into sending an expedition against us."

"Very well, but be careful, Colonel."

"Careful of what, sir?"

"Sometimes you allow your loathing of your enemies to cloud your judgment. Take care not to incite the nations of the Iroquois League. They're already acquiring arms from Boston and Fort Albany, which makes them doubly dangerous. If they should send a large force to join the English colonists in a march on Quebec, the outcome might well be in doubt."

Alain de Gramont made no attempt to conceal his anger. "No Iroquois warriors, not even the Seneca, are a match for my Huron!"

The old man shook his head wearily. "I don't dispute you, but I choose not to put your claim to the test, Colonel. Our task would be badly complicated if Seneca and Mohawk by the hundreds were to join the English colonists on the warpath. I forbid you to taunt them. Our enterprise will succeed only if the odds remain in our favor."

Since the untimely death of Agnes Hibbard, when it came to preparing meals for important guests, Mildred Wilson worked in the kitchen herself, spending several hours at the charcoal and wood-burning stoves before hurrying back to change her clothes for dinner. This night, however, she was delayed when she encountered her son in the corridor.

Jeffrey's eyes were glazed, his step unsteady, and Mildred knew at a glance that he had been at Haggerty's tavern in Fort Springfield. The proprietor of the place was reluctant to serve him, but because of Andrew Wilson's prominence in the community, Haggerty felt he couldn't refuse the young man.

"I see you've been idling away another day, Jeffrey," Mildred said. "Your father could have used your help harvesting the pumpkins and late corn."

"Papa has enough hired hands," her son replied, trying to edge past her.

She continued to block his path. "I'd ask your father to speak to you, but he has vital matters on his mind, and I don't want to distract him." She wondered, as she often had, how her son and Andrew's could have become so lacking in any sense of responsibility.

He was useless in life on the frontier, and she was tempted to let him return to London, where he might mature once he grew tired of drinking and gaming and wenching. But something deep within Mildred refused to give in, and she continued to insist that Jeffrey remain, hoping for a miracle that would enable him to make a man of himself.

"If you have no more lectures for me, Mama," Jeffrey said, "I'd like to go to my room."

"Please do," she said, tight-lipped, "and see to it that you stay there for the evening. You're not fit company for our guest. Your father and I are tired of being embarrassed by your conduct and disgraced by your condition." She swept past him, unmindful of his glare.

Less than half an hour later, Brigadier William Pepperrell reached the Wilson house. Tom Hibbard took his horse to the stable, Andrew Wilson escorted the militia commander into the spacious drawing room, and Mildred, wearing one of her London-made gowns, greeted him cordially.

Pepperrell, dressed in frontier buckskins, preferred a small cup of sack to stronger drink. He settled himself beside the fire. "It's ladies like you, ma'am," he said, "who set the example for the fainthearted who are reluctant to set up their homes near the wilderness these days."

"I wouldn't dream of living anywhere else, any more than Andrew would," she replied.

"It's unfortunate that so many people are becoming discouraged by the new series of Indian raids," the brigadier said. "Everywhere I've been, from the Maine District and New Hampshire to Connecticut and New York, settlers are reacting in the same way. Those who have established farms and homes refuse to be driven out by the Indian raiders, but immigration to the frontier has virtually stopped. People are afraid."

"I can't blame them," Mildred said. "If it weren't for my confidence in Andrew and the militia he's trained here, Fort Springfield would be none too safe these days."

Andrew Wilson looked at the brigadier. "What strikes me, Will," he said, "is that all the raids follow the same pattern."

"No question about that," Pepperrell replied. "One or two men are killed, one or two houses are burned, but no prisoners are taken, and so far there's been no appreciable looting. These raids are being conducted for nuisance value alone."

"I hate to sound prejudiced against people who

may be innocent," Andrew replied, "but it's almost as though we're being challenged. Deliberately."

"That's absolutely correct. For a time I suspected the Seneca, perhaps the Mohawk, figuring that the firearms we sold them were making them overly bold, but that sort of conduct doesn't fit the pattern of any of the Iroquois nations." The brigadier shook his head. "They have their own code of honor, and we've given them no cause to raid our outposts and kill our settlers."

"From the descriptions I've heard," Andrew said, "the raiders appear to be Huron—and they have no valid reason for traveling this far from their own land only to harass us."

Brigadier Pepperrell stood, his gaze locked with that of his host. "Now we come to the crux of the matter, Andrew. The Huron might be responsible for an isolated attack here and there, but I'm convinced that this is a planned campaign being waged against us."

"All of which means," Andrew said soberly, "that the French in Quebec are behind the Huron, goading and prodding them."

Mildred looked at each of the men in turn. "But why would New France do something like that?" she asked. "We outnumber them; surely they don't want to provoke us into making war against them."

Andrew shrugged. "Human motives are sometimes hard to understand," he said. "Why will someone who is an inferior swordsman deliberately provoke an expert into fighting a duel? There's a perverse streak in people that's often beyond comprehension."

The brigadier smiled grimly. "I'd be inclined to agree with you, Andrew, but not in this instance. I've played a game of chess with the Duc de Vendôme across the border for many years, and I've learned how our Henri's mind works. Unless I'm very much mistaken, he's trying to challenge us into sending an expedition to march against Quebec."

"Oh, dear," Mildred said. "This is much too intricate for me."

Her husband caught the point. "We'd be taking grave risks by sending an expedition of any size all the way to Quebec, Will."

"Oh, we'll do it fast enough if we lose our tempers. Let these frontier attacks continue a few more months, and all the settlers in the wilderness lands will be so angry they'll demand that we punish Quebec and put a permanent halt to the killing."

"I don't deny that we could be goaded into launching a major campaign—in spite of the risks," said Andrew. "Our honor will demand it. The men who want to settle on the frontier will demand it for the safety of their wives and children. Even London will insist we do something specific once King William begins to realize that immigration to our colonies is grinding to a halt."

"We're not prepared for full-scale war," said Pepperrell. "The real purpose of this tour of mine has been to assess our strengths. Massachusetts Bay can enlist the help of New York, but no other colony will want to cooperate with us. Rhode Islanders are so bloody independent that they won't send one militiaman beyond their own borders. Connecticut will need to be convinced that the dangers are very great. And New Hampshire can't make up its mind. Only a shattering crisis will cause all of us to work together."

"Are you saying," asked Andrew, "that Massachusetts Bay and New York would be forced to carry the whole burden of a campaign?"

"No!" the brigadier retorted. "We'd be inviting certain catastrophe."

"Then how do we go about handling this problem?"

William Pepperrell sighed. "I don't know the answer."

"I'm afraid I can't suggest anything, Will."

"The reason I've come to see you, Andrew," Pepperrell said, "is because only you and I can solve this problem. No one else has our experience or our knowledge of all that's at stake. If my theory is correct, we've got to come up with a move that will checkmate the Duc de Vendôme. We may think of something overnight, or it may take months, and then we'll have to consider that move carefully before we make it."

"Until then," Andrew Wilson said, "these provocative raids will continue."

"God help us," said Pepperrell, "I'm afraid that indeed they will."

The winter was bitterly cold, the carpet of snow and ice on the ground thick, and the wind that blew steadily from the west was raw. But Deborah Alwin told herself she had no real cause for complaint. Certainly she was safer and more comfortable than she had dreamed she could be when the Huron had abducted her from Fort Springfield.

The hut was warm, the supper they had just consumed had been satisfying, and she knew she would never go hungry in the land of the Seneca.

Soon it would be time to retire, and Renno would make love to her before they dropped off to sleep. Deborah faced the issue squarely, forced to admit— without shame—that she would welcome his lovemaking, as she always did. She was still astonished that she and this white savage were such compatible sex partners, that each had the power to give the other complete gratification.

At the same time, Deborah was wise enough to know that a great deal was lacking in their overall relationship. Circumstances, combined with the unexpected compassion and kindness Renno had shown her, had caused her to become his partner, but now that the novelty had worn off, she was gaining a better understanding of herself and her position.

She knew she didn't really love Renno. To her, true love meant mutual compatibility in all things, and the gulf between them was too wide. He might have white skin, blue eyes, and hair almost as fair as her own, but he was still an Indian, incapable of understanding her ways, her thinking, her civilization. She found it impossible to know what he was thinking or why he might be thinking it, just as he had no idea of her mental processes or emotional needs.

Deborah's greatest fear, a terror that gnawed at her constantly, was that she might bear Renno's child and condemn herself to spend the rest of her days in this remote Seneca town, far from her own people. She could not tolerate the prospect that she, like Renno, might become a white Indian.

Renno watched the firelight playing on her face, and something in her expression gave him pause. He knew that in spite of her physical proximity she had drifted away from him.

"De-bo-rah is sad," he said at last.

The girl didn't want to lie to him, but she didn't know how to explain, so she merely nodded.

"You would like the mother of Renno to teach you to make moccasins?"

"She has taught me. And Sah-nee-wa," she added

before he could question her further, "has shown me how to make soft the meat of the buffalo that I will cook tomorrow night for your supper."

Renno felt she was drifting even farther from him, and he became confused.

"If Renno lived in the town of my people," she said, hoping she could communicate her feelings, "he would miss his family and his friends. He would miss his hunting trips with El-i-chi and his talks with the senior warriors."

All at once he knew. He remembered the story of an Erie woman captured by the Seneca, who had become the wife of a warrior and had been treated as an equal by everyone. But she had been unable to eat or sleep because she had missed her own tribe so much, and one day she had died, even though never mistreated.

"The words of De-bo-rah are true words." he said, getting to his feet. "I will think about them." Throwing his buffalo-skin cape over his shoulders, he walked out into the night, his departure so abrupt that Deborah could only hope her candor had not offended him.

Walking beyond the palisade and across the frozen fields, Renno made his way silently to a clearing that stood near the peak of a wooded hill. Here the air seemed even colder, but he was oblivious to the weather as he looked up at the stars that filled the blue-black sky. Strangely, he was not surprised by what the girl had revealed to him. When she had been unaware of his scrutiny, he had often seen the same lonely look in her eyes. Only Seneca women had been trained to tolerate any misfortunes that might befall them. De-bo-rah had demonstrated courage, but she was different. There was so much she didn't know about Seneca life, so much she had to learn. It was not surprising that Ba-lin-ta had become her constant companion, particularly during his own absences or frequent hunting trips, and that the child had become the young woman's instructor in the ways of the Seneca.

What troubled Renno was that De-bo-rah was his woman, which made him responsible for her. Had Iala or Anowara become his woman, he would have felt no concern because they were themselves Seneca, but De-bo-rah needed his protection and the help of his family in order to survive here.

He thought of asking the manitous for guidance, but he discarded the idea as rapidly as it occurred to him. A man was expected to solve any problems that might arise in his relations with a woman, and the spirits would mock him if he went to them for assistance.

Renno stood motionless, impervious to the cold, his arms folded across his chest beneath his cape. He realized that De-bo-rah was suffering from a sickness of the spirit, and somehow he knew that she was not blaming him. That much was a relief, but he had no idea how to solve her dilemma, no idea how to attack the problem.

The night passed slowly, and still Renno made no move. He heard an animal moving stealthily through the dry underbrush, but he ignored the sound. Renno continued thinking. A senior warrior was expected to know his own mind, so he could not go to Ena or Sah-nee-wa, for even though they might feel sorry for him, they would not respect him.

Little by little the sky became pale and turned to a muddy gray. A tiny speck appeared high overhead, and only one endowed with extraordinary eyesight could have seen it. Renno watched as it grew larger, and he felt no surprise when he saw it was a hawk.

Perhaps it was his hawk, the son of the Great False Face who was his mentor. He suppressed the thought, waiting to see what the bird would do.

The hawk flew lower, then lower, and circled twice above him, swooping down and soaring again.

Renno made no move.

The hawk flew toward the southeast, moving in a straight, unvarying line.

Renno continued to observe it until it vanished from sight. His burden was lifted, and he knew now what he must do. He returned to the sleeping town and made his way to his hut.

Pretending to be asleep, Deborah studied him as he removed his cape and sat before the fire, never once glancing in her direction. His expression was wooden, and she marveled again that the Seneca frequently could read the thoughts of their own people when she could see nothing in their eyes.

The day grew lighter, and the girl stirred, pretending to awaken. She thought it best not to indicate her awareness of his long absence from the hut.

"I will cook breakfast," she said.

Renno shook his head. "This day," he said, "I will eat with my father."

As he left the dwelling again, she knew that an important decision was about to be made.

The Great Sachem and his wife and daughter were eating their breakfast when Renno arrived, and Ena immediately made a place for her son to the left of his father, handing him a bowl of stew.

Renno ate in silence.

Ena gestured, and Ba-lin-ta followed her mother out of the hut, leaving Ghonka alone with his elder son.

The two men continued to sit in silence for a long time before Renno said, "De-bo-rah has a sickness of the spirit. She has not told me this, but she suffers because she misses her own people."

Ghonka chose his words with care. "What do you want to do with her?"

"I seek your permission to return her to her town."

"It was my hope," the Great Sachem said, "that De-bo-rah would become the wife of Renno because her skin is the color of your skin. But she is not a Seneca, so it may be for the best that she leave. You took her from the Huron, so it is your right to do with her as you wish."

Renno was satisfied, and he fell silent again.

Then Ghonka surprised him. "Renno will visit the land of the pale skins and learn their ways. He who is called Abe Tho-mas spent many moons here. Now Renno will go to their town."

Renno was so startled that he didn't know what to reply.

"Soon the day will come," Ghonka said, "when the Seneca and the other Iroquois nations will want many more firesticks and arrows of metal. We are not yet the friends of the pale skins and they are not yet the friends of the Seneca. But you will learn their ways and they will trust you. Then they will trust all of the Seneca."

Renno had to admit to himself that he was curious about the town and the ways of the pale skins, whose ancestors were his physical ancestors, even though he would never become one of them, would never abandon the Seneca.

"In a few moons," Ghonka said, "the English pale skins will ask the Iroquois to make a treaty of friendship with them."

Renno wondered how his father could make the prediction with such authority.

"Word has come from the small Seneca towns and from the Mohawk that war parties of the Huron have passed through their lands. The Huron have attacked many farms of the English pale skins."

"That is not the way of the Huron," his son replied.

The Great Sachem's nod confirmed the wisdom of the younger man's observation. "The French pale skins have paid the Huron to make these attacks."

No wonder Ghonka was the leader of the entire Iroquois! No other man in the League possessed his cunning.

"When the English pale skins ask for a treaty with us, I must go to the Iroquois Council. There the war chiefs and the elders and the medicine men will wait to hear the words of Ghonka before they decide. If it were on this day, I could not decide, for I need to know more about the English pale skins."

Now Renno began to understand what his father had in mind for him, and the Great Sachem spelled out his son's mission. "You will be my eyes. You will be my ears. You will tell me whether we can trust the English pale skins. You will help me decide whether we should try to buy firesticks from them or make a treaty with them."

Renno looked forward to the day when the Seneca, carrying many firesticks, would attack the Huron in force, but he would not let that desire color his judgment. He was being entrusted with a mission of great importance.

"You will take six full warriors with you when you return De-bo-rah to her people," Ghonka said. "You will allow no harm to come to her on the trail, and you will give her as a free gift to Wil-son, the sachem of the English pale skins. Then he will know you come to him with trust."

The matter was settled, and Renno returned to his hut to find Deborah finishing her breakfast. "In one day's time," he told her, "you will carry all that you own and you will come with me."

A sudden fear gripped the girl. She felt certain that he had become offended and planned to hand her over to some other tribe. "Where will you take me?"

He was surprised that she hadn't guessed their destination, but pale skins were a remarkably ignorant people in many ways. "I will take you to the town of your people, so your spirit will no longer be sick," he said, his tone slightly aggrieved.

Tears of joy and relief came to Deborah's eyes, and she tried in vain to blink them away.

Renno promptly turned his back so he would not see her disgrace herself. No woman of the Seneca would weep in a similar situation; it was just as well that their relationship was coming to an end.

All that day Deborah found it difficult to curb her mounting sense of excitement, and long before sundown she had made a bundle of her few possessions. That evening, she and Renno went to the dwelling of the Great Sachem for a final meal, and she tried in vain to thank Ena, Sah-nee-wa, and Ghonka for their many kindnesses. She was afraid she might burst into tears, and she didn't want them to think of her as weak, so she soon gave up the effort.

Sah-nee-wa divined what was in her mind. "It is good for De-bo-rah that she will go to her own people," she said, "but the hearts of the Seneca will be heavy."

The girl drew a deep breath, trying to control the tremor in her voice. "My heart will be heavy also."

Ghonka spoke the final word on the subject. "Always there will be a place for De-bo-rah at our cooking fires."

His words told her that she had won a permanent place in the affections of these Indians, and in spite of her eagerness to return to Massachusetts Bay she would miss them, something she wouldn't have imagined possible when she had first come here.

Thereafter, the adults ate in silence, and only El-i-chi, who was one of the full warriors assigned to escort Deborah back to her civilization, was cheerful. Ba-lin-ta enlivened the occasion by talking ceaselessly, scarcely pausing for breath. Her eyes wide and shining, she announced that someday she would visit Deborah, whose people she would surprise with her ability to speak their tongue. Deborah's broad smile told the child she would always be welcome at Fort Springfield.

When the meal ended, Ena extended a hand and placed it for an instant on the crown of Deborah's head. None of the others had any physical contact with her, no one spoke, and she parted from them in silence.

That night Renno was careful to sleep apart from Deborah, indicating that their relationship had changed.

They were awake long before dawn, and while Deborah reheated the previous day's stew for breakfast, she prepared for travel, taking care to wear the heavy leggings Ena had made her. As soon as the simple meal was done, she banked the fire, donned her hooded cape of buffalo skin, and was ready to leave. She carried the bundle containing her few spare clothes and other belongings on her back, for it was beneath the dignity of a senior warrior to be burdened with anything other than his weapons.

Renno, armed with a bow and arrows, a tomahawk and his metal knife, as well as his German-made musket, led the girl through the sleeping town to the palisade where the six full warriors were waiting. No greetings were exchanged as the braves formed a cordon around the girl and, with Renno in the lead, made their way across the frozen fields. They wore wide snow shoes to enable them to travel through the snow-swept wilderness.

Before they entered the forest, Deborah looked back over her shoulder, unable to see much except the thin plumes of smoke rising from the fires in the long-houses. Yes, she would miss this place, even though life here was primitive and brutal. She had matured to womanhood during her months with the Seneca, gaining a bettter understanding of herself as well as becoming more resilient. She could cope now with unexpected situations; she could exercise greater control of her fears; and she faced the future with new confidence.

She blamed neither Renno nor herself for the loss of her virginity. Their union had been natural. Aunt Ida might be shocked, but the girl herself felt no shame. Life with the Seneca, particularly her intimacy with Renno, had endowed her with a realism in which sham had no place.

Renno moved steadily through the forest, never slowing or halting, apparently unaware that he was setting a blistering pace. After several hours Deborah's legs began to ache, but she refused to complain, grimly determined to go on.

El-i-chi noticed her stumbling occasionally, and

moving to the head of the column, he murmured something to his brother.

Renno nodded, but he refused to compromise, and the march went on for another hour before he finally halted.

It was apparent to the girl that he expected her to keep up with the men and that he had no intention of catering to her. She had anticipated nothing less, but she realized anew the vastness of the gulf that separated him from the colonists she knew. All of them, without exception, would have deferred to her.

One of the warriors gave Deborah some dried venison strips and a handful of parched corn. The fare was tasteless, dry, and difficult to chew, but she forced herself to eat, scooping up snow to wash it down.

Renno drew apart to eat, and Deborah heard the sounds of an animal moving in the brush near him. She was startled, then alarmed, when an enormous brown bear materialized, and she caught her breath, certain she was about to witness a battle to the death. But Renno calmly approached the bear, one hand touching the claw necklace at his throat. To the girl's astonishment they stood facing each other, and Renno spoke at length in a soft voice.

The bear made no move to attack him, and when Renno had finished speaking they looked at each other for a long time. Then the bear lowered himself to all fours and lumbered away.

When the march was about to be resumed, Deborah could contain her curiosity no longer. "How did it happen," she asked, "that the bear who came out of the forest did not attack you? I thought you would have to kill him before he harmed you, but you actually seemed friendly with him."

Renno nodded as though nothing out of the ordinary had happened. "Ja-gonh, my brother," he said, "awakened from his winter sleep to wish me success in my visit to the land of the pale skins."

Watching him as he moved to the head of the column, Deborah knew she would never truly understand him. They had lived together for months, but he was still alien to her. His thoughts, his feelings, his whole approach to life were beyond her. It was right for them to part. It would have been the worst of mistakes for them to spend their lives together.

That afternoon Renno maintained the same brisk pace, and it dawned on the girl that he had reasons other than his own convenience. There was a sting in the wintry air, but by walking rapidly, just short of being forced to break into a run, she managed to stay warm. The chill created no problems for her, and she applauded the Seneca wisdom.

Shortly before sundown they halted near the shore of a small lake. Two of the warriors gathered dry wood and brush, two others made a fire, and El-i-chi, accompanied by the sixth, chopped holes in the ice that covered the surface of the lake and began to fish. Deborah knew her turn to work would come when the fish were caught. As the only woman in the party, she would be expected to clean and cook them.

As the watery winter light faded, she sat warming herself near the mounting fire, grateful to rest after the long day's march, when suddenly she heard a crackling sound in the underbrush. Renno and his warriors heard it, too, and reached for their weapons, and Deborah braced herself for an attack.

Instead, a bedraggled and sheepish little girl, bundled in a bulky fur cloak and wearing oversized snowshoes, hauled herself into the open. "I wanted to come now to the land of the pale skins," Ba-lin-ta said, "so I followed you all day." Apparently the child was afraid her brother might strike her, and she fled to Deborah, who enfolded her protectively.

Renno stared at the child.

El-i-chi and his companion, returning from the lake with an abundant catch, began to laugh, and El-i-chi called a greeting to his sister.

Renno's glare silenced him. "El-i-chi," he said, "send a message to our father on the drum that speaks. Tell him Ba-lin-ta has followed us. By now our mother must be worried about her. If it is his wish, we will return Ba-lin-ta to the town tomorrow."

Deborah had to admire the little girl's courage, but never had she seen Renno display such irritation.

Ba-lin-ta trembled in the older girl's embrace.

"Help me prepare the meal," Deborah whispered, determined to protect the child as best she could.

Together they scaled and split the fish and packed them in clay, which they placed on the coals of the fire.

Meanwhile El-i-chi pounded out a message on the party's one drum. The task took a long time, for obviously this was no ordinary communication.

Deborah and Ba-lin-ta exchanged glances as they heard the drums of distant, hidden Seneca outposts relaying the message to the Great Sachem. The little girl had to fight back a giggle, and Deborah wanted to laugh, too. They were joined in a conspiracy now, and both avoided the gaze of the stern-faced Renno. It was impossible to predict what he would do if they were to laugh aloud.

Only Ghonka would make the final decision, and the meal was almost ready before the party could make out the distant sound of drums, too far away to be interpreted. The young full warriors sat solemn-faced around the fire, and not even El-i-chi, who sympathized with his sister, showed any emotion. Renno stood with his back to the fire, ignoring everyone.

The return message was repeated, then repeated yet again by a closer drummer.

Ba-lin-ta's delighted shriek echoed through the forest. "My father allows me to go with you!" she told Deborah, hugging her. "Renno will bring me home when he returns!"

All the younger warriors relaxed now, and El-i-chi was plainly pleased that his sister had won her gamble.

Only Renno remained unyielding, accepting the Great Sachem's decision and the additional burden of responsibility it placed on him, yet in no way indicating his approval. At this moment, Deborah thought he looked remarkably like Ghonka, and it was no easier to read his mind than it was to probe the older man's thoughts. Renno's skin might be white, but he was more Indian than any of his comrades.

That night the two girls wrapped themselves in their buffalo capes and huddled together near the fire. Renno awakened them before dawn, and after a breakfast of the inevitable jerked venison and parched corn, the march was resumed. They were obliged to travel at a somewhat slower pace to accommodate Ba-lin-ta; it was astonishing that she had managed to follow so closely behind them the previous day, but the effort had exhausted her.

Renno was still annoyed, and he glowered at her occasionally, but late in the day, after El-i-chi and his partner returned from hunting and brought a pair of wild turkeys with them, he relented slightly. Carving one of the roasted turkeys with his metal knife, Renno made certain that the little girl received a generous portion, and for a moment a gleam of humor appeared in his eyes.

That brief signal was sufficient for Ba-lin-ta to know he had forgiven her. Until now she hadn't addressed him directly, but all through the meal she directed a stream of conversation at him, satisfied when an occasional nod indicated that he was listening to her.

On the fourth day of the journey the party was delayed by a heavy snowfall. Renno directed that a camp be made at the base of the eastern slope of a hill where there was some protection from the wind, and the warriors built a roaring fire.

Renno went hunting by himself and demonstrated his skill by returning a short time later with a large buck slung across his shoulders. While two of his subordinates butchered the carcass, Ba-lin-ta proved her worth to the party by discovering some edible roots nearby, and she cooked them near the edge of the fire while Deborah roasted the meat.

There was more than enough food to wait out the storm, and the entire party ate their fill. Then, to pass the time, Renno told a story about a great Seneca warrior who had lived many generations earlier and had performed such great feats of valor that the father-sun and mother-earth permitted him to return to the land of the living for one day each year.

He himself had seen the great warrior while hunting, Renno declared, and he repeated their conversation. Ba-lin-ta and the young warriors were wide-eyed, listening intently and believing every word.

At first Deborah was uncertain whether Renno was inventing a tale for everyone's amusement or whether he actually imagined that the incident had taken place. He was so serious, so scrupulous in his attention to detail that the girl concluded he had come to accept the incident as true.

When the trek was resumed the following day, Deborah and Ba-lin-ta carried what was left of the roasted meat. They encountered no other people, Indian or white, and Deborah was impressed anew with the vastness of the North American wilderness. Surely there was more than enough space here for the English colonists and the Iroquois nations to live side by side for generations to come.

Renno followed the route he had taken when he had escorted Abe Thomas home, and one day in mid-afternoon they reached the Connecticut River, and there was Fort Springfield on the other side. The Seneca stared in silence at the impressive bulk of the log fort.

Deborah wanted to go to the river's edge and shout, knowing that a boat would be sent for her and her companions, but Renno's dignity was ruffled, and he curtly vetoed the idea. "In the morning," he said, "we will take ourselves across the river."

Deborah realized that her homecoming would be delayed, but she had learned it was useless to argue with a senior warrior of the Seneca. "We'll have to be careful," she said, "that the sentries don't shoot at us."

He shook his head. "No one will shoot at us."

She thought he didn't understand. "They might think we're a raiding party intending to attack the town, and if they do, well, the sentries won't hesitate to fire at us."

"No one will see the Seneca," Renno said, "so no one will shoot at us."

The party retreated some distance into the forest on the west side of the river, and there a camp was made for the night.

314

Renno awakened the girls long before dawn, and Deborah was surprised to see that the warriors had fashioned a log raft so large and cumbersome that four of the young men had to carry it.

They traveled a considerable distance downstream, then floated the raft. Renno lifted Deborah and Ba-lin-ta onto it, and with the aid of makeshift poles, two of the warriors guided the craft across the water. There were chunks of ice floating in the river, some of them large enough to be dangerous, but the two braves negotiated the stream with nonchalant skill.

Dawn was breaking, and it crossed Deborah's mind that Renno had made good his boast. Presumably there were sentries on duty at the fort and, perhaps, in outposts up and down the river, but none seemed to be aware of the Seneca crossing.

The raft was beached on the eastern bank, and Deborah pointed. "This way is my home."

Renno allowed her to take the lead, but he took the precaution of walking beside her. He was still responsible for her safety, and even in her own land he was taking no chances.

In the early morning light Deborah saw a new little log house, built on the same spot as the old one. Joy swept over her in waves.

Smoke was rising from the chimney, and she paused to stare at the candlelight that she could make out dimly through the windows.

Ba-lin-ta, suddenly shy, came up beside her and clutched her hand.

Deborah felt as though she were dreaming as she walked slowly toward the house, the child still clinging to her.

Renno followed at a distance with his subordinates, then he halted and waited.

Taking a deep breath, Deborah rapped at the door.

Ida Alwin and the deaf-mute Walter were eating porridge and tea in front of the hearth when the tap sounded. Assuming that some neighbor was in trouble, the woman went to the door.

The sight of an Indian woman and child startled her, as did the presence of the armed warriors clustered behind them, and she tried to slam the door, but Deborah stepped across the threshold and threw back her hood. "Have I changed so much that you don't know me, Aunt Ida?"

Ida Alwin had shed no tears when her husband died or when she discovered that her only child was born with physical handicaps. She did not weep now. "Land sakes alive," she murmured, embracing her niece.

Then she became aware of a solemn-eyed Indian girl tugging at her apron. "I am Ba-lin-ta, the friend of De-bo-rah," the child said in English. "You are the aunt of De-bo-rah, and that is Wal-ter." Without hesitation she went to the boy and grinned at him.

The smile Walter gave her in return was dazzling.

"Land sakes alive," Aunt Ida repeated weakly.

Soon seven Seneca warriors were seated in a semicircle in front of the hearth, and Ida listened to Deborah's breathless account as the girl tried to tell her whole story at once.

"Wait!" Aunt Ida commanded, and even the Indians respected her tone. "It's enough for now that you're here, child. Help me get some food together for these—these ruffians."

"I will help, too," Ba-lin-ta said.

Deborah hugged and kissed Walter, then went to work carving a smoked ham. She had been home only a few minutes, but it was almost as though she had never gone through her incredible experiences.

Renno and the warriors tried the ham, but they found the taste alien, and the porridge didn't appeal to them, either. Instead they ate chunks of cold roasted venison that they took from the pouches hanging from their belts.

Aunt Ida was both fascinated and repelled by their lack of manners as they held the greasy meat in their hands, tearing at it with their strong teeth like a pack of dogs.

It was a shock for her to realize that the obvious leader of the party, his feathered headdress larger and more elaborate than those of his companions, had blue eyes and a blond scalp lock. It was evident, too, from the way he and Deborah occasionally exchanged glances, that they had enjoyed more than a passing acquaintance.

Aunt Ida warned herself not to make hasty judgments. Her prayers had been answered, her beloved niece had been restored to her, and for the present that was sufficient.

She was surprised at the way the little Indian girl was making herself at home. Carefully copying Walter, the child was cutting her smoked ham and eating it with a fork. What was more, she seemed to be enjoying the meal.

Ba-lin-ta was doing her best to communicate with Walter. Aware of his inability to hear or speak, she ate quickly, then tried to signal to him with her hands.

Walter, having used signs with his mother and cousin, knew what she was doing, and he made signs in return.

Aunt Ida could not bring herself to watch them.

"Ba-lin-ta will stay here with us, Aunt Ida," Deborah said in a firm tone. "She and her family were generous and good to me when I badly needed friends."

"Then she is more than welcome," the woman replied.

That much was settled. "Now, before I do anything else," Deborah said, "I must take Renno to Colonel Wilson. He has come here as the emissary of the Great Sachem on an important mission. The others will be returning to their own land immediately. Our kind of civilization makes them uneasy."

It was difficult for Aunt Ida to grasp so much at once. "It might be better if you stay here and let me send a neighbor to fetch the colonel," she said. "You might not be safe."

Deborah's laughter filled the room.

Renno stood and faced this woman who reminded him of Sah-nee-wa. If he wanted to establish trust in the land of the pale skins, it was important that there be no misunderstandings. "De-bo-rah," he said, speaking in slow but carefully enunciated English, "was the woman of Renno. She is safe with him."

Chapter XII

The return of Deborah Alwin to Fort Springfield created a sensation from the Maine District and New Hampshire all the way to the newest English colony, Pennsylvania, where settlers were beginning to move out into the wilderness beyond the recently established town of Philadelphia. In Boston, Governor William Shirley issued a formal proclamation stating that "the Seneca are an honorable people worthy of our highest respect."

Everyone in western Massachusetts Bay, or so it seemed, called at the little Alwin house to welcome Deborah back. She was gracious and charming, but she revealed little about her experiences other than to say that she had been kidnapped by Huron and then rescued by the Seneca, with whom she had made her home for months.

People noted that she sometimes spoke the Indian language with the little girl who had taken up residence in the Alwin house. Most of the visitors, including those who claimed they had no use for any

319

Naturals, were captivated by the child, whose command of English astonished them.

When the frontier dwellers tired of talking about Deborah, they turned to the subject of Renno. Not only had Andrew and Mildred Wilson taken the warrior into their house as an honored guest, but the visitor—who held a high rank in his own land and was the "son" of the leader of the entire Iroquois League—was actually a white man.

Both of Boston's recently established weekly newspapers speculated on his identity, and so much interest in him was generated in London that two plays about white men reared as savage Indians would be presented to audiences within the next year.

Ida Alwin said that Renno bore a strong resemblance to her old friends, Jed and Minnie Harper, who had died in the Great Massacre. Minnie had given birth to a boy only days before the terrible tragedy, but neither Aunt Ida nor any of the other survivors could remember whether or not the body of the infant had been found, so it was manifestly impossible to pursue the clue.

Inevitably there was gossip about Deborah and Renno. No one dared question the girl, and wise men preferred not to question the austere young savage about personal matters. Those who knew Aunt Ida best said that her tight-lipped silence was significant.

Abe Thomas was inclined to believe some of the rumors, principally because Deborah and Renno seemed so completely at ease with each other. Consequently, even though he discussed his feelings with no one, he was somewhat cool to the white Indian who had become his friend during his own sojourn in the land of the Seneca.

Obadiah Jenkins made his views on the matter plain to everyone. "We don't know what Deborah might have had to do, what compromises she may have been forced to make in order to survive in a strange and savage place. If she has trespassed in any way, I'm quite sure the Lord has forgiven her. Dare any of us do less? She has been restored to us safe and sound and whole, so let us rejoice for her and with her!"

Andrew Wilson was quick to seize the opportunity presented by Renno's unexpected appearance at Fort Springfield, and both Governor Shirley and Brigadier Pepperrell, with whom he communicated at once, were in hearty agreement. The white Indian was an instrument through whom closer bonds with the Iroquois nations could be forged.

The Huron attacks on frontier outposts were continuing, even in the dead of winter, and Colonel Wilson took pains to relate the stark facts to his guest. A full-scale alliance with the Seneca and their brother Iroquois was becoming a greater possibility.

Some of Fort Springfield's ladies felt sorry for Mildred Wilson, and they loved to talk about her problems as a hostess. The white Indian had been given a chamber furnished with a magnificent feather bed, but he slept on the floor beside it. He made no complaint about his meals, eating whatever he was served, but his table manners were revolting to some who were invited to dine at the Wilson house. He refused to drink anything other than water, and he had to be taught not to throw away a silver goblet after he emptied it. He had no use for a chamber pot, the ladies whispered, and went to the woods behind the Wilson stable to relieve himself.

No one could complain about his cleanliness,

however, even though he refused to use the buckets of heated water that the Wilsons' maids brought to his room. Instead, to the astonishment of the entire community, he calmly swam in the icy waters of the Connecticut River each day and apparently saw nothing out of the ordinary in the exploit.

He could not tolerate being confined in the small rooms for more than brief periods and frequently went into the open to breathe the cold, clean air. In deference to his host and hostess, he tried to sit on their divans and chairs, but he felt more comfortable when he lowered himself to a cross-legged position on the floor.

Renno's principal concession to the ways of civilization was his eager acceptance of a gift that Andrew Wilson presented to him. He discovered that a razor was a superb instrument, especially when used after applying a layer of soft yellow soap to his face and the portions of his head not covered by his scalp lock. He began to use his new razor regularly, although he insisted on keeping his metal knife sharp.

Andrew and Mildred went to great lengths to hide their son's contempt for the visitor. They had no idea that Renno knew precisely what Jeffrey Wilson thought of him, or that the Indian returned the feeling. Renno well remembered the young man who had tried to cheat him in friendly combat, but he was a guest in the Wilson house and therefore reluctant to challenge Jeffrey. He did not allow himself to forget that Ghonka had ordered him to learn from these pale skins and to establish friendly relations with them.

Renno was most impressed by the great fort, which he inspected on his second day in the town. Colonel Wilson acted as his guide, and not until Renno was shown the saws, hammers, and nails in use did he comprehend how men could have constructed such a structure. "All the trees of the forest," he said in English, "have come together to make this one place."

Several militiamen protested when the colonel planned to exhibit the fort's cannon to the visitor, but Andrew Wilson would not listen to them. "Are you afraid the Seneca will steal the secret of forging cannon from us?" he demanded. "What rubbish!"

Renno was awed by the firesticks that were so heavy they required three men to lift them onto wheels so they could be moved. And he shook his head when he saw round metal arrows the size of the melons cultivated by the women of the Seneca.

The colonel, using two cannon, put on a gunnery exhibition for the visitor, training both weapons on a barge that was anchored in the river some distance from the shore.

The roar of the first cannon was so loud that Renno was stunned. He couldn't see the huge metal arrow fly through the air, but the barge was unscathed, and he realized that the sachem of the pale skins was angry with the crew.

The shot of the second cannon was more accurate, and Andrew Wilson took his visitor down to the riverbank. The remains of the barge were hauled ashore, and Renno gaped at what had been stout logs, now reduced to kindling.

The English, he decided, could become valuable allies, just as the French would be ferocious foes. He remembered every detail to report to the Great Sachem.

The Wilsons invited Renno to accompany them to church on his first Sunday in Fort Springfield, and he created a stir by appearing in full war paint and regalia. He was armed with his bow, arrows, and knife, and only with difficulty was Andrew able to persuade him to leave his weapons in the front vestibule.

"We show respect for our God by not carrying our arms into His house," the colonel explained, and Renno reluctantly parted with his own weapons when he saw the muskets stacked in the entrance to the church.

Ba-lin-ta, wearing a dress that matched a new gown Deborah had just made, accompanied the Alwin family, and after crossing the aisle to hug her brother, she returned to her own pew and sat sedately beside Walter.

In Renno's opinion the hymns were dull, even though the entire congregation joined in the singing, and he thought they lacked the fervor of the Seneca chants. The prayers offered from the altar were more interesting, and although he found it difficult to understand some of the words, he realized that the English settlers asked of their God what the Indians requested from the manitous: bountiful crops, good health, the healing of the sick, peace between nations, and the serenity of the souls of the dead. Perhaps the pale skins were more like his own people than he had imagined.

He was fascinated by the sermon that Obadiah Jenkins preached. The clergyman rejoiced that Deborah had been returned safely to the colony, and Renno was deeply impressed when he and Ba-lin-ta were welcomed to the community. He liked the medicine man, he decided, just as he liked Sachem Wilson. They were honest, and he felt increasingly certain they could be trusted.

After the services, people gathered on the frozen earth of the lawn to chat, ignoring the cold, and again

Renno was reminded of the Seneca, who loved to stand around and gossip outside the community longhouse after a special occasion. The men had retrieved their weapons, and Renno felt more secure now that he was armed again. A number of people gaped at him, which he thought was rude, and his face at once became drained of expression.

Certain subtleties gradually dawned on him. Deborah was obviously popular, and people crowded around to congratulate her on her safe return. Abe Thomas kept his distance, Renno observed, not realizing that it was he who was the cause of the coolness.

Many people avoided the son of Sachem Wilson, and Renno couldn't blame them. Jeffrey Wilson glowered, exchanged curt nods with a few of the parishioners, and then went off on his horse in the direction of the town.

To Renno's surprise, another who was avoided was a young woman of about his own age who fascinated him because her eyes were green and her hair was red. Nettie was the first red-haired person he had ever seen, and in her own way, he decided, she was as pretty as Deborah. Only the medicine man spoke to her, going out of his way to be kind. Some of the men looked at her while pretending to take no notice, but the women looked through her without seeing her.

Nettie became aware of the white Indian's interest in her, and for a moment her gaze met his. She was bold, far more so than any of the other pale skins he had encountered, but at the same time she was shy, almost painfully withdrawn. While he pondered this strange contradiction, she lowered her eyes and quickly moved off, walking toward town. Her hips were swinging from side to side, and Renno, who had never seen such a gait, found it disturbing.

A number of guests came to the Wilson manor house for Sunday dinner, and Renno was pleased to discover that among them were the Alwins. Glasses of sack were served to the adults, but he preferred the berry juice that was given to Ba-lin-ta.

"Soon you will become a pale skin yourself," he told his sister, who wore her hair piled up on the back of her head, in imitation of Deborah.

He had the opportunity to speak privately with Deborah for a few moments, and he deliberately addressed her in the tongue of the Seneca. "You are happy now that you have returned to your people," he said.

"I am very happy," she assured him. "My heart will always be full of thanks to you."

Others were impressed by the girl's ability to speak the language of the Indians.

Obadiah Jenkins joined them. "It's wonderful that you brought Deborah back to us," he said to Renno. "And I can't tell you how pleased I am that you're paying us this visit. You belong here, too, you know."

Renno shook his head. "A Seneca remains a Seneca for all time," he replied gravely.

"No, you don't understand what I mean," the clergyman said. He paused. "Many bad people are doing wicked things that are bringing the English colonies and the nations of the Iroquois closer together. We need a bridge between our worlds. Renno, son of Ghonka, because you belong to both worlds, you are that bridge."

Ghonka had told him the same thing. Renno nodded. "What you say is true," he said; then he pointed to Ba-lin-ta, who stood in a corner with Walter.

The little girl was speaking to the boy, chattering in her usual fashion. Walter seemed to understand her, and Renno noted that she was tapping her fingers on the back of his hand and wrist. Perhaps her method of communication was not all that strange. The manitous favored those who could not hear or speak and sometimes made it possible for others to communicate with them in special ways. It was possible that the spirits had bestowed that gift on the child, but he could not offend the manitous by questioning her on the subject.

"The sister of Renno," he said, "will be a bridge, too."

Deborah smiled. "Ba-lin-ta soon will be as much a citizen of Massachusetts Bay as she is a Seneca. And she will always be both."

Renno was pleased by her depth of affection for his sister.

At dinner, the white Indian was seated next to Lieutenant Donald Doremus, the second-in-command of the militia, who owned the local inn. Sympathizing with Renno's discomfort, Doremus showed him how to spear food on his knife, making it unnecessary for him to use a fork as well, and Renno was duly grateful to him.

Portions of the meal were delicious. The soup was too thin for Renno's taste, and he was amazed by the pale skins' habit of cooking and serving vegetables separately instead of chopping them into bits and preparing them in one pot. But the roast turkey was the best he had ever eaten, and the beef, the first he had tasted, was even superior to elk chops or the steak of the buffalo.

His favorite was the bread—made of finely sifted wheat, far more delicate than Seneca bread of corn, and served hot. The pale skins spread a yellow substance on it, something made from the milk of cows, and

Renno could have made a whole meal of that and nothing else.

Curbing a desire to cram a whole slice of the buttered bread into his mouth, he watched the medicine man break off a small piece and eat it, and then he did the same.

Obadiah Jenkins, realizing he was being emulated, winked at the white Indian. Renno grinned in return, and at that moment they formed an unspoken bond. For reasons that Renno made no attempt to understand, the incident was as important to their mutual feeling as the medicine man's revelation to him that his skin was the same as that of these English colonists.

At one point Ba-lin-ta stunned the company by announcing quietly, "Walter would like more bread and another slice of turkey meat."

Everyone stared at her.

Aunt Ida caught her breath, then exercised great self-control as she asked quietly, "How do you know, child?"

"He told me," Ba-lin-ta said, exchanging a quiet grin with Walter, who nodded emphatically when he was served the additional portions.

It was true, Renno thought, the manitous had given Ba-lin-ta special powers to communicate with this boy.

When the conversation turned to politics and war, Colonel Wilson grew serious. "I'm totally convinced," he said, "that Brigadier Pepperrell is right in his assumption that the French are responsible for the Huron attacks on our settlements. Only last week a farm just fifty miles to the north of us was destroyed, and the two survivors have positively identified the raiders as Huron. The same war party apparently worked its way into New York and murdered a family living only a short distance from Fort Albany."

A gaunt Tom Hibbard, still grieving for his wife, had no idea that others could hear him as he murmured, "Every Huron town and village should be burned to the ground."

Renno found himself in hearty agreement with this man who worked for Sachem Wilson. "There will be no peace," he said, "until every Huron is dead."

Some of those present were surprised to hear such vindictive candor, but Andrew Wilson saw an opportunity to pursue the subject from another angle. "Renno, son of Ghonka, suppose we wanted to make the Huron our friends. How could we do this?"

"Those who are the friends of the Huron are the enemies of the Seneca," was his uncompromising reply.

The choice was plain, and a treaty with the Seneca—and through them the other Iroquois—seemed preferable to trying to wean the Huron from the side of the French. The colonel sighed. "We hope the Seneca will become our brothers."

Renno's expression was inscrutable. Only Deborah guessed, from his failure to indulge in any negative gesture, that such an alliance might be feasible.

The total destruction of an Indian nation was too staggering a concept for Andrew Wilson to contemplate, but the white Seneca might be able to provide him with some clue to how they could end the present attacks on isolated frontier farms. "Then how can we make peace with the Huron?" asked Andrew.

Renno's reply was incisive. "Take many scalps."

Andrew Wilson had no intention of revealing to the Seneca emissary that Massachusetts Bay lacked the means to wage a full-scale war. "If we and the Iroquois band together," he said thoughtfully, "perhaps we could persuade the French, the Huron, and the Ottawa not to cross our borders."

Renno considered the suggestion, aware that the entire group was listening. He knew nothing about the French, but he was certain that their Indian allies could not be cowed. "Only the Algonquian," he said, "pay peace wampum rather than fight. The Huron are not cowards; the Ottawa are not cowards."

The colonel realized that this should have been a private discussion, but now seemed the right time to speak his mind. "How could we and the Iroquois beat the French and their friends—without sending all of our warriors into battle against them?"

A hush settled over the company. Renno thought hard and long, but he knew that only war chiefs who had fought in countless battles could find the solution to a dilemma of this magnitude. "When I go back to the land of my people," he said, "I will ask the Great Sachem what you have asked me. He will listen to the voices of his council, and then he will tell me what to say."

A decision had to be reached by early spring, at the latest, the colonel reflected, in order to prevent the Duc de Vendôme and Alain de Gramont from taking the initiative. But he saw his wife frowning at him and knew he could not prolong the discussion in the presence of ladies who were becoming restless.

A welcome diversion was provided by the serving of the dessert, made from a recipe Mildred had developed. It was a deep-dish pie of apples, raisins, and currants, enriched with brown sugar and cinnamon and topped with thick cream.

Ba-lin-ta and Walter ate rapidly, and the little

girl announced that both were ready for another portion. Walter grinned at his new friend when their wish was fulfilled.

The pie was too sweet and too filling for Renno. He would have left the table immediately, but he remained because all the others stayed seated. The customs of the pale skins were foolish.

Andrew poured a mellow brandywine, brought to the colonies from England at great expense, into small crystal glasses, which he himself passed to the adult men.

Renno was astonished by the glasses, the first he had ever seen, and he hoped Mildred Wilson would give him two that he could take to his mother and Sah-nee-wa. Even the firesticks of the pale skins were less miraculous than these containers that were almost invisible but as strong as gourds or bowls of clay hardened by fire. The contents of the glasses did not appeal to him, however. They burned a man's mouth, then scorched his stomach, and he couldn't understand why the English found pleasure in torturing themselves.

Everyone adjourned to the parlor after the meal, and Mildred smiled to herself when she saw Ida Alwin place an arm around Ba-lin-ta's shoulders. The child's loving ebullience, combined with the close relationship she and Walter were establishing, were eroding Aunt Ida's hitherto uncompromising loathing for all Indians. If Aunt Ida could be influenced, the concept of an alliance with the Iroquois was not farfetched.

Renno saw the medicine man and Deborah exchange a few words, then noted the unguarded expression in the man's eyes after the girl turned away. Startled by the realization that Jenkins wanted Deborah as his woman, Renno nevertheless approved. They would be a good match, he thought, feeling no jealousy. He wanted and needed a woman himself, but he knew that he and Deborah would not sleep together again.

Renno wished the medicine man well, but decided not to mention the matter. He knew Abe Thomas was jealous of him, and he had no desire to lose the budding friendship he was forming with Jenkins. As for Deborah, she would make up her own mind. On the surface she seemed softer than Ena and Sah-nee-wa, but he had learned that in her own way she was equally as resilient and independent, and he had been wrong to think of her as weak. Deborah would mate only with a man she wanted, and she would resent Renno's expression of approval.

Without realizing what was happening to him, Renno was becoming more mature, but at the moment, he knew only that his body longed for physical exertion, so he suggested to Lieutenant Doremus that they go out into the open and practice throwing tomahawks, an art that the pale skin had expressed an interest in learning.

"Wait until Reverend Jenkins escorts the Alwin ladies home," Donald Doremus muttered under his breath. "He doesn't approve of sport on the Sabbath." Renno had no idea what that meant, but he forced himself to wait.

Just before Aunt Ida departed, she unbent sufficiently to ask Renno to have supper at her house later in the week. "I don't want you sneaking up on us and scaring us half to death. Reverend Jenkins is coming for supper, too, so he'll bring you. And see if you can't learn some table manners by then!"

Renno and Doremus slipped off into the woods behind the barn, and the white Indian demonstrated the art of tomahawk throwing. He performed with such ease, clipping small branches from trees, that the act looked simple, but to his dismay the young militia officer could not hit a target, and the blunt end of the blade frequently struck first.

The lesson continued, and Renno promised to make Doremus a tomahawk of his own. In return, the lieutenant demonstrated ways to reload a pistol or musket quickly after firing, and Renno went through the process many times until he mastered it. He would need to practice alone for days in order to become efficient, but now he had a new goal, and he was pleased.

Later, Doremus had a private talk with the colonel, explaining the young Seneca's eagerness to learn English methods of warfare, and the next morning Andrew Wilson took the visitor to the fort and turned him over to a gun crew. "By the time these lads are through with you," he said, "you'll know how to load, fire, and maintain a cannon."

Renno spent the day with the crew, and they taught him how to swab and clean a cannon, how to move it into position, and how to load it. The following morning, his instructors showed him how to aim by raising or lowering the gun's trajectory.

He was beginning to understand firearms, so he was not surprised when he was told that the distance a cannonball traveled depended on the size of the charge. They warned him not to make the mistake of using too much gunpowder. "These cannon ain't too reliable even at their best," said the sergeant in charge of the crew. "Every artilleryman knows of times when a gun has exploded and killed every lad nearby."

Not until the third day did Renno actually fire a cannon. First he cleaned the weapon, then he aimed it, and only then did he load it, leaping as far from the barrel as he could after applying a lighted taper to the fuse.

His first two shots landed harmlessly in the Connecticut River, far from the target barge. Renno's new comrades teased him, as did Lieutenant Doremus, who had come to the fort to watch the pupil at work. Determined not to look foolish again, Renno remembered everything he had been taught. He threw a bucket of water over the barrel to cool it, and then, with complete concentration, he changed its trajectory slightly. It was common knowledge that he was endowed with remarkable eyesight, so the crew fell silent as he made minute alterations in the angle of the barrel.

He measured a precise amount of powder, making certain it contained no lumps before he poured it; after gently rolling a cannonball into the barrel from the muzzle end, he lighted a taper with a marvelous pale-skin device called a tinderbox and flint. Applying the taper to the wick, he raced for the relative protection of a log barricade a few yards away.

The cannon roared, the smoke cleared, and from the ramparts the little group could see that the projectile had landed at the far end of the barge, crushing it.

"Lieutenant," the sergeant said, "this here lad is a natural-born soldier. The members of my crew have been working together for three years, and not one of 'em can aim a gun the way he does!"

Doremus invited the elated Renno to dine with him that afternoon at his inn. He had to leave now, he explained, because he was expecting some well-to-do merchants and traders to arrive at the inn.

The gun crew had work to do. None were full-time militiamen, they explained, but each volunteered for two days' service a week. The sergeant and one of the men had to get back to their farms; a third was an apothecary who had closed his shop for the morning; and the fourth, the oldest, served at the bar in Haggerty's tavern.

Renno walked into the town with the apothecary and the barman. "Come with me," the barman said, "and Haggerty will set you up a mug until it's time for you to join the lieutenant. His place is right across the street from us."

A number of people greeted Renno as they walked toward town, but many strangers merely stared at the blue-eyed painted warrior.

The main room at Haggerty's was large and cheerful, and a fire was roaring in the hearth. The unvarnished pine tables and the piles of rushes on the floor reminded Renno of the longhouses in his town. Three men, all of them expensively dressed, were seated at a table drinking from pewter mugs, and Renno noted that one was Jeffrey Wilson.

Haggerty himself was a barrel-chested, balding man, and after hearing of Renno's exploit as a cannoneer he chuckled and slapped the startled Seneca on the back, a gesture rightly interpreted by Renno as a sign of fellowship.

"Damned if I knew what to think when I heard that a white Indian had come to Fort Springfield," the taverner said, "but damned if blood doesn't always tell."

Renno did not understand what he meant.

He noticed Jeffrey and his companions peering toward the bar.

"Pay them no mind," Haggerty said in a low tone. "I'd throw young Wilson out if it wasn't for his pa being who he is. And the other two are worse. Land speculators who visit frontier towns and buy properties cheap from folks who get discouraged, then sell the land at a highway robber's prices to people back in the cities who don't know any better. They're real scum."

Renno knew nothing about land speculation, buying, or selling. It was enough that Haggerty, whom he liked, had a low opinion of all three, so he turned his back to them.

The barman poured the visitor a mug of ale, and Renno sniffed the contents dubiously and took a mouthful, but the taste was so vile that he spat the ale onto the floor. Jeffrey and his companions laughed loudly, but Renno remembered his mission and had no problem controlling himself.

The apologetic barman handed him a mug of cranberry juice, which was more to his liking, and as he sipped it Renno became aware of someone else in the taproom. It was the girl he had seen outside the church. The shimmering firelight played on her red hair, which was tumbling down her back in loose waves, and her low-cut gown that concealed less than it revealed of her breasts was strangely exciting. In summer, Seneca women frequently wore no shirts, so the sight of female breasts was no novelty to Renno, but this artful partial hiding was new to him, and his throat became dry. He noted, too, that the girl's lips were very red and her eyelids smudged with a pale green substance that emphasized the extraordinary green of her eyes.

Nettie returned Renno's gaze, her expression the same combination of boldness and shyness that he had observed on the church lawn. Somehow he was reminded of the women who lived in the special longhouse of the Seneca, but he dismissed the notion.

Haggerty chuckled. "So you take a fancy to our

Nettie, do you? Can't say as I blame you, lad. She's a choice morsel. But I warn you, she's mighty expensive, and she has a fierce pride. I let her rent quarters here because she brings in so much business, but there are those who are stung by the nettles before they can pick the peach from the tree."

The three seated men had transferred their attention to the girl, and Renno saw that Jeffrey Wilson was saying something to her.

"Mind your manners, Jeff Wilson," she said angrily. "You could be anything in this world and have whatever you wanted if you stopped your drinking and behaved yourself."

Again he said something, and his companions laughed.

"What's your price, tart?" one of them called. "Provided you do no talking, of course."

Nettie's temper flared. "You don't have that much gold in your purse, bucko, and you never will."

The land speculator went to her table, caught hold of her wrist, and cursing her, slapped her hard across the face.

"Here, now, none of that!" Haggerty called as he and the barman started forward.

Before they could advance more than a few paces, Renno was across the room like an arrow in swift flight. Neither the participants nor the spectators knew precisely what happened, but the land speculator was crumpled over the table, Jeffrey Wilson lay sprawled on the floor, and the third man was cowering behind a chair. Renno's eyes were cold, and he was not even breathing hard.

The barman expelled the frightened land speculator, then half carried, half dragged his groggy com-

panion to the door and threw him out, too. Haggerty
helped Jeffrey to his feet. "Wilson," he said, "you've
created trouble in my tavern for the last time. You're
no longer welcome here. Step inside that door again
and I'll have the constabulary lock you up as a
nuisance!"

Jeffrey sauntered out, donning his greatcoat, and
did not look back.

The barman handed Nettie a small glass of brandywine.

"I smelled trouble," Haggerty told her, "and I
should have rid us of them earlier. I'm sorry."

"It's no matter," she replied. "They weren't the
first to insult me and they won't be the last." She
gulped her drink in a single swallow, and no feat
could have impressed Renno more.

Nettie looked at him and said, "Thank you very
much. I'm in your debt."

The green of her eyes had a hypnotic effect on
him, and once again reminded him of the women who
lived in the special longhouse, he could not look away.

Haggerty and the barman exchanged a knowing
glance, then discreetly retreated.

"If you like," Nettie said, "come with me."

Somewhat confused, Renno followed her out of
the taproom and up a flight of stairs, his state of mind
further disturbed by her swaying hips. The girl led
him into a large room that was furnished with several
chairs, tables with oil lamps on them, and heavy
drapes that had been opened to admit the sullen winter
light. The chamber was dominated by a huge canopied
feather bed, the biggest sleeping place of the pale skins
that Renno had ever seen.

Nettie bolted the door, took a decanter and two

glasses from a shelf, and offered Renno a drink. He wanted no part of the burning liquid, and he shook his head.

As she had done in the taproom, the girl downed her own drink quickly. "Now, then," she said, "I hope you'll satisfy my curiosity. I've never seen a white man who dresses up as an Indian. Who are you?"

"I am Renno, senior warrior of the Seneca, the son of Ghonka, the Great Sachem."

She ran a slender hand through her hair.

Still uncertain that she believed him, he gestured toward the scalps hanging from his belt, aware that the English settlers regarded them as repugnant.

Nettie didn't seem to mind. "Oh, I know you aren't joking," she said, "but I can't help wondering. You do know you're white?"

"My skin is the color of your skin," Renno said with great dignity, "but I am a Seneca."

The girl seemed satisfied with his answer. "You're like me," she said.

Her words were simple enough, but their meaning eluded him. English settlers were less precise than the Indians in the meanings of what they said.

"Sit down." Nettie motioned him toward the most comfortable chair in the room. "I can't talk to people when I'm standing."

Renno would have preferred sitting on the floor, but he politely moved to a chair, puzzled by the young woman's intensity.

"God knows, I'm no lady," she said, "although there are those who tell me I look like one when I try. I earn my living the only way I can, the only way I've ever known. In London, in Boston, and now here. And I've never yet met the man who condemns me for it. In private, that is. When they see me at church or on the street they pretend they don't know I exist. If you see what I mean."

He shook his head. She was more than pretty, and he thought he saw in her the sensitivity he had found in Deborah, the quality that had been missing in Iala. But she still wasn't explaining herself in concrete terms.

"They pay my price—and it's high—when they want a whore," Nettie said. "The rest of the time they act like their wives. Their pious two-faced women are jealous of me, and that much I can understand. But it's the men I can't abide. If they hate me, let them be honest about it. What I can't tolerate is being treated like an animal."

Renno thought of Ja-gonh, the noble bear. "Many animals," he said, "are better than people."

Nettie's tension lessened, and she laughed. "I never thought of it that way, but you're right. Anyway, I just wanted to tell you that I know how you feel when scum like Jeffrey Wilson sneer at you because you're an Indian."

He was surprised, and the expression in her luminous eyes indicated that she really did understand. He stood and inclined his head, glad that he had come to her aid when she needed help. "You are my friend."

A dimple appeared directly below the beauty spot pasted on her cheek. "Not exactly." She walked to him and stood directly in front of him. "I won't pretend I'm returning a favor, but I want what you want."

Again he was puzzled.

Nettie realized she had to be even more blunt. "You're a man and I'm a woman."

Comprehension dawned, but he knew that men

paid her, and he had none of the wampum so important to the English colonists. He couldn't recall their word for wampum, so he showed her the empty pouch hanging from the belt of his loincloth.

Deliberately, slowly, she opened the thongs at the front of his shirt and slid her hand up and down his chest. "Sometimes I need a man, not just a client."

Renno needed no further urging. Already aroused, he carried her to the feather bed, guessing she would prefer it to the floor and wondering how he himself would like it. There he removed her clothes.

"You learn fast," Nettie said with a husky laugh.

From the outset their lovemaking was urgent, explosive. Renno couldn't recall wanting a woman so badly or feeling such a surge of desire. Apparently the girl felt as he did, and they found gratification together. Later, Renno wondered that the feather bed hadn't broken. He guessed that the furniture of the pale skins was sturdy.

"I knew it would be like this," Nettie murmured. "The trouble with me is, I'm greedy." Her hand slid up the inner side of Renno's thigh, enticing and teasing him.

Laughing aloud, he fondled her in return, and again their passion mounted swiftly, resulting in a climax as intense, a release as complete as their first experience together.

"I'll see you again before you leave Fort Springfield," Nettie said as they dressed. "You have no idea how much you've done for me. The good ladies and gentlemen of the town can snub me all they please now. I just don't care."

Renno was on time for his dinner at the inn, and Lieutenant Doremus noted that the visitor was relaxed, seemingly at home already in these surroundings that were so strange to him.

That week, Colonel Wilson broached the all-important subject to his guest. "Massachusetts Bay Colony," he said, "would like to make a treaty of alliance with the Seneca and the other Iroquois."

"I, too, would like this," Renno said, "but only the Great Sachem and the Iroquois Council will decide."

"Will they meet with me and our war chief, Brigadier Pepperrell?"

"My friend is always welcome in the land of the Seneca."

Andrew Wilson seized the opportunity, and it was agreed that he and his militia superior would pay a visit to Ghonka before the winter ended. "Tell the Great Sachem," he said, "that I hope we can work out a plan—together—that will make it possible for us to make war successfully on the French and their Indian allies before they launch a major attack on us."

Renno hoped that his father, the sachems of all the other Iroquois nations, and the pale skin war chief would agree to become allies, for he was eager to make war against the Huron, and he was also hoping to meet Golden Eagle. He now felt mature enough, strong enough, and clever enough to defeat the older white Indian in personal combat.

The future was very much on his mind on the evening that he accompanied Obadiah Jenkins to the Alwin house for supper. There, he noted that Ba-lin-ta and Walter had grown even closer, and Ba-lin-ta was becoming more expert in her interpretations of what the boy wanted to express.

Renno had some news that would probably make

his little sister unhappy, and he waited politely until the meal was finished before he spoke. Then, as Obadiah Jenkins lighted a pipe, Renno said to his sister in their own tongue, "In two days we will begin our journey to the land of our people."

Deborah quickly translated his words for the benefit of the clergyman and her aunt.

Ida Alwin was quick to express her disappointment. "We'll miss the child," she said. "I've enjoyed her so, and she's been wonderful with Walter."

Deborah nodded, and Obadiah said, "It's true. She can understand him in ways I can't even fathom."

Ba-lin-ta looked at each of the adults in turn, hoping they would support her before she said to her brother, "Wal-ter wants to come with us to the land of the Seneca. And I want him to come. He can live with us in the house of our father and mother."

Ida Alwin gasped. "But that's impossible! Walter is helpless. I dread to think of what might happen to him in a world of sav— I mean, of Indians."

"I don't agree, Aunt Ida." As always, Deborah didn't hesitate to express herself. "I know the Seneca, and I think Walter has a good chance of becoming more self-reliant among their people."

"My view hasn't been asked," Obadiah added, "but I think Deborah may be right. The Almighty has granted these two children the ability to communicate with each other. You can see the change in Walter. In a short time he's become so much more self-confident and independent. Don't you think it might be wrong to separate them now?"

Deborah reached out and squeezed the clergyman's hand in gratitude, then she drew back so he wouldn't think she had been too forward. Renno saw the expression in Obadiah's eyes. It was surprising that

343

neither the white medicine man nor Deborah realized that she would become his woman.

Ba-lin-ta waited for her brother to speak. In her view, the wishes of Walter's mother counted for less than the decisive opinion of a senior warrior.

Renno realized that Walter was watching him with anxious eyes.

"I—I'd be afraid," Ida said.

"The family of Renno and Ba-lin-ta treated me well," Deborah said quietly.

"But you aren't deaf and dumb!" Aunt Ida retorted.

"Colonel Wilson will go to visit the Great Sachem in the Seneca town in a few weeks in the hope that he can arrange an alliance," Obadiah said. "I'll gladly go with him again, if he'll have me, and I can bring Walter back with me."

Ba-lin-ta shook her head. "Wal-ter wishes to come for a long visit. It is also my wish that he stay in the land of the Seneca for many moons."

The boy's mother looked stricken.

Renno saw that everyone was waiting for him to speak, so he composed his thoughts carefully, folding his arms across his chest. "Those who cannot speak or hear," he said at last, "are granted other powers by the manitous. These people are given honor by the Seneca people. It may be that the manitous will come to Wal-ter in visions and will offer him their help."

Ba-lin-ta clapped her hands in glee and relief, and a gleam appeared in Walter's eyes.

Deborah was afraid that the idea of pagan deities would cause the clergyman to change his mind, but Obadiah surprised her.

"We must commit ourselves to the way of the Lord, which is full of mystery," he murmured. "It is not our place to tell Him what road He should take. Let the spirits of the Seneca help the child, I say. He would go with my blessing."

Ida's last defenses were shattered, and only her fear remained. She was torn, wanting a more normal life for her handicapped son, anxious to do what was best for him, but unable to help him herself. She bowed her head.

Renno knew how Sah-nee-wa would react in similar circumstances, and he felt sympathy for this proud woman. "No harm will come to Wal-ter," he said, making her a solemn pledge. "As Ba-lin-ta is the daughter of Ghonka, the Great Sachem, and Ena, the medicine woman, so will he be their son."

Aunt Ida could allow no one to see her weep, so she stood and turned toward the fire. She, who had hated Indians with such passion, was facing the dilemma of entrusting her precious son to the care of these people in the hope that they could do for him what his own people could not.

Ba-lin-ta went to her and silently took her hand, and the child's loving gesture swept away the last of Ida's reservations.

"Take my son with you, then," she said.

Ba-lin-ta and Walter danced and leaped around the room, but the adults remained somber out of deference to the boy's mother. Renno was pleased to accept his new responsibility, and he promised himself he would teach Walter to hunt, fish, and survive in the wilderness. With the manitous to guard him, the boy would flourish.

Later that night, when the Wilsons learned of the plan, they approved heartily. The colonel found a sharp double-edged knife that he wanted to present to Walter, and the following morning, Mildred, after conferring with Renno, began to prepare food for the journey. Strips of beef were smoked, bags of cornmeal—in lieu of parched corn—were packed, and a side of bacon was quartered. Renno insisted that no other food would be needed.

On the day before their departure, Renno discovered that Ida was sending Walter off with too many belongings, so he stripped the boy's gear to the essentials necessary for a winter march through the forest. He made certain that Walter's boots were oiled, and he allowed the boy to keep his yarn hat, vest, leather breeches, and the pea coat he used when he chopped wood for his mother. But two of his three blankets were discarded, as were the rusty black breeches and coat that he wore to church on Sundays. In response to the pleas of Ba-lin-ta, who was learning to read English, Renno permitted the packing of a Bible, a book of stories by a man called Chaucer, and a third book of something called poems by someone named Milton.

Andrew Wilson arose in time for a predawn breakfast with his guest, and then they gripped forearms. "In one moon's time," the colonel said, "our war chief and I will come to the town of the Great Sachem." Renno felt that his mission had been accomplished.

Ida Alwin's farewells were simple. She kissed Ba-lin-ta and remained dry-eyed as she embraced her son. Then she turned to Renno. "I think I'm doing this because Minnie and Jed Harper were such good people —and such close friends."

There was nothing more than friendship in Deborah's eyes as she said good-bye to Renno. "We shall meet again," she told him.

Militiamen rowed the travelers across the river, and the journey began. The first problem arose when

Walter, unable to hear, crashed loudly through the underbrush as they walked. But Ba-lin-ta explained things to him by drumming her fingers on the back of his wrist, and thereafter he watched the way Renno walked. The boy was surprisingly quick to learn, and by the end of the day he was much improved.

Renno soon discovered that Walter was endowed with eyesight almost equal to his own, as well as a keen sense of smell and a sensitive touch. Traveling at a leisurely pace, Renno took time each day to teach the boy to use a bow and arrow. Walter proved adept and agile, and one day he succeeded in killing a large rabbit, which Ba-lin-ta insisted on cooking for their supper. The little girl's cooking aptitude left much to be desired, but she and Walter ate heartily. Renno, watching them enjoy the fruits of their accomplishments, secretly ate strips of smoked beef.

The small party's approach to the Seneca town was heralded by drums, and the waiting crowd stared at Walter, whose eyes were shining with excitement.

Renno explained the boy's presence to his parents, and when Ena instantly accepted Walter into her dwelling, the boy was ecstatic.

Renno joined his father at the fire outside the hut and told him the essentials of the visit to Fort Springfield, including his own experiences in firing the mammoth firestick. Wilson and Pepperrell would soon come to the land of the Seneca, he said, and the English colonists wanted an alliance.

"Can they be trusted?" Ghonka demanded.

Renno did not hesitate. "Yes, my father, because their interests are the same as our interests. They want to defeat the French, and we want to win against the Huron and Ottawa. They will need the cunning of the Great Sachem to make a war plan that will save the lives of our warriors and the English braves. And I am sure they will give us many more firesticks. Also, if we ask, they will give us many soft blankets and pots of metal for cooking."

Ghonka's face remained expressionless. "Much has happened since you have been gone," he said, and wasting no words, he explained that a large party of Ottawa, maddened by the strong drink given them by the French, had burned a Seneca village to the ground and destroyed a village of the Mohawk. No prisoners had been taken, and there had been no survivors.

"Did the French goad them into making these attacks?" asked Renno.

Ghonka shrugged. "I think not. That would have been foolish. But the French gave the Ottawa the drink that burns in the throat. Now our brothers and our cousins have been killed and scalped, so the French have become our enemies, too. We need the alliance with the English as much as they need it, for our people are crying for vengeance."

Chapter XIII

F ive weeks after Renno returned home, the snow was still thick on the ground, and Brigadier William Pepperrell and Colonel Andrew Wilson, accompanied by a small escort, came to the principal town of the Seneca. In addition to the many gifts they brought for their hosts and the letters for Walter Alwin, they carried a document from Governor Shirley authorizing them to conclude a treaty with the Indians on behalf of Massachusetts Bay.

The sachems of all the Iroquois nations had already gathered in the town to await them. The two leaders of the English delegation were given a dwelling of their own, and Renno shared his hut with Obadiah Jenkins, the highest honor that the visiting clergyman could be paid. The others in the party, including Abe Thomas—who greeted Renno coolly—were given lodging in various longhouses.

The sachems and the chieftains of the visiting delegation went without delay to a new building constructed for their conclave. The situation they faced was urgent, so no ceremonies were held to open their meeting, but a ring of senior warriors stood guard outside the building, indicating that the hosts were taking no risks of a surprise attack.

It was still midafternoon, and Obadiah was anxious to see Walter.

"Soon he will return," Renno told him, volunteering no information.

"How is he?"

Renno smiled.

"His mother grieves for him, but she's a courageous woman, and I'm certain her prayers will be answered. Deborah is of the same opinion."

Renno saw Obadiah's face come alive when he mentioned Deborah, and he reminded himself not to make any reference to the girl having lived with him in this very hut.

Obadiah changed the subject abruptly. "If we form a joint expedition, as I hope we will, I've decided to go on the march."

Renno didn't realize that English medicine men might serve as warriors. "You will fight the enemy?"

"No, my profession forbids it. But I'll go as their chaplain—their chief medicine man," he explained. What he left unsaid was that he could still wield a sword better than most—and a man of the cloth was not forbidden to defend himself if attacked.

Renno stood up and beckoned. Obadiah walked with him beyond the palisade and they stood in a field where the snow was calf-deep. Renno was motionless for what seemed like a long time, and the clergyman became restless.

At last a group of boys approached from the forest, walking in single file, each carrying a string of fish. Renno grinned. The second boy in the line was

350

Walter Alwin, attired in a loincloth, moccasins, and a buckskin shirt embroidered with porcupine quills. He carried a small bow and a quiver of arrows on one shoulder, and his head had been shaved, with only a scalp lock remaining. He had lost his excess weight and he looked stronger, but the astonishing differences went deeper: he walked with confidence, and his eyes were at peace.

When he saw the clergyman, Walter gravely raised a hand, palm outward, in the Seneca greeting, and then he laughed. Obadiah returned the gesture with as much dignity as he could muster.

Subsequently, a meal was carried to the hut where the leaders were still conferring, and Obadiah went with Renno to the dwelling of the Great Sachem, where Ena and Sah-nee-wa made him welcome. Sitting beside the fire, he saw more of the remarkable transformation in Walter. Under Ba-lin-ta's tutelage, bolstered by the respect he was shown by everyone in the community, the boy was making rapid progress in lipreading, a skill he had never acquired at home. Even more encouraging was his use of a sign language that he and Ba-lin-ta were developing together. Not only were the two children able to communicate rapidly, but Walter had learned to make some of his simpler thoughts known to others, and for the first time since he had known the boy, Obadiah found that he could understand things Walter was telling him.

Renno and his guest retired to their own hut long before a weary but erect Ghonka returned to his dwelling for a few hours of sleep. Ena gave him his breakfast at dawn, while Sah-nee-wa made herself responsible for serving Brigadier Pepperrell and Colonel Wilson.

The deliberations were resumed at sunrise, and no one but the participants knew any of the details of the discussions. It was not the way of the Iroquois to reveal information before a settlement was reached, and the pair from Massachusetts Bay, out of deference to their hosts' customs, said nothing to their own subordinates.

By noon, a treaty was concluded. The five Iroquois nations and Massachusetts Bay formed an alliance, which New York and the other English colonies could join if they wished. As a sign of friendship, Massachusetts Bay would provide the Iroquois with a thousand muskets as well as ammunition and gunpowder. In return, also in the name of friendship, the Iroquois would send a thousand beaver skins to Boston. Each side would be free to send trade missions to the towns of the other, and each pledged to come to the aid of the other in wars with their common foes.

Both invoked that clause of the treaty immediately, so the conference was resumed in the community longhouse, with the Iroquois war chiefs, Lieutenant Doremus, and Brigadier Pepperrell's aides also participating. The Seneca warriors and their visiting cousins from other Iroquois nations rejoiced, convinced that a great war of extermination would be launched against the treacherous Huron and Ottawa. Perhaps even the Algonquian would be invited to join, given the alternative of choosing one side or the other, and the greatest Indian war in history would be waged.

But the leaders on both sides were more restrained than their enthusiastic subordinates. On the surface, the prospects for a major campaign were encouraging. The weight of numbers was heavily in favor of the new allies. Massachusetts Bay could send a thousand reliable militiamen into the field, all thoroughly familiar with firearms, all at home in the forests; the Iroquois could provide a minimum of three thousand warriors, about two-thirds of whom were seasoned veterans.

In Quebec, the French maintained a garrison of only twelve hundred men, and the Huron and Ottawa could send them another fifteen hundred warriors. According to information Brigadier Pepperrell had received recently from London, additional troops from France would arrive soon, but no more than two regiments of infantry, approximately five hundred strong, augmented by about one hundred cavalrymen, were expected.

But other vital factors had to be considered: allied supply lines would be extended over vast distances on the long march into Canada; the Citadel was protected by seventy cannon, and the Great Sachem had been deeply impressed by his son's awed account of the power of these huge firesticks; and three or four French warships would be docked in the Saint Lawrence River at Quebec. None of the Iroquois had even seen vessels that could carry hundreds of men and thousands of pounds of cargo, but Pepperrell and Wilson assured them that these ships also carried cannon of varying sizes, the armaments of some more numerous than those guarding the Citadel.

Consequently, the French would take a terrible toll of any attacking force. Brigadier Pepperrell somberly estimated that at least one out of every four members of such an expedition would die, and another two would be wounded. As well as suffering humiliating defeat, the allies would be weakened for many years to come, and they would only be able to offer feeble resistance when the French and their Indian friends decided to launch a countercampaign.

A full-scale attack in strength, Pepperrell said flatly, would succeed only if the colonies of Connecticut, New York, Rhode Island, and New Hampshire sent their largest contingents of seasoned frontier dwellers, and these colonies were not prepared to make such an effort. The alternative would be certain suicide.

After an exhaustive discussion, Ghonka proposed that a joint war party be sent to Quebec, strong enough to inflict severe damage on the French and their allies yet small enough to escape before the defenders, presumably stunned by the blow, would be able to follow in force and annihilate the invaders.

Everyone agreed that the risks would be great; however, if the effort succeeded, the French, Huron, and Ottawa would be thrown off-balance. The Iroquois villages and the isolated farmers of the colonists would be safe for a year or two, at which time it was likely that a more conclusive war would have to be fought. The chances would be worth taking; the rewards would be great, the possible casualties relatively small.

After an overall strategy had been determined, the leaders turned to a discussion of specific tactics. By this time mutual respect had developed on both sides in spite of the sharp differences in backgrounds. The colonists realized that the Indians were well versed in the business of waging war, and Ghonka understood, as did the other sachems and principal war chiefs, that these pale skins were not novices who relied only on the power of their firesticks.

Agreement on the first question raised was unanimous: in order to hold casualties to a minimum, only experienced men would be sent on the mission. This meant that there would be no Indians below the rank of senior warrior and that Massachusetts Bay would dispatch only veterans of wilderness combat. Inexperienced amateurs, no matter how great their zeal, would be more of a handicap than a help.

The problem of numbers took more time. Long discussion was needed before it was agreed that no more than four hundred men should participate. Each man would carry his own food, and the column would live off the land on the march, so no supply train would be attached. Individuals would be responsible for their own weapons and ammunition.

Massachusetts Bay would send two hundred militiamen on the campaign, all from the western sector of the colony and from the Maine District. Brigadier Pepperrell would be in command himself, with Colonel Wilson acting as his deputy.

It was more difficult for the Iroquois to work out their ratios, for all five nations clamored for representation. The Mohawk, who were demanding vengeance against the Ottawa, were permitted to muster a contingent of seventy-five warriors. Twenty-five Oneida also were included because they were more familiar with Canada than any of their cousins. The remaining one hundred Iroquois would be Seneca, and on this point there was no argument.

It was decided that the Mohawk and the Oneida would be led by their own war chiefs; then Ghonka electrified the gathering by announcing that he would assume the overall command of the Iroquois party and would also lead his own Seneca.

Some of his fellow sachems protested, saying he was too valuable to the League to risk his life on such an enterprise, but he was adamant.

"The honor of Ghonka and of the Seneca demands that I wear war paint on the trail," he said, "but there is more than honor that makes me go. Other war chiefs are wise and wily, but who among all the Iroquois is stronger or more cunning than Ghonka?"

His subordinates were forced to concede that no other living war chief was his equal.

"That is why Ghonka will go," he said, his tone forbidding further discussion. "Our enemies need more than a lesson. They must be crippled so badly that they cannot go on the warpath again for many moons. When they learn that Ghonka leads the warriors, there will be fear in their hearts, and they will be right to be afraid. Many Huron and Ottawa will die. Many French will die. Many houses and forts will be burned."

Only after the talks came to an end was a feast held, and even on this occasion ceremony was kept to a minimum. An appropriate celebration would come when victory had been achieved.

The next morning, before the white men returned to Massachusetts Bay, there was a meeting to resolve one final matter.

Brigadier Pepperrell was in favor of waiting until spring before the campaign was launched, but Ghonka demurred. "When the weather is warm," he said, "the enemy also will stir. Man is like the bear. When the sun grows strong, he becomes active."

Andrew Wilson smiled thoughtfully. "The Great Sachem is right," he said. "The French and their allies won't be expecting an attack while there's still snow on the ground. We may find the march more difficult, but we'll be better able to surprise Quebec and carry out our mission if we attack before the end of winter."

So it was decided that the march would start in fourteen days, which scarcely gave the colonists time to return home and muster their troops. Pepperrell and Wilson departed at once, and later that day the sachems of the various Iroquois nations left for their respective villages.

Not until allies and relatives had gone did Ghonka let it be known that his principal assistant would be senior warrior Sun-ai-yee, who had earned the honor.

All the full warriors were bitterly disappointed, and no one was sadder than El-i-chi. However, he could not dispute his father's word, so he consoled himself with the thought that his day would come.

Renno hoped desperately that he would be included in the party, but he did not dare raise the subject. Throughout the afternoon other senior warriors were notified that they had been selected, but Sun-ai-yee did not send for him, and he became more and more apprehensive. That night he went to the dwelling of his parents for supper, but nothing in his father's attitude indicated that he had been either accepted or rejected, and Renno had to exercise all his self-control to remain silent.

After the meal, the Great Sachem rose, donned his cape, and beckoned to Renno, who was surprised when Ghonka led him out into the fields beyond the palisade. In the past they had always followed the ancient tradition of holding talks of consequence in front of the cooking fire. Now the young warrior was doubly afraid he would be left behind, and he braced himself for the disappointment.

Ghonka halted, staring toward the forest. "It is wrong for a senior warrior to know fear in anything," he said, "but my son fears he will not go on the warpath with me."

"That is true." Renno knew better than to lie to his father.

"You carry ten scalps in your belt. I am proud of

you for that. But you have not fought in many battles at the side of your comrades."

Renno nodded glumly, making no comment.

The Great Sachem glanced at him, an unexpected gleam of humor in his eyes. "Do you think I would deny you the pleasure of going on the warpath with me? Do you think I would deny myself that joy?"

It was impossible to remain passive. In spite of a lifetime of training, Renno couldn't help grinning broadly, his relief almost overwhelming.

But Ghonka quickly shook his head. "I am speaking with you because you will not be an ordinary member of the band. If the manitous of war will it, you may fight in battle at the side of your brothers, but perhaps you will not."

Renno inhaled sharply, his face suddenly expressionless.

"Since the times of our fathers' fathers," Ghonka said solemnly, "the Seneca have gone to war at the side of their Iroquois cousins. Now we will go to war at the side of the English. Their way of fighting is not our way. Their way of thinking is not our way. To fight with them against the same enemy will not be easy."

Renno was forced to agree, and he wondered why he was being honored with such confidences.

"You have visited a town of the English," the Great Sachem said. "You have learned to speak the tongue of the English. Because your eyes and hair are the color of their eyes and hair, they do not think of you as a Seneca. For all these reasons I have a special mission for you to perform on the warpath."

Renno knew it was better to wait patiently than to leap to groundless conclusions.

"My son will be the messenger who travels between me and the sachem of the English. You will carry my words to him and his words to me. When the time comes for us to fight the enemy, you will stand with the English sachem, Wil-son. You will tell him what the Seneca are doing and why we do it that way. Then he will not make mistakes that will cost his band many lives."

Renno felt as though he had been immersed in the cold waters of the lake. Perhaps he would have an opportunity to use his firestick or his bow and arrows, but it might well be that his duties as a messenger and an adviser to Colonel Wilson would make it impossible to add more scalps to his belt.

Not even a favorite son dared question the decisions of the Great Sachem. It was the duty of a senior warrior to do precisely as he was ordered. Only a few moments ago he had been afraid he would be left at home with the women, children, and the young full warriors who were junior to him. Other senior warriors, even more experienced in the waging of war, would also be left behind, and it would be wrong to protest that his one desire was to show valor against the Huron and Ottawa, to inflict a damaging blow to the French, and, most of all, to meet his personal enemy in hand-to-hand combat.

"I hear the words of the Great Sachem," he said, "and I will do as I am bidden."

Ghonka turned on his heel so abruptly that Renno had to hurry to keep up with him as they returned to the town.

Andrew Wilson looked sharply at his guest, who stood warming himself before the fireplace after his ride from his own small farm.

"Reverend," Wilson asked, "are you quite certain

you want to come with us on this expedition? The presence of a chaplain in the company will be a luxury, but since we're marching with only a hundred men, you well may be drawn into the fighting."

Obadiah Jenkins turned from the fire and smiled somewhat defensively. "I'm well aware of the risks, Colonel."

The older man laughed. "It strikes me you won't be too sorry if you're obliged to use arms."

"I was a swordsman before I became a minister," Obadiah said. "And ever since I've been old enough to think, I've yearned for peace between nations. Since coming to the New World, I've seen settlers scalped, I've seen women and little children murdered, I've seen homes that were carved out of the wilderness burned to the ground, I've seen livestock slaughtered and property wantonly destroyed for no purpose other than the creation of terror. Well, Colonel, the French haven't frightened us yet into leaving this land the Almighty has led us to settle, and we have no intention of being driven back to England."

He was so intense, so sincere that the colonel was deeply impressed.

"Forgive me for sounding as though I'm delivering a sermon from my pulpit, but I've had enough. The French must be taught a lesson they won't forget, and their Indian allies must learn to live in peace with us. Some of your militiamen have been calling me the fighting parson, and I tell you truly, I'm not ashamed of the nickname, sir. I flatly refuse to be left behind!"

"Under the circumstances," Andrew said mildly, "I accept your offer, Reverend. Now, will you stay and have supper with us?"

Obadiah shook his head. "I thank you all the

same." He hesitated for a moment. "To tell you the truth, I have a rather delicate mission. I'm going to the Alwin house to let Deborah know that I'm marching with you. I'm afraid she may be opposed to the idea, particularly since her own experience has taught her something about the rigors of Indian life."

The colonel lowered his voice as he accompanied his guest to the front door. "Ladies," he said, "sometimes don't understand that there are times when a man must resort to violence in order to win real peace." He refrained from remarking that the friendship between Deborah and the clergyman seemed to be swiftly blossoming. It was not his place to comment on the personal lives of others. "I have something of the same problem in my own family."

Obadiah was surprised. "Mistress Wilson doesn't want you to march against Quebec, Colonel?"

Andrew shook his head, but he abandoned the subject when he heard his wife coming down the stairs. "I'll have to explain some other time, although I hope the question will have been resolved before then."

Mildred Wilson, who made it her practice to change into one of her handsome gowns before supper, repeated her husband's invitation as she greeted the clergyman.

"I'm afraid I can't stay," he said, then added to the colonel with a wry grin, "Wish me luck, sir."

When she and Andrew were alone, Mildred said, "What was that all about?"

"Reverend Jenkins and I have a problem in common, my dear. Would you mind having a word with me before dinner?"

She accompanied him into the library, refusing a glass of sack and watching him as he poured himself a small drink.

Andrew decided that a direct confrontation was preferable to a flanking approach. "I completed the roster of men who will take part on the march to Quebec," he said, "and I've included Jeffrey on the list."

Mildred did not flinch. "You know he hates militia service. He's a member of the company only because you've insisted. Why ask for trouble when it could so easily be avoided?"

"For the simple reason that even greater trouble lies ahead if I don't take him." He drew a deep breath. "Jeffrey is our only child, and I love him as much in my way as you love him in yours, Mildred, even though he infuriates me beyond measure."

"You confirm what I'm saying," she replied. "You're asking for aggravation."

"I regard that as irrelevant."

"Irrelevant?" Mildred cried. "If Jeffrey disobeys military orders—"

"He won't. He's been a member of the militia long enough to know that even my position as regimental commander wouldn't save him from a court-martial trial."

She sank wearily into a chair. "Then I don't understand."

"Jeffrey is in a sad state. Between drinking and wenching, he has no time for anything else. He refuses to work on the property, and he's so imperious and unpleasant to people that he's antagonized everyone in the neighborhood. To an extent, you and I are to blame, Mildred, because we gave him too big a taste of a different sort of life in England."

"I'll grant you we spoiled him. But we've tried so hard to make him see reason and make something of himself." Her voice trembled slightly. "I'm afraid of what might happen to him on an expedition into Canada. A man needs self-discipline and determination for such a venture, and as we both know—to our sorrow—Jeffrey is sadly lacking in both. He's so reckless and headstrong, he'll be killed."

A sad smile crossed Andrew's face. "The need for self-preservation sometimes changes a soldier's outlook. That's my hope. Jeffrey isn't yet a man; he's an overgrown boy, and I've included him on the roster simply because this campaign could make him realize his potential. However, I can honestly say that his excellent marksmanship will make him valuable to the mission. I'm taking risks, I know, but I'm willing to accept them. Now I'm asking you to take them, and I know it must be terribly difficult for you. After all, you brought him into the world, and you've cherished him all these years in spite of everything."

"What are the risks I'd be taking?" she asked.

"If this effort fails, and it well might, your first reaction could prove prophetic. Only the strong can survive as hazardous a march as this will be. You might find it impossible to forgive yourself—or me— if something should happen to Jeffrey. You might even feel we sent him to his death."

Mildred stared into the fire, tugging absently at a tiny lace handkerchief.

"If you're too afraid, my dear," Andrew said, "or if the whole idea overwhelms you, I'll remove his name from the list. I'll include him only if you and I are in complete agreement."

Her smile was tremulous when she looked at her husband. "Has it occurred to you that I'll be worried about you, Andrew—above all? You'll be risking your own health and life, yet you take it for granted that you must go. And that I won't object."

"Do you?"

She bit her lower lip as she shook her head. "In two decades of marriage, I've never stood between you and your duty, and I don't intend to begin now. We gave up a meaningless life in England so we could help create a new civilization here. We've endured a great many hardships and we've made more sacrifices than I care to recall. Now, when everything we've worked to achieve is being threatened, I don't think you have a choice. You're needed in the militia, just as Will Pepperrell is needed. There's no one who can take your place or his. So you'll go—in spite of all my fears—with my blessing and my love."

Her husband went to her, bent down, and kissed her tenderly.

She lifted a hand to his face, her fingertips stroking his cheek, her eyes luminous, and Andrew realized how their love had grown over the years, more precious now than it had ever been. Afraid he might become too sentimental, he took a step backward and clasped his hands behind him.

"Yes or no? Do I take Jeffrey to Quebec with me?"

Mildred became pensive. "I'd like to tell you about a strange feeling I've had of late. During the brief time that white Seneca stayed with us, I've wondered about him. If Ida Alwin is right, he's the son of a couple who died right here in Fort Springfield during the Great Massacre. How different his life would have been if he'd lived to grow up as an English settler in Massachusetts Bay."

Andrew didn't see the connection, but he exercised patience. "Similar thoughts crossed my mind," he said.

"He's lived as a savage all his life, but what a fine and honorable young man he is! Renno has all the qualities we've wanted Jeffrey to display. How

roud and happy I'd be if Renno of the Seneca were
ur son."

He nodded.

"I don't know whether it's too late for Jeffrey
to change. I don't even know if he's capable of mend-
ing his ways, Andrew. But—if the wilderness can make
a man of him, if the dangers and rigors of a campaign can cause him to turn over a new leaf—then take
him with you. If he dies, you and I will know a
permanent loss, but he may live. For the first time in
his life. So the risk is worth taking! Yes, I give him to
you freely, and may he be transformed into the son I've
always wanted!"

At the fort, the arriving militiamen reported for
duty to Lieutenant Donald Doremus. Then Sergeant
Abe Thomas checked their equipment. Some of the
men were already grumbling because each had to carry
a seventy-five-pound backpack containing a blanket,
a change of boots and linen, ammunition and powder,
and emergency rations of jerked beef, flour, and bacon.

As Brigadier Pepperrell and Colonel Wilson had
determined, no packhorses would accompany the men.
Speed and mobility would be critical factors, and the
militia would be required to keep pace with their
Iroquois allies.

"We're not soldiers, we're animals," Jeffrey Wilson complained.

None of his comrades was willing to go that far,
but it was obvious to everyone that the march would
not be easy.

After the mustering procedures were completed,
the members of the company went off to the mess hall
for a cup of tea and a last chat with families and
friends who had gathered to see them off. A log fire

burned in the hearth, and in spite of the early hour, more than 250 residents of the area were there to say farewell. Parents and brothers and sisters, wives and children congregated in small groups, surrounding their loved ones. Conversation was subdued, befitting the solemnity and tension of the occasion.

Some were surprised to see Nettie, the red-haired trollop, on hand. She had elected to appear to say goodbye to the men who had no relatives. Even though he was a complete stranger, she spoke to the laconic Tom Hibbard, and, of the other three men she greeted warmly, only one had been her client.

Dressed in buckskins rather than a militia uniform, his sword at his side and a pistol in his belt, Obadiah Jenkins moved from group to group offering comfort to those who appeared to be on the verge of breaking down. Then he saw a girl with shining blond hair coming into the mess hall, and he went to her at once.

"Well," he said, his clergyman's glibness deserting him, "this is a surprise . . ."

Deborah Alwin was ill at ease. "I decided I couldn't let you leave without coming to see you off," she said, "even though I still can't quite understand why someone in your position should have to go."

"I'm going because the principles I hold dear are more important to me than my own comfort and safety."

"So you told me the other evening." Deborah sighed, an expression of grudging admiration in her eyes. "You've paid two visits to the land of the Seneca, so you have some idea of what lies ahead. I—I don't envy you."

"No, I don't envy myself, frankly, but I'm doing what I must. So my conscience will allow me to live with myself."

Deborah was silent for a moment. "Would it be presumptuous to ask a man of God to be careful?"

"A man of God is like anyone else. He's flattered and touched when someone who is—important to him—shows concern for him."

Deborah's pale eyes widened.

Suddenly Obadiah caught hold of her arm and led her to the private alcove that the colonel used as a dining room when entertaining prominent military guests.

"There's a matter I fully intended to raise with you only after I returned from Quebec," he said, "but I find I must bring it up now." Nervousness assailed him, and he had to regain some measure of poise before he could continue. "I'm a poor man, Deborah; I'll never be wealthy. It may be years before my congregation can afford to pay me wages that will make it possible for me to give up my farm. All the same, I ask you to share my poverty with me. Will you marry me when I return?"

The girl was even more shaken. "Thank you, Obadiah," she murmured. "You'll never know how much this proposal means to me. But I can't accept."

He looked stricken.

"Not because of any lack in you," she added hastily, "only because of my own weakness. There are incidents in my past that would make me an unsuitable wife for a clergyman."

Obadiah smiled, then became firm. "I've heard rumors about your life in the land of the Seneca. I'm indifferent to those stories, regardless of whether they're true or not. I neither know nor want to know any more about it. You did what had to be done to survive, and I'd be proud to have you take my name."

Tears came to Deborah's eyes.

"I'm no saint," he told her. "Someday I'll tell you the details of what no one else in all of the New World knows or even suspects. I fled to Massachusetts Bay from England after I killed a man in cold blood."

Deborah was surprised by the feeling of protective loyalty that surged within her. "Then I'm certain you had good cause. And it wouldn't influence my opinion of you. I have a greater respect and a higher regard for you than for anyone I've ever known."

Obadiah's eyes glowed. "Regard and respect are important feelings. I have both for your aunt, let's say, or for Mistress Wilson, just as I have for you. But I have an additional feeling for you that takes precedence. During the months when you were off in the land of the Seneca, when no one knew whether you were dead or alive—I realized that I loved you."

Deborah reddened. "I—I can't pretend I thought of you in any special way while I was in the wilderness," she said. "It wasn't until I returned home and began to see everything here in a new perspective that I came to know how you stand above every other man."

His grasp gentle, he caught hold of her arms. "Are you telling me that you've come to love me?"

She nodded.

"I hereby pronounce us betrothed," Obadiah said, kissing her.

As their lips met, Deborah knew this was the man for her, the only man who mattered, the man with whom she wanted to spend the rest of her life. Circumstances and a sense of gratitude had led her to become Renno's mistress, and although she wasn't denying to herself that she had wanted him as he had wanted her, proximity had been a vital factor in their relationship.

Now she and Obadiah looked at each other, smiling in their mutual discovery. Obadiah removed a gold signet ring from the little finger of his left hand and slipped it onto her ring finger. "This," he said, "is my inheritance from my mother. I'd ask you to wear it until I can buy you a more appropriate ring in Boston, but I know it will be many years before I can afford the luxury. So you'll probably wear this one for all of your life."

"It's the only ring I'll ever want," Deborah said, and she moved into his embrace again.

When they returned to the mess hall, Aunt Ida knew at once that they had reached an understanding. She went to them, rejoicing and relieved. Both kissed her, and for once in her life she had nothing to say.

Andrew and Mildred Wilson arrived, having said their own farewells privately, and Lieutenant Doremus promptly assembled the militia company.

The men fell into a double row, with the lieutenant and Sergeant Abe Thomas bringing up the rear.

Colonel Wilson took his place at the head of the line, and Tom Hibbard joined him. Newly commissioned as an ensign to celebrate his long years of militia service and, even more important, the end of his indentureship, Tom still looked as forlorn as he felt.

Nettie was sorry for him and favored him with her most brilliant smile. She had no way of knowing that he was still grieving for his wife.

Absently returning the trollop's smile, Tom made a silent vow. Agnes, my love, he promised, I'll make the Huron pay dearly for your murder. May the Lord have mercy on them, for I'll show them no pity.

The colonel drew his sword and gave the order to march.

369

Obadiah Jenkins looked out of place as he walked behind the commander, his bearing and gait those of a civilian, but to Deborah Alwin, no man had ever looked more dashing.

Mildred Wilson prayed that her husband would return safely to her side, and only when he had left the mess hall did she turn her attention to her son. Jeffrey walked with his customary swagger, his arrogant expression indicating his contempt for the ordinary men and women who were taming the wilderness of western Massachusetts Bay. At the last moment he raised his hand in a final salute to his mother. Thy will be done, Mildred thought.

Lieutenant Doremus drew his sword and, before moving out into the field, raised it with a flourish in a final gesture to the settlers whose future depended on the outcome of the campaign. Several little boys cheered, and a woman's dry sob was almost obliterated by their noise.

The bitterly cold morning seemed like any other. The Great Sachem and his family sat around the fire calmly eating breakfast. Ena had arisen early to prepare the customary stew, and although she had little appetite she pretended to eat with relish.

Ghonka seemed serene and untroubled. Only those who knew him well could see changes in him. He had shaved his head the previous night. In place of his usual headdress, his scalp lock was adorned with a single feather of the white eagle, the symbol of his tribal esteem. His face and torso were smeared with fresh war paint, his metal knife was honed, and the pistol in his belt was loaded. Beside him lay his bow and a quiver of arrows.

Renno, also ready for the trail, was ravenous, and

he was secretly elated because Sah-nee-wa had appeared with cornmeal cakes swimming in maple syrup, one of his favorite dishes since early childhood. It would have been unseemly to thank his aunt, but three times he politely handed her his gourd for another helping.

This campaign, Renno thought, justified his entire existence. No man was more of a true Seneca than he, yet no warrior was so different. Very well. His father had given him a unique role, a role that no other warrior in the land could play, and he would live up to his responsibilities. His parents would be proud of him. If the hawk who watched over him would guide him now, perhaps he could begin to perform the exploits that someday would win him enduring renown. Perhaps it might happen that chants about his deeds would be sung while he was still alive, as they were sung about his father.

Surreptitiously, he checked his weapons. He had honed his own metal knife when he had sharpened his father's, and it was as sharp as the razors of the English. His tomahawk was perfectly balanced. He carried pouches of metal arrows and powder for his musket, which he had cleaned with care the previous night, and his quiver was filled with arrows. All was in readiness. The mere thought spurred his appetite, and again he handed Sah-nee-wa his gourd. The old lady, who really obeyed no rules except her own, grinned openly at him.

El-i-chi ate silently, methodically, still disturbed because he could not go on the warpath, but in no way resentful. That would have shown a lack of respect for the father and brother he admired above all living men. He would hunt, and he would be there to protect the town, particularly if the Erie were foolish enough to launch an attack while so many of the senior warriors were absent. Someday his turn would come. Then he, too, would win his share of glory.

Only Ba-lin-ta chatted, pausing only to take bites of stew and eating more rapidly than usual. She knew the cornmeal cakes had been made for her father and Renno, but she was certain that if she finished her stew in time they would share the delicacy with her, for neither ever denied her a special treat.

She had to be careful of Ena, however, who would not allow her any of the cornmeal cakes if she left even one scrap of her stew unfinished. Perhaps the exciting story of yesterday's quarrel in the longhouse of the maidens would have to wait until she made certain that she received a heaping helping of cornmeal cakes. Her father and Renno would be sad to miss that story, but she would do her best to remember it so she could tell it to them when they returned from their war.

Ba-lin-ta cleaned her gourd, then glanced obliquely at her mother. Ena nodded, averting her face to hide her smile.

At last the meal came to an end. Ena rose, then handed her husband and son large pouches filled with jerked venison and parched corn. These rations would last a long time, she knew, because the men would hunt and fish on the trail. No Seneca ever went hungry in the wilderness, no matter the season.

Ghonka and Renno stood.

Sah-nee-wa hauled herself to her feet, faced her brother for an instant, then turned to her nephew. Her lips moved silently, and they knew she was asking the father-sun and the mother-earth to protect them.

When it was Ena's turn to bid them farewell, she smeared ashes on the palms of the departing warriors'

372

hands, but she spoke no word to either, as that would have been a sign of weakness. Then she went out to join Sah-nee-wa.

Ghonka turned to Walter Alwin, who had remained unobtrusive throughout the meal, and deliberately treating him like a man, exchanged firm forearm clasps with him.

The boy stood erect, his eyes aglow with pleasure.

"Wal-ter," Ba-lin-ta said, "tells you he knows you will come home with many scalps."

Her father's expression remained unchanged, though a hint of determination appeared in his eyes. "We will bring home scalps for him to see," he replied. The pudgy little girl relayed the message, and the boy's eyes widened.

Now it was Renno's turn and, like his father, he exchanged forearm clasps with Walter before the boy went out into the open and waited for Ba-lin-ta to join him. Ba-lin-ta disregarded custom and hugged her father, and the Great Sachem returned her embrace, which he never would have done had she been his son.

Then she threw herself at Renno. "Will you bring me—?"

"I know," he interrupted. "A French doll. A Huron doll. An Ottawa doll. I make no promise, but I will do what I can."

Ba-lin-ta skipped off to join Walter, and they walked hand in hand toward the field.

El-i-chi stepped out of the shadows to bid farewell to his father. His manner was dignified, befitting a full warrior, but anyone who knew him could read the pain behind his eyes. He did not falter as he exchanged forearm clasps with the Great Sachem, for patience was as necessary a virtue as courage, and he intended to be ready to prove he was worthy of promotion when the appropriate time came.

Renno found it difficult to say good-bye to his brother. He could well imagine himself in El-i-chi's shoes, and he knew all too well the lonely frustration that could choke a young man.

"While I am gone," he said, trying to strike a cheerful note as they clasped forearms, "visit often with Ja-gonh. You will lift his spirits."

El-i-chi understood his brother's purpose. The suggestion was a reminder that the warrior who remained at home was required to fulfill obligations to his family, the community, and the nation. There was no need for him to feel ashamed of being left behind. On the contrary, he would carry a heavy burden of responsibility, and he would accomplish nothing by feeling sorry for himself.

As Renno had discovered, the transformation from youth to manhood was a painful, delicate process. He could almost see the growth taking place in his brother. El-i-chi seemed to stand taller as he squared his shoulders, nodded, and left the dwelling without a backward glance. He would join his comrades, and together they would hunt, fish, perform sentinel duties, and keep the town and its inhabitants safe during the absence of the older warriors.

Alone now, Ghonka and Renno swiftly smeared grease on their arms and legs—the only portions of their bodies where there was no war paint—to protect themselves from the elements.

Picking up their weapons, and donning webbed snowshoes, they walked with rapid strides through the town to the field where the war party was assembling. Virtually everyone in the town had gathered, but no one spoke, no one moved; the women and the elders knew that a smaller number of warriors would return, yet no one showed any sign of grief. The men who would die would be honored for all time, and their spirits would join those of the countless Seneca who had distinguished themselves in the past.

Some of the children, particularly the girls, found it impossible to contain their excitement. Ba-lin-ta couldn't resist smiling broadly at Renno as he walked past her. He could have reached out and touched her. No one was watching him, he decided, so he took the risk of smiling at her. She giggled aloud, but Walter, who stood close beside her, remained grave, never forgetting he was a male.

Three of the party's senior warriors who would act as scouts broke away from their companions when the Great Sachem gave an almost imperceptible signal. Fanning out, they headed for the forest at a trot, their snowshoes keeping them from sinking into the deep snow.

Ghonka took his place at the head of the column, with Sun-ai-yee directly behind him, and they moved off in the wake of the scouts, neither one indicating an awareness of the people they were leaving behind, and one by one the senior warriors fell in behind them.

At last it was Renno's turn, at the tail end of the line. Too well disciplined to glance at either Ena or Sah-nee-wa, he trotted at an even pace that kept him six feet behind the man in front of him. Rarely would they move faster or slower, and at no time would the distance between them vary.

Renno was thrilled to the core of his being. As far back as he could remember, his deepest wish had been to join a war party headed by his father. Now his dream was being realized. Renno, the son of Ghonka, would find an opportunity to make his mark at the side of the legendary Great Sachem.

The hazards that awaited the party were spurs to greater achievement, challenges to be overcome. Life was sweet, but death, if it came, would not be avoided.

Chapter XIV

The Oneida scouts appeared out of nowhere to join the Seneca, and the augmented party went on to the principal town of the Mohawk, where the group was joined by seventy-five more warriors. Tarrying only overnight, Ghonka and his braves headed north, skirting the shores of the lake known to the French as Champlain, called the Long, Thin Lake by the Mohawk. Arriving at its upper end, they turned eastward. Even though the snow was still thick on the ground, the hunters and fishermen in this group of seasoned veterans were so skilled that food supplies were ample and there was no need for anyone to use his emergency rations.

Meanwhile, Andrew Wilson and his militiamen, also wearing Indian-style snowshoes, trekked up through New Hampshire into the Maine District of Massachusetts Bay where they were met by Brigadier Pepperrell and his contingent of hardened frontiersmen.

Like the Indians, the militiamen lived off the land and managed to eat well.

One night, as the commanders of the expedition sat apart from their subordinates at a campfire, Pepperrell expressed uneasiness over the venture. "I can't help wishing you had arranged for us to meet the Iroquois at a specific place, Andy," he said. "This forest is endless. We don't even have a definite border to tell us when we leave Maine and move into Canada. I'm damned if I know how we'll get together with them."

Wilson's smile was confident. "I have faith in Ghonka," he replied. "I told him our general line of march, and he wants us to halt and make camp on our sixth night. He said he would find us, and I have no doubt that he will."

The battalion followed instructions, and on the evening of the sixth day of the joint march, larger than usual campfires were made near the shore of a small lake. Some of the men cut holes in the ice and dropped their fishing lines into the water, and the next morning a small group of men went hunting, returning at noon with enough game to keep the battalion supplied for several days.

In midafternoon, Pepperrell's apprehensions vanished when three Oneida scouts appeared, and an hour later the entire Iroquois war party arrived at the rendezvous. The Indians, who had obviously suffered no ill effects from their strenuous march, built their own fires several hundred yards from those of the colonists, and although there were no obvious tensions, the two groups were wary of each other, and there was no mingling or visiting.

That night, Ghonka, Sun-ai-yee, and Renno ate roasted venison and boiled roots at the fire of Pepperrell and Wilson, and the leaders made their joint plans.

"It seems to me," said Pepperrell, "that we'll want to stay far to the east of the village the French call Montreal. It might be easier to follow the Saint Lawrence River, but we'll risk being seen by the enemy. The river is their principal line of communication, and there's always traffic on it, even at this time of year."

Ghonka nodded gravely. "The trees that stay green in the winter will shelter and hide us," he said. "We must not leave the forest until we come to the town of the French."

"There's one major problem," Andrew Wilson interjected. "Quebec lies on the far side of the Saint Lawrence, which is very wide there. And we'll face the additional obstacles of ice floes that will need to be avoided. How do you propose we cross the river?"

Ghonka and Sun-ai-yee conferred in undertones, then tried to explain what they had in mind. The colonists couldn't understand the words they used, and Renno was asked to translate.

"At another time of year," Renno said, "we would make Indian boats—canoes. But the river ice makes many dangers. So we will put logs together and float them across. But we will make paddles for them so they will go where we want them to go."

Pepperrell was dubious. "I don't see how we can cross the Saint Lawrence under the noses of the French garrison in the Citadel, especially if we're going to do it in rafts," he said. "They'll be waiting for us when we land."

Ghonka was unaccustomed to having his word disputed. "The enemy," he said flatly, "will not see the Iroquois or the English."

Pepperrell still had reservations. "I don't plan to

see a hundred of our best men butchered," he said.
"I'm reserving judgment until I find out precisely how
this miracle is going to be accomplished."

When the march resumed the following morning,
Renno was ordered by his father to stay at the side of
Colonel Wilson. The colonists were better marksmen
with their firesticks than were the Iroquois, but it was
astonishing how little most of them knew about the
wilderness.

The rate of march had to be reduced drastically
because the colonists couldn't keep up the pace set by
the Iroquois, and Renno winced inwardly when the
heavy boots of the settlers thudded on the ground and
ice. They were almost as noisy as a herd of stampeding
buffalo, he decided, and at the end of the first day's
joint march he went to his father.

"The English cannot be quiet," he said. "The Huron and Ottawa surely will hear them as we draw
nearer to the town of the French."

"Then we will march more slowly," Ghonka replied. "And you will tell Wil-son that his warriors
must walk with lighter feet."

Renno conveyed the message, and the militiamen
did their utmost to tread more lightly. With the exception of a few hunters who had enjoyed years of experience in the forests, however, the English colonists
lacked the lifelong training that enabled the Iroquois
to glide like ghosts through the deep woods.

To compensate for the problem, Ghonka changed
his approach. The twenty-five Oneida scouts spread out
in a wide circle surrounding the column, and whenever they discovered Huron or Ottawa in the vicinity,
even in small numbers, they gave the call of the snow
owl. Whenever that warning sounded, the entire line

immediately halted, and a rule of total silence in the ranks was observed.

At Ghonka's request, Pepperrell directed the battalion not to use firearms under any circumstances, and the Iroquois took over the hunting duties for the entire company, using only their bows and arrows.

Renno developed a measure of sympathy for the colonists. In spite of their limitations, they were men of courage. They made no complaint on the long trek even though they were bothered by the footing and the cold. They were accustomed to a variety of foods, but they ate roasted game and boiled roots quietly, and when they grew tired late in the day they did not slacken their pace. There were no stragglers.

Gradually Renno and Tom Hibbard came to know and like each other. The former indentured servant, much older than most of his companions, seemed endowed with inexhaustible energy, and Renno came to the conclusion that he would be a reliable comrade in battle.

Another whose company Renno enjoyed was Lieutenant Donald Doremus. The innkeeper, so amiable in Fort Springfield, was a different man on the march, constantly ranging up and down the line, encouraging his men, quick to chastise those who forgot themselves and spoke too loudly. He, too, was tireless, and he was the first to rise each morning, the first to supervise the building of campfires.

Some of the militiamen were uncomfortable in Renno's presence because they were uncertain how to deal with him, but Jeffrey Wilson was the only member of the battalion who was openly hostile. Renno, who had no desire to provoke a needless quarrel, took care to avoid him.

The attitude displayed by Abe Thomas was disturbing to Renno. Jealous because of what he had heard or imagined about the young warrior's relations with Deborah, Abe acted as though they had never met, and Renno waited patiently, hoping that something might happen during the campaign that would enable them to resume their friendship.

One afternoon, the Oneida who were scouting in advance of the column brought word that the Saint Lawrence River was only a half day's travel away. An immediate halt was called, twenty-five Mohawk were assigned to augment the Oneida as sentinels, and both Ghonka and Brigadier Pepperrell banned the lighting of campfires.

For the first time the Iroquois and the colonists worked shoulder to shoulder, chopping and trimming trees, and twenty-four hours later they had succeeded in constructing twenty rafts, each large enough to carry twenty men. Then the entire group of Mohawk, who had the greatest experience in traveling by water, began the task of fashioning paddles.

Warriors and militiamen alike were reduced to eating cold meat, and the Indians were somewhat surprised when they heard the colonists grumble. Many of the settlers still had a great deal to learn about wilderness warfare.

Only now did Ghonka reveal his plan. "Some days, before snow falls," he said, "the air becomes very thick. At night the thickness is even worse. We will wait for such a night. Then not even the best of Huron warriors will see us. The Mohawk will paddle us across the water, and we will enter the great longhouse of the enemy before they know we are there."

Pepperrell and Wilson exchanged glances, and both were impressed. The appearance of heavy fog was a common phenomenon in this part of the world, particularly in the vicinity of the Saint Lawrence. Everything would depend on the ability of the Mohawk paddlers to guide the rafts across the river.

"It's going to be difficult," the brigadier said. "The current in the river is swift, and any raft that strikes an ice floe is almost sure to sink."

"I'll grant you, the risks are enormous," Andrew Wilson replied, "but we have no real choice."

Several of the Oneida were sent back to the river to await the arrival of propitious weather, and the sentinels doubled their vigilance. If the French and their Indian allies learned that four hundred heavily armed men were this close to the capital of New France, the campaign would have to be abandoned even before the attack was launched.

Tension mounted as the warriors and militiamen waited day after day with nothing to occupy their time. The Indians displayed their customary stoicism, and some of Pepperrell's troops marveled at Renno, who squatted on his haunches, impervious to the elements, lost in thought for hours at a time.

On the third day of waiting there was a near brush with disaster. Two Huron traveling to Quebec ventured close to the invaders' camp without realizing it. The Oneida gave the alert, and the Seneca immediately went into action, Sun-ai-yee leading a small party of warriors to cut off the Huron.

The militiamen anticipated the sound of a battle, but the wilderness remained enveloped in profound silence, and William Pepperrell began to fear that the Huron had managed to avoid the ambush.

Then Sun-ai-yee and his braves returned as quietly as they had departed, and there was no need for the war chief to explain that his mission had been successful. Fresh scalps were hanging from the belts of two of his warriors, who were also carrying the bows, arrows, and metal knives of the slain Huron.

Well aware that he had struck the first blow of the campaign, Sun-ai-yee couldn't resist grinning in triumph at Pepperrell and Wilson.

But the incident did nothing to reduce tension, which actually became greater. Other enemy warriors might inadvertently slip through the screen of sentinels, and the campaign could still be lost before it was launched.

Early the next morning, Ghonka came to the militiamen's bivouac area just as the commander and his deputy were forcing themselves to eat a breakfast of cold venison. Ghonka came to the point immediately. "Snow tonight," he said. "Soon thick air will come."

Pepperrell and Wilson were incredulous.

"The Great Sachem knows," Renno told them. "Always he knows more than other warriors."

The brigadier was reluctant to break camp and advance to the river. "If the Seneca's hunch—or intuition, or whatever it is—proves wrong, we're taking a terrible risk based on one man's whim."

Ghonka listened to Renno's translation, then looked at his son without commenting.

Renno knew his throughts. "If the English are cowards," he said, "the Iroquois will attack alone."

Pepperrell reddened.

Colonel Wilson made an instant decision and, not wanting to offend their allies, did not wait to consult privately with his superior. "Wherever the Great Sachem leads," he said, "our militiamen will follow!"

Ghonka's brief grunt indicated that he was satisfied.

Both groups broke camp at once, and the march

began, with fifty Oneida and Mohawk forming a screen. The advance was slow, partly because of the need to maintain strict silence, partly because the warriors who were carrying the rafts could not move rapidly.

The final stage of the march was concluded without incident, and late in the afternoon an Oneida scout signaled that the great river lay directly ahead.

Renno accompanied Pepperrell and Wilson when they went forward to join Ghonka and Sun-ai-yee at a spot just behind a screen of trees that prevented them from being observed from the north bank.

A fog was beginning to boil up from the river, and already Quebec was partly obscured in the haze. William Pepperrell, speaking in a low but earnest tone, offered his apologies to Ghonka. Concentrating on the far bank, the Great Sachem nodded. Renno, awestruck, peered hard across the river. Never had he imagined that such a place could exist.

The entire area was dominated by a cliff, known as Cape Diamond, that rose more than three hundred feet from the river. At its apex stood the Citadel—a testimonial to the ingenuity and hard labor of its French builders. Facing the almost sheer drop to the water, the huge fort was surrounded by a palisade of tree trunks, sharply pointed at the top, all of them more than thirty feet tall.

It was obvious that no man could scale that palisade. On the inner side, near the top, was a sentry platform, and Renno could see soldiers patrolling back and forth.

On one side, where the little Saint Charles River flowed into the Saint Lawrence, the ascent was more gradual. There were houses, churches, and other buildings clustered in the lower portion, and still others had been constructed on the rising plateau below the Citadel. Quebec consisted of two towns, not one, with the upper part virtually impregnable.

Even as the group of attackers examined their target, the fog became thicker. The combination of approaching nightfall and an increasingly leaden sky made it extremely difficult for the observers to see clearly, and only Renno, with his extraordinary eyesight, could make out any details.

"Find two paths," Ghonka told him. "One for the Iroquois in the back of the town, one for the English in the front of the town."

Devoting his full attention to the task, Renno was able to make out two winding streets, one further inland, and one near the riverfront where several warships were moored. He studied them at length, memorizing every detail of their twists and turns.

"I see a gate on the front path that opens onto the wall of the great longhouse," he said, speaking in the tongue of the Seneca. He could not afford to lose concentration by trying to translate his words into English. "But I cannot see whether there is another gate for the back path."

Ghonka shrugged. "If there is a gate, we will find it. If there is none, the Seneca will make their own."

It was growing dark now, and before night fell Renno had to pass along what he had learned. Picking up a small branch from a dead tree, he traced both of the streets on a large patch of snow.

The leaders studied the sketch until they were able to commit it to memory.

"At its narrowest point," Andrew Wilson said, "the river appears to be about five thousand feet wide."

"A crossing of a mile," said Pepperrell, "would be

difficult under the best of the circumstances. Those ice floes racing downstream make it all the more dangerous. But we seem to have no alternative."

Turning away from Renno's sketch, the group looked again at the river. The fog was even heavier, the north shore had become an indistinct blur, and the ramparts of the Citadel looming above the crest of the cliff were no more than a dark, almost shapeless shadow.

Ghonka had already determined the final attack plan. "The Iroquois are silent," he said. "We will take the longer trail and go to the great longhouse from the rear. The English will take the short path near the river."

His reasoning made sense, and Pepperrell and Wilson immediately concurred.

"My son," the Great Sachem said to Renno, "you will go with the English and lead them to the gate you have seen."

Renno nodded.

"I hope," Andrew Wilson remarked with a smile, "you can remember how to get to that gate!"

Renno grinned at him. He was learning to judge men, and he had faith in Wilson as a leader.

"If we start now," Ghonka said, "it will be night by the time we reach the town."

Colonel Wilson demurred. "We must wait at least an hour," he said. "The French garrison will eat now, and they will drink much wine with their meal. Soon they'll become sleepy and will grow more careless."

Ghonka nodded. "We will wait."

"Speed is absolutely essential," the colonel continued. "Once we open fire, we'll have to kill quickly, then set our fires just as swiftly."

"Any warrior who falls behind will join the spirits of his ancestors," agreed the Great Sachem.

Sun-ai-yee spoke for the first time. "When the attack is done," he said, "let every man return at once to his own raft. Let the raft return to this shore as soon as it is filled."

His suggestion was wise, for casualties would mount rapidly if the first men to leave the town had to wait for the others.

"I imagine the French will try to follow us," Colonel Wilson said thoughtfully, "so we shouldn't try to meet too close to the riverbank. Let's set a rendezvous farther south."

Again Ghonka turned to Renno. "Did you see the great maple that stood beside a small clearing—the tree that looked like three trees?"

After a lifetime of observing every detail in the forests, Renno knew his father was aware that he had seen the tree, which was located two or three miles to the south. "I saw it, my father," he replied.

"We will meet there," Ghonka ordered. "You will bring the English warriors to that tree. The Iroquois will be there waiting, if the manitous will it."

More than ever, Andrew Wilson and William Pepperrell knew that their future lay in the hands of their Indian allies.

"We will go without delay," Ghonka said. "If we wait until the father-sun rises in the morning, the Huron and Ottawa will come, too."

The militia leaders understood the Seneca tongue sufficiently well to grasp the significance of that statement. There would be no rest for the invaders tonight. No matter how tired they might be, they would be obliged to begin their retreat as soon as both wings of the attacking force were reunited.

The leaders returned to their respective groups, and Renno lingered for a moment with his father.

Ghonka grasped his forearm. "It is good that you are a Seneca," he said. "It is good that you are my own son."

"It is good that you are my father," Renno replied.

They each turned away abruptly, and Renno went on to join the militia battalion.

The tension had reached a peak. Silence had been imposed on the men, who were spending the time checking their weapons, and some, including Jeffrey Wilson, had dipped into their rations.

Renno wanted to tell them they were wrong to take food now. The Seneca believed that a warrior fought more vigorously and that his head was clearer when his stomach was empty, but he had learned enough about the colonists to realize that his advice would be resented.

He squatted near the militia commanders and waited with them. Occasionally one or the other reached into his pocket for a metal object that made a loud ticking sound, and he hoped that later he could ask them the use of such objects.

At last the colonel said, "We've waited an hour."

"Very well, we'll march now," Brigadier Pepperrell replied, "and may the Almighty show us His favor tonight."

The militiamen filed down to the riverbank where the Mohawk boatmen were waiting.

As soon as the colonists arrived, the Iroquois shoved off, heading for the north bank, and disappeared into the fog when they were only a few feet from shore.

Renno accompanied the militia commanders onto their lead raft, acknowledging the presence of the Mo-

389

hawk warriors with a solemn nod. The night was damp, the air raw, and the young Seneca knew that a chill would settle into his bones on the long ride across the river. But he showed no sign of discomfort. He moved to the front of the raft, balancing on two logs with his feet planted apart.

Colonel Wilson gave the quiet order to shove off.

The Mohawk boatmen proved marvelously adept, and Renno admired their skill. Four of them guided the boat, the fifth used his paddle to ward off chunks of ice, and all seemed to be guided by instinct. Although they could not see the raft carrying Iroquois warriors that was directly ahead of them, they managed to stay close behind it.

Renno's eyesight made it possible for him to see ice chunks bearing down on the raft, but he remained quiet, leaving the task of dealing with the floes to the Mohawk who had been given that responsibility. The warrior fending off the floes seemed endowed with a sixth sense, and each time one approached he deftly maneuvered it out of the way with his paddle. The militiamen watched with amazement.

"Thank God they're on our side," the colonel muttered.

Someone's teeth began to chatter, and the man drew a deep, noisy breath. Tom Hibbard turned to glare at him, and even Obadiah Jenkins looked annoyed. Renno could almost sympathize with the culprit, for the cold was numbing, turning a warrior's hands and feet to ice. The boatmen maneuvered superbly, never fighting the current, but using it to work their way toward the north bank.

The fog combined with the heavy clouds overhead made Quebec invisible. Even Renno was surprised when two of the Mohawk leaped from the boat and began to pull the raft onto dry land. He jumped ashore, too, and sensed the presence of dark shapes directly ahead. These were the dwellings of the people who lived in the lower portion of Quebec.

Soon the other rafts were discharging militiamen, and Renno was aware of Obadiah Jenkins's relief when all the rafts landed safely.

Brigadier Pepperrell gave a signal, and as the men moved into a double line, their muskets ready, he moved back in the column to take command of the main body.

Colonel Wilson, who had taken on the difficult task of commanding the vanguard, stationed himself directly behind Renno; and Obadiah, refusing to be denied his share of the excitement, took his place beside his most distinguished parishioner.

Renno was pleased when Tom Hibbard moved up to join him. Here was a determined comrade who would need no instructions.

Then Andrew Wilson tapped Renno on the shoulder. The white Seneca started forward slowly, groping until he oriented himself, and soon he came to a narrow lane with houses on either side. Lamps and candles glowed softly behind the oiled paper that covered the windows, giving off a faint light that almost—but not quite—managed to penetrate the fog.

Turning left, advancing several paces, and then turning right again, Renno knew he had found the trail. Only his years of wilderness living and his instinct could help him now, and he made no attempt to apply reason to the problem.

Inside one of the houses a young woman laughed, and the sound of her voice echoed through the night.

In another house, two men were arguing in a language Renno could not understand.

The ascent grew steeper, the snow and ice underfoot were treacherous, and Renno could hear the heavy breathing of the militiamen.

He felt a few soft, wet drops on his face, and he realized that it was beginning to snow, further reducing visibility and offering the invaders slightly better protection. Ghonka, as always, was right in his prediction.

Someone in the line coughed, and Colonel Wilson turned to glare at the offender, but the man couldn't be seen even though he was no more than a few feet away.

The street continued to wind its way up to the crest where the Citadel stood. Although the actual height of the bastion was only a little more than a hundred yards above the level of the river, the attackers had to walk at least three times that far to reach the summit.

Renno sensed rather than saw the high palisade looming directly ahead, and halting, he raised a hand in warning. Colonel Wilson followed his example, as did those in row after row behind him, and the entire column stopped.

The combination of the fog and the snow, which was falling more and more heavily now, made it almost impossible for anyone to make out objects more than three or four feet away, but Renno concentrated on the log wall, calling on his hawk manitou to sharpen his vision. A hawk could see anything, at any time, anywhere, and the white Seneca prayed for the assistance of his guiding spirit.

Gradually the blur in front of him grew more distinct, and after a time he made out two figures: a Huron warrior and a gold-and-white-clad French soldier were standing guard duty outside the gate that Renno had seen from the far side of the river.

If the sentries became aware of the approaching column now, an alarm would be raised and all would be lost.

The Huron sentinel was impassive, as befitted a warrior, standing still with his arms folded across his chest. The Frenchman rubbed his hands and began to stamp his feet, paying no attention to the man beside him.

The warrior was by far the more dangerous of the pair, and Renno knew he had to be immobilized first. How much more valuable were the weapons of the Seneca, which made no noises betraying their users!

Renno took his bow from his shoulder, reached for an arrow, and fitted it into the slot. Tom Hibbard leaned closer, raising an eyebrow, and Renno indicated in pantomime that the two sentinels were nearby.

Colonel Wilson understood, too, and realizing that he had to leave matters in the hands of the two men who led the line, he nodded, taking care not to draw his pistol. Tom Hibbard had waited a long time for this moment, and his hand closed over the hilt of his long knife as Renno released an arrow. The shaft penetrated the left side of the Huron's chest, and the Indian collapsed without a sound.

Tom leaped forward, his long knife raised. He didn't see the French sentry until he was almost on top of him, but he was fully prepared for his stroke of vengeance, and the knife blade cut into the sentinel's heart.

Before dragging the Huron out of his path, Renno scalped him swiftly and efficiently and placed the dripping trophy on his belt. Then he and Tom put their shoulders to the massive gate, it creaked open, and the members of the column squeezed through, leaving the gate ajar, and entered the Citadel.

Colonel Wilson needed a few moments to orient himself. He had studied sketches of the great town within a town, but the snowfall was becoming a blizzard, the fog remained thick, and he had to figure out where in the complex they were standing. At last he knew, or hoped he knew, and gestured toward his right.

With Renno and Tom Hibbard still in the lead, the militiamen moved forward, their boots crunching on the snow, and when they reached the parade ground, Renno paused, and listened intently. The Iroquois were already at work inside the Citadel, and the faint sounds he heard indicated that they had invaded a building off to the left and found many victims.

The colonel, certain of the enemy unit's location now, gestured sharply to the right.

Again Renno led the colonists, and after a few moments they came to a log building that resembled the Seneca longhouses but was much larger.

The colonel drew his pistol and cocked it, and the entire column heard the sound. Muskets were cocked, too, and the unit was ready.

A door stood directly ahead, and as Tom pushed it open, Renno fitted another arrow into his bow. The firesticks of the English were powerful, terrifying weapons, but he preferred to use his own reliable weapon in this moment of crisis.

The building they were entering was a barracks, and French soldiers who had recently finished their evening meal were taking their ease. Most had removed their tunics and boots and were in their shirt sleeves reading or writing letters as they lolled on their beds. One large group was playing cards, and a few others were engaged in conversation.

The colonel was quick to note that the French muskets were stacked in racks near the door, rendering the defenders helpless as the English colonists poured into the barracks and opened fire. The carnage was swift and terrible, and within minutes at least thirty members of the garrison lay dead, and many more wounded.

Renno shot two men with his arrows and calmly proceeded to scalp them.

Then the attack ended as suddenly as it had begun. "Withdraw!" Brigadier Pepperrell shouted above the roar of musket fire. "Withdraw!"

The militiamen retreated, leaving the shattered survivors behind, but the problems were just beginning. As the unit approached the parade ground, intending to leave the same way they had entered, muskets began to roar, their flashes momentarily casting a glow that could be seen through the snow and fog.

Renno heard a high-pitched war cry, and he knew that the Seneca, also withdrawing, were locked in combat with the French and their allies. Guided by the sounds of the battle, he made his way to the portion of the parade ground where the Seneca, Oneida, and Mohawk were engaged in a ferocious struggle with the defenders of the Citadel. For the moment, at least, the Iroquois were giving better than they received, for the warriors were using their bows and arrows, which did not give away their positions in the gloom.

The English colonists drew up beside their allies and formed a double row, those in the front rank dropping to one knee while those behind them continued to stand.

"Fire at will!" Brigadier Pepperrell ordered, and Colonel Wilson moved up and down the line, ignoring the French musket fire and hail of Huron and Ottawa arrows. Only Obadiah Jenkins refrained from taking part in the battle.

Renno caught a glimpse of his father and moved closer to him. Ghonka, displaying remarkable calm, was not shooting blindly. Instead, he waited until he saw an enemy musket or pistol discharge and then sent an arrow in that direction.

The raging snowstorm handicapped both sides, but sheer logic indicated that the defenders, vastly outnumbering the invading force, would triumph. The retreat must be resumed.

The French, well aware of their foe's problem, were determined to make the situation untenable for the attackers. A rush was organized, and Huron warriors and French light infantry raced forward, the Huron clutching their knives, the Frenchmen holding muskets with bayonets attached.

"We've got to pull out before we're overwhelmed," Colonel Wilson said.

Brigadier Pepperrell agreed and called for a full retreat.

A hard core remained behind to ward off the counterattack as the militiamen and Iroquois streamed toward the gate, and Renno found himself beside his father.

Ghonka set the example for the rear guard of both warriors and militiamen. Not budging from his position, he waited until an enemy came close enough to be seen and then dispatched the foe with an accurately aimed arrow. Corpses began to pile up in front of him.

Andrew Wilson was fighting in the same manner, and at last there was something practical for Obadiah Jenkins to do. As soon as the colonel fired a pistol, he handed it to the clergyman, who reloaded it while the militia leader fired a second weapon.

No one was shooting with greater accuracy than Tom Hibbard, who was concentrating exclusively on the Huron. The flashes of his musket attracted the Indians' arrows, but he seemed to be leading a charmed life, and he sent round after round at the enemy, reloading with grim precision.

Renno's lifetime dream was coming true. He and his father were standing shoulder to shoulder, fighting the enemies of the Seneca, and the young warrior's spirits soared. Never had his aim been more accurate, his eye keener, his reflexes more rapid. He, too, began to accumulate a pile of corpses in front of him as the defenders of the Citadel, ignoring their heavy casualties, sent forward wave after wave of light infantrymen and warriors.

Suddenly a French officer who looked vaguely familiar to Renno loomed up in front of him. The man, caught unprepared for battle, was in his shirt sleeves, although he was wearing his powdered wig. In one hand he carried a pistol and in the other he gripped a sword, but apparently he had suffered a wound in his sword arm, which was hanging at his side.

The officer stumbled over a musket, and his wig was knocked from his head.

Renno knew him: it was the white Huron who was his mortal enemy.

At the same moment, Alain de Gramont recognized the young white warrior whose life he had spared. Now the situation was changed, and there was hatred

397

in the man's eyes as he shouted in the Huron language, "You! Again! I should have killed you sooner!"

He raised his pistol, fired at Renno, and there was a clicking sound, but the weapon failed to discharge.

Renno drew his metal knife, intending to end his enemy's life, but even as he took a step forward, Alain de Gramont was too quick for him. Throwing the useless pistol at his foe's head to deter him for a moment, Gramont withdrew, melting back into the fog and blinding snow.

It was not their destiny to end their feud now, Renno realized. He and the white Huron would meet again. In some strange way their fates had been linked, perhaps by the manitous, and only one of them would emerge alive after their next encounter.

There was a brief lull in the fighting, and Ghonka was the first to sense it. "We will leave now," he said quietly. He looked at his son for an instant, and never had Renno seen such love and pride in his eyes.

There was no greater praise that Renno wanted, no trophies of war he would have preferred. If he died right now, his life would be fulfilled.

As the rear guard began to depart, Ghonka and his warriors slipped away silently. Andrew Wilson and his small band of volunteers tried to emulate them but made enough noise to reveal their presence, and the Huron became aware of the exodus. Some of them, better attuned to the situation than their French allies, moved toward the gate in an attempt to cut off the retreat, and muskets roared, knives flashed, and arrows sang through the snow-laden air. Before any blow, each man had to make certain he was attacking a foe rather than a friend.

Renno fought his way toward the gate, aware that Tom Hibbard was still fighting furiously at his side. Only belatedly did the young Seneca realize that Obadiah Jenkins was no more than a pace or two ahead of them.

Then they heard a loud shout. "Go on, Pa!" Jeffrey Wilson cried. "I'll cover you and I'll be right behind you."

As Renno, Tom, and Obadiah neared the gate they saw Jeffrey Wilson and Abe Thomas holding off a small band of Huron, although the storm was so ferocious that it was impossible to determine how many.

Renno sprang back into action, driving his knife into one of the hated Huron, withdrawing the blade and striking another. Tom was equally energetic, and using his musket as a club, he grasped it by the barrel and chopped viciously at any approaching shadow.

For the first time, Obadiah Jenkins was drawn into the fight. He fired his pistol at a Huron who came close to decapitating him with a tomahawk, then quickly drew his sword and skewered another of the enemy.

The defense overwhelmed the Huron, who retreated into the fog and fell back toward the parade ground.

Now Renno became aware of the two young militiamen who had been directly ahead of him and his companions. Jeffrey Wilson was sprawled in the snow, knocked unconscious by a tomahawk blow on the side of the head, and Abe Thomas was bleeding from two nasty knife wounds, struggling for breath as he lay flat on his back on the wet ground.

Renno dropped to one knee beside him and read death in his eyes.

Abe peered hard at him and finally recognized him. "Renno," he said, fighting for breath, "I—I'm sorry. You're a comrade. A friend." And he closed his eyes, then breathed no more.

Early in childhood, a Seneca learned to be practical, and in spite of the feeling of grief that welled up within Renno, he knew that Abe Thomas had gone to join his ancestors. His lifeless body had to be left behind.

But the colonel's son was still very much alive, and Renno quickly picked him up and threw the unconscious Jeffrey across his shoulders, much as he would carry a buck he shot in the forest.

His companions needed no urging, and they dashed out through the gate, Obadiah Jenkins in the lead. A silent Tom Hibbard brought up the rear, thirsty for more combat if another enemy appeared.

Renno ran easily, almost unaware of the burden draped across his shoulders. Only a Seneca could have kept up the pace set by Obadiah as they ran and slid through the narrow, twisting street toward the Saint Lawrence River.

Many of the lower town's residents undoubtedly had heard the sounds of musket fire at the Citadel, but they had the good sense to remain behind the barred doors of their cabins. They were protected by the troops of King Louis and by the Indian allies of New France, and they had no intention of becoming embroiled in a battle they knew nothing about; therefore, no civilian appeared on the road to impede the flight of these last members of the rear guard. The attack had been so swift that the cannon of the warships could not be manned in time to bombard the attackers.

No one followed from the heights, either. Perhaps

the French, Huron, and Ottawa didn't yet realize that their attackers were escaping.

Obadiah became confused when he saw the black waters of the river directly ahead. Renno, however, turned sharply and, still carrying the unconscious Jeffrey, led his companions to the last of the rafts. Andrew Wilson was on the verge of giving the order to shove off when he saw the young Seneca appear out of the blizzard with a soldier slung across his back. Recognizing his son instantly, Andrew was both alarmed and relieved.

Renno placed Jeffrey on the raft as Obadiah and Tom boarded; the colonel gave the order to leave; and the raft moved out into the swirling waters.

Renno stood at the front of the crude craft paying no attention to the ice floes or the current. For the first time since the march began, he felt weary, and even though the mission had been a success, he was surprised that he was not exhilarated. He had enjoyed fighting at the side of his father, but he was sorry he had not taken the scalps of the last two Huron he had killed. Those prizes had been legitimate booty. He would fight the Huron again, he promised himself, and he would seek a final confrontation with the older white Indian who was his personal enemy.

The river had become more turbulent, and the Mohawk had to use all their skill and strength to steer the little raft toward the south shore. Their progress was painfully slow.

"Renno."

The young warrior turned and saw Jeffrey Wilson, ashen-faced, half supported by Obadiah Jenkins. Apparently the colonel's son had just come to his senses.

"I owe my life to you," Jeffrey said, speaking slowly. "I—I guess I needed some sense knocked into my head." He smiled painfully, then drew in his breath. "I don't deserve your friendship, but I'd like to shake your hand."

Renno reached out to grasp young Wilson's forearm, then shook his hand in the English manner.

"We are brothers," Renno said.

It seemed like a long time before the raft reached the south bank where the bulk of the militia battalion had already gathered. Giving no one time to pause and rest, Renno plunged into the forest, leaving those who were strong enough to carry the wounded.

The battalion followed, and a half hour later they reached the clearing where Ghonka and his Iroquois were waiting. The Indians had already made litters for carrying the injured, and the entire party moved on without delay.

"The snow," the Great Sachem said, "will hide the signs of our feet on the ground. It will not be easy for the Huron and Ottawa to follow."

The march continued until long after daybreak. The Iroquois, particularly the Seneca, could have gone on all day, but many of the militiamen were so exhausted that a halt had to be called. Sentry outposts were set, and the snow continued to fall as men dropped off to sleep, their weapons close at hand.

A scant four hours later, Ghonka gave the order to resume the march. The Iroquois were content to dip into their emergency food supplies, but the militiamen would need more substantial fare later in the day, so Sun-ai-yee sent several hunters ahead of the main body.

Before the column moved off again, a head count

was made, and it was learned that casualties had been remarkably light. Two Seneca, two Mohawk, and eight militiamen had paid the supreme price for the daring invasion. Fourteen men were wounded, but Obadiah Jenkins, attending them in the absence of a physician, predicted that all would recover, and the grueling march continued, the men resting for no more than a few hours at a time. After many days, the colonists became haggard, and the strain began to tell on even the hardiest of the Seneca.

Soon after Brigadier Pepperrell estimated that they had crossed the border from Canada and were now in the Maine District of Massachusetts Bay, the weather changed. A warm, brilliant sun appeared in a cloudless sky, the snow began to melt, and there was a strong hint of spring in the air. A real bivouac was made, and a hunting party returned with venison, wild turkeys, and small game. The fishermen were equally successful, catching many salmon in a swift-moving stream, and for the first time since before the battle, campfires were built.

That night the victors feasted, free of fear, militiamen and Iroquois warriors mingling freely. Renno sat at a campfire between Tom Hibbard and Jeffrey Wilson, none of them feeling the need for talk.

After the meal, a senior warrior came to Renno with word that the Great Sachem wanted to see him, and Renno accompanied the warrior to the fire where the officers of the high command were eating. Ghonka stood as his son approached. Then he took the eagle feather from his own scalp lock and placed it in Renno's. Renno, overwhelmed by the honor, bowed his head so no one would see that he was badly shaken.

Pepperrell and Wilson watched the brief ceremony, conferred in low tones, and then the colonel spoke.

"Hear me, leaders of the Iroquois," he said. "Brigadier Pepperrell and I were given the special assignment of this expedition by Governor Shirley, our leader. We have won a victory by defeating the French in Quebec and teaching them a lesson they will not forget. Now, however, they will seek revenge. They will stir more hatred in the hearts of the Huron, Ottawa, and other Indian nations. They will send more troops to Quebec from France, and by this time next year our danger will be greater than ever."

Colonel Wilson's words made sense, and Ghonka nodded thoughtfully as he lighted his pipe.

Wilson continued. "Our governor wants to send an emissary who will explain the situation in North America to our great King William, who lives in England. Only if King William and the members of his Privy Council know and understand what is truly happening in the New World will they send us the help we need to defeat the French for all time."

Again Ghonka nodded.

"Only if we send a very special ambassador will the King and the members of his council listen," said the colonel. "And we know of only one man who can perform this vital task on which the future of our colonies in this land depend. Great Sachem, will you send your son to England?"

Renno's joy turned to dismay. After the rigorous campaign, he was tired of war. He had seen enough of the English colonists. He wanted to return to his town, where he would be reunited with his mother, his aunt, and his little sister; he wanted to enjoy the admiration of the entire community. He needed a respite—some time to hunt and fish with El-i-chi, as they had done in other days.

Ghonka puffed on his pipe. "My son is a senior

warrior who has won many scalps. Now he also wears an eagle feather. I will not give an order to such a man."

"It would be helpful to the Seneca and the other Iroquois," Colonel Wilson said. "Our King is generous, and he will send you many more muskets, iron pots to cook your food, and blankets to keep you warm at night."

"My son," Ghonka said firmly, "will make up his own mind."

Renno's face remained impassive. Turning from the fire, he walked slowly into the forest where he could wrestle with the problem alone. Did he owe anything to the pale skins from whom he was descended? He didn't know, even though he did not doubt his identity as a Seneca.

It was true that he despised the Huron and Ottawa; by gaining support for the English colonists, he would be hurting his own foes as well as the French. On the other hand, he had done his duty, he had fought well and courageously, and he deserved a time of rest.

He had to admit that he was also apprehensive about making a journey that would last for more than a moon. He had only heard vaguely about the great sea, and he couldn't imagine sailing on a huge boat. In addition, he felt uneasy about visiting a powerful monarch in a strange land.

He asked the manitous for guidance, but they showed him no sign. He knew then, that he must make his own choice, and this was fitting for one who had become a senior warrior. A man must determine his own destiny.

Renno returned and met his father in private.

They sat opposite each other, and Ghonka spoke

to his somber son. "When a warrior becomes a leader of men," he said, "the choices he makes are not easy. The boy learns in the trials of manhood that he must be patient. But the leader learns he must not hesitate too long."

"It is true," Renno replied, "that I have done all that the English have asked of me. It is right that I wish to return to my own land, where I will see my mother and the sister of my father. I have earned the right to hunt with El-i-chi and to be at peace in the great forest."

"You have earned that right," Ghonka said impassively.

Renno stirred uncomfortably. "It is true also," he said, and looked intently at Ghonka, "that the English have become our brothers. Standing together, they and the Seneca have such great strength that no Indian nation will dare to break the peace, no army of the French will dare to invade our lands."

"It is so," Ghonka said and offered nothing more.

At last Renno forced himself to face the heart of this crisis, the words coming freely, as his thoughts revealed them. "Of all the warriors of the Seneca," he said, "I am more the brother of the English than any other. My skin is the color of their skin. My eyes are like theirs, although my heart is Seneca. It is plain to me that I have been chosen by the manitous to bring the Seneca and the English colonists together."

There was admiration in the Great Sachem's eyes.

"I have no choice," Renno declared, speaking slowly, his heart wrenched at the thought of leaving his people. "It does not matter that I have earned the right to rest now. It is my duty to go off to the land of the English Great Sachem. I must do what no other warrior can."

"You do that which is right, my son," Ghonka said, his own heart torn at the prospect of his son leaving.

Renno, his decision made, sat as stoically as his father. No matter what the hazards and uncertainties of the future, no matter what the cost to his own happiness, the fate of children as yet unborn lay in Renno's hands. He could not fail them.

★ WAGONS WEST ★

This continuing, magnificent saga recounts the adventures of a brave band of settlers, all of different backgrounds, all sharing one dream— to find a new and better life.

☐	26822-8	INDEPENDENCE! #1	$4.95
☐	26162-2	NEBRASKA! #2	$4.50
☐	26242-4	WYOMING! #3	$4.50
☐	26072-3	OREGON! #4	$4.50
☐	26070-7	TEXAS! #5	$4.99
☐	26377-3	CALIFORNIA! #6	$4.99
☐	26546-6	COLORADO! #7	$4.95
☐	26069-3	NEVADA! #8	$4.99
☐	26163-0	WASHINGTON! #9	$4.50
☐	26073-1	MONTANA! #10	$4.50
☐	26184-3	DAKOTA! #11	$4.50
☐	26521-0	UTAH! #12	$4.50
☐	26071-5	IDAHO! #13	$4.50
☐	26367-6	MISSOURI! #14	$4.50
☐	27141-5	MISSISSIPPI! #15	$4.95
☐	25247-X	LOUISIANA! #16	$4.50
☐	25622-X	TENNESSEE! #17	$4.50
☐	26022-7	ILLINOIS! #18	$4.95
☐	26533-4	WISCONSIN! #19	$4.95
☐	26849-X	KENTUCKY! #20	$4.95
☐	27065-6	ARIZONA! #21	$4.50
☐	27458-9	NEW MEXICO! #22	$4.95
☐	27703-0	OKLAHOMA! #23	$4.95
☐	28180-1	CELEBRATION! #24	$4.50